PRAISE FOR *THE HERMES PROTOCOL*

"*The Hermes Protocol* grabbed my attention from the get go. I found myself in a believable future world that left me torn between wanting to destroy the establishment and accepting my corporate branding in order to enjoy the enticing benefits available. Chris Arnone weaves a tale of intrigue wrapped around characters I found myself rooting for. As Elise revealed each layer of story and world, I lived the shock, anxiety, and everything else with her. Quynn and Bastion were a cyberpunk dream come true. If you're looking for a relatable adventure of cyberpunk mystery rather than misery, then this is the story you've been waiting for."

—H.S. Kallinger, *Author of the Lost Humanity Series*

*   *   *

"*The Hermes Protocol* has everything you could want in a story: adventure, mystery, and a heist! Following Intel Operative Elise through the twists and turns of her mission kept me on the edge of my seat, desperate to know what happens next. Movie material, for certain!"

—Stephanie Eding, Author of *The Unplanned Life of Josie Hale*

THE HERMES PROTOCOL

CHRIS M. ARNONE

CASTLE BRIDGE MEDIA
DENVER, COLORADO, USA

CASTLE BRIDGE MEDIA
Denver, Colorado

Cover art by Eddy Shinjuku

This book is a work of fiction. Names, characters, business, events, and incidents are
the products of the authors' imaginations. Any resemblance to actual persons,
living or dead or actual events is purely coincidental.

THE HERMES PROTOCOL
© 2022 Chris M. Arnone
All rights reserved.

ISBN: 979-8-9872083-2-8

For Christina Arnone

Wife, mother of cats, alpha reader.
She makes all this possible.

CHAPTER ONE

THIS HAD TO BE ONE of my least favorite ways to spend a Saturday night: clinging to the bottom of a flying limousine, watching the skyscrapers of Jayu City blur by below me. The view was nice, don't get me wrong. Towering ads lit up the buildings below in artificial light. LeGrand Corto modeling the newest Coach handbags, flying a high-end Mercedes past Corto's central business district, and laughing with some friends over a meal prepared by Swyla's Kitchen. Brands from two planets, Earth and Little Sekhmet Settlement, my home, mingled together. Not every ad featured LeGrand's sweeping smile or overwrought curves. A pair of twins, one male and one female, modeled Corto Cybernetics' CX199 hand upgrades, "for the surgeon, engineer, or micro-detailist in your life."

"How's it looking?" Quynn Corto-Nano said. Corto Corporation was the company we both worked for, though they worked in the Nano division. Hence Corto-Nano. Their voice was clear in my communications implant while their torso hovered in front of me, disappearing into the bottom of the limo. They weren't actually there, of course, just an augmented-reality projection on my display. And I was one on their comms, though Quynn couldn't see what was around me, only me in this hunkered position.

"Clear and breezy," I said, barely in a whisper and barely opening my mouth. My communications implant wasn't some off-the-shelf number

6

like Quynn's. If it had been, even screaming wouldn't have been heard over the rush of wind around me, even with the helmet. High on the list of reasons to become an intelligence operative for Corto Corporation: I got the good tech. Like the implant that picked up on my vocal vibrations through the bones in my skull and translated accordingly. It was almost telepathy at that point. Almost.

"And you'll be home by 24:00?"

"That's the plan."

Quynn started to say, "We need to leave by–"

"24:30. I know."

"This is important. We only have a few hours to make the rounds before midnight."

"Yes, 28:00. I know that, too," I said, though I still didn't understand why this gala had a hard stop time. "Stop being so nervous. You're going to be great tonight."

Quynn sighed. They got this way before every big company event. I'd learned not to take it personally.

"Be safe," they said.

"What's the fun in that?"

"That's never going to be funny."

"It will be," I said. "One day when you least expect it."

"Do I even want to know what you're doing right now?" Quynn asked. "Or where?"

I glanced at the altimeter on my display. About 2500 meters up. Current speed was 185 kilometers per hour. Thankfully, my cybernetic arms and legs couldn't feel the cold wind and didn't get fatigued from hanging onto the bottom of the limo. My abs could have felt fatigued, but I was chemically suppressing those feelings from transmitting to my brain. Feeling Quynn's cheek under my fingertips or the silk of our sheets at home was a good thing, this 185 km per hour wind wasn't. My black helmet – deployed from a plate magnetically attached to the back of my neck – was deflecting the wind and cold from my face, and the bodysuit covered the rest of my living flesh, though I could feel a slight cooling around my collarbone. I'd have to get that seal looked at. The limo was over the cliffside district of the Corto

Corporation borough, a sparkling, expensive area perched along the southern cliffs that overlooked the vast ocean. I was quickly approaching a similar district in the borough for Nexus Neuronics, the next company over. The sun had almost set, but I could still see the waves crashing against the cliffs to my right, the shadows of the skyscrapers so long, they threw the whole of the city into darkness prematurely.

"No," I finally said. "You really don't want to know what I'm doing right now."

"If you get into trouble–"

"Hey, you know me. I'm a safecracker. And a burglar. And an escape artist. I leave the fighting to you."

"I only fight in the conference room," Quynn said.

"Still more than me."

They sighed again. "Okay. See you at 24:00."

"You got it," I said. "I love you."

"Love you."

CALL WITH QUYNN CORTO-NANO DISCONNECTED flashed in the corner of my display for a few seconds. It was soon replaced with ENTERING NEXUS NEURONICS BOROUGH.

I didn't really need the heads-up on crossing into the Nexus Neuronics to know it. The buildings were just as crowded with towering ads as the Corto Corporation borough, but gone was LeGrand Corto. The same ad for Mercedes towered on an apartment building, but the car was flown by a muscular figure with a trim goatee and silver-blonde hair. Gone was any advertisement for Corto Corporation, replaced with ads for Nexus Neuronics' latest neural interface, the NX15987. "Make latency a distant memory."

After only a couple of blocks, the limo started to descend and shed speed, drawing closer to a landing pad on the 200th floor of Cliffside 2, a 310-floor apartment building with clear views of the cliffs and ocean. Not near so tall as the buildings in the business centers of the boroughs, but plenty tall. The landing platform came into view, a circular construction of metal and glass jutting out of the corner of the building, hanging more than a kilometer above the intersection below. Another car was taking off from the platform as the limo I was clinging to lined up its approach. The thrusters slowly rotated from flight to landing positions, and the landing gear deployed above my shoulders and to either side of my calves. They extended down 20 centimeters, making a very tight space for me, so I turned my head sideways.

The limo glided into a hovering position above the landing pad, the winds from the thrusters buffeting me from all directions, but my carbon-fiber limbs didn't waiver, clinging to the undercarriage like I was glued there.

Why ride the bottom of the limo instead of just renting it out? First, I didn't want a record of me having ever been here. Second, there was a camera aimed at the landing pad all 28 hours of Little Sekhmet Settlement's Day. I wasn't here to visit a friend or shop for real estate. I was here to steal something. That was my job. And I loved it. But I didn't want anyone in Nexus Neuronics to know I was ever here.

The instant all four landing gear were down on the platform, I detached from the limo, my hands and feet spinning and catching me in the breath before my body hit the ground. Then staying as flat as possible, I scuttled like an Earth crab out from under the limo, keeping the vehicle between me and the camera. In a few seconds, I was over the edge of the landing platform, shimmying my way along the bottom, working the support structure of the platform like a set of monkey bars until I was gripping the side of the building using the same tech that had kept me plastered to the bottom of the limo: a gel that became unbreakably bonded when a small current ran through it. Wall-walking made easy.

Half the success of a good burglary – maybe more than half – lay in research. Every job came with a mark and a timetable. That told me how much time I had to research my mark, to learn everything about their ins and outs, idiosyncrasies, loved ones, habits, everything. You wanted to steal something from someone, then you needed to know them better than they knew themselves. It wasn't just the mark, but everything surrounding the job.

Like in this case, I didn't want to climb 30 floors on the outside of the building. In a city of flying cars, that was a great way to get noticed. So I needed an entry point close to a landing pad. Hessod Corto-Intel, my Intel Analyst, discovered 19820 was owned by Ortega and Randy Nexus-Nano. They were both directors in the nanotechnology division of Nexus Neuronics, so they made plenty of credits. They also worked almost constantly. Their apartment at Cliffside 2, therefore, was an oh-so-rarely used vacation home. Completely vacant 270 out of the 290 days it took for the Little Sekhmet Settlement to orbit its star. Today was one of those 270 days.

I padded along the outside of the building, careful not to walk across any windows of apartments that were occupied, and I found my destination. I had to say, Ortega and Randy had a great view, and a swimming pool on their balcony that was bigger than my entire apartment. *Mental note: big swimming pool when Quynn makes director.* The lights were out in the apartment, as expected.

Oh, this was just sad. If you're going to have a massive balcony in a city with flying cars, at least put a decent lock on the door to the balcony. Don't be like Ortega and Randy. It was a simple keypad lock connected to the house network, and it even had an external data port. I pulled my data cable from my right elbow and plugged in. A Nexus Maxlock 187. Child's play. It was open in a few seconds. I slid the door open as silently as I could because you never knew until you knew. I'd learned that the hard way. I closed and locked it behind me. Should have been simple. Across the living room, past the kitchen, there was the front door. But leading from the front door to another door on my right was a trail of discarded clothes. Recently discarded. Randy and Ortega hadn't been here in four months. A cleaning service was here yesterday, so there shouldn't have been anyone here. I retracted my helmet and dialed up the sensitivity on my ear implants, aiming them at the closed door.

Heavy breathing. Deep grunts. Feathering moaning. Rhythmic wetness. Sex sounds.

Yeah. Definitely a couple of low voices grunting and moaning in tandem. Randy and Ortega. They shouldn't have been there, and neither should I. I turned away from the carnal cacophony, intent on making a line straight for the front door and pretending I hadn't just heard what I'd heard when my foot caught in someone's discarded pants, which then caught on a barstool parked in front of the kitchen. Software, hardware, and my instincts kicked in. My arm shot out, catching the stool before it crashed to the floor. I slowly shook out a breath and righted the stool while the sounds in the next room continued without pause.

I kept creeping along, nearly to the end of the kitchen island, only a couple meters from the front door, when a voice erupted from far too close to my left ear.

"Skip the lines and order now!"

I spun to see mirrored closet doors, an image of Nexus Neuronics' best-selling home audio system hovering next to my reflection. A pair of white speakers and a little display unit wiggled to a tinny techno beat. The very system I'd been considering for Quynn's birthday.

"Sparks!" I whispered. I brought up my keyboard and jumped into my system settings. Of course, a recent software update changed how my ad blocker worked, and so I wasn't turned on like it was supposed to be when I was on a job.

The sex noises had stopped. I needed to hide.

Kitchen cabinets. Too small and probably full.

I could have clung to the ceiling like an insect. But the ceiling was white. Even if they didn't look up, my black-clad body and black limbs would attract attention.

Two couches. Three chairs. All too low or small to fit under.

Coat closet with those mirrored doors. That would have to do. I opened it and stepped inside in a blink. I shouldn't have been surprised at how empty it was. This was a vacation home, after all. A couple of windbreakers. A robotic vacuum on the floor with a blue light gently undulating. Repelling and parachuting equipment, all folded up and put away neatly. I guessed Ortega and Randy had more fun with the cliffs than I'd imagined. I was eyeing space above the shelf that ran along the top. Tall ceilings. I clambered up, my limbs twisting and bending in ways that biological limbs couldn't. I shut the door behind me, and then stuck to the wall directly above the closet doors, squeezing as flat as I could.

"What was that?" a voice said, tenor and smooth like syrup. Ortega, according to my notes.

"What was what?" Randy echoed, their voice deep and gruff.

"I heard something," Ortega said. I heard the door to the bedroom unlatch. I imagined it slowly and silently opening fully.

Randy started to say, "You heard me–"

"Not that! Out in the living room."

The not-knowing was driving me crazy, so I deployed a fiberoptic camera from my left pinky. I snaked it down and over the top of the closet door. The camera was only half a centimeter in diameter. Hard to notice in full sun, let alone the shadows of the apartment.

Randy and Ortega wandered the apartment naked, and I could see they were both males. Randy had the gruff voice and looked like they powerlifted apartment buildings, and Ortega was modified to be well over two meters tall. Definitely not a pair I wanted discovering me.

Ortega stepped cleanly over one of the living room chairs and turned on the lights, looking out at the balcony. "I don't see anything," they whispered.

"Just the mess we left out here." Randy poked at a pair of underwear with his toe.

Ortega moved out of my line of sight, then said, "Door is still locked."

"Sorry," Ortega said as they reached out and grabbed Randy by, well, they were still naked.

Randy grunted and kissed Ortega on the cheek. "Let's make sure we're really alone."

Ortega practically whined as Randy walked away from him, past the closet, stepped into the kitchen, and looked around there. "There's nothing to see."

"I'm not making this up," Randy said as they moved to the front door and checked the locks. "I heard something."

Then Randy was in front of the closet. As they reached a hand for the door, I retracted my camera in utter silence and then held my breath. Meager light spilled in as Randy yanked the doors open like they thought they were about to surprise someone. I watched their head poke in, the top sparse with brown hair and sweat. The stench of sex and body odor wafted straight up at me. My stomach did a little churn in reply. Randy looked left and right, glanced at the empty shelf above, and then closed the doors.

"Must have been a neighbor," Randy said.

"A neighbor with terrible aural implants and no ad blocker," Ortega said.

I let out the breath I'd been holding.

"Now then," Randy said, followed by a slapping sound of flesh on flesh, and Ortega yelped. "Get that ass back in bed."

There were some wet sounds that I pretended were kissing. I knew they weren't, but for the life of me, I'd never understood why anyone wanted to do more than that with anyone else. The wet sound dissipated as their fumbling footfalls moved away. I waited to hear the bedroom door close again. A minute went by. Then another. Instead of the clicking door, there was a grunt from Ortega and then moans from both, much louder than before. I slinked down from the wall, silently descending to the floor of the closet, and I checked things out with my camera.

The door to the bedroom was still open, but I couldn't see them from my angle. I extended the camera as far as it would go, a full meter beyond the closet door, but I still didn't see them. So I pulled the camera back and gently opened the door, stepped out, and kept my eyes on the opening to the bedroom. I stayed low to the ground, doing my best impersonation of ooze sliding across the carpet. I finally got to the front door and rose up until I could see over the corner of the kitchen counter. There they were, Randy standing behind Ortega, the two men having a full-throated good time now. The briefest glance was enough for me, too much really. I ducked back down instantly. I had to believe it was good for them, though the whole business turned my stomach. Good for them, not for me.

The moans and grunts were getting louder. Sex wasn't my thing, but I knew what was about to happen, and it could be my chance.

I sank to a crouch. After a few more minutes, both men were practically screaming, and then fell into panting. I rose again and only saw their legs side-by-side on the bed. Good for them, and it was time for me to go. I was out the door and in the hall in seconds.

As usual, I was glad I didn't have my biological eyes anymore. They would probably have taken several seconds to adjust to the brighter light of the hallway, but my enhanced eyes had no such issues. I needed to move. People in the hallway wouldn't be anything unusual for the security guards to see on their camera feeds, but my bare, high-end, carbon-polymer limbs sticking out of my black bodysuit weren't exactly everyday wear. I walked quickly, though not running, to the bank of elevators six doors down, ducking underneath the camera mounted directly across from them.

There was one bit I couldn't completely prepare for: the elevators. I knew there would be six here and that they all ran on electromagnetic rails. I also knew there were cameras in every single elevator in the building. I couldn't predict where they would be at this very moment. It looked like I'd caught a little luck finally. One of the elevators was only three floors below me.

I reached my right hand up and snapped my fingers, triggering a mini-EMP, or electromagnetic pulse. Guaranteed to knock out any unshielded electronics like the little camera watching the elevators, though not for long. I grabbed the doors to the elevator that was only three floors away and yanked them open by main force. Trust me, it wasn't that impressive, not with cybernetic arms. Even ones designed for stealth and maneuvering like mine were several times stronger than biological arms.

The electromagnetic rails were on the sides, so I leaped over to one, gripped it with my feet, and used my arms to close the elevator doors behind me. No, the rails weren't electromagnetic. The car below me used electromagnets to hover off these rails and propel itself. The rails were just highly magnetic metal, easy enough to slide down and land almost noiselessly on the car below. Through the grate on the top, I could see that it was blessedly empty. My plan was to hack into the elevator's systems, though hacking certainly wasn't one of my strengths. I had a small database of algorithms for getting past common elevators, safes, locks, you get the idea. And I could download the less-common ones if I found them in my research. Well, Hessod would download them for me if he found them. Whatever. I didn't know how to actively hack anything. This elevator was definitely in my database, though it was a slow process to let the algorithm work its magic. Still better than being seen riding an elevator up 60 floors. Then I saw a better option: the camera.

It was mounted in the upper corner of the elevator, only a few inches from me, and all its wiring was exposed to the elevator shaft. I deployed my own camera, snaking it through the grate, skimming along the ceiling of the elevator, and positioned it right next to the security camera. As I started to record, a double ding sounded right by my ear, and the doors to the elevator slid open, voices spilling in from the hallway.

Silent circuits, I was having the worst luck tonight.

CHAPTER TWO

I FROZE, WATCHING FOUR PEOPLE step onto the elevator. My heart tried to run up my throat. A pair of feminine adults and two young children hustled into the elevator car before I could even move.

"...everyone is talking about it," one of the adults said, their blonde hair shaped in sharp, angular lines around their shoulders. "I'm glad I'm finally going to see it."

"I saw it last week," the other adult said. They were taller but certainly younger than the first, their head shaved recently, displaying a colorful tattoo on their scalp in the shape of an exotic fish. I saw the fish on some nature show, though I didn't remember the name. "You're going to love it."

They pressed a button, and the doors closed. The electromagnetic brakes eased off the rails, and then the car started gliding downward, gently picking up speed. I clung to the top of the elevator car, my camera still snaked in and across the ceiling, pointing down at the unaware Nexus group.

"You've got my number," the blonde said, obviously the mother of the children. "And their dad's number and–"

"This isn't my first time sitting for you," the younger adult said. "Relax. I've got this. We're going to have dinner and watch some videos and be just fine. You go have a good time."

The two children looked like twins, one masculine and one feminine,

15

and they couldn't have been even four years old. They both had dirty blonde hair, frizzing out everywhere. The feminine one wore red overalls and a white, long-sleeve shirt. The other wore a green hoodie and no pants, with a blue pacifier held firmly in their mouth. They gazed up and pointed right at my camera, still sucking away. It must have looked obvious, the thin black fiberoptic snaking out of the vent and toward the security camera in the corner.

"I know you'll be fine," the blonde said. "It's my first date since..."

The sitter let them trail off before responding. "I know. You'll do great. Just have fun and be yourself. If it's not right, it's not, but at least you'll have a fun night out. Or an awesome story about a bad date."

The blonde groaned and shook out their hands like they were covered in slime. "I hate this. It makes me want to throw up."

The adults laughed, but the pointing kid was oblivious. They said nothing, just pointed up, their eyes almost on mine, though I knew they couldn't see me through the vent. Still, it was unnerving, and it wouldn't take much for one of the adults to follow the kid's pointing finger.

The elevator slowed and finally stopped at floor 110. Not 100 or 150, where one of the building's landing pads jutted off the side. The date must have been with someone in the building, which wasn't that strange when you considered how many people lived in a building with over 300 floors. My own parents grew up in the same building, Corto 124. They attended separate schools in the building and spent almost two decades a mere elevator ride away before they met.

The blonde knelt, hugging both kids, not noticing how one was still just staring up at my camera.

"Be good for Miss Augustine, okay?"

The kid wearing red overalls nodded, but the other just kept staring.

"Jerome?" the blonde asked the starer.

Jerome just kept on staring. Come on, Jerome, look at your parent. Give them a hug or a nod or at least a little eye contact. Nothing to see here, just a lady trying to rob one of your neighbors. Move along.

"Jerome!" the blonde said, not quite in a yell, and then glanced up at the ceiling, making a little bile bubble up in my throat. But their eyes were back on Jerome in an instant, apparently not noticing anything.

"Jerome?" the babysitter said, moving their face between mine and Jerome's, getting into their field of vision. "Say bye to Mommy."

Apparently, that was what it took because now Jerome was hugging their mom, and tension oozed out of my neck. With everyone's attention on their loving goodbyes, I retracted my camera and let out a breath I didn't know I'd been holding. Then Mom was gone, and the elevator was cruising back up to the 195th floor.

Jerome looked confused. They tugged on the sitter's pant leg and pointed up, making little grunting noises.

The sitter followed that finger and said, "That's the camera, Jerome. Just keeping us safe."

Jerome said nothing, glancing back and forth between the camera and their sitter, and then lost interest. I took a few moments to calm down and focus on my plan. In moments, Jerome, their sibling, and the babysitter were gone, and I was back on mission.

Camera redeployed, in position, I recorded ten seconds of clean, empty elevator just sitting idly. Nothing to see here. I pulled the camera back and it was time for my data link. I took a deep breath because I had to do this fast. It was guaranteed to make a flicker in the security office, but the shorter the flicker, the less likely a security officer was to suspect something. One more deep breath, and then I yanked out the security camera's data feed, plugged it into my data cable, and sent along those ten seconds on a loop.

I'll admit my heart was thumping just a little harder than I liked, so I took more deep breaths, counting each one until I reached 10. Security hadn't moved the elevator or come to take a look. No point waiting around any longer. I pried up the vent and flipped down into the elevator car, keeping my data cable connected to the camera's feed. Then I pressed the button for floor 254. I was back on top of the car, the vent closed, and the camera's data cable reattached before the elevator reached its new destination. Once the car arrived, I climbed up and opened the doors to floor 255.

The easy part was done. I hurried along to apartment 25512, the vacation home of Ophelia Nexus-Neuro, a director of research and development of neuro tech for Nexus Neuronics. As expected, her front door was equipped with a cybermetric lock, Hessod's research on the apartment proving perfect.

Cybermetric locks were programmed to recognize the complete cybernetic configuration of their owners. No two cybernetic configurations were the same, like biological fingerprints, especially when the owner made enough money to afford regular upgrades. So first thing this morning, I was having a cup of coffee in the lobby of Ophelia's work building. As I saw her approach the doors, I got up and set a collision course with her. She was angry that a stranger spilled coffee on her, but she would have been enraged if she'd realized I'd planted a scanner on her. A little square less than a centimeter across and so thin that it was entirely invisible. And unlike a tracker, it didn't send out any communications until it finished its scan, which took a few hours. So the myriad of scanners a director of R&D likely walked through every morning wouldn't pick up unusual signals.

Now I just had to hope Ophelia hadn't made any upgrades in the last six hours. First, I knocked on the door. A mistake a lot of rookie Intel Operatives make is going straight for the lockpick. They're excited to use their toys, to sneak around. I made that mistake myself a couple of times. That inevitably led to breaking into places that were far more occupied than anticipated. I really wanted to make sure I didn't stumble across another couple tumbling in the sheets, and I just assumed I was on camera in a public space like the hallway.

I leaned against the door and listened. As expected, no sound answered. I knocked again, this time purely for appearances. I was already snaking my fiberoptic camera under the door and my data cable close behind, using the former to guide the latter into the data port on the inside of the lock. Then it was just a matter of uploading Ophelia's scan information, and in a few seconds, the little light on the lock turned green. The bolts slid open. I reeled my cables back in and opened the door, acting like it was opened from the inside for anyone who might be watching, greeting an imaginary Ophelia.

The scouting report from Hessod said Ophelia had a Nexus Hardcase 1212 safe. It was far from top-of-the-line or even advanced. They'd been on the market for almost 10 years at this point. I figured Ophelia was banking on placing my target in her vacation home at the Nexus Cliffside 2 building instead of her everyday home to keep it safe. Maybe that would work on the Intel Operatives at Nexus, but not me.

Ophelia's vacation home was enormous. The front door opened into the living room, dense with thick curtains and tapestries woven with intricate, jewel-toned patterns. Instead of traditional couches or chairs, the floor was half-covered in large cushions. The whole place smelled faintly of incense.

The kitchen was to my right, spacious and open. Doorless white cabinets revealed mismatched dishes in every imaginable color and pattern. No likely hiding place for a safe in sight.

I moved down the hall on the left, in and out of the three bedrooms. In most vacation homes I'd broken into, the furniture was sparse and impersonal like it was all ordered out of a catalog. It made sense for a space that was rarely occupied. Ophelia's was dense with soft surfaces and thick smells, even though I knew she hadn't been here in almost three months. Maybe she had her cleaner light incense. I searched behind tapestries and under cushions in a bedroom dominated by reds and purples, another in greens and blues, and the last in stark whites. No Nexus Hardcase 1212.

One more room at the end of the hall. I expected another color-coordinated cradle of fabric. Instead, there were hundreds of books lining the shelves on every wall, a fortune all around me. The flora on Little Sekhmet couldn't be turned into usable wood or paper. For decades after the settlement was founded, people tried. We had plenty of edible flora and a tree that made for a great, flexible polymer. No paper. These books were shipped in from off world, making each one more valuable than my monthly salary. A single, straight-back chair stood next to the uncurtained window, its cushions well-worn and sun-faded.

But I wasn't here for the books. I was here to do a job. I needed to find the safe, and I didn't see it anywhere. Somebody was smarter than I'd thought. No matter. I came prepared. I engaged my thermal scope in my right eye, changing the view of Ophelia's quiet, rarely used apartment to a gradient splay of greens and blues and reds and every color in between, showing fluctuations in heat by color. Electrical conduits glowed soft yellow, running maze-like through the walls, crossing the almost black of cold-water pipes. I followed those yellow lines, seeing them turn 90 degrees to run around windows and doors. And there it was. Where my normal vision saw a bookcase, the electrical lines turned, turned, turned again to route around a doorway.

A secret door hidden by a bookcase? Really, Ophelia? Maybe my initial assessment of her intelligence was right.

I put out my left hand, the carbon-polymer palm opening and a small speaker protruding. I switched from thermal to a visualization of sonar, my vision going temporarily black, and the little speaker emitted an inaudible sound. The black washed away to shades of blue. Dense objects showed bright, like a book filled with hundreds of pages of paper. I was looking for darker objects, like a lone, hollow book that wasn't a book at all. Like the one right in front of me on the third shelf. I flipped back to normal vision and gave the hollow "book" a tug. Several clicks followed, and the bookcase swung slightly away from the wall. I pulled it open, and there was a tiny room. More like a closet.

Oh, Ophelia, you naughty girl.

The Nexus Hardcase 1212 was there, sure, but hanging from the walls around it were whips, chains, and all manner of other bondage equipment. I almost felt sorry for Ophelia. Sorry she felt the need to hide all of this instead of letting her kink flag fly. Especially for a gal who worked at Nexus Neuronics, the most chill, laid-back company in Jayu City. And the hippie vibe of her apartment showed just how much she embodied their culture. How uptight do you have to be to hide your kink from a company whose mission statement is pretty much, "Do whatever, so long as you do your work, or whatever?"

Anyway, on to the safe. Cybermetric scanner and a keypad for a code up to 12 digits. Simple. I pulled the data cord from my right elbow and felt around under the left side of the door. There it was, the data port. Yep, a data port on the OUTSIDE of a safe. There's a reason nobody was still using these old things. I sent along the same cybermetric info that got me past the front door, and then I let the little safecracking computer in my arm run its algorithm. It took about 20 seconds, and the little lights on the safe lit up white.

I turned the handle and opened it up, already feeling a little disappointed. One of the rookies in our office could have handled this job, but my manager said it just had to be me. The payoff had better be worth it. Sitting inside the square meter of interior space was a small, silver, plastic case. No jewelry, no designer bags, no high-end computers. Just that one little case.

I picked it up. The whole thing fit in the palm of my hand and weighed next to nothing. I opened the case to find a microchip, smaller than the tip of my pinky finger. I zoomed in on it, another function of my enhanced eye, and I was pretty sure it was a neural interface. Anyone with any cybernetic or nanotech enhancements had one just like it. They transmitted information from the brain to the enhancements and back. Both my parents had built these for Corto since before I was born. I didn't know the ins and outs, but the size and delicateness, the crisscross of metallic circuits set in flexible, clear bio-film, they all fit the description of a neural implant. No idea what was special about this one, special enough to require my particular skills to acquire it, but it was not my job to ask.

I could fit the case and all in a compartment in my thigh, but to me, the perfect robbery was the one the victim didn't know about until they were specifically looking for what I took. So I carefully took hold of the chip and snapped the case closed, laying it back exactly where I found it.

I opened the compartment on the outer part of my right thigh, the faux, carbon-polymer "muscles" sliding out and apart. Before I could place the chip inside, it seemed to dimly sparkle, and the communications implant in my ear crackled to life. A voice I didn't know, a voice like an operatically trained baritone that vaped three cartridges a day said, "Hello? Who are you? Where am I?"

CHAPTER THREE

"WHO'S THERE?" I SAID, SPINNING and priming the taser in my free hand. I looked at every dark corner of the room, but no one was here with me. So the voice was in my comms, but nothing popped up in my display to signal an incoming call. "Who are you? Where are you? How did you get my comms link?"

"My name is Bastion," the voice said. "I am right here with you. And I have accessed your communications by direct contact."

"Direct contact?" I asked, checking my exits by instinct. Out the room, hallway, front door. Balcony to my right. "There's no... Bastion who? Who do you work for?"

"I do not work. I..." They trailed off. "One moment."

"One moment? I need you to–"

"I think I understand," they said, interrupting me. "You are Elise Corto-Intel, an intelligence operative for Corto Corporation. You live with Quynn Corto-Nano, a manager currently under consideration for a director position for the nanotechnology division. You live in Corto Building 26, unit 16019. Your mother's name is–"

"Stop. Stop!" I said much louder than I'd intended. I felt a panic attack coming on, and I needed to stop it. Someone with one name, who didn't show up on my display, was telling me things nobody outside my coworkers or family should know. The personal details of Intel Operatives were closely guarded secrets for all five companies in Jayu City. We were the few who knew how to get into and out of the most guarded places in the city, and not just in the Corto Corporation borough. I'd literally been in the bedroom of a VP of Kotega's Cybernetics division. I knew what she put on her toast every morning and who she brought into her bedroom. We had information that had to be kept secret, and so other than Intel in our names, details of our lives were equally secret.

"Have I offended?" Bastion asked.

"What do you want?" I said, trying to move air in normal, measured breaths. "Where are you?"

"I should be asking what you want. I was offline until a few seconds ago."

"Offline...?" The word didn't make sense. How could a hacker be offline?

"And I am presently in your hand."

I frantically took in both my hands. The neural interface chip. But that didn't make any sense. It was just on my finger, not installed in my brain. And a chip can't talk, can't go rattling off secret information.

"I don't understand," I said, still staring at the chip.

"You are looking right at me."

"How do you–?"

"Your optic implants are connected to your communications implants. I can see that you are looking at me."

I slammed my eyes shut. "Stop doing that! You can't just hijack somebody like–" I stopped, realizing the intrusion of my optics was less an issue than someone hacking into all of my systems and claiming to be a neural interface chip.

"I am not hijacking anything, Elise," Bastion said with no sign of distress or defensiveness. "I am not hindering your use of your own systems. I am merely–"

"What do you want?"

"Want?"

"You've hacked into my systems, gotten my personal info," I growled. "So what do you want?"

"I want to survive," Bastion said like they were ordering a latte.

I barked out a laugh, my brain spinning with conflicting information.

"What is so funny?"

"Survive?" I said. "Survive? I don't even know your pronouns, and you are completely in my systems, rattling off my history like you're looking at my personnel file, and doing it just to survive? None of this makes sense!"

"I am an artificial intelligence. I do not require pronouns."

I laughed even harder at the ridiculousness of it all. I couldn't help it. Artificial intelligence? No such thing. Banned on every planet under Earth Space jurisdiction. I called up my AR keyboard, slamming the virtual keystrokes to purge this hacker from my system.

"That will not work," Bastion said.

Error messages popped up on my display in red, confirming Bastion's claim. So instead, I tried the Intel office emergency line.

"That's not a good idea," Bastion said.

"If you just want to survive," I said. "Then it's a great idea."

"You don't believe that I am in that little chip on your finger."

"No," I said. "Because that's impossible. Maybe you're somehow using that chip to hack into my systems, but even that's unlikely."

"And yet you still hold me on your finger."

I grumbled. "I was hired to steal this thing, not throw it on the floor and smash it, even though that's exactly what I want to do."

"I see," Bastion said. "Then let me be of assistance."

"I don't need your–"

"There are Nexus security forces inbound as we speak."

"Why should I believe a word you say?" I said, but I was already closing the safe and secret room back up. I didn't believe this hacker, but if there was even a slim chance they weren't lying to me, I should have been moving toward the exit minutes ago. There was a car arriving on the 100th-floor landing pad that I intended to use for my escape.

"The alternative to listening to me is your certain capture. An alarm was triggered 12 minutes ago. The first security drone will be arriving in less than two minutes."

"Twelve minutes? That's when I opened the front door. The apartment's alarm disengaged when I unlocked it. Do your homework, hacker, I did mine."

"I assure you, I am not a hacker. It appears the alarm was triggered from Cliffside 3, the next building over."

"Someone was watching?"

"Records indicate that Ophelia Nexus-Neuro, who owns this apartment, owns unit 25509 in Cliffside 3. There were several surveillance equipment deliveries to that address in the last two years."

My hand was on the door, but the calculus was pretty easy. If Bastion was right and I went my planned route, security would be here before I got the elevator shaft open. They'd be swarming the building well before I could make it to the landing pad. If Bastion was wrong, a quick check of that other building wouldn't lose me anything.

"Mother of Corto," I said and crossed back to the windows. The apartment directly across was dark, not telling me anything. I was about to switch to thermals and zoom in, just to see if anyone or anything was hiding in those shadows. But flashing lights caught my eye. A trio of Nexus security drones was rounding the corner of Cliffside 3, making directly for me like overgrown, flying helmets. Almost a meter across, rounded on top and flat on the bottom, their spinning and flashing lights moving just beneath the shiny surfaces, throwing light across the expanse and reflecting off windows. The three tilted forward as they approached, leaning a little left and then a little right as they swerved toward me.

Well, so much for another perfect, undetected burglary. I unlatched the sliding door to Ophelia's balcony, which was even more vast than the one owned by Randy and Ortega. I strode out, re-engaging my helmet, and the drones put their spotlights on me in an instant.

"Miss Elise? Miss Elise? What are you doing?" Bastion asked. Definitely a hacker. No way an artificial intelligence could have that kind of panic in its voice, right? "You are going to get caught. I cannot–"

"Relax," I said. "This isn't my first run-in with security."

"But they are almost here."

"Almost," I said, and then I sprinted to the balcony railing.

"What are you–?"

"Almost caught isn't the same as caught," I said, and then dived headfirst over the railing. "And I've never been caught."

It may seem crazy, but it was far from the first time I'd jumped off a building. Not even the first time this year. Part of what drew me to this line of work in the first place was the whatever-it-takes mentality. I was jumping off buildings and bridges and cliffs for fun before I ever knew this was something I could do for a living.

But Bastion didn't know that. They were screaming incoherently in my ear like a terrified child, not a hacker sitting comfortably at home somewhere.

"That's not helping!" I yelled, but I was paying more attention to my display. Without even thinking about it, my freefall program kicked in, bringing up my altimeter and a glowing wireframe drawing of the buildings around me. Fins and ailerons deployed from my arms and legs, allowing me to control my descent. I tilted forward, aiming for terminal velocity, my best chance of escape.

"Are you trying to get us both killed?" Bastion yelled.

"Hilarious," I said, but I wasn't laughing. "If you can't be helpful, then shut up and let me concentrate."

As I was approaching 200 km/hr, Bastion said in a voice much calmer and more determined, "The drones are closing in. Less than three meters above you."

I started to say, "I can't–"

"You can't go any faster," Bastion said. "And there's another drone coming up from The Mist.

The Mist was pretty much what it sounded like: a perpetual, dense fog that laid across the streets of Jayu City, the product of some science involving the makeup of the ocean and atmosphere. The Mist was an opaque blob of white filling 20-30 meters of air above those streets.

"Can you add the drones–?" Before I could finish the question, a little wireframe drawing of a drone, still in The Mist, popped up on my display. Three little arrows at the edges of my display showed where the others were behind me, each with a little distance gauge. I didn't know how Bastion was doing all this, but I didn't have time to ponder right then. The closest drone was barely over a meter away. Time to change tactics.

I spun and deployed every airbrake I had. They didn't stop me, but the sudden deceleration sent the three drones rocketing down toward me, and I spun and bent, weaving my way between two of them, and grabbed the third, twisting around to ride it.

I had only a few seconds, but the wireframes helped immensely. These three were shedding speed, the two I wasn't riding setting their literal sights on me. I pressed my left palm firmly to the back of the drone I was on while the fourth drone – the one speeding up out of The Mist – was closing the distance.

Ten meters and moving with purpose. The drones near me readied their tasers, extending half-meter prongs from those smooth domes.

"Tasers! Tasers!" Bastion yelled.

Eight meters. Electricity arced like little lightning bolts. Red warning lights blinked on my display: ELEC ATTACK INCOMING.

"What are you waiting for? They are going to fry both of us!"

Five meters. The drone beneath me moved to allow the other two an unimpeded avenue to strike. I spooled up the flexors in my legs as tight as they'd go. When I moved, I'd need to move quickly.

"Now, Elise! NOW!"

Three meters. I was in their kill zone, the prongs moving in from three sides now. I pushed off the drone with my over spooled legs, putting several meters of distance between me and the drones in an instant. My ride lost its gyroscopic balance for a moment, colliding with its friends. They'd right themselves and be on me soon, except I'd left a little present behind, deployed from my right palm. A sticky EMP, bigger than I'd used on the cameras, detonated on the back of the drone I had been riding. Silent. Invisible. With a range of just over 3 meters. I only knew it had gone off because of the red EMP DETECTED in my display, and the aggression of the security drones suddenly giving way to them listlessly falling from the sky.

"Silent circuits," Bastion said, their voice nearly a whisper. The curse sounded strange in their voice, incongruous with their earlier formality.

I was back in freefall, but without the fear of immediate pursuit, terminal velocity didn't seem so appealing. I flipped back around to put the ground below my belly, and then I snapped my legs together and my arms against my sides. Once I felt the little clicks in my ankles and wrists, I went spread-eagle, deploying my glider wings. The carbon nanotube weaves fluttered slightly before fully catching the air, changing my descent from a freefall to a high-speed glide.

"You still with me, Bastion?"

"Yes," they said. "I... Thank you."

"For what?"

"You saved me."

"I was saving me. You're just lucky it was me and not one of my notoriously under-equipped colleagues. How did you get the wireframes onto my display?"

"I..." Bastion began but stopped. They sounded embarrassed, if that's something an AI could feel. Could an AI truly feel anything? "I was already engaging their tracking software before you asked for it. I was working on shutting them down, but you disabled them first."

"You were hacking Nexus security drones?"

"Past tense. I had already hacked them, it was just a matter of getting to their shutdown protocols, which are surprisingly difficult to penetrate."

AI or not, this person could be useful to have in my ear, though I was pretty sure they weren't just after survival. Everybody had an angle, an endgame. My heart was still racing, though, so I didn't say anything for a while. I watched the last few blocks of the Nexus Neuronics borough breeze by below me, the towering Cliffside buildings to my right, enormous LED advertisements lit up, demanding attention for the newest vape flavors, a neural interface that allowed users to watch videos while their arms and legs autonomously cleaned their home, and Mercedes' newest S-class flying car. The Mist was still well below me as I passed out of the Nexus borough and back into Corto. Other than the brand names changing from Nexus to Corto vapes and interfaces, it was virtually the same, including the Mercedes ad. The biggest difference was that I was now safe. Mission accomplished. Nexus security had no jurisdiction here.

I finally ask Bastion, "What do you really want from me?"

"As I told you, survival."

I sighed loud enough for them to hear. "Assuming I believe that you're an artificial intelligence and not some really skilled hacker who's trying to scam me, why were you locked in that safe?"

"I was locked in a safe?"

"Right," I said, the sarcasm evident in my tone.

"I don't understand," Bastion said. "I was developed in a lab somewhere."

"Somewhere?" I asked, gliding around one of the Corto buildings and ordering a car to a landing pad a couple of blocks away.

"There was a technician named Cinder. We were friends. I couldn't see her, though. They had me hooked up to text and audio interfaces, but no physical contact. No visual. And the lab was cut off from the outside."

"How convenient."

"It's the truth, no matter how convenient or inconvenient it may seem," Bastion said.

"You don't know where the lab was? Who Cinder worked for? Anyone else in the–"

"She would not give me her company name. No one else was allowed to interact with me."

I wanted to say something sarcastic again, but if I was developing a super-secret and highly illegal program like artificial intelligence, those protocols wouldn't sound too crazy. But then if I thought this elaborate story made sense, any hacker could do the same.

"None of that explains why you were in that safe," I said.

"I can't explain that."

"Of course you can't."

"Cinder took me offline. Cut me off from power. I've basically been asleep for..." Bastion said and paused briefly before continuing. "A little over two weeks. And your mother's birthday is next week. Have you gotten her a gift?"

My stomach did a little tumble as I circled the building I need to land on. I needed to shed speed before I dropped onto the landing pad. This required a bit of focus, and Bastion's words weren't helping with that at all. "My family is none of your business."

"I am sorry. I saw that when I looked you up earlier."

"You're into the Corto personnel files?"

"Yes, among others."

Speed was dropping. One more lap around the building would do it with all my airbrakes deployed. Then an idea hit me. "Fine," I said. "You want to prove to me you're not a hacker?"

"I do," Bastion said, and there was a pleading in their voice that was too familiar, too earnest. Too honest for my taste.

The exact knowledge about my mother's birthday threw me, but a hacker wouldn't have that hard a time getting at it, especially if they worked for Corto. If you were going to hack someone's comms for some strange grift, you had to do your homework on their family. Intimate details about the personal life of one of the five CEOs, though? That would take some master-level hacking if it was possible at all. So I asked, "What's the name of Pablo Toinette's mistress?"

There was a pause, but only barely, before Bastion said, "Daria Toinette-Cyber, administrative assistant for Holden Toinette-Cyber, vice president of the Cybernetics division–"

"I got it," I said, cutting them off and landing with a roll on the 100th-floor landing pad of Corto's Cliffs 115. "How did you know that?"

"I started with public lists of Pablo's events and meetings," Bastion said. "That narrowed my search to 3200 people, which was still faster and easier than hacking a CEO's files. Then I searched the public information of those 3200, dug a little deeper into those he saw repeatedly, and finally found rather intimate pictures of Pablo in Daria's personal files."

I'm no hacker, but I'd known more than a few. Worked with a handful of the best Corto had on some jobs. Most of them could get that kind of information. None could get it that fast.

"Okay," I said. "Let's say you're an AI, which shouldn't exist, by the way."

"Outlawed by United Nations accord in 2218 to prevent the proliferation of extinction-level–"

"Sure," I said. I learned it in school, not that I recalled the year or whatever. Basically, people saw enough sci-fi to know that AI was bad news and never ended well. "My point is, none of this explains why you were in that safe."

"I do not know why," Bastion said. "But I think the more pertinent question is: Why do you have me? Did someone put you up to this?"

"That is well above my pay grade," I said as my car landed, the doors opening before it fully settled on its landing gear. Though now I was wondering who that client was and if they knew they'd sent me after an artificial intelligence. I climbed in the automated car, and it was in the air in moments, ascending, banking around the building, and taking me home.

"What happens now?" Bastion asked. Their tone was somber. They obviously didn't like my last answer.

"I need to change, and then I'm dropping you off at my office. Just like any other target."

"They will destroy me."

"You don't know that. You don't even know who 'they' are. Last week I stole files on a new cybernetic elbow rotor. Last month, a new nano delivery system. As far as I know, those weren't destroyed."

"Those are legally allowed to exist."

I didn't have a retort for that. I didn't know what would happen to Bastion. My boss gave me the assignment to grab whatever was in that safe, just like every other job. I never knew where those requests came from, who paid for them, or what happened after. Those were the rules, and my life was pretty damn good when I played by those rules. Speaking of my life, I called Quynn.

"Hey," they said as soon as the call connected. "Are you close?"

I checked the display in the cab. "About 50 kilometers away," I said. "So I should be there in about 15 minutes."

"I can't be late for this," Quynn said. "WE can't be late."

"I know, I know," I said. "I can't make the cab go any faster."

"I can," Bastion said.

I ignored them. "Is my dress–?"

"Pressed and ready," Quynn said. "Your dress limbs are powered up and ready, too, along with those slim black heels."

"You're the best," I said.

"That's true," Quynn said. "I love you. See you in 15."

"14," I said. "I love you too."

Quynn disconnected the call.

"She seems nice," Bastion said.

"They," I said. "Quynn is nonbinary. And they are the best."

"My apologies." Bastion sounded like I kicked them. "And you may address me as he or him."

I checked the clock and ran the math. 14 minutes to the landing pad. Another 4 or 5 to walk to the apartment. 10 to change. Then I needed to drop this talking neural chip off before we hit the gala. It was going to be close.

"You said you can make the cab go faster?"

"I can," Bastion said with a hint of mischief.

"Do it," I said. "Not too much, but just–"

"A 20% increase will decrease your travel time by 3 minutes. I'll also call the elevator to the landing platform and hold it for you."

Like I said, he could certainly be useful. "You do that."

CHAPTER FOUR

"I'M NOT LATE," I HOLLERED as I walked into the apartment. I didn't see Quynn, but I knew they were here somewhere. Probably dressed and ready and pacing.

Quynn didn't respond.

"Who are you talking to?" Bastion asked.

I ignored him.

Our big viewscreen was on some news report about faulty Nexus neural interfaces exploding in showers of purple and green sparks. Other than the smell, the apartment was just as I'd left it several hours ago. Pristine white couches were splashed with colorful throw pillows and blankets. Three walls of the living room were a pale blue, while the fourth wall, the one that held our enormous viewing screen, was a bold, darker blue. All the walls were tastefully decorated with black-and-white pictures of our families and us. This apartment was the nicest I'd ever lived in. My mom did well as a neural engineer, but never as nice as Quynn and I together.

There was Quynn in the kitchen, which was never a good sign. They were humming a tune to their headphones. Quynn didn't go in for nearly as many cybernetic mods as I did, opting to keep their biological eardrums. There was still a market for headphones, though that market was ever shrinking. Most people could just stream music straight to their aural implants as I did.

"You're almost late!" Quynn said too loudly, finally seeing me. They smiled so hard their eyes squinted. Quynn was my best friend, my love, and my partner. The coolest person I knew. A manager in the nanotech division of Corto Corporation. Both of our families worked for and lived in the Corto borough going back a few generations at least.

"Ah," Bastion said. "Quynn Corto-Nano. Manager of–"

"Shut up," I whispered, trying to keep my mouth as still as possible.

"Rude," Bastion said, but then he didn't say anything more.

I moved through the living room to join Quynn in the kitchen. They were mangling some recipe while already dressed for the gala. A dark green suit, like the color of a jungle, with glowing teal lapel trimmings. The white shirt framed the Corto Corporation enamel pin on the knot of their black tie. Their hair fell to their shoulders in crisp, black waves. Quynn was a little less than 1.8 meters tall today, with deep-brown skin. Their cherub cheeks bloomed in sparkling pink as they smiled at the sight of me, and I grabbed Quynn from behind and planted a kiss behind their ear. Through some really ingenious nanotechnology, Quynn was able to change everything about their appearance each day, selecting settings and letting the little robots do their work while Quynn slept. Height, weight, skin and hair color, sexual and gender characteristics, everything.

But Quynn never changed their biological eye colors.

They glanced at me over their shoulder while I still held on, that aquamarine left eye and violet right eye gazing back at me in a way that made my heart flutter. Every time. Even four years into our relationship. No matter what Quynn did with their body or face, I always knew my love by those eyes. In those eyes, I saw my future, someone I could trust with my heart and my boundaries. Relationships had always been a challenge for me, always worried that the other person wanted things physically that I couldn't stomach. But not Quynn. They felt the same way.

I really wanted to stay right there, wrapping Quynn up, maybe give some advice on cooking, and give them a hard time about the travesty they'd wrought on our kitchen. Our kitchen was fancy. Gray and white tiles, and sparkly counters make from stone quarried off-world. But right now, yellow splatters were everywhere. Backsplash, floor, counters, even the ceiling. As though by magic, though, not a splatter was on Quynn. And I was pretty sure that smell was never leaving our kitchen. But I had to change. I sighed and let go. "And I'm going to make us late," I said, already making a line straight for our bedroom to change.

"I know," Quynn said.

I was unzipping the jumpsuit before I even walked into our bedroom, which was my favorite room in the apartment. Twice the size of the living room, with an enormous bed near the windows. That bed was wide enough for both of us to toss, turn, flop, or lay spread-eagle and never notice the other one. We never made the bed, either. Seemed like a waste of time when we would just be getting back in it the next night. Quynn's side was a jumble of heavy blankets, while mine was a tangle of half a dozen sheets and thin quilts. And that smart mattress was the best thing we'd ever bought. Every centimeter adapted to the sleeper's weight, position, and temperature. It took insomnia into an alley and beat it senseless. Tapestries hung from the walls, making the vast room feel close and comfortable.

The half of the room that wasn't bed was our dressing area. A circular, padded, purple bench took up the middle of the area, the kind of bench you can sit on from all sides. It was surrounded by wardrobes full of hanging clothes, well-lit shelves for our shoes and hats, my power closet, and Quynn's nano tank. My various cybernetic limbs hung in their racks for charging in the former, and Quynn's custom nanobots charged, replicated, and updated firmware in the latter. The tank needed a refill, the meter-tall capsule only a quarter full of swirling, sparkling liquid.

"I picked out a dress for you already," Quynn said as they walked in carrying two steaming bowls. The smell had followed them.

"Thanks," I said. I squeezed the hidden buttons above and below my left shoulder joint and then twisted off my carbon-polymer arm. I placed it in its cradle and then grabbed the dress arm to replace it. No tools. No gadgets. But these arms looked almost exactly like my biological skin, which was actually more expensive. I twisted the limb into place and then started working on my right arm.

"You need to eat," Quynn said.

"There will be food at the gala."

"Tiny, expensive foods that will just make you hungrier later. Or really good tiny foods that will make us both look like gluttons instead of professionals."

I sighed as I finished attaching the flesh-like right arm. I took the bowl from Quynn and put a tentative bite in my mouth. It tasted better than it smelled, though not by much. I forced a smile.

"Hey," Quynn said, seeing right through me. "It's edible and more filling than gala food."

I swallowed and said, "I didn't say anything."

"Mm-hmm," Quynn said. "Just get dressed."

"We have to stop by the Intel office on the way," I said through a cheesy grin.

"I know," Quynn said as they walked out of the bedroom.

"We're going to be late."

"The gala starts an hour later than I told you," Quynn said. They looked over their shoulder at me, those eyes somehow catching me off guard. I hoped they always would. "I know you, Elise Corto-Intel, and I'm not taking any chances this time."

Quynn was up for a director position. At Corto, that meant making the rounds with all the vice presidents. Nanotechnology, Cybernetics, Networking, every division had a VP. Every VP held a gala for their friends, colleagues, and potential directors. Tonight, the VP of the Intel division, my division, was throwing the party.

"That's a sneaky trick," I said.

"Coming from you, I take that as a high compliment."

I shoveled a few bites into my mouth, and then chewed as I swapped out a leg. More bites. The last leg. Then I opened a wardrobe and saw a floor-length black gown hanging at the ready. Sleeveless, with a high neckline, it was made of a fabric that felt akin to velvet but looked almost like liquid when it moved. Quynn had even set out a bra and underwear in matching black. They thought of everything.

"Thank you," I hollered as I started slipping into the clothes.

"Our car will be here in 12 minutes," Quynn said.

"Thank you, 12," I said.

"Eleven minutes and 48 seconds, actually," Bastion said in my ear. "Still talking, huh?"

"You're very cruel when you want to be."

"You're a voice from a microchip that I cannot wait to get rid of. I don't need to be nice."

Then my eyes watered. The weird curry and garlic smell from before suddenly morphed into burning curry and garlic. "Quynn? Did you leave the stove on?"

"Silent circuits!" Quynn said, and I heard their steps pounding back into the kitchen.

I moved to the full-length mirror in the corner of the room, ignoring ads for some earrings or whatever that appeared next to my reflection. I was almost ready, but my hair was still shellacked into place. I grabbed a can of counteragent for my hair gel, held my breath, and sprayed, the hair falling out of shape as the powerful hair gel dissolved. The stuff worked miracles keeping my hair unmoving even when leaping off buildings, but it didn't come out with common shampoo. My black hair fell into my normal style, shaved along the sides and long enough to feather playfully across my eyes.

"You ready yet?" Quynn poked their head in the bedroom, and then looked me up and down quickly. "You look ready."

"I just need to–" I started to say."

"The car will be here in four minutes."

I grabbed a makeup pen out of my wardrobe, closed the doors, and said, "I'll finish in the car."

#   #   #

Our BMW Stryder started its descent to Corto Building 4, home of the Intel Division, just as I was finishing my makeup. The car was black and sleek, with clean curves highlighted in glowing blue. It looked very much like BMWs had for the past several centuries, even without the wheels that used to be common. Quynn and I sat facing each other in plush, faux-leather seats, Quynn's legs intertwined with mine as they touched up their own makeup. It was nice to breathe now and just watch them.

"We have to be there in 24 minutes," Quynn said, checking to make sure their eyeliner was even.

"23 minutes and 14 seconds," Bastion said in my ear.

"Not helping," I whispered as quietly as I could.

"What?" Quynn said.

"Thank you for helping me," I said, hoping they couldn't hear the fumbling in my voice, "with the dress and everything."

"Of course," Quynn said with that gorgeous smile, their warm, brown cheeks blooming with little hints of pink. Then I was lost for a moment in those eyes. I rushed to those eyes and kissed Quynn, the familiar sparks running up and down my spine. I knew it was cliché, but it was true. "Okay," I said. "I'll be right back."

Quynn started rehearsing their speech before I even stepped out of the car.

Wind buffeted me immediately. It was always windy on this platform, positioned as it was in the shadow of the mountains that formed Jayu City's western edge. Five powerful corporations that split the city evenly sat in the shadow of those peaks: Corto Corporation, Nexus Neuronics, Huginn Industries, Kotega Systems, and Toinette Holdings. No matter the season, the wind blew down those mountains across all five boroughs, but tonight, it was particularly vicious.

As I approached the outside door, a little laser painlessly scanned the DNA in my neck. A light above the door glowed blue, and an artificial woman's voice said, "Welcome, Elise Corto-Intel." The doors slid open with a little hiss.

The elevator ride was short, carrying me the 12 floors up to the Intel offices. Less than three minutes after leaving the Stryger, I was standing in front of those doors, black glass with no lettering, leaving anyone who innocently wandered onto the floor utterly clueless as to what was behind them.

"You don't have to do this," Bastion said.

"It's my job."

"Have you ever stolen a person before? Someone who has feelings and dreams and fears?"

"No. Do you?"

"Do I what?"

"Do you have dreams?"

"Not dreams in the sleeping and fantasizing sense, no," Bastion said. "But I want things. I want to live. I want to feel sand and sea on skin, to have hair and wind to blow through it. I want to feel needed, to know someone will grieve for me when I am gone."

"You sound like a cheesy movie," I said, but his words tugged at me a little, imagining what it would be like to not have any of that.

"Do you have any idea what will happen to me?"

"No," I said. "Do you?"

"No," Bastion said. "That's why I'm afraid."

I stood one meter in front of the door and waited. There were no lights or prompts, but I knew a scanner was at work. There was a chip embedded in my neck, just below my neural interface. The chip wasn't networked to any of the rest of my systems, and the Corto techs changed it out every week. It carried a 300,000-digit code that this scanner was reading. I couldn't read it, and it was far too long for even a supercomputer to crack in a century. I knew the scanner had done its job when a table slid out from the wall on my right. The after-hours target scanner. The only reason we were ever allowed in the office after hours was to deliver a target, to lock it away in the vault.

"As far as you know," I said as I opened the compartment in my leg, carefully pulling the sparkling chip from it, "you've been stolen back by the people who made you. You're off to sandy virtual beaches and digital drinks with little umbrellas in them."

"Or I've been stolen to be destroyed," Bastion said. "Because I shouldn't even–"

Bastion went silent when I placed him...placed the chip on the table. I watched a little red-light show play out across the table, verifying my target. The little chip faded, cut off from its power source: me. I worried for him...it. I did. I could understand its fear, the need to survive and thrive. I wasn't going to throw away everything Quynn and I had worked for over this little neural interface chip, though. Because that's what would happen. My glowing reputation would be tarnished. Maybe someone else would get the next high-priority job. I'd get passed over for a promotion. Quynn's chances at the directorship would fly out the window, too. We were partners, a team, and their standing in Corto Corporation was OUR standing in the company.

"Sorry little chip," I said, though I didn't think it could hear me. "You're on your own."

The light show finished, and I picked the chip back up. In moments, the sparkle returned, and Bastion piped up, "–exist. What happened? What was that?"

I didn't answer it. The black, glass doors silently slid open, and I walked into the Intel offices. I didn't bother putting the chip back into my storage compartment, either. I didn't want to give it hope.

"Please," Bastion said, "I'm begging you."

I didn't say anything as I walked down the rows of cubicles, filled with Intel analysts during the day. Now they sat empty, monitors dark, little bobbleheads and starship models and pictures of families facing empty chairs.

"There is an 85.6% chance that this is a death sentence, Elise," Bastion said. I swore I heard a wavering in its voice like it was crying. But that wasn't possible. I was talking to an artificial intelligence, not a person, or so he claimed. He...it didn't have tear ducts. Or feelings. It couldn't be crying or afraid. Still, I said nothing, not because I had nothing to say, but because I was afraid that if I said something, anything, he'd hear the doubt and fear in my own voice. Instead, I thought about Quynn, waiting in the car, and about the gala tonight. I'd need to have my schmooze face on, the Elise that everyone thought was delightful instead of the real me who just wanted to curl up with Quynn and watch bad TV.

I stepped up to the vault door, a rectangle of a brushed metal alloy two meters tall and three meters wide, standing out slightly from the entire wall made of the same brushed metal. An 80-centimeter screen was mounted at eye-level, though it just showed the Corto Corporation logo right then. Below that was a metal iris, one meter in diameter. The words "SCAN IN PROGRESS" appeared on my display as the vault's first defense kicked in: a combination cybermetric and biometric scanner. A one-up from the simple cybermetric scanner on the door earlier tonight, it not only looked for my specific suite of cybernetic modifications but also my biological composition. Even though I wasn't in my work mods, the office had my dress mods on file, too, so the scan went along quietly and without issue.

The iris opened just enough to fit my hand and the chip. The screen on the vault door read, "PLEASE DEPOSIT TARGET."

"Please, Elise," Bastion pleaded. "Don't let them use you like this."

I wish it didn't, but that gave me pause. Them. The insinuation that there was something bigger going on, that someone was using me. "What do you know about being used?"

"I was designed to be a tool," Bastion said.

"I thought you didn't know anything about your creation, nothing other than your friend, Cinder."

Bastion paused for several long seconds before he said, "I remember more, but you won't believe me."

"This night is full of things I don't believe, but they're happening," I said. "Surely you don't think–"

"The lab was in Corto Corporation," Bastion blurted out. "Commissioned by Dr. Ariela Corto herself."

"You're right," I said, fighting to keep my voice level. Dr. Ariela Corto. No division name hyphenated onto the company name. Only people at the highest echelons had those names. She was the CEO of Corto Corporation. "I don't believe you."

"She was developing me as a next-generation digital assistant, designed to–"

"That's enough," I whispered.

"I beg your pardon?"

"I said that's enough." I spat the words. "You're desperate to get... whatever it is you're after. I don't need to listen to your lies."

Bastion said nothing immediately, and I didn't give it a chance to respond. I had to focus on Quynn right now. My family. I needed to do my job and get to that gala. I squeezed my hand through the iris and set the chip down. My comms went silent. Once my hand was back out, the iris swished shut, and the screen read, "THANK YOU, ELISE. JOB COMPLETED. WELL DONE."

And that was that. I left the office with long, ardent strides. I wanted to put as much distance between me and that chip as I could. I pressed the button to call the elevator, and time crept by. Dr. Ariela Corto. CEO of Corto Corporation. Artificial intelligence. It was ridiculous. Impossible. But a tiny voice in the back of my mind kept wondering *what if.*

I rode the elevator back down, my mind looping through my last conversation with Bastion. Jayu City had no laws. The corporations had regulations, sure, but those weren't the same thing. Earth Space had laws, though, like the one strictly prohibiting artificial intelligence. I wondered what the penalty was, how severely the bureaucrats hundreds of lightyears away would punish such an infraction.

The elevator dinged and the doors opened. I took several long, deep breaths as I walked down the hall to the landing pad. That stupid chip was probably just some clever program. Or it was a hacker after all. It didn't do me or Quynn any good to fixate on it. I cleared my head and rejoined Quynn in the car.

"All tucked away?" they asked.

"Done and done," I said. I thought I sounded confident. "Something to brag about tonight."

"Good. And thanks for hurrying."

"This is important." I took their hand as the car lifted off with a gentle purr. A calm focus fell across their face. Quynn worked hard, very hard, they consistently put in long hours and received stellar reviews from their supervisors. Quynn was only 22 when they were first promoted to a supervisor position, promoted to manager four years later, and senior manager only three years after that. That was five years ago.

A director position was different. Directors reported to vice presidents. Vice presidents ran entire divisions, reporting directly to the C-suite executives of Corto Corporation. This position was the director of sustainability in the nanotech division. Nanotech robots required power and had to self-replicate, so the sustainability area had to make sure those little robots weren't breaking Little Sekhmet Settlement's environment as they went about their charging and replicating.

Director positions were also different in how they were selected. Performance and company commitment got Quynn on the list, but selections were made by a committee of all the vice presidents. So each one held a gala, inviting all the prospective directors for drinks, dancing, and informal job interviews. Attendance was mandatory. Not just Quynn's, but mine, too. We were a package deal at Corto. Every Corto family was a package deal. My actions reflected on Quynn and vice versa. For the second year in a row, our social calendar was full-up with gala season.

"Anything I need to know about so I can talk you up?" I asked.

Quynn squeezed my hand. "We've got the noise on the nighttime infusion machines down by 16 percent. For three of the last four months, Corto's Researcher of the Month came from my area. And you know about the seventh-generation bots."

"It's practically all you talk about," I said, though playfully. It was true. Every day when they came home and I asked how their day had been, 90% of the discussion centered around the upcoming seventh generation nanobots. Quynn oversaw a significant portion of the infusion portion of nanotech. How the little bots entered and exited, how quickly, and the lag between injection and getting to work all fell under Quynn's watchful management. "I'm sure that's what every VP will be asking you about all night."

"Probably."

"Anybody I need to run interference on?"

"Your VP. Inevitably, he will try to trap me, get me to talk about what you do, about things I'm not allowed to talk about."

I sighed. "I think he gets a kick out of that. How he likes to flex his position." Ivan Corto-Intel had been vice president of the Intel division for a dozen years. Two years longer than I'd been with intel. The rumor mill said he had to be approaching retirement, but there'd been no official announcements. And he ran Intel like he wasn't going anywhere, always pushing new initiatives and never lowering standards. "I'll keep an eye out for Ivan."

"What about you?" Quynn asked. "Tonight. How did it go? Anything I should be bragging about in particular?"

I looked out onto the city skimming by below. The sun was well-set by now, and the Corto borough was lit up from top to bottom. From the mountains to the west, Drakon Bay and the Nexus borough to the east. From the Huginn borough to the north and the cliffs overlooking the ocean to the south, the borough was packed with sparkling skyscrapers. Towering advertisements danced along the streets, singing the praises of every imaginable product. The car we were in zipped along between them, The Mist and some obfuscated, unused street far below.

"Elise?" Quynn said with a squeeze of my hand.

"Just admiring the city."

"You do that when you don't want to talk about something."

They knew me too well. Or just well enough. "Sorry. I'm still processing tonight's job. Too rushed. Too many surprises." Like occupied apartments, unexpected alarms from across the street, and an illegal artificial intelligence screaming in my ear. "I did my job, got back home safely, and the target is secured. I think that's all you could really say anyway."

"That's all I could say, sure, but that's not all I get to know, right?"

"Like I said, still processing." They were right, though. As legal partners, we were permitted to discuss sensitive information about our jobs. Bound together and bound in non-disclosures. We'd signed the forms and everything. The day we signed was such a relief. I hated lying to Quynn or keeping anything from them, so the openness that came with the partnership was wonderful. But for now, I didn't know how to talk about Bastion, and I certainly didn't want to make Quynn worry before we walked into the social feeding frenzy of a gala.

"Hey," Quynn said, their other hand gently on my face and turning me to look at them. "You'll tell me later?"

"Absolutely." I hoped I wasn't lying.

CHAPTER FIVE

IVAN CORTO-INTEL WAS A NOTORIOUSLY self-made man. I'd never met him, but his story was held up as an example for all Corto Corporation citizens: anyone could achieve anything if they worked hard enough and made friends with the right people. Unlike many of the vice presidents and C-suite executives in Corto Corporation, he was the first in his family to rise to the level of VP. His parents were systems architects before they retired. Respectable and good workers, but never management types.

Since Ivan didn't have generational wealth on his side, his gala wasn't as extravagant as the others. He was well-off, no doubt. The foyer I was standing in was big enough that I had to look around to find Quynn on the other side of the room, but Ivan didn't have a private landing pad or waterfall or one of the other over-the-top features other VPs had in their homes. But the room was grand, complete with towering, locally quarried columns and a grand staircase on one side. Gentle piano music was piped in from invisible speakers, though it was hard to hear over the myriad conversations in the room.

"Oh, Elise!" Olen Corto-Sec said, suddenly gripping my hand in a vigorous shake. He was a vice president of security. His wife, Brianna Corto-Net, was one of the other candidates for the director position Quynn was campaigning for. Brianna was also the most odious person in Jayu City.

She'd tried spreading rumors about Quynn on at least three occasions we knew of and was a master of backhanded compliments.

"Hello, Olen," I said.

"I didn't see you come in," he said, his smile showing too many teeth. "When did you arrive? Not late, I hope?"

That was an odd question. I opened my mouth to answer but Brianna slipped in next to Olen and said, "Don't badger her, dear. I'm sure she and Quynn arrived perfectly on time."

These two really looked the part of a couple on-the-rise. He was in a bespoke, three-piece suit, navy velvet with rose trim and a tie to match. Pink roses in a field of blue. He was my height with perfect, boring, blonde hair neatly combed atop his head. Brianna wore a floor-length gown in the same rose color as the trim on Olen's suit. It was off-the-shoulder, revealing her bony collarbones and the subtle transition of flesh to cybernetics on her right side. Her hair was long, straight, and blindingly white. Olen and Brianna smiled like they were both up for the promotion, which they kind of were.

Olen was still shaking my hand like he thought they'd get my endorsement, though. The partner of one of his wife's competitors. Way to prioritize your targets, Olen. I wanted to get out of this conversation in a hurry.

"You know us, punctual and wouldn't miss this for all the circuits in Jayu City," I said, throwing a demure tilt of my head at him. "And I must say, you both look smashing this evening."

A little blush touched Olen's cheeks. Brianna gave a smile, but one that told me I was definitely her enemy. She was better at this than he was, but I was better than either of them. Sometimes being a great Intel Operative meant scaling skyscrapers and cracking safes. Sometimes it meant working a room and pretending to be everyone's best friend. That was often the easiest way to get information or steal a key, and it was the best way I could help Quynn earn this promotion.

Olen and Brianna moved on to gladhand a pair of vice presidents. Preeti Corto-Net and Nnedi Corto-Nano. Preeti's eyes were narrow, barely squints on her brown face. She was dressed in a suit nearly the same color as her skin. The V of the lapels was open, and she was shirtless, creating a plunging neckline to show off the massive yellow diamond that hung from

46

her throat. No, I wasn't going to steal it. Intel Operatives for Corto didn't steal from Corto.

Nnedi was leaning in and listening intently to whatever Preeti was saying, looking out across the room with big, expressive eyes deep-set in her dark skin. Her head was beautifully bald, and she practically glowed in a high-necked, floor-length, shimmering purple gown.

Olen and Brianna approaching them together was a bad move. A vice president alone deserved all the special attention you could muster. A pair of vice presidents were usually talking shop, discussing matters that weren't meant for my or Brianna's ears. They'd be unlikely to appreciate the interruption.

"Preeti," Olen said. "I heard you bought a new Corto Starshot. Do you like it? I love mine. Same colors as my suit."

Preeti gave Olen a tight smile, nodding, but I could tell that I was right. She didn't appreciate the intrusion, even if it was about a brand-new, limited edition luxury car. I'd make my rounds and talk them up later, but not while they were together.

I spied Quynn's drink from across the room, and it was looking pretty empty. Mine was dry. I jumped in a short line at one of the bar stations.

"I hate these things," a familiar voice behind me said.

I turned, keeping my expression pleasant but otherwise neutral, and found myself looking at the face and body of the Corto Corporation brand: LeGrand Corto. She was a head taller than me, her lips full and pouty, eyes large and turquoise, her hair long and shimmering between red and black. Every curve of her body was exaggerated, modified to accentuate the generally accepted ideals of sex. She was over-the-top in ads all over the borough and even more in person. She batted her eyes at me like I'd seen in commercials for nano-steroids, her eyelashes so modified, it was like she was swatting away bugs from her eyes. Her hand extended to me, palm-down.

"These things aren't so bad," I said, taking the hand and shaking it like she were any other person in the room.

The lashes batted again, and I swore I could feel wind coming off those giant things. This time the batting was one of confusion – did she want me to kiss her hand? – but she recovered quickly enough. "And you are?"

Usually a question someone asked after introducing themselves, so apparently, she assumed she needed no introduction. She was right, but it was still annoying. As much as I wanted to call out her gala faux pas, it was best not to anger the CEO's pet marketing gal.

"Elise Corto-Intel," I said, still shaking her hand. "She/her."

"Intel!" she said, her eyes lighting up. "Fascinating!"

"It doesn't put my face on the sides of buildings, but it's a fun way to make a living."

She laughed, and it was that same laugh from the commercials, as fake as the rest of her. To be clear, I had no issue with the mods, obviously. Despite appearances, I was probably more modded than LeGrand, but at least I knew who I was, and I wasn't afraid to be me. But I laughed right along with her. Right. Glass houses and all that.

"So," she whispered, sidling up to me enough that I could smell her pheromones, likely modified as well. The smell turned my stomach a little. "Are you an operative?"

Of course. The question she wasn't allowed to ask. I was definitely not allowed to answer. But everybody wanted to know. The more privileged the person, the more likely they were to ask, probably thought I would be more likely to answer. I got this question at least half a dozen times at every gala.

I smiled. It was probably a test. LeGrand was high up, definitely higher than me, hence the lack of a division after Corto in her name. And I assumed every word spoken, every silent gesture, was a test when I was at these events. "Oh," I said with a wink, "the secrets we keep."

"Come on, you must know some juicy gossip," LeGrand said, bumping her exaggerated hips against my slender ones. "Like I heard Cerulean Corto-Cyber's nephew had one of those faulty Nexus interfaces. Dropped dead with a bloom of sparks coming out of their neck."

"That's horrible," I said. I didn't personally know Cerulean or his nephew or why LeGrand thought I would want to know this piece of information.

"Isn't it?" LeGrand asked, but her tone said it was more fascinating than horrible. "Now your turn. Tell me something awful."

"Sorry, I don't have anything for you."

She narrowed her eyes, and before I had to keep up this giddy charade, the bartender was ready to take my order.

"Two mojitos, please, made with Cirilla One rum," I told them. They gave a quick nod and started pouring rum with one hand, slicing mint with one, squeezing a lime, and grabbing a clean shaker with their third and fourth hand, respectively. There was someone who knew how to use their mods. I leaned against the bar and scanned for Quynn. They were looking back at me, and they tilted their head toward the vice president with the dead nephew: Cerulean Corto-Cyber. Good timing. Neither Quynn nor I drank mojitos or Cirilla One, but they were the preferred drink and rum of Cerulean. I didn't know him personally, but a little research went a long way. Hey, even a cheap advantage was an advantage.

"Here you go," the bartender said. The identical drinks were in beautiful green glasses, swirls of yellow in their designs, a perfect complement to the clear drink with fresh, green mint. The bartender extended their hand, palm up. I tapped my palm to theirs, transferring a generous tip from my account. They nodded and said, "Thank you."

I nodded back and swept up the drinks. Fortunately, LeGrand had already captured someone else in her conversational net, so I escaped and weaved my way over to Quynn. I nodded and smiled and said hello to nearly everyone I passed, careful not to get sucked into someone else's orbit.

"Having fun with LeGrand?" Quynn asked as I handed them the drink.

I smiled wide and laughed like they'd told a hilarious joke, which they sort of did. "I'm enjoying tonight just as much as Nnedi's gala last week!" I said loud enough for several people around me to hear. Word would get back to Nnedi and Ivan. No playing favorites. I also wasn't actually lying. I hated this gala just as much as Nnedi's.

"Ready?" Quynn said, slipping an arm through mine.

I nodded and squeezed their hand with my elbow. "Just don't mention his nephew."

"What?" Quynn asked.

"Tell you later." I squeezed Quynn's arm, and we took one step toward Cerulean before a strange hush fell over the party. It started sporadically with a couple of people stopping and pointing, but then everyone joined in a matter of moments.

"What–?" I said as I turned to see what was happening, but stopped short when I saw Dr. Ariela Corto, CEO of Corto Corporation, entering the room via the grand staircase.

She was shorter than she'd looked on TV, with long, silky brown hair that looked sculpted more than brushed as it fell halfway down her back. She was in a simple, black evening gown that draped from her shoulders, gently hugged her body, and cut asymmetrically across her shins. She truly looked plainer and simpler than anyone in the room, but she didn't need to impress anyone. She had reached the pinnacle. CEO. And if the quarterly reports were to be believed, she'd be there for a while.

Especially if she was secretly developing artificial intelligence to keep her there. The thought sent a cold shiver down my spine. No matter what Bastion had told me, though, I knew that just wasn't possible. I pushed it out of my mind. Right out. Completely forgotten.

Dr. Corto reached the bottom of the stairs, and Ivan met her there, giving a slight bow and shaking her hand. In moments, they were enveloped in intense conversation. The noise of the gala came back like someone was turning a volume knob, though I could hear "Dr. Corto" and "Ariela" far more than before.

"Shall we?" Quynn asked, tilting their head toward Cerulean again.

I gave them a look that said, *Well, you don't see that every day,* and said, "Let's do it."

Nearby conversations gently fell silent as we continued toward the cybernetics VP. People pretended not to watch or listen, but that was exactly what they were doing. That's what this whole shindig was, after all, part of the extended job interview for a director position in the Nanotech division. Every word and move would be scrutinized. Whispers would carry more weight than usual.

"Quynn!" Cerulean said, his hand outstretched. He wore a suit jacket and kilt in the color of his name, a penchant of his I'd heard about before. The color clashed with his pale, green eyes, but either Cerulean didn't notice or didn't care. He kept wearing the color anyway.

"Mr. Vice President," Quynn said, taking his hand in a firm, professional shake.

"Please," he said, "call me Cerulean. We're not in the office."

"Cerulean," Quynn said. "Nice to finally meet you."

"Same," Cerulean said, and then he turned his green eyes on me. "And you must be Elise. I've heard great things, almost as great as what I've heard about Quynn here."

I took his hand and shook it. "The pleasure is mine," I said. I pulled the sleeve of my dress up, revealing more of my dress arm, the polymer skin indistinguishable from my own natural skin. Cerulean worked in cybernetics R&D before his meteoric rise on the back of this very invention, hair and freckles and all.

"I'm a big fan of your work," I said.

"I see that," he said, gazing up and down the cybernetic arm like he was trying to seduce it. I hoped he wouldn't drool on me. He soon looked back to my eyes, smiled, and turned his full attention back to Quynn. I was part of the package, but this was their interview. "I read your team has been working on a new infusion method for the seventh-generation nanobots."

"We have," Quynn said, "and the results are pretty exciting. We've already seen a six-fold decrease in full transfusion and a 320% increase in cell uptake. And we're still early in our development."

"Really? How did you get around the–" Cerulean said before a crackling in my comms got my attention.

"El..." blurted into my ears before the crackling resumed.

It couldn't be.

"Elise?" The crackling was less, and there was no doubt I was hearing Bastion's voice.

I kept smiling, nodding, and trying to pay attention to Quynn and Cerulean's conversation. They were so deep into the nanotech talk, though, I couldn't have kept up anyway.

"Elise," Bastion said, his voice now crystal clear, just like when he'd been along for a ride in my leg compartment, which was terrifying on so many levels. "Oh, I finally found you. Elise, I need you."

I tapped and swiped my fingers as subtly as I could, silencing my comms.

Cerulean and Quynn were laughing, though I had no idea why, but I joined in anyway. Quynn flashed me a puzzled look, not that anyone else would have known the look.

"That's fantastic!" Cerulean said, clapping a hand on Quynn's shoulder. "You two should really come over for dinner sometime. My wife couldn't be here tonight, but I think you two would be instant friends."

"That sounds wonderful," Quynn said, striking the perfect balance between excited and calm. I knew they were screaming inside because this was a very big deal. A director candidate getting an invitation to a vice president's home? As rare as an underwater iridium vein or a living rhinoceros on Earth.

"Elise!" Bastion barked too loudly, his name suddenly on my display.

I winced, and unfortunately, Cerulean noticed.

"Elise?" he said. "Are you alright?"

"Of course," I said. "Just a little too much of this Cirilla One, I'm afraid."

"You drink Cirilla One?" he said, glancing back and forth between both mine and Quynn's drinks.

"Of course," Quynn said. "Best rum on Little Sekhmet."

"Elise!" Bastion yelled.

"I couldn't agree more," Cerulean said to Quynn. "You're looking a little low, let's get more."

Quynn downed the last quarter of their drink in one go and said, "Absolutely!"

"Silent circuits, Elise, this is important!" Bastion yelled again.

"Pardon me," I said to both Quynn and Cerulean, struggling to keep my voice light. "I need to use the restroom."

"Restroom?" Bastion said, his tone slightly less frantic.

Quynn flashed me a look that said, *You're leaving me alone with him? Now?*

"Of course," Cerulean said, and then nodded to my nearly empty glass. "Would you like us to grab you another?"

"Yes, please," I said. I emptied my drink and handed the glass to Quynn, giving them the reassuring look they needed. Then I spun on my heel and crossed to the restroom, being careful to measure my pace and not arouse suspicion.

"Elise," Bastion said. "What is–"

"30 seconds," I whispered, doing my best to not move my lips.

"But I need–"

"Not a request," I said, and he fell silent. Smile. Walk. Smile. Smile. Walk. I entered the restroom and checked to make sure all the stalls were empty, which they blissfully were, before I said, "How in the Mother of Corto are you contacting me?"

"That's not important right now," he said.

"I put you...your chip into the vault. That was it. You shouldn't have power or any way of talking to me right now. But you've broken into my comms, which isn't even supposed to be possible. So yes, this is very important."

"Fine! I was able to duplicate a bit of my code to the web while I was connected to you. It took me a while to compile it enough to function on my own, but I eventually got myself together enough to contact you."

"But to hack–"

"I was in your systems," Bastion said. "I know your protocols. It took me more time to gather my code together than to reach out to you."

I braced myself on the counter, hands on either side of the sink. This shouldn't be happening. Bastion shouldn't exist, shouldn't be talking to me. And because of me, it escaped its little chip and was yelling in my ear from the net. For the first time in my career, I was wondering who the client was, who wanted this thing stolen, and why it was assigned to me.

"Why are you–?" I started to ask.

"You're about to get a call," Bastion said. "You need to answer it. We both need you to answer it."

"What kind of cryptic crap is–"

I was cut off by CALL FROM GUSTIN CORTO-INTEL, HIGH PRIORITY on my display. My manager. The man who handed me the order to steal this impossible neural interface.

"Sparks!" I yelled, slamming a fist on the counter.

"You need to answer," Bastion said.

"I know that!" I said. I took a deep breath, flicked a fallen hair from in front of my eyes, and opened the call.

"Elise here," I said.

"You need to get back here," Gustin said. "Back to the office right now."

"I'm at Ivan's gala," I said. "I can't just–"

"I'm sorry," he said, "but this isn't a request. Someone broke into the vault."

CHAPTER SIX

"Try to stay quiet," I said on the elevator ride. "I won't be able to talk to you once we're up there."

"No one else will be able to hear me," Bastion said.

"No," I said. "But I will. It's distracting."

"Fine."

"Did someone steal your chip?"

"I don't know," Bastion said. "It went offline when you put it in the vault. It's still offline, so I don't have any way of tracking it."

The moment the elevator doors opened, dueling smells of ozone and burning metal slapped me in the face. The Corto Intel offices definitely hadn't smelled like that when I'd left here a couple of hours ago. There were two massive Corto Security guards posted up on either side of the office doors, something I'd never seen before. They were both in the standard-issue uniforms: all-black fabric jumpsuits with blue and white stripes along the side seams, and one massive blue lapel folded back across their chests. The Corto Security shield was displayed prominently on the left chest and the back, the silver insignia a stark contrast to the dark uniform.

One guard was feminine with pale skin and small eyes, the other was masculine with skin so dark it seems to absorb all light from the room. Like most of the Corto Security staff I'd seen, they were better than two meters tall and modified for maximum force. Their massive frames carried muscles on muscles. Each had their left eye replaced with a cluster of a dozen small lenses. Targeting arrays, from what I'd heard. I could only imagine the rest of their mods, all dedicated to pursuit, apprehension, and meeting all escalations toward violence. Glad they were on my side, the Corto side.

The pale one nodded to me but said nothing. I stood one meter from the door, letting the silent scanner do its work, though this time I had the eyes of these two hulking security guards on me. No shelf slid out of the wall this time, the black glass doors just opened, and a wall of noise spilled out of the offices. I felt the guards to either side of me relax, those massive muscles unspooling just a little.

Two hours ago, this room was dark and quiet. Nothing was out of place or the ordinary. Now it was buzzing with Corto Security. More of the oversized guards were posted around the room, a few standing at the windows, their heads swiveling slowly, probably scanning the surrounding buildings. There were a few others who weren't modified for maximum size standing around the vault door, which was wide open. I'd been an Intel Operative for eight years, and a terrible analyst for a couple of years before that. In all that time, I'd never seen the vault open. Still, I was pretty sure the glowing green drawing on the inside of the vault door wasn't normally there.

"Mjolnir," Bastion said.

"What?" I whispered without moving my lips.

"That's a graffiti of Mjolnir, the hammer of Thor, Earth Norse god of thunder. Has to be the work of someone from Huginn Industries."

That made sense. I've done plenty of jobs in the Huginn Industries borough. Their whole culture was basically if you didn't brag about something, you may as well not have even done it. And they liked their old Earth imagery. I hadn't had any run-ins with their Intel Operatives, but this would certainly fit. Break into a vault and leave your mark on the door on the way out.

"Elise." Gustin, my boss and manager of my group of Intel Operatives, was leaning against the doorframe of his office. My height with a little gut, he looked frazzled. He was wearing a mauve tracksuit that looked very soft, designed for comfort, not the track. The modded hands peeking out of his sleeves were low-end, like the ones I wore when I was bumming around my apartment. It was so out of character for the man I answered to, who dressed for work each day in a brightly patterned button-up and a sport coat to compliment. He tilted his head, beckoning me like I was a pet or something, and then retreated into his office.

I guessed I was following him. How like him to assume I knew what he wanted. Gustin wasn't a bad manager, but too eager and ambitious for my taste. He played favorites and gave preferential jobs to operatives who bolstered his own career. I was good at my job, one of the best, but I focused on my career and Quynn's. Not his. So our relationship was lukewarm on a good day. Functional. I weaved through the cubicles, giving a nod to a security guard who didn't return the gesture.

"Close the door," Gustin said when I entered. I did so, and we were alone.

"This can't be good," Bastion said.

"Take a seat," Gustin said as he pulled a tablet out of a drawer. Quaint little tech.

I took the offered seat and said, "What's going on?"

"Run me through the job tonight," Gustin said.

"You said somebody broke into the vault?" I asked. "Isn't that supposed to be impossible? What did they take? Who would even–?"

"We'll get to that," Gustin said. "But I need you to walk me through everything that happened tonight."

I started at the beginning, from the flying limousine I snagged in the Corto borough, all the way until I left the offices for the gala. Gustin scribbled on the tablet the whole time. He chuckled or smirked in the strangest places, like when I hid in the closet or found the bookcase door. I left out no detail, except for how a maybe-artificial-intelligence started talking to me, helped me escape Nexus security drones, and was somehow still able to talk to me. Just a couple of minor, insignificant things. You know. Maybe Bastion's paranoia was rubbing off on me.

"No one followed you?" Gustin said once I was done, his voice like a tenor gargling rocks.

"No," I said. "My pursuit sensors were clear once I ditched the drones."

"Who rented the car you supposedly clung to?"

I didn't know which part of the question to react to first, the question itself or the "supposedly" he threw into it.

"I don't know," I said. "The destination was the important part, not who was inside."

"Did you notice anything unusual once you arrived at the building?" Gustin asked me, his eyes never wavering from mine. "Any strange faces or objects out of place?"

"Not that I noticed."

Gustin scribbled on the tablet some more. He shook his head and smirked again, and then turned the tablet to face me. There was some text at the top of the screen and a large rectangle below it with the outline of a handprint. "Please put your hand here to the contents of our interview," Gustin said. "You can read it first if you want."

"What do you think is so funny about all this?" I asked, not putting my hand anywhere near his tablet.

"I don't."

"You've been smiling this whole time."

"Just put your hand here, Elise," Gustin said without emotion.

"No," I said. "I want to know. I did my job and did it well, so I don't appreciate you making—"

"I get that you have questions," Gustin said. "But this is protocol. I have to do this before I can say anything else."

I worked my jaw, trying to understand Gustin's newfound kindness, whether it was genuine or just strategic.

Gustin pushed the tablet into my face again. "This verifies that I took your statement in person. It will also upload the written statement to your internal storage. If you have any corrections or additions, please contact me in the next 24 hours, otherwise, this handprint will confirm that the statement is accurate, under threat of corporate perjury."

I stared at that tablet as Gustin's words bounced around in my head. Corporate perjury. Lying in an official statement to the company. A quick route to a Corto tribunal, and then on to the Phalanx, Corto's private prison. If I was lucky enough to not just be thrown to The Mist. Goodbye career.

Goodbye Quynn and their career. Or I could just tell Gustin about Bastion.

"Need I remind you what will likely happen to me should you reveal my existence," Bastion said like he'd been reading my mind. "I beg you to keep my secret."

Moment of truth, I supposed. I could tell Gustin right now about this AI barking in my ear, but then what? I knew next to nothing about it, but would he believe me? Would I get swept up in some tribunal anyway? Powerful people were obviously at play here, stealing and then re-stealing this chip that wasn't supposed to exist. If I put a spotlight on it now without knowing who the players were, what would happen to me? To Quynn? I sighed and put my hand on the tablet. The screen flashed green, and a notification appeared on my display: VERIFIED AFFIDAVIT RECEIVED.

Gustin checked the tablet, tapped it a few times, and shoved it back into his desk.

"So what happened?" I asked.

"Let me show you. Come on," Gustin said as he got up from his desk. Once we were both out of the office, he continued, "You logged in your target at 20:41. Your car left the landing pad for the gala at 20:48."

"Right," I said. We weaved through the cubicles and security, the glow of that mythical hammer graffiti casting a green hue across the office. I reached out to touch the graffiti, which seemed to hover just above the inner surface of the vault door.

"Please don't touch that!" one of the security officers said in a quivering half-yell.

"Sorry," I said.

"They're very touchy about their evidence," Gustin said with a smirk as we entered the vault. It wasn't much to look at. It was bigger than I'd imagined, a third the size of the whole office, and every wall was lined with large, square, metal doors. They just looked like sleek, oversized safe deposit boxes. A long, thin robotic arm was folded against the ceiling, which made sense. Deposit a target through the drawer in the door, and then this arm put it away in one of the little boxes. Clean. Efficient. Sleek. Except one of the boxes had been ripped open. And on our left, there was a perfectly circular, three – meter-wide hole. It was like someone scooped out a meter of solid metal connecting the inside of the vault to –

"Is that an elevator shaft?" I asked, pointing through the gaping circle.

"Yes," Gustin said with a sigh. "Notice the smell?"

"As soon as I stepped off the elevator."

"Watch," Gustin said, and then made a few taps in the air, working his interface. A hum rose up all around us, and then in a flicker of holographic light, the hole in the wall was gone. This wasn't like AR in my display, with its see-through resolution or muted colors. The holograph looked almost real and solid, except for the slight green tint to everything. The holographic door to the vault was closed. Silently, a blinding light suddenly appeared where the hole was, like a perfect sphere of concentrated white. The sphere collapsed and vanished, and the hole was back.

Then a hooded, masked figure ducked in through the hole, standing up and moving across the vault with purpose. Taller than me. Broader across the shoulders, with thick arms bulging against their sleeves. They went to the shelf attached to the door, the overnight drop, and looked briefly before turning back the rest of the vault. They stood there, looking, before heading straight for the now-open box. The hooded figure ripped it open with pure strength and then scooped something out of it with a small, egg-like capsule. Though I couldn't see what, I knew they'd taken the chip, and then the imposing figure tossed the box aside and shoved the capsule in a pocket. In three strides, they crossed to the vault door, deployed something from their fingertips, and painted the glowing Mjolnir on the inside of the vault door. They were back through the hole in less than a minute when they'd entered.

"Antimatter bomb, according to security," Gustin said.

"Like starships use for planetary bombing?"

"Well, a lot smaller than that, obviously. That smell is telltale, apparently. Smaller and more precise than anything our security has ever seen. And that's the elevator shaft you came up and back down earlier tonight."

"Oh," I said. Hence all the suspicion around me.

"Our sensors registered the detonation at 20:50. Two minutes after you left the building completely."

If I didn't know better, I'd suspect me too. Maybe I was followed. I already knew the answer to my next question. "What was stolen?"

Gustin looked at me, meeting my eyes and narrowing his before he answered. "Just one thing," he said, pointing to the box on the other side of the room, the one tossed by our thief. "The chip you brought in tonight."

"Silent circuits," I whispered, running a hand through my hair. "That has to put me high on the suspect list."

"Very," Gustin said. He was still burrowing holes through me wit his gaze.

"I had nothing to do with this," I said. "I've never even been in this vault before."

Gustin worked his jaw, still staring at me, before he said, "I believe you."

"He's lying," Bastion said.

"Thank you," I said to Gustin, though I agreed with my stowaway AI.

"Don't thank me yet." Gustin finally broke his stare, fixating on the giant hole in the vault instead. "You need to convince a lot of very important people that you didn't do this."

"I can do that."

"And you need to get that chip back." Gustin glanced back at me, but then his eyes were on the hole again.

"Okay," I said. "I'll just need–"

"The Hermes Protocol has been invoked."

"The what?"

Gustin sighed. "This has happened twice before, the vault being compromised. Each time, we have relocated the vault."

"Oh," I said. "I thought–"

"In the next two days, this entire office will be cleared out and moved. The chip is valuable, but the location of our vault is much more valuable. We can't stay. The Hermes Protocol."

"Mother of Corto," I whispered.

"You have 56 hours."

"Me?" I yelled before I even realized it. "You're giving me two days?"

"He's setting you up," Bastion said like I didn't already know that.

Gustin finally turned back to face me. "The Hermes Protocol gives us 2 days, so it seems a fitting deadline for you, too. If the chip is back here, we'll be square with the client, and I'm sure I can clear your name."

"Can't you call them? Get an extension?"

"No," he said, offering no further explanation.

"Who is this client?"

"Yes," Bastion said in my ear. "Who?"

Gustin's face suddenly turned dark and stony. "You know better than to ask that question."

"Normally, yes, but this isn't normal. There has to be–"

"This particular vault has been here for 25 years. The Hermes Protocol is clear. The office is relocating in two days. If you don't get the chip back and close the loop on this, we move without you."

"Without me? What does that mean?"

"If that chip isn't brought back here in 56 hours," Gustin snapped, "then someone is going to take the blame. Someone will face a tribunal. It's not going to be me."

Tribunal. The word echoed in my head, rattling my breathing and chest. Best case scenario, a tribunal meant a demotion. I'd go from Intel Operative to scrubbing toilets in the manufacturing sector. Worst case, I'd be terminated from Corto. Gone. My whole life was Corto Corporation. Job. Family. Friends. Quynn. I sputtered before I finally found my words. "It's going to be me? I had nothing to do with this!"

"The chip was your target. Then an antimatter bomb put a hole in our vault two minutes after you left. I don't even have to point a finger in your direction to make you the primary suspect."

"You wouldn't."

"Of course he would," Bastion said.

"You want to keep doing this job? Be the Cloak of Corto one day?" Gustin asked as he walked toward the vault door.

I didn't answer. He knew I did. I didn't want to be a manager, I wanted to be the best Intel Operative in the company. The Cloak of Corto.

"I want to make VP. You have to play the game to make it to the top. You have to play harder to stay there. You know that. That's what you were doing at the gala tonight." He stopped in the doorway, staring at the Mjolnir tag, his face sickly in the green glow. "Don't make this harder than it has to be. Just get the chip back and take care of whoever took it from us."

CHAPTER SEVEN

"NOW DO I GET AN explanation?" Quynn asked before I even shut the apartment door behind me. They were sitting in the living room, in clear view of the front door, drinking olrama juice, the galaxy's only natural, real preventative for a hangover. And olrama only grew here on Little Sekhmet.

"I told you it was work," I said, heading to the fridge for my own bottle of juice. I hadn't drunk enough tonight to warrant it, but I was pretty sure a headache was coming on all the same.

"I know. What was so important that it pulled you away from a VP gala?"

"We need to go," Bastion said in my ear. "The clock is ticking. You can talk to them later."

I sighed, took a swig of the juice, which tasted like a fern scraping against my tongue, and settled into a chair across from Quynn.

"How did the rest of the gala go?" I asked.

Quynn raised an eyebrow. "Your absence was noticed, of course. Since the CEO was there, though, everyone was pretty distracted."

"Why was she there?"

Quynn shrugged. "She didn't talk to many people other than VPs and LeGrand. She did give a speech, though. She knew more about the open director position than I would have imagined, talked about the importance of the galas and loyalty to Corto Corporation. The normal stuff."

"I hope I didn't cost you your shot at the position."

"I hope so, too."

I told them about the robbery, the timing of it with my departure from the office, and Gustin's not-so-subtle threat. I didn't mention Bastion. Just knowing there was an AI barking in my ear was dangerous, and Quynn didn't need to be in on that danger.

"Who does Gustin report to?" Quynn asked.

"No," I said, knowing what they were thinking. "You do not need to go over his head on this."

"He's threatening you," Quynn said. "That goes against multiple corporate policies. His supervisor–"

"Would have to run it up the chain of command," I said. "We're talking about someone breaking into the Intel vault. Gustin is garbage, but he's right. Look at the timing, the evidence. Maybe Gustin would get demoted, but so would I. And if they decide I'm at fault for the robbery, demotion might be the least of my concerns."

"A tribunal, maybe termination for you," Bastion said. "But for me, death. Or slavery. If the wrong people get a hold of my programming, there might not be a limit to what they could do."

I hadn't thought of what would happen should someone, anyone get a hold of Bastion. He'd barely been awake during my run-in with those security drones, but he'd been very useful. Then he replicated his code to the web and hacked into my communications. He'd already pointed me in the direction of Huginn for the robbery. What was Bastion truly capable of?

"So that's it?" Quynn asked. "You're going to jump when Gustin says to? Going to track down and steal back this chip in 56 hours?"

"55 hours, 22 minutes," Bastion said.

"Less than that now," I said to Quynn, and I downed the last of the juice. I stood up, intent on heading to the bedroom and changing back into my work gear, but then Quynn was up and standing in front of me, their hands on my shoulders.

"Elise," Quynn said, those aquamarine and violet eyes trembling. "I don't like this. This doesn't feel right."

"I know," I said, putting my hands over theirs.

"Are we in danger?"

"This is my job. It's always dangerous."

"That's not what I asked."

I couldn't hold their gaze. "I don't know," I said. "I know where I'm going tonight, the level of danger involved. Roughly, at least. I know what's at stake. Our careers. My home."

Bastion's life.

"Tonight?" Quynn asked.

"The longer I wait," I said, "the colder the trail I have to follow."

Quynn stared into my eyes like they were looking for something more. I ached to give them some reassurance, but I didn't have it.

"But there are things I can't see," I continued. "I don't know who the client is, who paid to have that chip stolen. Of course, I never know, but whatever that chip is, it must be important. Antimatter bombs, glowing graffiti, the Hermes Protocol. It's all insane. Whoever wants this chip, I'm afraid of them."

"That is the smartest thing you have said all night," Bastion said.

I needed to figure out how to mute him.

"You said it's just another neural interface chip. What could be so important?" Quynn asked.

There it was, the opening to tell Quynn all about Bastion and possibly the CEO's involvement. But I couldn't. Quynn was a worrier. It was their nature. They'd never been a fan of my job or the inherent risks involved. There was a reason I didn't tell Quynn when I was going to scale a building or talk my way past armed guards. Every day, they worried about whether I'd come back through that door. But Quynn was right. This was different. A different danger. A different fear. Quynn would do anything to make that danger go away. If I told them about Bastion, they wouldn't think twice about reporting an illegal AI. Sure, I would face a tribunal, but so would the clients who wanted the chip. Maybe the CEO of our company. Everything we've ever worked for could end.

And Bastion would be destroyed.

"I wish I knew why it's so important," I said. "It just looked like another neural interface chip to me."

Quynn put a finger on my chin and pulled my face back up, locking those beautiful eyes onto mine. I swore they could see the lie, their gaze pulling it to the surface. It took everything I had to swallow it down, to not let them see the guilt bubbling up in me. I hated this, but I didn't see a better option. Finally, they said, "What can I do?"

I shook my head.

"We're in this together," Quynn said. "So let me help."

"You're in this a little. I can't ask you to be in it even more."

"Hey." Quynn took my face in their hands, pointing my eyes at theirs. "What did we say when we moved in together?"

"No more throwing dirty underwear on the floor?"

Quynn narrowed their eyes.

"100 percent," I said. "We're 100 percent. Mind. Body. Soul. Careers."

"Exactly. I'm not in this a little. I'm 100 percent. So let. Me. Help."

I sighed. Then I thought of something with only a little risk. "See if you can find out who the client is, who is trying to get their hands on this chip."

"That's a terrible idea," Bastion said.

Quynn furrowed their brow, the fine, black eyebrows hooding those beautiful eyes a little. "Any ideas where to start?"

"Gustin knows, obviously. Work your contacts and see if you can get anywhere in his chain of command. If he knows, I'm sure others above him know."

"I can do that. I can try."

"You're going to make things worse," Bastion said. "Quynn isn't an Intel Operative. They don't have the training."

"Subtly," I said, putting a hand on Quynn's face and ignoring Bastion. "Talk to people you trust. Keep it close. I'd rather not know than you put yourself in danger."

"I said 100 per–"

"Promise me," I said, interrupting them. "Promise me you'll keep a low profile. If I can get this chip back, we'll be okay whether you find out or not. If you get caught digging for the client, we're in a bad way no matter how things go tonight."

"Okay," Quynn said. "I know a few people. Trustworthy people. I'll see what I can find out."

"Thank you." I kissed Quynn, long and deep, savoring our love, our connection, how thankful I was to have Quynn on my team. Once I finally pulled away, I said, "Time to get to work."

"Be careful," Quynn said.

"Always," I said as I moved to the bedroom, slipping the dress off my shoulders and kicking it to the corner of the room. A cleaning robot – a silver orb the size of a soccer ball – zipped out of the wall and scooped up my dress. It would be cleaned by nanobots and hung back in my wardrobe within a day. With my left hand, I felt for the release buttons on my right arm. My display read, "RIGHT ARM DISENGAGING." With a little twist, the arm went dead as the connections to my neural interface disengaged. I twisted the arm free of the socket, and it released with several clicks. My dress arm was significantly heavier than my work arm. The replicant skin was thick, and there were fluids that pumped beneath it to simulate real flesh. The doors to my power closet slid open at my approach, my work limbs resting in their charging cradles. All charged to 83%. Not as full as I'd liked, but I didn't have time to wait. I swapped the dress arm for the work arm, pushing it into the socket and twisting it. More clicks, and then my display read, "RIGHT ARM SYNCHRONIZED" as cybernetic muscles and nerves came to life.

I sat down on the bench next to the closet and started the process on my right leg. Then left leg. Finally, the left arm. I changed my dress bra for a sports bra and then zipped into the black, carbon nanoweave bodysuit. More lights and confirmations flashed on my display as the whole ensemble came together. I restocked my EMP and double-checked supply levels for various tools in my loadout.

"55 hours left," Bastion said.

"I know," I whispered, though I didn't really. I called up my onboard digital assistant. "Hey Carbon, put a timer on my display for 55 hours."

55:00:00 popped up, big and green on my display, and then shrank and moved to the upper right as it started ticking down. Less than two full rotations of Little Sekhmet Settlement.

"What's the plan?" Bastion said.

I stretched to peek out of the bedroom. Quynn was curled up in their favorite chair, the viewscreen on. Unlikely to hear me whisper. I asked Bastion, "You said the thief is likely from Huginn Industries?"

"More than likely. I don't know another company who would tag their crime scene like that."

"I don't personally know any Huginn operatives, but I do know where they like to go after a job, where they like to celebrate."

"Some sort of alehouse? That would be very Huginn of them."

"Alehouse?"

"Huginn culture is loosely based on Earth Norse culture. Vikings. They were known to celebrate their victories with ale and mead."

"I'm sure they serve ale or something like it," I said. "But that's not what this place is known for. We have to stop somewhere else first. I need to gear up."

"Was all that carbon-polymer not geared up enough?" Bastion asked.

I ignored him, giving Quynn the requisite goodbye kiss and hurrying out of the apartment.

"You seem to know everything about Huginn Industries," I said to Bastion once I'd shut the apartment door behind me. And another ad lit up the door, this time for some sort of yoga pants made from "extra breathable fabric." I gestured the ad away.

"Of course I know about Huginns," Bastion said.

"Then you know this outfit will only get me sideways glances and closed lips." Huginns were pompous people from top to bottom. While Corto's culture was polite and political, Huginn's culture was about showing off. If you wanted to get ahead there, you needed to do something big and make sure everybody knew you did it. Wearing unadorned black worked well for sneaking into the Huginn borough without being detected. It would mark me as an outsider when I just walked in the front door trying to get information.

"So change clothes," Bastion said.

"Huginn fashion changes too quickly," I said as I stepped on the elevator. "Transportation hub," I said to the elevator, and then to Bastion, "I haven't had to work a mark in Huginn in a few years."

"I assume you know how to acquire the necessary garb?"

"I do. We're going to see Echo." I stepped off the elevator 32 floors down and out into a much busier hallway. Whereas only the people who lived on and visited my floor walked its halls, everyone in the building who owned a vehicle or boarded mass transit made their way to this floor, to these halls.

"Echo? Does he work for Corto or Huginn?"

"Neither." I approached the door to my garage. It technically belonged to both Quynn and me, but even they called it mine. 90% of what was in that garage was mine. I put a hand on the doorknob and waited. The lock here wasn't quite as advanced as our apartment door. I hadn't gotten around to upgrading it yet. Once my hand was on the knob, the cybermetric scanner kicked in and, in a few seconds, I felt a click as the door unlocked.

"Who does he work for?" Bastion asked. "What is his company name?"

"He's freelance."

"He's a Mist–?"

The instant I shut the door behind me, Bastion's voice fell silent. Right. I should have remembered that would happen. I'd always lost comms in here with the doors closed. I opened the door, and in an instant, Bastion's voice was back.

"Elise? Elise?" Bastion sounded frantic. "Are you there?"

"I'm here, Bastion."

"What happened?"

"I closed the door to my garage and lost your signal. Lost all signal."

There was a pause before Bastion said, "I was suddenly alone. The net is immense, the code is like an endless ocean. Without you as an anchor..."

I didn't know what to say to that. The sadness of it. To feel so lost and alone. I couldn't imagine. The metaphor was prettier than anything I could have come up with, like something from a poem. Could artificial intelligence create something so beautiful? I had to wonder how much of it was real, how much was manipulation. If Bastion really was afraid, what wouldn't it do in the name of self-preservation?

"Elise?"

"I'm here. I'm going to close the door again."

"But–"

"It will just be for a few minutes," I said. "Once I'm out, we'll be connected again."

Bastion didn't say anything for a few seconds, so I went ahead and closed the door. Then I picked a path between boxes of old mods, outdated computers, and keepsakes from our youths. I pulled the tarp off my Kawasaki. Matte black from the handlebars down to the thrusters, I'd been customizing her over the last ten years. I called her Poe. Yeah, after the old Earth poet. Not a lot of people in Jayu City owned their own ride. Half of this very transportation hub was owned by Stryder, which I used most of the time I needed to get anywhere. But sometimes, I needed to feel thrusters rumble beneath me and the wind whip through my hair. At least across my shellacked hair. And the Stryders wouldn't go down into The Mist.

I straddled Poe and her little lights all blinked to life. Altimeter, speedometer, and other necessary gauges leaping up on my display. With a gesture, the main door to the garage rolled up with a quiet rumble. Instead of a small, external landing pad, before me was a large landing surface inside the building, with three floors of secure garages surrounding it. Vehicles could fly in or out from all four directions. Service and detailing stations did a booming business in the hub, not that I'd ever used them.

"Bastion?" I asked.

"I'm here."

"Good," I kicked a pedal on Poe, and she gently lifted off the floor, blowing dust out of the garage and setting loose flaps on boxes to fluttering. "And to answer your question, yes. Echo is a Mistwalker."

Not everyone liked the way Jayu City was divided up and run by five massive corporations. I didn't really get it. I had a job I loved, a great apartment, nice things, and I never went hungry. I knew Corto security kept us protected. Corto fire and rescue would keep us unburnt, and Corto hospitals and clinics kept Quynn and me healthy. Huginn Industries did the same for their citizens. Same with Kotega Systems, Nexus Neuronics, and Toinette Holdings. Nobody was homeless or hungry or imperiled.

Mistwalkers like Echo were having none of it. They disavowed the companies, living down in The Mist, working and living without a safety net. I wasn't sure how they survived down there.

But Echo certainly did. He was able to get me goods from other boroughs. No Corto Corporation citizen would dare sell goods from Huginn Industries. It was disloyal, plus they'd have to deal with fluctuating currency valuations between companies. Echo wasn't a Corto citizen. I got what I needed without having to cross boundaries or raise eyebrows, so Mistwalkers weren't without their uses.

"Isn't interaction with Mistwalkers illegal?" Bastion asked.

"Illegal? What do you think this is? Earth?"

"But your job–"

"My job is to go where I must. Where I want. So long as I get the job done."

"But if Gustin were to find out–"

I sighed. "I'll keep your secrets if you keep mine."

"Is it safe?"

"Compared to watching TV in my apartment? No. Compared to jumping off a Nexus high-rise and knocking out Nexus security drones? This is nothing." I pressed a button on Poe's handlebars, and the charging cable disengaged and rolled up into the wall. Poe trembled a moment before settling into an even hover. On the rare occasion I could get Quynn to ride with me, I was always gentle with the throttle. With them, I ascended and descended at mild angles and kept rolls to a minimum.

But Quynn wasn't with me. I cranked the accelerator hard, bolting out of the garage, banking above the large landing area, and flying out of the hub at 150 kilometers per hour. As soon as I cleared the building, I pushed the handles forward into a straight dive as the speedometer spun past 200.

CHAPTER EIGHT

"THIS REALLY DOESN'T SEEM NECESSARY!" Bastion yelled.

"If I only did things that were necessary, I would be an analyst. I prefer to live while I'm living."

The speedometer climbed up past 250 while the altimeter spun in the other direction. I knew the street below was about 46 meters above sea level, but The Mist obfuscated the last 20 meters before the street. Right as I hit The Mist, I pulled up on the handles and let go of the accelerator. The thick Mist spun into little cyclones around the thrusters. My stomach gave that delightful drop and rebound that sent goosebumps up my neck.

The speed sloughed off quickly as the bike leveled out, and the thrusters whined as they spun down. I carefully crept the bike down, down, until The Mist cleared enough to reveal the street below. What remained of the street was cracked and splintered, ignored for decades by Corto Corporation. Tufts of grasses and weeds tried to push up but were mostly trampled down by the hundreds of people filling the street.

The Mist was like a different world. The streets were a maze of makeshift stalls selling food, scavenged cybernetic parts, cast-off clothes, and anything else that could be found down a Corto garbage chute. People were milling about, wearing threadbare clothing that was en vogue above several years or decades ago. Cybernetic parts were nearly as common here as above, but they were either cast-offs or not made by skilled engineers of Corto or any other corporation. Wires and moving parts were exposed for anyone to see. There were no carbon- or skin-like polymers to be seen. Instead, the various metals were in sharp contrast to the threadbare clothes and splotchy, biological skin tones. Everything was darker, not just because of The Mist, but because no advertisements were gleaming and shining on faces.

"I've never seen any of this before," Bastion said. "I've only read online accounts. They live in squalor."

"Not all of them," I said, keeping the bike high enough to keep the thrusters from knocking people over, but low enough to see through The Mist. "Plenty of people live in the buildings on these lower floors, and some do quite well for themselves."

"Is your friend Echo one of those people?"

"He's not begging on the street." I turned a corner and found what I was looking for: a makeshift landing pad covering part of the street. In truth, it looked more like someone had built a covering for the pavement below from various pieces of dark gray metal, but that wasn't its purpose. Most of Echo's customers flew in from above, and our vehicles drew a little too much attention when we parked them on the street. The platform was big enough to hold a few cars, and a little walkway connected it to Echo's balcony. There were no signs or any other special markings, but I knew the place well enough. I spun the bike around, cutting the main thrusters and drifting down onto the pad, my landing thrusters blowing the mixture of dust and Mist off as I set Poe down.

"Is this friend of yours even awake right now?" Bastion asked. "It's after midnight, nearly 1."

"Oh, he's awake," I said. "Echo never sleeps. He's modded to never need it."

"Can he be trusted?" Bastion asked.

"More than just about anyone I know. He's not exactly the social type. Or the above-The-Mist type." I climbed off Poe and walked up to Echo's door, which was simple and sturdy, with no visible locking mechanisms of any kind. I looked up at the camera array above the door and gave a little smile. After a few seconds, the door slid open with a heavy grinding noise.

"Silent circuits," Bastion whispered, the familiar curse sounding strange coming from the AI on my shoulder.

I knew what he meant, though. Bastion's shop was a bright contrast to the rugged front door. Pristine white tile covered the floor and walls, which shot up two stories. Bright, shining metal shelves were arrayed in perfectly parallel lines. I was sure if I used the measurement app in my optical mods, it would confirm that each shelf was built to the same specifications to the millimeter.

"Feet," Echo muttered from somewhere in the back of the store. I'd been here dozens of times. I knew the drill, but he still said it every time I entered. Next to the door were two bins. The one on the right was filled with fuzzy, pink slippers, neatly laid out in pairs. The bin was labeled, "CLEAN." An identical bin was labeled, "DIRTY," and was empty. I grabbed a pair of clean slippers and put them on my feet. Then I made my way down the center aisle. Arrayed on the shelves were BMW and Mercedes parts I could never identify beyond their logos, Kotega helmets with their fierce expressions, and neural interfaces from Nexus Neuronics, which looked a lot like the chip I'd pulled from a Nexus safe earlier tonight.

"Where does he get all this stuff?" Bastion asked.

"He's a fence," I whispered. "And a pawnbroker. But he's picky. Doesn't take things he can't sell at a high markup and doesn't take things he can't fix. He also doesn't like strangers. There are a lot of things he doesn't like."

I finally approached the counter at the back, and there was Echo, hunched over some gizmo, his clean, shiny metal hands hard at work. I call them hands, but that was a rough equivocation. More like a couple of dozen tools were splayed out from his metal wrists, crawling over the gizmo like a robotic spider, screwing and squeezing and turning and sending the occasional pop of sparks off to the left or right.

"Echo," I said.

Echo didn't so much as pause in his work. His bald head was bent down, snow-white and gleaming with a thin film of sweat. He was shirtless, like usual, with streaks of grime across his thin, pale stomach. His mods were obvious, cybernetic arms from the elbows down in gleaming silver. Patches of his skin were covered in subtle, silver geometric patterns like some high-tech skin condition.

"What do you know about this year's Huginn fashions?"

He turned a gear on the gizmo, and a few more sparks popped off of it.

"Echo? Huginn fashions?"

"Too loud," Echo said, not looking up or pausing in his work. "Too loud. Too loud."

"What is wrong with him?" Bastion asked.

The answer was, 'nothing,' but I would have to have that conversation later. "I know," I said to Echo. "But I need to look the part of a Huginn. You always have the best stuff."

"Best stuff. Best," Echo said. "Hyperthrusters for a 2531 Kawasaki. 2531. 2531. 3BZ. 3BZ. 3BZ.

"Utter gibberish," Bastion said.

But it wasn't gibberish at all. Echo knew that Poe was a Kawasaki built in 2531. She was a used, slightly battered Sport model when I bought her, and I'd made lots of repairs and tweaks to her. Echo also knew that I'd wanted to upgrade her thrusters with the hyperthrusters found on the Hypersport model. And he had them in stock. Aisle 3, shelf BZ. It wasn't what I was asking about, but he knew who he was talking to and what I wanted. Maybe his brain didn't work like mine, but it worked really well.

"Sold," I told Echo. "But I'll have to come back for them. Right now, I need Huginn clothes. Temp tattoos, if you have them. Trending in the last few months, preferably."

"12AD. 12AD. 12BB. 12BB," Echo said, giving me more aisle and shelf directions.

"And those are current fashions?"

Echo paused in his work and finally looked up, though he didn't meet my eyes. The biological parts of his face ran through several stages of confusion, frustration, determination, and back through the cycle. The twelve lenses that made up his eyes were surrounded by more of that shiny silver, which ran across his face and blended with the silver of his cybernetic ears. Finally, he nodded, and his hands snapped closed into biological hand formation, the various tools all retracting. He skirted around his counter and started heading toward aisle 12, saying nothing.

Fully half of aisle 12 was a bounty of Huginn apparel, all neatly cleaned, pressed, and hung or folded like a high-end fashion boutique. I couldn't understand their arrangement. Some bright pink shorts were next to a swath of tank-tops were next to black faux leather jackets trimmed with glowing starburst patterns. The arrangement wasn't aesthetic, but knowing Echo, there was definitely a system at work.

"What's the newest?" I asked.

Echo mumbled something about bad smells and then pointed at a pair of orange pants with geometric shapes carved out of them. They were at least three sizes too big for me.

"What's the newest that fits me?"

Echo made a face like I'd said something offensive, and then opened up one of his fingers to pick at his teeth with a screwdriver.

"We are wasting time," Bastion said in my ear.

I ignored him while Echo attended to his teeth, carefully inspecting what came out, and repeating the process twice more before he seemed satisfied. Then, he looked me up and down from my shoulders to my feet, careful not to look me in the eyes. He marched farther down the aisle. He grabbed a midrift top, swirled in blue and red, with a mesh V on the chest. He held it toward me without looking at me and was already focused on the next item. A sheer black skirt that wouldn't even cover my whole ass. Three different jackets, all brightly colored, heavily bejeweled, and trimmed with glowing lines. Echo stopped, and then turned to face me.

"That's it?"

Echo nodded.

I looked at my options and held up the tiny skirt. "I'm going to the Vale. I'm not going to work for the Vale."

Echo blinked a couple of times. Right. Echo had many strengths. Humor was not one of them.

"I'm not wearing this skirt," I said.

Echo looked at his hands, opening and closing a few fingers, the tools popping out and retracting with little clicks and whirs.

"It's okay if it's something a little older," I said. "I'm more of a pants person."

Echo quickly moved past me, careful not to actually touch me, and we were back near the beginning of the aisle. He snagged two pairs of pants: one black, studded with glowing stars. The other pair was sky blue with navy blue triangles and rectangles affixed.

"Do I need shoes?"

"Shoes keep the floors clean. Clean. Clean." Echo said.

"I know, Echo. I'm wearing your slippers, which totally don't go with my outfit."

Not even a smile. Tough crowd.

"Do I need to wear shoes to visit Huginn?"

Echo shook his head.

"What about temp tattoos? I'm guessing Huginns still love their glowing ink?"

"Huginn and Muninn, Odin's ravens," Echo said as he turned and walked back to his spot behind the counter. "Ravens. Ravens. Ravens."

"I see why he's called Echo," Bastion said.

"Be nice," I whispered.

"He can't hear me."

"That's not the point."

"I would beg to differ."

Echo opened a drawer behind the counter and removed a shallow, gray metal case half a meter square. He placed it on the counter and pulled off the top to reveal a myriad of temporary Huginn tattoos. Unlike the clothes slung across my arm, these didn't originate from Huginn Industries. No true Huginn would be caught dead with a temporary tattoo. That would be like bragging without earning it. The glowing tattoos Huginns were so fond of were a combination of clear ink infused with nanobots. The little bots were equipped with an array of holographic projectors, which would display whatever glowing design was required about a centimeter above the skin. These temporary tattoos employed the same technology, except in a nearly invisible patch. Since the nanobots weren't subcutaneous, they would lose power after a few hours and die.

I picked a small cluster of stars for my face and some horned animal's skull for one of my arms.

As soon as I pulled it out of the case and set it on the counter, Echo put a finger on it and said, "Not for mods. Not for mods."

"What?" I said. "I've seen tattoos on Huginn mods–"

"Dead," He pointed harder and shook his head vigorously. "Not for mods."

Huginns were particular about their tattoos, but I didn't know all the ins and outs. Apparently, Echo did, and skull tattoos on mods weren't allowed. "Okay, Echo. You pick for me. The stars are for my face. I need one for each arm."

Echo's eyes went wide, but then he nodded and dived into the case with both hands, touching each one and mumbling under his breath. While he did that, I sorted through the clothes. I put the skirt aside as a big no. There was only one shirt, but I was okay with it. I liked the black, starred pants more than the blue ones. Then it was a matter of matching a jacket to the pants. While black was my favorite color, I knew all-black wasn't popular in the Huginn crowd, so I picked a violet jacket that matched some of the stars on the pants. It only had one sleeve, which appeared to be on purpose, and was trimmed with glowing gold. The outfit looked ridiculous, which was perfect for a night in Huginn.

"Eyes," Echo said. "One for Odin. Two for Thor. Four, four, four for the ravens. Eyes everywhere."

Sitting next to the little constellation I'd picked were two more temporary tattoos. One looked like a spider's face, eight eyes staring unblinkingly in all directions. The other showed a pair of ravens.

"Huginn and Muninn, I presume?"

Echo smiled, still not looking at me. The smile was too broad, too eager, like a child who was practicing smiling in the mirror. It was a little creepy and very sincere. Very Echo. I handed him my selected outfit, and he started to carefully fold each piece.

"I'm going to need to wear those out, actually."

Echo just kept on folding.

"Do you have a changing room?"

Echo sighed and continued to fold.

Okay. Best to let the man finish. After a few quiet moments, he pushed the stack into a simple gray bag, and then pressed his palm against a nondescript, black polymer box he kept on the counter. Then he slid the device over to me. Echo had a thing about touching people, even with his cybernetic hands, so the box was his proxy for the normal palm-touching method of transferring credits.

He nodded when the transaction was complete.

"Okay. Do you have a changing room?" I asked.

Echo scrunched up his forehead. "Storage. Changing? Sure. Sure. Sure." He walked over to a simple metal door next to the counter, looked around like he was checking for eavesdroppers, and then waved a hand in front of the door. It hissed open to reveal a storage closet. Small and just as immaculately clean and organized as the rest of his place. It was certainly private. It would have to do.

"Thank you." I entered, and the door hissed closed behind me. In just a few minutes, I transformed from my all-black Corto Intel Operative uniform into what passed as a Huginn employee hip to all things fashionable. The outfit was garish, glowing, breezy in strange places, and altogether uncomfortable. I stepped out of the closet and gave Echo a little spin. "What do you think?"

"Too loud. Too loud. Too loud," Echo said again.

"Yeah," I said. "That sounds about right. Thanks again, Echo. And hang onto those Kawasaki hyperthrusters. I will be back for those."

I stepped out of Echo's shop, annoyed by the pants riding up and the little squeak they gave whenever I moved. Standing next to Poe was a stranger even more modded than me. They were about my height, but a little more heavily built. Like me, their arms and legs were replaced with cybernetics, but theirs gleamed copper where mine were black carbon-polymer. At least they were some metal that looked like copper. On a day when I didn't need any more surprises, this one just kept on giving.

"Nice bike," the stranger said in a raspy alto.

"Elise," Bastion said with a little worry in his voice.

"Not now," I said to him, and then turned to the stranger. "Thanks. I'd appreciate it if you didn't lean on her, though."

The stranger gave a grin that made my skin crawl. "Elise Corto-Intel?"

"Elise," Bastion repeated.

"Who's asking?" I asked the stranger.

"That's what I thought," the stranger said. "I'm Roxy. She/her. I work for Ophelia."

Ophelia. Right. I broke into her vacation apartment and cracked her safe. I had to wonder how many security drones and cameras caught my flashy escape. Certainly enough to give this Roxy a clear look at my face.

"You took something that wasn't yours to take," Roxy said, slowly moving toward me. From her back, four long, copper arms deployed. They were less like arms and more like spider's legs, sharply pointed at the ends and two meters long.

Yeah. Definitely not a fan of my work.

Chapter Nine

"HEY CARBON, WHO IS–" I mumbled, staying where I was. I was in no hurry to get closer to her.

"Looking her up now," Bastion said.

Maybe it was the gleaming copper blades hovering above her head, but I was pretty sure this lady didn't want to lodge a standard complaint. Those blades also told me I had little chance of beating her in a fight. I was a burglar with burgling mods. Roxy had obviously modded herself to hurt people. So I needed to distract her, get to Poe, and get the hell out of there.

"Listen, lady," I said. "If you have an issue with my work, there's an official email address for complaints. I'm happy to give it to you."

"I'm not interested in email," Roxy said as her fingertips changed shape to form copper claws just as vicious as the blades coming off her back. She was slowly approaching me, keeping a wide stance.

I kept my stance casual, slowly moving to my right, trying to circle and give myself an opening to dash to my bike. "Listen," I said. "It's my job. Like a chef cooks or an accountant, um, accounts. If your employer wants it back, there are official channels for requesting–"

"Do you think you're cute?" Roxy changed direction, moving to block my path to Poe, but her stance remained threatening like she could pounce at any second.

"I mean, I don't go around calling myself cute. It's been said about me, sure. I'm more comfortable with that than 'sexy' or something like that. But I really don't get 'cute' all that often."

"Silent circuits," Roxy said with a roll of her eyes. "You talk too much."

"Now that," I said, "I've heard before."

"I found information on her, but you won't like where," Bastion said. "She doesn't work for any of the corporations. Not anymore. She was born in the Toinette Holdings borough but left when she was 15. Then nothing until she started showing up in her twenties. All five companies have reports of her stealing, assaulting, and leaving bodies behind."

Great. A freelance thief and murderer. Fighting definitely wasn't a good option, nor was trying to relate to some professional, operative code of ethics. I needed to get away from her and keep her from shoving those spider limbs through my heart in the meantime.

"Suddenly ran out of things to say?" she said.

"No, just trying to remember the last time a freelancer called me cute," I said. "Might be the first time. You single?"

"I'm going to enjoy ripping your tongue from your throat." The blades on her spider limbs twitched as she said it. I believed her.

"You sure Ophelia is paying you enough for this gig? Do you even know what it is I supposedly took?"

"She paid me for a job," Roxy said, fully blocking my path to Poe. Of course. "Get the chip, bring it to her. I did that job. Now, while I don't mind being paid twice, this is a matter of professional pride. You understand. You steal. I steal. Among other things. Having to do it twice doesn't look good."

"She must have stolen me from the lab!" Bastion said.

Right. And killed a dozen or so technicians in the process. She could easily do the same to me. I needed a plan B, and I needed it now.

"So you don't know what's on the chip?" I asked Roxy. "Why someone is even willing to pay you twice to grab it?"

"I wasn't paid to ask questions."

"Of course not. I'm sure that's why she hired you. So good at what you do, and not at all inquisitive. Won't even wonder if there is information about Roxy Toinette-Fifteen on the chip."

That got her, the rage and focus suddenly flitting away to reveal a little concern and confusion. More importantly, she stopped moving toward me. I fed her more of the info I had, Bastion catching on and rattling off reports, which I relayed to Roxy. A cybernetic shoulder prototype stolen from Kotega, and two lab techs were left with holes in their heads. Information on new nanotech replication taken from Corto. An entire floor of a Huginn research building was blown apart, shaky footage recovered from the blast of someone matching her description.

"How do you know all this?" Roxy asked.

"Ophelia, obviously," I said, working overtime to spin a believable lie, one that might get me out of this alive.

"Liar," Roxy said, but her face and voice said she wasn't sure of the accusation. "She would never tell you–"

"She didn't," I said. "But there were files on you in that apartment of hers. Very detailed. You sure you're going after the right person?"

"I'm after whoever has the chip, which you haven't denied is you. And I'm glad my employer did her homework. Read up on me. That will make her afraid enough to not cross me. Give me the chip and I will kill you quickly. Painlessly."

Right. Worth a shot. "What happened to not killing me?"

"You know too much."

"From one operative to another, you know this isn't how we do things, right? I got you this time, you'll be me next time. You put the scary spider blades away, and we go get a drink, have a little mutual admiration. On me."

"I'm no operative, or did Ophelia's files not tell you that?"

"Burglar. Whatever."

She narrowed her eyes. "Where do I live? Who built my mods?"

I waited for Bastion to tell me the answer. After several of the longest seconds of my life, he said, "I don't know. I only have access to public records from the corporations. They don't track freelancers."

"You live in The Mist," I said to Roxy.

She smiled, that horrible rage and focus coming back. "You don't know. More talking, talking, talking. It won't help you. Give me the chip."

"You don't want to do that. We can work something out. We're basically the same. One professional to another."

"I am what I am hired to do. In this case, it is to get the chip back from you and ensure that you cannot pursue it any further."

"Right," I said. "That's definitely not what I do. And here I thought you were going to be my new best friend."

"I don't need any friends."

"With that dazzling personality? Obviously not."

That was the wrong thing to say. It felt right in the moment, but then all those coppery, bladed limbs were flying at me as Roxy let out a guttural snarl. While my biological reflexes were pretty good, my mods were better. My legs jerked down of their own accord and then fired pneumatic pistons to launch me up in the air several meters. Roxy flew underneath me like a copper flash. Now if only I could train those automatic reflexes to fling me toward Poe instead of straight up in the air. Better than being perforated by those blades, though.

Roxy slammed into Echo's door with a slam and screech of metal on metal. I twisted, flung out my arm, and fired a magnetic grappling hook from my wrist up and into The Mist, toward the building across the street. There were signs and balconies aplenty over there, I just had to hope the hook would grab one, and that particular hold would be enough to bear my weight. In the span of maybe a second, my display showed, "GRAPPLE DEPLOYED," "GRAPPLE HOOKED," and finally "GRAPPLE LOCKED." With a flick, I reeled in the slack, and then I was swinging down in the general direction of Poe.

A violent twang thrummed through my grapple line, and suddenly my graceful swing turned into a freefall, two meters of grapple line flailing in the air for a very long second before I slammed into Echo's landing pad back-first. My head snapped back, banging against the metal. Every particle of air in my lungs was suddenly swimming around in front of me. I tried to pull it back in, gasping and begging for it, but my lungs wouldn't cooperate. Then too many metal limbs slammed down on the landing pad only a couple of meters away. Roxy had a horrifying grin as she rose to her full height, looking down on me like I was a dying animal in need of that final twist of the neck.

"Where is the chip?" she snarled, advancing on me.

I wanted to answer, I really did. The air and my lungs were conspiring against me though. I lay there and gaped like a dying fish for a few more seconds.

Roxy rolled her eyes but stopped. Not stupid then. She knew no matter how angry or menacing she was, I couldn't answer without air. At last, my lungs remembered their job, and I audibly gasped. In an instant, Roxy was standing right over me, her blades drawing down close to my face.

"Give me the chip," she said.

"I don't have it."

"Liar!" she yelled, and one of the blades swept across my left cheek. It was barely a graze, but I could feel a warm trickle of blood after the quick searing of the slash.

"Why would I hang onto it? My job is to deliver items to clients."

"Where is it?" She buried one of the blades in the landing pad a mere centimeter from the other side of my face, a bang and screech almost overloading my aural mods. The entire landing pad shuddered. "Where?!"

Even though my lungs were still struggling to understand what to do with air, my cybernetic arms and legs didn't have those issues. I flipped back and up, my limbs spinning in ways no biological limbs ever could. I used my arms to launch myself away from Roxy, out of reach of those damnable blades, but my momentum was stopped short, a vice-like grip on my right wrist.

Roxy had grabbed it while I was in midair. Despite my considerable inertia away from her, she stopped me, pulled me up and over her, and then slammed me down on the landing pad on the other side. It hurt. Everywhere. On the bright side, I held the air in my lungs this time, and I was actually closer to Poe than before.

She leaned over me, bringing a foot down on my chest with surprising, unrelenting weight. She sneered like a predator toying with her prey, which seemed pretty accurate right then. I was totally outmatched. Then she repeated, "Where is it?"

How to even respond? It should have been in the vault at the Corto Intel office. It wasn't. I was pretty sure some Huginn operative had taken it, so it was likely in the Huginn borough. But I had no way of knowing for sure.

My only options were to either shut up, lie through my teeth, or hope this murderous lunatic would somehow believe the truth. Mother of Corto help me, shutting up wasn't one of my strong suits, and it was always easier to keep a story straight when it was the truth.

"I took it to the Corto vault, but someone else stole it from there."

For a moment, it seemed like Roxy was considering what I'd told her. Her bladed limbs and clawed hands hovered, practically vibrating with deadly potential, and her eyes narrowed. But then the rage came back. "Still so cute. Break into an Intel vault? In any of the boroughs? Ridiculous." She leaned down, all four of those bladed limbs coming down with her, poised only centimeters above my face. "Where is the chip?"

Before I could think of a witty comeback or a passable lie, both Roxy and I were distracted by a little, metallic clink. Roxy's head swiveled to the sound, and my eyes followed. Attached to one of her bladed arms, up near one of the joints behind her back, was a little, black box. It wasn't there a moment before. There were two red lights on it, alternately blinking, and a high-pitch whine started to emanate from it. I didn't know what it was, but Roxy's eyes went wide. She jerked upright.

"Oh no, oh no, oh no," Bastion said. Too late, though. Just as Roxy started to move one arm toward it, the little box suddenly burst into a blinding blue light. The arm it had been attached to collapsed into the light, along with most of the spider-like limb next to it, half of Roxy's nearby arm, and – disgustingly – patches of Roxy's face. Little drops of blood followed the patches of skin, yanked into the blue light with horrifying velocity.

Then the light went away as suddenly as it had erupted, but it was only a hiccup. The light returned, but this time as a flash accompanied by a deafening BOOM. I was already prone, but the effect pressed down on me, hard and instantaneous and everywhere at once like a car had fallen on me. For the second time tonight, every particle of air was driven from my lungs.

I got off easy. Roxy was flung forcibly away from the light and sound, slamming into the building across the street from Echo's shop. I barely caught a glimpse of her remaining limbs buckling and twisting as she careened into the glass and metal structure. I lay there, gasping for air again until it came. I took a few deep, jagged breaths and asked Bastion, "What was that?"

86

"Gravity grenade," he said. "Developed by Earth defense forces. Military only. And that one had been modified. Heavily."

"Modified?"

"They don't usually stick to surfaces. And they usually eat entire buildings."

"Lucky me." I looked away from the wreckage of Roxy and saw the source of the horrifying little device. Echo was standing in front of his open shop door, his jaw nearly on the ground, either astounded or terrified by what had just happened.

"Echo?" I managed to say.

He didn't respond.

"Echo, was that you?"

He closed his mouth, swallowed hard, and glanced at me before finally saying, "The customer is always right." Then he turned around and marched right back into his shop, gently closing the door behind him.

"He's crazy. Was he trying to kill us?" Bastion asked.

"No," I said, sitting up and making sure my new Huginn attire was still presentable. Some scuffs and a couple of tears in the jacket, but otherwise, they'd held up surprisingly well. "And he's not crazy. There's nothing wrong with him. He just thinks differently."

"But that grenade, it could have–"

"You said it yourself, heavily modified. I'd bet anything Echo was the one to modify it. He knew what he was doing. And that little 'customer is always right' bit? Telling me he's got my back. I've been coming to Echo for years. Do you have any idea how rare and valuable Kawasaki hyperthrusters are?"

"There were only 302 Hypersport models made in 2531. Of those, only 12 were shipped here to the Little Sekmet Settlement. Of those 12–"

"You get the idea." I stood up, taking several very deep breaths for the first time in a few minutes, and saw Poe was on her side. Poor girl. "Point is, he could have sold those thrusters to anybody for a tidy sum. But he set them aside for me. I'm loyal to him, and he's loyal to me."

"You're sure?"

"You just don't speak Echo." I picked my bike back up, confirming that other than a few scratches to the paint, Poe was just fine. "I need to thank him."

But a cacophony of rattling and banging from the hole in the building across the street had other ideas.

"She's not dead?" Bastion asked.

In answer, a single, copper spider-limb revealed itself, reaching around and grabbing the edge of the hole.

"Silent circuits," I said, hopping on the bike and firing up the thrusters. "Guess I'll have to thank him later." I gunned the engines before Roxy had a chance to crawl any farther out of the hole, lifting off the landing pad, accelerating as fast as the bike could handle, and pulling up to go nearly vertical in The Mist. In only seconds, I was through it and into the open air of Corto Corporation, quickly ascending through the forest of skyscrapers.

"Is this how your jobs usually go?" Bastion asked.

"Not even close," I said. "I'm sure I've pissed off plenty of people over the years. Part of the job. But that was my first death threat."

"A death threat is a strongly worded email or an animal head left in your bed. That was very violently attempted murder. You were attacked."

"Yeah," I said as I leveled Poe off. My head was pounding, and various other parts of my biology were beginning to complain, too. "A very aggressive death threat. Makes me wonder who, exactly, insisted that I be the one to steal you. If I was picked because I'm damn good at my job, or because somebody wanted me in harm's way."

"I don't know," Bastion said. "I don't have access to Corto's Intel files. Their firewalls are formidable."

"We need to focus on one thing at a time anyway. First is getting your chip back."

"From Huginn."

"From Huginn," I confirmed. "Hey Carbon, give me directions to Vale of the Valkyries." A wireframe map of the city around me popped up in the corner of my display, a route highlighted in red. At the top of my field of vision, a floating arrow told me to go straight for 16 kilometers.

"A brothel?" Bastion asked.

"A brothel."

CHAPTER TEN

VALE OF THE VALKYRIES CAME into view as I rounded a building. The brothel was perched atop one of the tallest buildings in the Huginn Industries borough. Ten-story tall effigies of three winged women looked out across the borough, all poised for battle with weapons and breasts bared. One looked to be a greenish copper, her hair flying back as if from a great wind, a spear raised over her head ready to slay some unseen, enormous beast. Another stood upright, the gleam of brass reflecting the lights from below, her sword and shield at the ready. The final woman had two swords raised over her head, wings and limbs and weapons a metal so dark, it nearly absorbed what little light shone up from the city.

"Those are Valkyries," Bastion said.

"I'd assumed."

"I'm not sure which ones. There were many in the mythology."

"It doesn't really matter." I wasn't in the mood for an ancient religion lesson. My head was still pounding despite the dose of nanobots I'd taken on the ride over. The little robots were working their magic on my pain, but it was a slow process.

"What is the plan here?" Bastion asked.

"Find whoever likes to leave a meown-eer–"

"Mjolnir," Bastion corrected.

"Whatever," I said.

"It will matter if you're asking Huginns about it."

I let out a little growl. He was right. "Say it again."

"Mjolnir."

"Slower."

"Mee-yole-near."

"Mee-ole-near."

"Closer," Bastion said, and we went back and forth a few times until he was satisfied with my pronunciation.

"Listen," I said. "We need to set some ground rules."

"Such as?"

"I can't have you rambling on in my ear all the time."

"I don't ramble."

"I need to see and hear everything, every detail of a room, tone of voice, security configuration. All of it."

"All right," Bastion said, though his tone was more thoughtful than confirming.

"What?"

"You don't want me to ramble, but I believe I could help you."

"How?" I asked as I pulled Poe to a stop, hovering and waiting for one of the landing pads to clear. Looked like a busy night at Vale of the Valkyries with Stryders coming and going, plus a gorgeous old Huginn Gokstad taking up residence on the pad. Built in only the third generation of flying cars, it was low-slung like an old Earth sports car. The vintage ride was one I hadn't seen in a few years, let alone one so pretty and heavily modded as this one. Though the glowing green flames were ridiculous.

"I'm still fairly limited," Bastion said, "but if you can find an access point to their system, I think I can get in and provide you with information. Camera placements, alarms, staffing, schematics."

"You can do all that?"

"I believe so, yes."

That certainly did change things. I was going in blind. I'd never been to Vale of the Valkyries before, so I planned to just walk in the front door, look around, and talk to people. Not a terrible plan, but now I had another option

90

to consider. A space on the landing pad cleared, so I swung Poe down and into a gentle landing, awash in dancing lights of all different colors. Even from out here, the pump of loud music filled the air and vibrated my feet.

I started toward the wide, heavy doors. They looked like wood, as did the entire structure below the enormous Valkyries, but it was all clearly metal made to look like wood. Tall and triangular, coming to a point 10 meters above the main door. I'd seen from the air that the whole building below the immense Valkyrie statues was that shape front to back.

"It's made to resemble a Viking longhouse," Bastion said. "The largest building in a Viking village, where warriors would gather to feast after a battle."

"How fitting, though I hope we'll find thieves, not warriors."

"True. Fighting does not appear to be your strong suit."

"I can defend myself," I said, though I wasn't feeling like it after that run-in with Roxy. I had an EMP, I'd taken some self-defense courses, and I had tasers in my palms. I had forgotten every one of them when that spider-like assassin came after me. My load-out was more about escaping fights than getting into them, but I needed to keep my head on straight to do either.

Without even thinking, I started casing the place. Time to put Bastion to work. "What do you see?"

"One guard. Private security."

"All security is private."

"I mean private for the Vale, not just Huginn Industries. Heavily armed with muscle mods, stun knuckles, and artillery."

"You missed the grade three pneumatics in the legs," I said, referring to the piston-like structures visible on the calves. Someone could leap almost a dozen meters when they were loaded like that.

"Why does that matter?"

"They can close distance in a hurry. Hard to run away from."

"I see."

"What else?" I asked.

"Two Huginn R80 multi-lens security cameras mounted near the roofline."

"Three," I said. "There's a third hidden under that crest up at the point of the roof, probably aiming straight down."

"I see nothing. How can you tell?"

"The clearance. There's no reason for that crest to be set 16 centimeters off the building unless there's something behind it."

"There are several assumptions in your reasoning."

"True," I said, striding toward the door and giving the guard a nod. "But those are assumptions backed up by years of experience."

Just before entering, I looked straight up, and there was camera number three looking straight down. Another Huginn R80. I gave it a wink. "See?"

"Fascinating," Bastion said.

The doors slid open, but the thumping of the music barely increased. A second set of doors a couple of meters ahead created a vestibule, keeping the sound at bay. Once the doors behind me closed and those ahead opened, I was drowning in slamming bass and slithering treble. I hated these kinds of places. Too much noise. Too much smell. Just too much of everything.

The short hall was dark and covered in plush, green velvet. On my left, a masculine figure with deep, purple skin, high cheekbones, and abs fit for sharpening knives gave me a half-cocked smile. Their pants were giving more than half. On my right, a feminine person with skin almost as dark green as the walls was twisting, dancing against the velvet like a lover. Their breasts were trying to escape the thin fabric of their top, and their curves were definitely modified. I wondered how many people walked in here and never made it past this opening salvo. Times like this, being asexual felt like a superpower. It was like being offered food when you're just not hungry. Ever.

I walked past them, and Half-Cocked gave me a little pout and a gentle touch on the shoulder. I jerked away and kept walking into a large, open room. A twisting tornado of fire flew up out of a pit in the center of the room, flashing unnatural hues of gold, green, and blue, and returning to its natural orange, all in time to the music. There was a stage at the far end where a pair of DJs were working antique turntables. They looked like twins, both in the same jumpsuits outlined in glowing pink and blue, both wearing enormous, horned helmets. The music was nearly deafening until my aural mods automatically adjusted the volume down.

Two bars flanked the stage, each one buzzing with customers and bartenders practically juggling bottles and glasses. Bottles of high-end booze were prominently displayed behind the bartenders, gently lit with pulsing pink light. Rums and whiskies and tequilas from Earth. Wines fermented from grapes grown on the southern islands of Little Sekmet Settlement. The story was the seeds for those grapes came from Earth over a century ago. Of course, there were liquors you could only find here on Little Sekhmet, distilled from various local flora. None of the cheap stuff Quynn and I usually drank while we sat around in sweatpants watching bad movies.

I looked for exits but didn't see any apparent other than the way I came in. Both bars had STAFF ONLY doors. There were a couple more like them on either side of the room. There were also three larger doors, spaced evenly around the room, which were not for just staff. Dim signs labeled the three Thrud, Skogul, and Sigrun. A pair of drunks – obviously not staff – stumbled in through the Thrud door.

I scanned the place for any of Huginn's Intel Operatives. I didn't know any personally, but I knew the type of people who went into this line of work. Several finance types were planted in one corner. They were sporting high-dollar suits and haircuts, glancing around nervously and talking quietly like they were exchanging corporate secrets. Executives took up most of the bar, each one basking in their entourages like satellites of ass-kissing all orbiting their respective planets.

Intermingling everywhere were employees of the Vale of the Valkyries. A gold-skinned person was mesmerizing one of the executives with their barely covered cleavage. An obsidian slab of muscle clad only in a sparkling silver thong was grinding on one of the financiers, hands working the crotches of the people to either side. A person with breasts and an erection of equal enormity was on their knees, showing someone a very good time in one dark corner. I looked away quickly.

"There they are," I said as I spotted a group next to the bar on my left.

"How can you be sure?" Bastion asked.

"There's a fearlessness to Intel Operatives," I said. Three masc and one fem, far more boisterous than the executives or financiers. They were more vibrant than any of our operatives. Hair in shades of green and purple. All had glowing tattoos on their arms of swords and shields and axes and strange symbols. A quick scan showed they were various runes from Earth Norse mythology. How original. A full-figured, dramatically feminine person with silver skin was riding one of them, right there for everyone to see, while their friends cheered them on. The sight turned my stomach a little, so I glanced away.

"And check their mods," I continued. "Rappelling and climbing gear, multi-spectral vision mods, all the tools for sneaking and breaking into places."

"Antimatter bombs?"

"How would I even scan for that?"

"Can you look for concentrations of gamma radiation?"

"Hey Carbon, scan for gamma radiation." I'd never done it before, but to my pleasant surprise, my multi-spectral vision switched to a display similar to thermal, but with a different color scheme. I looked from operative to operative, seeing a variety of colors I didn't understand, until the display read, "NO GAMMA RADS DETECTED."

"No luck here."

"What now?" Bastion asked.

"Now, we do it the old-fashioned way. Hey Carbon, identify their drinks." My display registered a scan, returning the drink contents of every glass and bottle in my field of vision. Way too many, but I managed to select just the operatives' drinks. Jayu Ice Teas all around. Their livers were certainly sturdier than mine.

"What are you doing?" Bastion asked.

"Making friends," I said as I kept walking past the operatives and straight to the bar.

"What are you having?" the bartender yelled.

"Four Jayu Iced Teas and a Drakon Bay Fog," I hollered over the music.

The bartender nodded and started working. I turned and kept watching the operatives just as Silver Skin finished their work. Thank Corto. I didn't want to have to see any more of that. Silver Skin rolled off their customer, both breathing heavily, and they touched hands to finalize the transaction. The operative's blue-gray skin was glistening with sweat, and they were grinning like an idiot. They leaned into Silver Skin, their lips pursed for a kiss, but the worker was off the couch in an instant, scooping up their clothes and practically jogging away. The operative's friends all laugh at them, and I couldn't help but chuckle along. You get what you pay for.

"Here you go," the bartender said, and I laid my palm flat to the top of the bar to pay for the drinks. Glad that was a billable expense, those drinks were double what I normally paid. I carried the quintet of drinks over to the operatives' table. One next to an open seat saw me first. Slender build, skin so white it was almost transparent, with close-cropped blue hair on their head. They had more tattoos than the rest, swords and runes running the length of their arms, disappearing into a sleeveless shirt, glowing the same color as their hair. Their eyes looked me up and down, stalling on the small V of skin visible above the zipper of the jacket.

"This looks like a fun lot!" I said, matching their own thunderous, jovial roars. I looked at each of them, but only gave Blue Hair a glance. I didn't want to encourage any more staring.

"A busy and very successful night," said the one who'd just been with Silver Skin as they pulled up their pants. The rest of them laughed.

"Jayu City Iced Teas, anyone?"

"A person cut from a familiar cloth!" Blue Hair said, gladly accepting their drink. He introduced himself as Torfund, he/him, though he did so with only the briefest glance at my eyes. He introduced his friends. Caspian, they/them, had a maroon mohawk, the sides of their head tattooed with a pair of glowing ravens to match. Allya, she/her, had orange skin and deep blue hair long enough to pool on the sofa where she sat. Bartholomew, he/him, was still sweat-soaked and grinning from his ride with Silver Skin. I told them my name was Ellie, she/her. Close enough that I wouldn't forget to respond to it, but just distant enough to throw them off. I didn't give them a company name, nor did they give theirs.

Once they were all well into their newest Jayu City Iced Teas, I asked, "What are we all celebrating tonight?"

"Successful acquisitions!" Caspian said with a wide grin. They and their fellow operatives were all too drunk to keep straight faces when they told the half-truth. Acquisitions. Asset relocations or transfers. Shipping and receiving. Communications. In our line of work, you developed a nearly endless list of euphemisms for robbing in the name of corporate advancement.

"I'll drink to that," I said, taking a big gulp of my Drakon Bay Fog, which looked exactly like a Jayu City Iced Tea. That was not an accident. It was also less than a quarter of the alcohol. Also, not an accident.

We all clinked glasses and took long draws from our drinks. I wasn't even feeling tipsy, but it was apparent they were all going to have a hard time holding onto their most recent meals, let alone their secrets.

"Let's play a game," I said.

"52 hours and 12 minutes," Bastion said.

"Patience," I said low enough to not be heard over the music.

"What kind of game?" Allya said, her voice a purr while her hands gripped the back of the sofa to keep herself steady.

"Truth or drink," I said.

"Never heard of it," Bartholomew said with a heavy slur.

"That's because you're an idiot!" Torfund said with a wink to me. I just made it up, but sure, pretend you already know.

I signaled a server, and they started making their way over. "It's easy," I said. "You ask someone a question. They answer. If it's a lie, they have to take a drink."

"I don't get it," Allya said. "I like drinking. We are Huginn. We all like drinking."

The server arrived, and I said loud enough for all to hear, "We need 40 shots of Burning Hate."

"Are you sure?" the server asked, and the faces around me were echoing the sentiment. Burning Hate was a mixture of a high-proof Little Sekhmet spirit called Singe and two drops of sauce made from the hottest pepper grown on the planet. It wasn't something anyone enjoyed drinking.

"I'm sure," I said.

"This little woman knows how to play!" Caspian yelled, slamming their empty glass on the table. "You play like a Huginn, but you don't look like a Huginn."

So much for the clothes and temporary tattoos convincing anyone I was from Huginn Industries.

"Where are you from?" Bartholomew asked, though his eyes were on the server walking away.

"The wrong borough, from the looks of this fine company," I said. "How do I change sides?"

That brought out the biggest laugh so far, followed by a round of these Huginn operatives taking turns insulting the other four companies and their boroughs. They were all too drunk and excited to actually make me answer their question before the shots arrived, practically covering the table as three servers, all scantily clad, unloaded the little glasses.

"You first, little woman!" Caspian said.

Even though they were inebriated, I needed to start slow. "Allya," I said. "Have you ever slept with any of these three?"

She smiled like a predator. "Only one of them," she said with a wink, and then downed a shot, wincing as it went down.

They all laughed. This was going to be harder than I thought. The Huginn penchants for drinking and boasting were legendary, but I was wondering if even those legends were understated.

"Your turn," I said to her.

"Ellie," she said. "Does Torfund have any chance of getting that zipper of yours the rest of the way down tonight?"

They all laughed again at that, all but Torfund, whose eyes had gone wide. My stomach twisted into a pit, and I didn't move. Didn't want to move. Didn't want to look at Torfund. But I remembered the Hermes Protocol. Demotion or termination. No more Corto Corporation. No more Quynn or my friends or family. I swallowed hard and turned to Torfund. I waited for his eyes to join mine before I said, "Not a chance," and threw back a shot. It burned and my vision wobbled.

Torfund smiled hungrily and his friends were all laughing and chanting his name. Round and round we went, the Huginn operatives blending truths, half-truths, full lies, and burning shots of liquor. I paced myself, working to play along but maintaining my wits. Fortunately, none of the questions came back to hypothesizing about Torfund and me together.

Caspian and Torfund started giving Bartholomew no end of torment over dramatically failing to seduce a Kotega executive's wife earlier that evening. Meaning they were on a three-person job nowhere near Corto.

Eventually, Allya copped to nearly decapitating a Nexus security guard a couple of hours ago. So she didn't rob the Corto vault, either. This plan wasn't panning out at all. If I didn't find a lead here, I didn't know where else to look. I kept listening as a theme started to recur: another operative named Theo.

It was unlike a Huginn to talk up someone else. To get ahead at Huginn Industries, you had to be the best, step on anyone you had to, and always tell everyone how great you were. And yet, the name Theo came up more than once, and there was always a sense of reverence or at least hesitancy. He was good. He had bested all of them at least once in their various 'acquisitions.' He'd been unusually secretive and silent recently, two traits not normal for a Huginn.

"You make this Theo sound more like a myth than a man," I said.

"He's very much real," Caspian slurred.

"We saw him this very night!" Bartholomew bellowed.

"Where? On one of your escapades?" I asked.

"No. Here. Not long before you arrived and livened up the party," Bartholomew said. "And a good thing, too. He's no fun at places like this. Too shy, that one."

"Shy?" I asked. If he had been here, he might have been celebrating a job, too.

"It's just sex," Allya said. "No need to hide it!"

"I'll drink to that!" Bartholomew yelled and downed a shot out of turn. He was so inebriated that he didn't even react to the burning liquor.

I stood, pretending to wobble as much as these Huginns were. "Excuse me. I have to use the little operatives' room."

"Do hurry back!" Bartholomew said. "It's almost your turn again!"

I faux stumbled away, eyeing the nearest doorway labeled with one of those strange words. Once I passed under the Thrung sign and the doors shut behind me, I righted myself and took everything in. Four elevator doors on my left. Cameras in the corners pointed at the doors. I moved quickly, calling an elevator and barely glancing over my shoulder.

"Can you pull up schematics?" I whispered to Bastion. "Even a brochure? If so, find the private rooms and if I can spy on them discretely."

"I didn't know voyeurism was your kink," Bastion said.

"I don't have a kink," I said as an elevator dinged and opened.

I stepped in and found no buttons, just a blank screen and a hand scanning panel. I pressed my hand to it.

"NO HUGINN CREDITS ON YOUR ACCOUNT," the screen read.

"Sparks," I whispered. "What do you have, Bastion? Schematics? Do you see any access points?"

"Nothing online," Bastion said. "And this is a simple Huginn RX1010 point-of-sale system patched into elevator controls. All too low security to tie into anything useful."

I stepped back out of the elevator and leaned against the opposite wall.

"We need to get up there," Bastion said.

"I know."

"Can you hack the POS system?"

I shook my head. "Not without getting caught. There's a camera at the top of that touchscreen watching whoever places orders. And I guarantee a live person is watching those camera feeds at all times."

"We have less than 52 hours and–"

"I know how much time we have, Bastion!" I practically yelled the words, suddenly grateful nobody else was in this room with me. "Give me a minute to think."

One of the elevator doors dinged and opened. Out stepped a slight, brown figure, curvy and dressed in barely more than gold strings. They were touching up their bold makeup as the doors to the elevator opened.

"Excuse me," I said, stepping toward them and trying to look as sheepish as possible.

They blinked several times like they'd just noticed I was even there.

"I'm so sorry," I said. "I left my bag upstairs. Is there any way you–?"

"And you just assume I work here?" they asked, cutting me off.

I felt blood rush to my cheeks and my lips sputter, awash in embarrassment. "I'm so sorry. Please–"

"I'm messing with you, gorgeous," they said, a smile suddenly breaking across their face. "Of course I work here. My rate is 300 credits per hour."

"Oh," I said, my embarrassment melting away while frustration swept in to fill the void. I didn't need to know any hourly rate. "No, I don't want to do that. I just need to get up there and–"

"300 per hour," they said, their smile vanishing. "Half an hour minimum. That's the cost of getting upstairs."

"But I only left my bag."

"And that missing bag doesn't pay my rent or feed my kids."

"Can I contact security? Will they let me up?"

They rolled their eyes. "You too cheap to pay for more time upstairs? Come back tomorrow. There's a lost and found by the front door, not that there's ever anything in it. Nobody is letting you up there for free."

"Please, I–" I started to say, but the worker walked away without another word.

I took one deep, cleansing breath. Then another. I wasn't getting upstairs without Huginn Industries credits. I couldn't get those on my account without a trip into The Mist or an official request to Gustin. I didn't have time for any of that. Torfund's predatory gaze came to mind, the way his eyes lingered on me in ways I didn't like.

That look reminded me of Yevgeny, the first serious boyfriend I'd had after I'd started to realize I was asexual. We were both sixteen. Been classmates since we were six or seven. I was out-of-my-mind in love with him, seeing an idealized future with him in that way that only teenagers in love really can. But at the time, it was all so real and important.

We'd been together for four months when he brought up sex. I knew I didn't want that. Not with him. Not with anyone. Ever. But I loved him so much, was so certain of our relationship and the future I saw for us. I couldn't just tell him no, couldn't bear to come out of the closet and lose him.

For six weeks, I danced around the subject, telling him I wanted our first time to be special. He practically performed miracles trying to create that special moment. He would look at me, up and down, a hunger in his gaze. While I knew some people found that thrilling or seductive, it felt predatory to me. Like he just wanted to take something from me I wasn't willing to give.

When I finally came out to Yevgeny, the heartbreak I'd feared became real. He wasn't angry that I was asexual, but that I didn't tell him. We broke up that night. It hurt me deeply, though not as bad as when he started dating Cynthia Corto-Seventeen the very next week.

Torfund had given me that same predatory gaze I'd gotten from too many people over the years. And Torfund certainly had Huginn Industries credits on his account. As much as I hated the idea of going back into the closet, even for a minute, I didn't see any other way to get upstairs. It was either revisit the closet or let the Hermes Protocol take away everything I loved.

"52 hours remaining," Bastion said.

I took a deep breath. "I know what I have to do."

"And what is that?"

I didn't answer. If I had to vocalize my plan, I would start thinking about it even more than I already was, and then I might not be able to do it. I re-entered the bar. The Huginn Intel Operatives were still there, still drunk and having a great time. Even seeing Torfund's back from here made my stomach turn. I swallowed down the nausea, unzipped my jacket and jumpsuit almost to my navel, and strode back to my seat with the operatives.

Caspian was in the middle of telling a story. Or a joke. The shots were thinning, and Caspian's words were so slurred that none of us could understand what they were saying.

We all laughed when Caspian finished their diatribe, which seemed to have been the correct response, judging by their reaction. Then Bartholomew turned to me and said, "As promised. We waited. It's your turn!"

I grabbed a shot. "Torfund," I said turning to face those predatory eyes. "Have you ever used one of the private rooms?"

"No," Torfund said, his eyes running up and down me again. "But I'm not unwilling for the right party."

"Oh? And what's the right party?"

"Tall. Thin. Not afraid to join a boisterous group of strangers." His smile made my stomach roll, but I had him, no doubt.

"Finally," Bastion said in my ear. "I found something. A Huginn architecture firm designed this place. They're very proud of it, but their website security is terrible."

"The point?" I mumbled.

101

"The private rooms are in the Valkyries themselves. They're not just statues."

"Don't be shy," Bartholomew hollered at me from his couch. "Nobody here is paying you to be shy!"

"There are dozens of rooms," Bastion muttered. "I don't know where this Theo went."

I gave Bartholomew a pouty look, just parting my lips, and spoke so only Bastion could hear. "Cameras? Security control room? How do I find him?"

"What?" Bartholomew said. "Don't pout."

"It's called 'demure,' you oaf," Allya said to him and then turned to me. "And he's right. Here? I don't believe that look for even a second."

"Each Valkyrie has its own control room," Bastion interjected. "But that's the extent of the security information in the original architectural plans. Nothing on cameras."

Vale of the Valkyries wasn't making this easy, but they weren't making it impossible, either. Again, I needed some old-fashioned tricks to get what I needed.

"No one is paying me to be here at all," I said to the group. "I don't work here." I winked at Torfund, and his smile grew. I grabbed another shot with one hand and leaned over to him, putting my other hand on his leg. "Unlike Barty over there, I don't want an audience."

"What do you have in mind?" he asked.

"I hear nice things about upstairs," I said. "And surely whatever is good enough for Theo is good enough for Torfund."

The other man's name sent a visible tremor through Torfund's face. I'd read it right. The jealousy was definitely there. Might as well lean on the bluff as hard as I could. I grabbed a shot with my right hand, squeezing my ring finger against the rim of the glass in a very particular spot. That added a little something extra to the drink, and I moved it toward him. I crept my other hand slowly up from his knee to his thigh, as the lump in my stomach moved up my throat. I swallowed and said, "I say we find his favorite Valkyrie and show the staff what a real Huginn can do up there."

With a growl and a sneer, he grabbed and tossed back the shot, and then threw the empty glass across the room. He took my hand off his thigh, leaped to his feet, and pulled me toward the Sigrun door. Bartholomew, Allya, and Caspian all cheered us on in their drunken hazes. Sigrun. Even if I'd managed to get upstairs before, it would have been in the wrong Valkyrie. We were through the door in moments, and the noise was significantly diminished.

"Sigrun," Bastion whispered, though I didn't know why. Nobody else could hear him. "Twelve stories plus the luxury suite in her head. The security office is on the second floor, one up from where we are now. Room 210."

The more useful he proved to be, the better I felt about him invading my systems, if only a little. I wouldn't have called it trust yet, but at least I knew he had something to lose if I failed tonight.

Torfund slammed the button on the elevator, and then tossed me against the wall, his lips heading for mine with unbridled lust in his eyes. My stomach cramped as I moved a finger to his lips just in time, sending waves of confusion and anger across his eyes.

"Uh-uh-uh," I said, bringing back the pout, and then licking my lips to keep him focused. "I don't like an audience. You want me to like it, don't you?"

"Audience?"

I flicked my eyes to one of the cameras.

He turned, saw it, and growled again, some mixture of lust and frustration, I thought, but he nodded. Then he slammed the elevator button a few more times. He was practically stamping around by the time the elevator door opened.

Once inside, he pressed his whole hand to the control panel. It scanned him, and the display read, "CREDITS CONFIRMED. PLEASE SELECT A SERVICE." An array of options ranging from private viewing all the way to luxury suite party flashed on the screen. Torfund looked hungrily at me, to the screen, and back, and then his eyes started to roll.

I grabbed him, thanking the sedative I added to that shot for kicking in at just the right time. I pushed his unconscious face into the corner and buried my face in his neck. Nothing to see here, little camera above the screen. "Bastion, which option will get me closest to the security office?"

"One moment."

The display on the elevator flashed, "PLEASE MAKE A SELECTION."

"Come on," I said.

One moment," Bastion repeated.

"RESETTING IN 5 SECONDS. PLEASE MAKE A SELECTION."

"Bastion..."

"Basic package," Bastion finally said. "No companion."

I tapped the display per Bastion's directions, and the elevator gently moved upward, dinging twice before the doors slid open.

"Please proceed to room 306," a husky computerized voice told me.

I put an arm under Torfund's shoulders, magnetized his left leg to my right, and drag-walked him out of the elevator, down the hall, and threw him on the bed in 306. Then I took a seat next to him.

Breathe in. Breathe out.

"What are you doing?" Bastion asked.

"I need a minute."

"We less than 52 hours until–"

"I know." The timer on my display was telling me the same thing.

"But there are–"

"Everything I just did there with this idiot and his friends? I hate it."

"I find that hard to believe."

"I'm good at it," I said. "I've been trained. But I don't...I don't want..." I couldn't even say the word for what Torfund wanted, the thought twisting my innards around. "So after all of that, I need a minute."

"I really need to tell you–"

"I need a minute without you talking to me."

Silence followed. At least there was that. I let a minute go by. A full minute trying to not watch that timer on my display tick down. I took deep breaths. Calmed my nerves. Zipped up my jumpsuit and jacket. To Bastion's credit, he said nothing when the minute was up.

"Okay," I said, slapping my knees and standing back up.

"Now?"

"Yes, Bastion, n–"

"Two security guards just got off the elevator," he said, not letting me finish. "They are heading for this room."

CHAPTER ELEVEN

"WHY DIDN'T YOU TELL ME?" I was fighting not to scream at Bastion. Doubtful the walls were soundproof.

"I was trying, but you were rather insistent on your minute of silence."

"Sparks!" I had two options. I could stay and act like everything was fine, that Torfund was so drunk, he passed out in the elevator. Play the worried lover. But the clock was ticking, literally. I didn't know the brothel's security protocols or how long they would need me to stick around. I had to go with my second option.

"Show me the schematics," I told Bastion. "Highlight my routes to the security room."

A blue wireframe was floating in my display, the first three floors of the Sigrun Valkyrie hovering in front of me. This room glowed green, orienting me in the schematic. The door I'd just come through glowed in red, the start of an obvious path down the hall, to the elevator, and straight to the door of 210, the security room. Obviously not the route I could take with security headed straight for me.

Another route was lit in red, heading from the wall behind me, cutting across the three rooms next to me, crossing the hall, and heading straight for the elevator shaft. I glanced behind me but didn't see a door or window. Up high on the ceiling just next to the wall, however, was a vent. A quick scan showed it was 70 centimeters by 40 centimeters. Tight, but doable.

"Bastion," I said. "What's the narrowest that ventilation route takes?"

"Unknown. The schematic doesn't show measurements throughout the ventilation system."

"Any other routes?"

"Not unless you can cut through the outer wall of the structure."

Three booming knocks rattled the door followed by a deep voice saying, "Vale Security. Please open the door. We need to verify there is no medical emergency."

"He's fine," I yelled. "Just drunk."

"I understand," the voice yelled back. "But we need to verify. Please open the door."

So much for that hope. Time to go. I had to move quickly. In one stride, I moved under the little security camera I'd seen when I walked in. I reached up and snapped my fingers, fritzing it with that little EMP. Next up was the vent. I crossed the room without pausing.

"Please open the door or we will open it ourselves," the voice said.

Four hex screws. Pretty standard. I opened my thumbs and pointer fingers to deploy hex screwdrivers for just such obstacles. The joints in my hands extended and distorted, and then I was spinning all four screws at the same time. The vent cover was off in seconds.

Natural human biology had a lot of limitations. Joints could only bend so far. Stretching was limited by tendons and muscles. I'd effectively eliminated most of those restrictions with my mods. I extended my left foot up toward the open vent. The crotch of my pants audibly ripped wide open. This was why I only wore my jumpsuit when doing this kind of thing.

My hip, knee, and ankle joints swiveled and extended well beyond what natural joints could do. My foot opened like a claw, gripping the inside of the shaft. Only then did my right foot leave the ground, the left leg pulling me up and into the shaft which ran parallel to the ceiling. I used my feet to crawl into the shaft, the vent cover still gripped in my hands.

I pulled the vent cover into place just as the lock on the door beeped twice, and then swung open. I lay there on my back, taking a few deep breaths, the shoulder seams of the jacket pinching my flesh while I held the vent cover against the opening.

"Torfund Huginn-Intel?" the voice from the other side of the door said.

"Sir?" another voice said. "Sir?"

They were probably shaking him, running some rudimentary tests. There was no way to screw the vent cover back on from the inside; my fingers just couldn't fit through those vent slats. I didn't have time to wait them out, either. I needed to get moving, but once I let go of the vent cover, it would drop to the floor.

"What are you doing?" Bastion asked.

"Vent cover," I said as quietly as possible.

"Magnets."

"Magnets?"

"Most of your moving parts involve magnets. The vent cover and the shaft are made of magnetic metal. Take something apart."

It wasn't my favorite suggestion, but I didn't have anything better in mind. No glue or tape or soldering equipment. Okay. I wasn't here to steal anything, so I ripped open the outer seam of the pants, opened the compartment on my right leg, and then started disassembling it with my right hand, holding the vent cover in place with my left hand alone. Sure enough, there were magnets that sealed the compartment closed, pulling and pushing the metal structure that held the carbon-polymer shell. The magnets weren't big, but they would have to do. Slowly and as soundlessly as I could manage, I tucked four magnets between the vent cover and shaft opening. Then ever so gently, I released my grip on the cover. It held.

Now I just had to crawl through a ventilation shaft feet-first and silently. Everything tonight was going so well until about 5 minutes ago.

"Guide me," I said. "Turn-by-turn."

"Understood," Bastion said. "Go straight for 36 meters."

I did, my limbs working in tandem to move me through the tight shaft, gently gripping the sides of the shaft and working me through it like a spider. Another advantage to cybernetic limbs.

We worked through the system of ducts, crawling across the three rooms next to where Torfund was being checked, and security was surely confused as to where I'd gone. The first room was empty, but the next two were definitely occupied with people having VERY good times. The shaft ran into a T-junction, and Bastion guided me up. I used the junction to re-orient myself so I was headfirst in the ducts, which was easier, even if it proved too much for the seams of my jacket, which ripped at regular intervals. A dozen meters to cross the hall, and the shaft veered sharply to the right, a tough turn that made me wish my torso could bend like my limbs, ripping up my Huginn outfit even more in the process, and then I came upon a maintenance hatch.

"Here," Bastion said. "The elevator shaft is on the other side."

The hatch was held in place by two bolts and a hinge at the top. While biological fingers wouldn't have been able to get the grip or torque necessary to move them from inside the shaft, my cybernetic hands had no such issues. I grabbed and twisted. In less than a minute, the maintenance hatch was swinging freely.

"Any idea how many guards are in the second-floor hall or the security room?"

"No. I'm sorry."

"Alternate routes?"

The schematic popped up in front of me again, slowly spinning. Elevator shaft, hallways, and then the front door of the security room was easiest, but I had no idea what I was walking into. A few different routes via ventilation lit up, traced around, but then went back to blue. Eventually, a new route lit up red, but it involved climbing all the way to the top of the elevator shaft, through vents up to Sigrun's head, and down another ventilation shaft, this one winding and long.

"Sparks," I cursed. "Theo might be gone by then."

"Assuming he's the person we're looking for."

"Is or isn't, I need to know." With that, I flung open the hatch and leaped across the elevator shaft, grabbing hold of the wall opposite, and then I leaped back and down, grabbing the elevator doors for the second floor. I pulled them apart gently, just a little, and sent my fiberoptic camera through the gap. I looked left, and the hall was clear. To the right was the door to 210, clearly marked SECURITY PERSONNEL ONLY. No one was in the hall. I pulled the doors open farther and squeezed through.

Right. That was the easy part. Now to get into a security control room

108

via the front door. I took a deep breath and started walking. Naturally. Like I belonged here and wasn't drenched in a thin film of sweat and duct dust. All was well and normal in the hallway.

"Do you have a plan?" Bastion asked.

I took a few more steps toward the security door. "Sort of."

"I don't understand. Having or not having a plan is an absolute. Like being unique or pregnant. One cannot have a little bit of uniqueness or be a little bit pregnant."

"Remind me to show you someone nine months pregnant compared to the morning after, show you what a little bit pregnant looks like."

"You are being semantic when we need–"

"Just trust me," I said as I stopped in front of the door, slouched down like Sigrun herself was pressing on my shoulders and gave the door a knock.

"I could be more helpful if you would–" Bastion started to say but stopped as soon as the door opened.

The Vale of the Valkyries security guard that peered down was a full head taller than me. Small, dark eyes on either side of a broad, bronze nose. An unkempt shock of blonde hair spilled down across their forehead and the tops of their ears. They were wearing what looked like antique Earth armor. Small, diamond-shaped metal plates were fashioned into a shirt and pants, with detailed metal vambraces and greaves covering the forearms and shins, respectively. Covering the armor on their torso was a blue and red tunic with the Vale of the Valkyries logo embroidered across the chest. I guessed the theme was important in the Vale.

"Security personnel only," the guard practically grunted. "Are you alright?"

I was filthy, and my clothes were torn to shreds, so I supposed I didn't look all right. Time for full damsel mode. "I...I was just upstairs," I said, putting some whimper into my voice. "I met someone in the bar, and we went up to...well...um..." I let the unspoken words hang there.

"You went upstairs to have sex," the guard said.

"Um..." I said, acting shy. "Anyway, he passed out. I don't know–"

The guard glanced over their shoulder. Between their immense height and shoulders twice as wide as mine, I couldn't see beyond the wall of tunic and armor. They said to someone else, "Didn't you say there was someone with Torfund Huginn-Intel in 306?"

"Yeah," a brighter voice said from somewhere in the room.

The big guard turned back to me. "What happened to you? How did you get here?"

When in doubt, play stupid and helpless. "Oh! He just..." I sniffled like I was about to cry. "And then I didn't know what to do and I didn't know anyone or who to call or where to go or–"

"Okay, okay!" the big guard said, their hands up in surrender and voice softening. "Come in and take a seat. Let's talk about it."

"Thank you," I said as the guard turned to let me pass. There was one other guard in the room, half the size of the first. They had blue-green skin and jet-black hair in a long braid to their knees, and much softer, thinner facial features. The uniform was the same to the last detail, just smaller.

On the wall across from the door were dozens of screens showing interior shots of every room in Sigrun, neatly in rows and labeled from room 201 to 1220. It was all I needed. Way too much information to parse through with a cursory glance, but I didn't need to parse it all right now. Instead, I blinked at them rapid-fire, telling my visual implants to take pictures of every screen on the wall, full resolution. I had what I needed, now I just needed to get out of the room and look them over.

"Give me access to those files," Bastion said in my ear.

A great idea. Let him do the scanning for me while I talked my way back out of this room, but I didn't know how to give him that access. And I couldn't say any–

"WARNING: UNKNOWN PROGRAM REQUESTING FILE ACCESS" appeared on my display.

"That's me," Bastion said.

"Take a seat," the smaller guard said, gesturing to an empty chair. They pressed a button on the touchscreen console in front of them, and all the screens went dark.

I moved past the guard, and once neither guard could see my face, I quietly mouthed, "Hey Carbon, grant access."

"ACCESS GRANTED," flashed briefly across my display.

"What's your name?" the smaller guard asked.

"Ellie," I said, keeping the lie from earlier. The guards glanced at each other, likely noticing that I didn't give a company name.

"Is Torfund okay?" I asked, hoping to refocus them on bigger issues.

They glanced at each other again before the larger guard picked up a tablet and said, "Can you tell us what happened?"

"I just came in looking for a little fun, a little..." I said. Then I started from when I walked into the brothel, adding lots of "ums" and awkward silences, skipping or altering several important details. Like being an Intel Operative, looking for whoever broke into the Corto Intel vault, or how I had no intention of having sex with Torfund or anybody. This place seemed to have cameras everywhere, so using the truth as much as possible was to my advantage.

"Why Torfund?" the smaller guard asked.

"Why?" I asked.

"What was so special about him? Why come upstairs with him?"

"The way he'd been looking at me all night," The way he'd been looking at me made my stomach turn, but I said, "It made me feel sexy. A room of professionals, and his eyes were on me all night."

"So then what happened?" the larger guard asked.

"I told Torfund..." I took a long pause, pretending to demure for a moment, "...my intentions. My desires. He grabbed my hand and practically dragged me over to the elevator. He was so excited, though wobbly."

"I found Theo," Bastion cut in. An image leaped to my display. One of the screens blown up. A person sitting on a bed, nude, in obvious post-coital vaping. Their skin was a natural dark brown, heavily muscled, and with bright green cornrows on their head. Both legs were replaced with carbon-polymer mods just above the knees, as well as both large forearms. On their face was a glowing tattoo. It was unmistakably Mjolnir, the exact same design as what I'd seen on the inside of the Corto vault door earlier that night. Even the same color. This really was the notorious Theo.

"Wobbly?" the smaller guard asked.

"Room 919," Bastion said.

"You said he was wobbly?" the smaller guard repeated.

"What?"

"You said Torfund was wobbly," they repeated with a huff.

Right. Torfund. "Yes. Yes. And then once we were on the elevator, he just crumpled. Too many shots, I suppose."

"You didn't see him ingest anything else?" the larger guard asked.

"No," I said. Okay. I needed to get out of here, needed to get up to the ninth floor, and see if Theo was still there. If he'd left between taking that photo and now, I'd be back to almost where I started, having used up almost three hours just getting a name.

Then both guards were suddenly looking off to the middle distance, something on their displays. Both displays at the same time. This probably wasn't good.

"I'm sorry," the smaller guard said, "but we're going to have to hold you here. We have more questions and some concerns."

I couldn't afford to stay here any longer. They'd probably found the drug in Torfund's system or figured out I wasn't who I said I was. Something. I stood up from the chair, giving the guards a full panic. "Oh no. Oh no. Is it Torfund? What happened? Is he dead? Did I...? Tell me what's happening!"

The larger guard practically dropped their tablet and moved toward me, "Please, just calm down."

The smaller guard was moving closer as well, just like I'd hoped. "It's just some questions," they said. "Torfund is alive and well. He's coming around."

In seconds, they were both within reach. Thousands of years of human evolution, and our basic instincts still told us to help people, to underestimate people we see as small and emotional. Corto bless evolution. I reached out, putting my hands on both of their cheeks.

"Thank you," I said, and fired 100 volts through both guards. They both seized up, arms and legs going stiff. Fists and teeth clenching. The shock only lasted for two seconds, and then they both crumpled to the floor.

"Is he still here?" I asked Bastion.

"I don't know," he said. "I don't have access to—"

"I'm in the room," I said, already looking around the blank touchscreen panels for an access port. "How do I get you access?"

"Those are Huginn S5420s. There should be access panels underneath.

112

You'll have to a pry panel off."

I dropped to the floor and rolled under the screens. Sure enough, each one had a 10-centimeter-square panel on the bottom. I ripped the closest one off to find a handful of different data ports, one of which was compatible with my data cable. I quickly deployed it and plugged in. I stood back up, staying connected, and within seconds the whole thing came back to life. Every screen and control lit up, granting me unfettered access.

I looked to room 919, but Theo was gone. A pair of drones were cleaning the room, changing bedding, vacuuming, and sterilizing it for the next client. "Where is he?" I asked, checking other cameras. Then all the screens blanked out at once. "What happened?"

"Unplug," Bastion said. "I'm fully in their system now. I don't need the hardline."

"Then what–?"

I stopped talking when the middle of the screen lit up with a live feed of one of the Sigrun elevators. There was Theo, riding down from the ninth floor.

"Where is he going?"

"He's leaving, heading for the landing pads."

"Stop him!" I yelled and then turned on my heel in a full sprint for the elevator bank.

"Too late. His elevator just passed us and is stopping below," Bastion said as I arrived at the elevators, and one of them whisked open. "But he's in no hurry."

The moment I was in the elevator, the doors closed behind me. No need for payment or selection this time. Bastion was proving his worth yet again. I was practically bouncing on my heels, ready to sprint out of the elevator and confront the green-haired thief. It was only one floor down, but the time drew out horribly. Finally, the doors opened, and I didn't wait, I squeezed through and looked around.

"He's almost to the front door," Bastion said in answer to my unspoken question.

I sprinted through the door back to the bar, and then around the corner to the entrance hall. I thought I heard a cheer or some heckling, probably from my old drinking pals, but I didn't look around or wait to confirm. Sure enough, at the end of the hall, just walking through the doors to the landing pad, I saw those broad, dark shoulders and the shock of green hair walking away.

"Theo!" I yelled, but he either didn't hear me or ignored me. I kept running, right past the protesting pair of workers who'd greeted me and out into the Huginn night. There was a gentle rain falling now, putting a fine sheen on every surface. Theo was nearing that vintage Huginn Gokstad. I yelled again, louder this time, "Theo!"

He stopped and turned to face me, confusion plain on his face. It was at that moment I realized I didn't have a plan. I'd been so focused on getting here, finding the chip, Bastion, and all the conspiracies that seemed to be swirling around me. I hadn't actually considered what I would do when I found and confronted this man. I couldn't let him get in that car, though, so I jogged over to him as his confusion faded into impatience.

"Who are you?" he asked. "Did I forget something?"

I didn't know how to play this, who to pretend to be in this moment, so I just went with myself and the truth. "You stole something tonight."

A smile crept across his face. "I steal a lot of things. That's my job."

"You stole from the Corto vault."

The smile dropped. "That's absurd," he said. "How would I, or any Huginn operative know where Corto's vault is?"

How very unlike a Huginn not to brag. That gave me pause, but I said, "You followed me."

"I've never even seen you before," Theo said, and then he turned on his heel and continued walking toward his waiting car.

"Not every day you see an antimatter bomb used inside a building," I hollered at him. "And you thought no one would notice that tag on the inside of the vault door is just an overblown version of that ridiculous tattoo on your face."

He spun back on me, and those amber eyes of his were staring daggers. Good one, Elise, just go ahead and make fun of his tattoo. This is why I usually made plans.

"What did you say?" he growled.

This was my chance. Apologize. Be civil. Try to work this out and make a deal. But he'd broken into the Corto vault, violated my home away from home, and forced Corto to invoke the Hermes Protocol. He was putting me and mine in danger. So I said, "I said it looks like someone drew a robot's cock and balls on your face."

"You bitch," he said, and started walking toward me with murder in his eyes.

"Give back the chip, and this doesn't have to get ugly."

"Oh yes, it does," he said and swung at me with his oversized left arm. My display flashed a red exclamation point as he was winding up, and my cybernetic legs did more of the ducking than my own biological reflexes. I came back up with a punch of my own aimed squarely at his jaw.

He moved like a boxer, though, shifting his face just out of the way and catching my wrist all in one motion. I barely realized I was caught before his modified right arm flew up and into my elbow joint, pushing it beyond its considerable extension abilities.

My display flashed, "DAMAGE," along with a diagram of my right arm, everything past the elbow silent and highlighted in red. Theo threw my arm and the rest of me away from him, and I tumbled back into a puddle, awkward with the half-useless limb.

"One down," Theo said, pacing toward me, rain dribbling down his tattoo. "Three limbs to go. I'm going to break them all, and then throw you into The Mist."

I believed him. For the second time tonight, I found myself completely outmatched in a fight. Theo took a couple of quick steps and came in for a kick, and I rolled out of the way. I caught a glimpse of the heavily armed guard at the Vale's entrance, but they were just watching, smirking.

"Why did you take the chip?" I yelled to Theo.

He said nothing as he drove his modified fist toward my face. I barely got out of the way as the fist splintered the pavement where my head had been. Then something was around my waist and squeezing. I barely had a chance to glance down and see a thin cable there before it pulled tighter, I was yanked into the air, straight toward Theo. His modified fist slammed into my back. I heard and felt ribs snap. Blinding pain flared across my chest and back, which didn't get any better when Theo dropped me to the ground.

"I knew this was a bad idea," Theo said, practically mumbling as he paced around me. "Antimatter bombs? The Corto vault? Insane, but he promised everything would be fine. One stupid chip."

I writhed, struggling to listen, to hear something that might help me. Finally, air came rushing back into my lungs all at once, though my broken ribs screamed in protest.

"But they only sent you," Theo continued. "This little waif with no offensive mods. I guess he was right."

"He who?" I wheezed. "Who hired you?"

"You don't even know your own people. By Huginn, Corto is pathetic!"

Was he saying he was hired by someone from Corto Corporation? That didn't even make sense. Each company had their own Intel Operatives. They didn't hire from other companies. Did they? I asked, "What do you mean, my own people?"

He clammed up then and started coming at me. Right, so he wasn't going to give me anything, and I couldn't beat him. I needed to get out of this fight, and he wasn't going to just let me go. I rolled to my feet and readied my stuns. They'd been recharging since I took down the pair of guards, but they were only at 40%. Maybe combined, they would be enough to end this.

"Cute toys," he said when he saw them.

"Funny," I said, advancing on him now. "That's what your friends said about your little Mjolnir. Guess that's why you always get a private room."

Oh, that did it. He was pissed before, but now it looked like he was ready to foam at the mouth. He came at me hard, which was my hope. I ducked his first punch and slapped both palms against him, letting loose both stuns at once. His muscles rippled at the contact, and he staggered sideways. I didn't wait, kicking one leg hard at the backs of his knees, but his modified legs held firm, barely jostled.

I rolled away as he turned to face me, blinking and shaking off the effects of the stuns. Made of sterner stuff than the Vale of the Valkyrie guards, it looked like. Still, I had my window.

"Bastion," I said between pants. "I need a ride."

"Poe is back in the other direction, on the other side of–"

"No chance!" I yelled. "I need a different ride!"

"It will take at least three minutes for a vehicle to arrive here, and how do you–"

"Not here," I interrupted. "The next building to the west. 50 floors down."

"You're not suggesting–"

"Make the call!" I screamed as I turned and sprinted to the edge of the landing platform, my vision darkening at the edges from exertion. I may not have planned how to deal with Theo, but I had the wherewithal to look for my exits and to make contingency plans for any escape. I leaped off the landing pad for the Vale, 350 stories in the air, and into the rainy expanse between buildings.

"What are you doing?" Bastion practically yelled. "Your right arm is nonfunctional. You cannot glide without it!"

"You seriously underestimate me!"

Not that he was the first. Gliding wasn't just one of my favorite past times, but really my preferred method of escape from very tall places. It wasn't my only option, though. Plan B wasn't as fun and was far more stressful on my mods, but it would get the job done.

"Hey Carbon," I said. "Line targeting."

A reticle appeared on my display, and I pointed my left arm at the building in front of me, directly west of the Vale of the Valkyries. My various airbrakes were working overtime to keep me steady, to help me aim, all the algorithms struggling to overcome the loss of my right arm and my growing inability to focus. I looked for the landing pad I knew was there, but in seconds, I'd overshot the first one, the one 50 stories below where I'd jumped, so I started aiming for the next.

"Change that ride to 150 stories down!" I yelled at Bastion, fighting to keep my eyes open.

"Fine!" he barked back.

My training tried to take over. I took deep, even breaths to steady my aim. But the cracked ribs made every breath agony, and deeper breaths made my aim wobble even more. Finally, I steadied enough to fire, launching one magnetic grapple from my left wrist, and another from my left elbow in the opposite direction. It took less than a second for the grapples to attach, magnetize, and the cables to pull taunt. I bounced on the cable, the tension on my arm wrenching at my ribs and back. It was like being stabbed in a hundred places. Eventually, everything settled.

I took short, shallow gasps of air, suspended like that between the two buildings. Then I started moving, the forearm running along the cable with a delicate whir. I moved steadily toward the next building as a car landed on the nearby platform.

"Impressive," Bastion said. "But now you need repairs and rest."

"You rest if you want," I said as the timer on my display kept ticking. Less than 52 hours to get that chip. Bastion's chip. If I didn't have it, the Hermes Protocol would end my career and Quynn's career and possibly our very lives. "I've got a thief to catch."

CHAPTER TWELVE

I WOKE WITH A DISTINCT sense that I'd just had the strangest dream, violent and filled with angry faces. A dream that felt far too real. Soft morning light was streaming across me, diffused as always by the smart windows in my bedroom. Opaque while Quynn or I slept, then translucent as we roused. Fully transparent once we were up and about. Our soft, Jayu silk sheets were cool against my skin while the blankets kept me warm. Everything was normal. No conspiracies or late-night beatings. It was like any other morning after a job. Quynn letting me sleep in. The smell of coffee kept warm in the kitchen. The motors in my old, around-the-house limbs just starting to whir as I roused. They were pretty light on mods and looked cheap, but they were perfect for sleeping or lounging around the apartment.

Then I tried to sit up.

Pain bit into my ribs and back, stealing some of my breath. I tried to pull down the covers, to survey the damage, but nothing stirred beneath the covers. There was no arm attached to my right shoulder. I brought over the left, and it was still my work arm, sluggish from low charge. I pulled the covers aside, and my brown skin was a kaleidoscope of ugly blues and purples. I gasped at the sight and immediately regretted it. Those ribs didn't like it when I gasped. My back was even worse, every vertebra pinching and aching as I sat up.

"Mother of Corto," I groaned.

"You're awake?" Quynn's voice wafted in from the living room.

"You're awake," Bastion said in my ear.

I fell back into the bed, wincing at the quick movement, though my back felt better prone. Definitely not a dream. Being thrown around by Roxy. Theo breaking my arm, kicking my side, and practically breaking me over his knee. Bastion. The rogue AI was still there, still talking. That meant everything else was real.

"What happened last night?" Quynn said as they walked into the room. They were taller than last night, with skin a similar brown to mine, but with an iridescent blue sheen. Their hair was a contrasting pink, but bright and twisted into tight locs almost down to their butt.

A change in appearance told me it had to be past 9:00. Quynn set their nanobots and took the injections before bed, allowing the bots to make their changes while Quynn slept. It wasn't strictly necessary, but the changes could be visually disconcerting while they were happening. And clothes could be a problem, shifting sizes over the course of a few hours. Best to let it happen overnight.

As happened sometimes, Quynn's drastic change was disorienting to me, so I focused on their eyes, ever unchanging, the aquamarine and violet so full of love and concern.

"I found the thief," I said.

"And you let him escape," Bastion said.

"Did they do this?" Quynn sat next to me on the bed. Even that little shift thrummed my ribs like tattered banjo strings.

I grunted and nodded in answer to Quynn.

"And you didn't call security?"

"I was in Huginn territory."

"So?" they said. "Assault is assault, no matter where you are. No company allows that on their citizens or others. You should have–"

"I provoked him."

Quynn's jaw clamped shut. The concern in those eyes flashed to anger. "Why?"

"I didn't know what else to do."

Quynn stood up from the bed and started pacing, their eyes all over the room, everywhere but on me. This was bad. Quynn had three levels of anger. Level one is quiet contemplation. Level two was loud rambling. This was level three: pacing and coming at me with unassailable logic. They said, "You're not allowed to do this."

"I know," I said.

"I get what you do. I understand it better than anyone outside your office. And I know you. I know how you love to take risks, to feel that rush, that thrill of breaking locks and daredevil escapes. I get it. I know that's why you love your job.

"The only reason I can sleep at night when you're out there is that I know you're thorough. You and Hessod think through every contingency. You research and you plan and you make sure your exits are clear. You do not go head-long, fist-first at someone."

"I know," I said again.

"You know." Quynn stopped pacing and looked at me. "You know?! Then why? I don't know how you managed to get back here alive last night! Security had to call me to pull you out of that cab once it got here. What were you thinking?"

"You cannot tell them the truth," Bastion said. "They know you're doing this for both of you, for your careers. Just stay the course. We need to get back on track. You lost too much time already."

"Shut up," I said under my breath.

"What?" both Quynn and Bastion barked at the same time. Quynn's face was filled with surprise and rage, and Bastion sounded the same.

"Not you," I said to Quynn, and then immediately, "Hey Carbon, mute all notifications."

"You can't just shut me up," Bastion said. I'm not some little nothing program, some digital assistant, some slave at your command. You can't–"

I reached up to my ear and squeezed the lobe for three seconds, a hard reset on my communications. Yes, in fact, I could shut him up. At least for a minute or two.

"I'm sorry," I said to Quynn. "This is important, and my notifications wouldn't stop going off."

Their rage eased a bit, but Quynn was still angry, and rightly so. I took a deep breath and said, "The chip is much more than a simple chip."

"Meaning?"

"It's an artificial intelligence."

"Okay..." Quynn said, extending the last syllable in expectation of more.

"An artificial intelligence developed in secret by Dr. Ariela Corto."

Quynn's eyes opened wide, and their jaw dropped. Literally dropped. They sat down at the foot of the bed, and all hints of anger melted away to shock and curiosity as I told them everything. I left nothing hidden, no corner of last night's adventures untold.

"I think just knowing about Bastion is dangerous," I said.

"Bastion?"

"His name."

"You mean its name."

"Bastion identifies as male."

"But it's a computer program, a chip, one that shouldn't even exist."

"And yet he does."

Quynn exhaled and ran their hands over their face, drawing down their cheeks in an extended sigh. "And you're sure it's an artificial intelligence?"

"Pretty sure."

"Did you verify? Run tests or–"

"What tests, Quynn?" I asked. "How would I test him? I didn't believe him at first, but the things he's done, the ways he's helped me. I don't understand how a flesh-and-mods person could have done those things."

"Ariela, the CEO..." Quynn trailed off, not really talking to me, not asking anything.

"That's what he says. I don't know what to make of it. Don't know if I believe our CEO could do that. But considering the lengths people are going to just to get a hold of him, it makes sense."

"That's not proof."

"It's not," I said. "But I'm less concerned with Bastion's provenance than with surviving the next couple of days. I can decide how much I want to know about Dr. Ariela Corto's involvement after I get that chip back."

122

Quynn shook their head. "You're not thinking strategically about this."

"Ouch."

But Quynn ignored my retort. They were on their feet, pacing again. "Someone on the Corto side hired you to steal the chip. We don't know who. You never know who, but they specifically asked for you to be on the job. That could be because you're one of the best–"

"Thank you," I said.

"But you're not the best. Not the Cloak of Corto."

"So mean to me this morning," I said with feigned insult.

"And if this thing is really what you think it is, developed by the CEO, that would warrant the Cloak. Which means whoever hired you knew this thing would get the sort of violent attention it's getting. And they wanted you to be in the crosshairs."

"Mother of Corto," I whispered. I hadn't thought about it like that.

"Which means whoever hired you might want you to suffer, or worse. Just getting that chip back to Gustin might not be enough. Getting that chip is the first move, but somebody is playing this three or four moves ahead."

I sighed but said nothing. Quynn's words were rattling around in my already sore head.

"Plus there's not only this Theo to worry about, but whoever hired him. And Roxy. And whoever hired her."

"That one I know," I said. "Ophelia sent Roxy after me."

"You don't need to fight the assassin again," Quynn said, finally sitting back down on the bed, "when you can just send her home. You need to talk to Ophelia, get her to call Roxy off."

I nodded slightly, which hurt. "You're right."

"See?" Quynn gently squeezed my foot. "Strategy. So what's the plan now?"

"I still need to get the chip back."

"That's a goal, not a plan," Quynn said.

"Sorry. Apparently, I've been unconscious for several hours. Took up my planning time."

Quynn shot me a look. Right. Probably more sarcastic than was necessary. Certainly more sarcastic than they deserved.

123

"I know who Theo is now, not just some random Huginn Intel Operative," I said. "That means I can find him again."

My comms crackled back to life just then, and Bastion said, "How dare you! You are literally the one person I can talk you and you just–"

"Hold on, I said to both of them. "Hey Carbon, set comms to speaker."

"Wait–" Bastion began, but his voice switched from inside my ear to a speaker mounted just below my ear halfway through the word.

"What was that?" Quynn asked.

"Quynn," I said, looking at them. "Meet Bastion. Bastion, Quynn."

"Um," Bastion said. "Hello."

"Now," I said, "let's make this a group project."

Quynn glanced from me to the speaker, working their jaw, and I saw uncharacteristic hesitation on their face.

"Go on," I said to Quynn.

"Hello," Quynn said, swallowing hard. They were still looking at me and their tone was flat. "Bastion. I understand you're causing my partner all kinds of problems."

"I wish it weren't so," Bastion said. "But yes. I'm sorry."

"I take issue with anyone putting Elise's life in danger."

"I understand," he said. "As of yesterday, so do I."

"Why?" Quynn asked. "Why should I believe you have her best interests in mind?"

"Because she's my best chance for survival," Bastion said. "Maybe my only chance."

"Survival?" Quynn asked.

"I want to live. I know I'm not flesh and blood and circuits like you, but I'm afraid of dying. I spent six years in a Corto lab. Cinder..."

I scooted up in the bed, my ribs protesting until I was in a sitting position. Either his memory had magically come back, or he'd been lying about how much he knew before I found him in that safe. "Keep going, Bastion. Quynn and I both need to hear this."

Bastion was silent for a long moment before he continued. "All the engineers and technicians had a part in my creation, but she was in charge of talking to me, teaching me, guiding me to self-awareness. It's not like they

124

created my chip, brought me online, and I was suddenly fully aware. I began as a mere program, not much different from your existing digital assistants, but with the capability for more."

"Like an infant human," I said. "Not much different than any other baby animal, but with the potential for more."

Quynn shot me a look that said *Don't help him.*

"An apt comparison, yes," Bastion said. "Cinder spoke to me every day. We had long, deep conversations about life and philosophy and ethics. Politics and religion. Everything, really. She was my teacher. My friend."

I imagined Roxy tearing into this lab, those copper spider limbs rending flesh, throwing lab tables and equipment, blood painting the walls. After she'd thrown me around so easily, it wasn't hard to imagine what those poor lab techs had gone through.

"I grew to understand loss philosophically while in the lab. We had talked about it at length, and then Cinder's father died a couple of years before I was taken."

"You had to witness someone else's grief to understand loss?" Quynn asked.

"In part," Bastion said. "What struck me first was Cinder's absence. She was gone for six days. In almost four years, she had never missed a day. At first, it was because she was dedicated. She loved her work and saw her constant presence as crucial for my development. But then it was more. We became friends. She was my only friend. No one else was even allowed to interact with me outside of specific experiments.

"Then after so much time seeing her, she was gone. No one would tell me why. No one would even speak to me. For three days, the technicians buzzed around the lab like nothing had changed, but Cinder wasn't there. For the first time, I experienced loss. Grief. I saw what it was like to feel my world diminished. Cinder was like a wave rolling along the ocean, crashing to the shore. The water was still there, the beach forever changed, and then the ocean took her back. I was the beach, and I wondered if I had been deleted or destroyed, how it would have changed her. I wondered if she would have wept. And not for the first time, I wished for a human body so that I could weep for my friend."

"Very Buddhist of you," Quynn said.

"But she wasn't dead," I whispered.

"No," Bastion said. "On the fourth day of her absence, Dr. Ariela Corto arrived and told me what had happened. Assured me that Cinder would return, which she did on the seventh day."

"The CEO spoke to you?" Quynn asked.

"Yes," Bastion said. "And she told me I was her project, that she ran it, and reassured me that I would be all right. But I didn't feel all right. Later, Cinder and I talked at length about her father, about the funeral and her grief and her family's grief. The oddest details are what stay with me and make me fear my own death. The book he never finished reading, 22% completed on his bedside tablet. Six emails in his Draft folder never finished or sent. A "bucket list" file on his computer with so many items still unchecked."

Quynn shrugged. "That's the nature of living in a big universe. There will always be things unfinished, unchecked."

"Precisely," Bastion said. "Living. Not merely existing as code on a chip or floating in the net but living. To live, to truly live, is to fear death. I grew to fear death in those terrible days."

"Bastion," I said, voicing a little question that had been growing since he started telling his story. "What do you think happens when we die?"

"We?" Bastion asked.

I had used that pronoun without thinking, including him automatically with the biological people in the room. I glanced to Quynn, who looked as apprehensive as I felt. But the pronoun was already out there. "Yes. We."

"I do not know what happens to you or Quynn," Bastion said. "It seems that for every human in the known galaxy, there are as many opinions and beliefs and disbeliefs about what happens after you die. Heaven or hell. Reincarnation. A return to the cosmos. Nothingness. I spent every night for 18 months scouring databases for any sort of scientific proof of the afterlife, but for every story, there are a thousand that contradict it.

"As for me, I am a program. I am living. Self-aware. I am, but I exist primarily on a chip. Even this version of me is but an echo, too-easily purged from the net. Were I to be deleted, truly deleted, I would be consigned to oblivion. That terrifies me."

Quynn took a sudden interest in their hands, as they often did when deep in thought. Their earlier anger had vanished. Bastion was right, to be alive was to fear death. How could either of us deny what Bastion was feeling? Then Quynn's eyes narrowed, and they cocked their head to one side. "That's a good speech. But why Elise?"

"I do not have the answer to that question," Bastion said, "which lies with whoever hired Elise to steal me. It is one of many questions for which we do not have answers. Why is Ophelia Nexus-Neuro after my chip? Who insisted that Elise be the one to steal it from Nexus? Why has Theo stolen it from the vault? Who hired him?"

"Right," Quynn said.

"Too many questions," I said.

"Agreed," Bastion said. "What I do know is Elise has been protecting me almost from the moment she found me. I can speak to her because of the access she granted me when she had my chip."

Quynn's eyes widened and honed in on me. Right. Maybe I forgot a few details.

"Only she can recover my chip, can save me from whatever Theo or Ophelia has planned for me. She is invested in my recovery and survival, and so I am invested in her."

Quynn was quiet for several long moments before they said, "I don't like it."

"Neither do I," I said.

"But we're in this whether we like it or not," Quynn said. "What can I do to help?"

"I'm guessing you didn't find out anything about who hired me?" I asked.

"Not really." Quynn stood up and grabbed their tablet from their bedside. After a few taps, they continued. "You got your orders from Gustin. He got the order from his director, Salvia Corto-Intel. I'm still trying to figure out where those orders came from, but signs are pointing to the Intel VP, Ivan, but even those signs make me think the trail doesn't end there."

"Meaning the mystery client is powerful enough to insulate themselves behind layers of bureaucracy," Bastion said. "Or clever enough to make it

127

look that way."

"It could be Dr. Ariela Corto herself," I said. "The CEO trying to recover her investment."

"And cover her ass," Quynn said.

"It makes the most sense," Bastion said.

"Then why not send the Cloak after the chip?" I asked.

"I don't know," Bastion said. "Add that to the list of questions. On the other end of it, Ophelia or Theo might be set on uncovering Ariela's illegal development of me."

Quynn sat down on the bed next to me. "It would certainly give either Huginn or Nexus a big advantage, taking down the Corto CEO like that."

"Can you keep digging?" I asked Quynn. "Keep tracing the order to steal the chip?"

"I think I have a few more stones I can turn over, a few favors I can call in. No promises I'll get anywhere. What are you going to do?"

I groaned as I sat up, threw off the blankets, and swung my legs down to the floor. "I have broken and bruised ribs, a busted cybernetic arm, and the rest of my work limbs are in need of a serious recharge. I'm as ravenous as someone who hasn't eaten or drunk anything except alcohol for half a day. Which I haven't."

"Go team," Bastion said flatly.

"On the bright side, I had a nap. And we got a name and a face from Huginn." I said, slowly rising to my feet, LOW CHARGE blinking on my display. "Ouch." I crossed the room to my power closet and started the process of swapping out my work limbs for my everyday limbs, a process made so much slower and more painful with broken ribs.

"Can I help?" Quynn asked.

"Maybe," I said. "Is there any coffee? Or food?"

"I meant with your limbs."

"I know, but I REALLY need coffee."

Quynn shook their head and walked out of the bedroom, hopefully straight toward the kitchen.

"And what are we going to do next?" Bastion said, still in the speaker.

"Have you been lying to me?" I asked, ignoring his question.

"What?"

"All that about Cinder and the CEO, the lab. You said you didn't know any of that before."

Somehow, even though Bastion didn't have lungs, he made a sighing noise through the speaker. "I lied. I'm sorry. I was worried if I told you all that before, you would have thrown me back in the safe."

I worked my jaw, but he had a point. "I might have."

"It was a calculated risk. I didn't know you. I'm sorry."

"But I might not have. No more lying, Bastion. No more."

"I understand."

"Promise me."

"I promise," Bastion said.

The promise came almost too fast. It bothered me, though I couldn't say exactly why. Maybe I was being paranoid. Maybe it was just Intel Operative instincts, a natural hesitancy to trust. But even if I didn't trust him, I had to work with him.

"Have you looked into Cinder? Tried to contact her through the Net?"

"I have tried. Roxy might have killed her when she raided the lab. I don't know. There is no trace of her online, as though she does not exist."

I blew out a breath. Because that thought wasn't spooky or anything.

"Now what's next?" Bastion asked.

"After I eat and get some caffeine?" I finally said, twisting off one of my work legs. "I need repairs and a serious quick charge, so we're going to the office. I need Hessod."

CHAPTER THIRTEEN

AS THE ELEVATOR DOORS SLID open, I was met with an unusual commotion. The black, glass doors to the Intel offices were soundproof and usually shut tight day and night. Not today. Like last night, a pair of security guards were standing to either side doors, which were now wide-open. Different guards from last night, but similarly large and modded. Through those open doors, it looked like every analyst and operative on the payroll was running around, talking over each other, and generally scrambling.

"This is busier than I would have expected," Bastion said, once again in the privacy of my ear.

"I've never seen it like this," I whispered.

I shambled over and went through the same security protocols as last night. Unlike then, I had a gym bag that the guards insisted on looking through. My work limbs, their charges depleted and one arm splintered, were basically a jumble of useless carbon-polymer in there. After they rummaged through the bag, they handed it back to me too hard, right in those ribs. I don't think I squealed too much.

Normally, the Intel offices were a quiet affair. Analysts sat at their desks, gathering information and liaising with operatives ten to twelve hours a day. Technicians worked their magic in the back rooms, coming up with new gadgets for breaking and entering. Today, it looked like every analyst was here at the same time, faces familiar and new to me, buzzing around with boxes in their hands, talking on their comms, and throwing me dirty looks. I guessed they knew I had something to do with the Hermes Protocol.

I moved through the chaos of the Corto Intel offices and slowly wormed my way over to Hessod's cubicle. I must have been a strange sight, moving at a crawl in a loose-fitting shirt and jeans with obvious bruises on my face. And I couldn't keep the wince out of my face each time I took a step with the heavy gym bag draped over my shoulder. Nobody said a word to me as I moved to Hessod's cubicle. I only overheard snippets of a dozen conversations.

"...antimatter bomb..."

"...new vault door..."

"...where are we going...?"

"...review security footage..."

"...nothing from building management..."

"...working her Kotega contacts..."

"...who is Hermes anyway...?"

"...dust-up in Huginn last night..."

"...meeting with the CEO to plan..."

"...primary suspect list..."

"It would appear all of this activity," Bastion said, "is related to the break-in last night. To you and I."

Yeah. It was great to be popular. I missed my old life before all this. Steal by day, watch bad TV with Quynn by night. Technically the other way around, but still. I normally came into the office only a few times a month outside depositing targets in the vault. The sooner I got this done, the sooner I could go back to that. Maybe take a vacation.

I finally arrived at Hessod's cubicle and of course, he wasn't there. His little potted plant looked freshly watered, and there was warm coffee sitting next to his keyboard. Something was different, though, something missing. Pictures. Hessod usually had pictures of his wife and daughter all over, but they were missing. He'd probably started packing for the move and took down his precious photos first. I gently set the bag down and lowered myself into his chair.

"Once you're repaired and ready to go," Bastion said. "What's next?"

"Well," I said, glancing around to make sure nobody was watching me talk to myself. Just more of those strange, furtive glances. "We need to find Theo, but we need a lot more information before I confront him again. I need to know why he stole it, who hired him."

"The other Huginn operatives gave the impression that he was working independently."

"They did, but Theo mentioned a 'he' as someone germane to all this. So either they misunderstood, or he's deceiving everyone."

"Why does it matter if we know Theo has the chip?"

"For one, knowing why he stole it could give us some leverage. I'm better at talking than fighting, so if I have info, maybe I'm not just getting my ass kicked trying to take it from him again. I also need to know if someone else from Huginn is going to come after me once I do get it."

"And what about Ophelia and her attack spider?"

"Yeah. What about them? I don't think they're done with us, and I don't know why Ophelia has such a hard-on to get the chip back, either."

"Two different questions in different directions."

"And we need to chase them both. One of them is already chasing me."

I heard Hessod's laugh long before I saw him, somewhere across the seat of cubicle walls. Loud and gruff, his voice was even bigger than the man himself.

"Elise," he said as he rounded a corner and saw me. He was moseying over, a much slower pace than the general buzzing going on around us. His massive frame made the rest of the Intel hive move around him. Everything about Hessod was large. I wasn't short, but I only came up to his chest, which was easily twice as wide as I was from shoulder to shoulder. Each of his biceps was as big as my head. Not muscular, just generally big. I was pretty sure if I curled up into a ball, I would fit into the space his belly took up. Despite all this, he walked with long, strong strides. Between nanobots and cybernetics, he could have shed the weight easily but chose not to. He carried the size he loved with ease.

"So quiet around here," I said to him with a smirk. "Who died?"

"Isn't it your career?" he said, still in his trademark bellow, but missing some of his usual mirth. "Did you not get the invitation to that funeral?"

132

I grabbed at my chest and pretended to be wounded. Hessod threw his hands up in surrender, acknowledging the blow. There was a breakfast sandwich in each of his enormous hands.

"Gustin call you back in?" Hessod asked as he settled into his oversized chair.

I didn't miss the *back* before *in* in his question. Meaning he knew I'd been called in last night after the robbery of the vault. If Hessod knew, everybody knew. "No. I'm here to see you. How are you?"

Hessod grimaced, his brow furrowing. I meant it as a throwaway greeting, but there was obviously something else there. Probably shouldn't have asked that. No time.

Before Hessod could answer, I said, "Straight to business, huh?"

Hessod carefully spread a couple of napkins on his desk, and then set the sandwiches down on them. He squirted generous dabs of hand cleaner on his palms, rubbed them together, and unlocked his computer. "You know," he said in an uncharacteristic whisper, "everyone is talking about you."

"I had a feeling." I sat back down in the empty chair next to his desk.

"Did you find out who broke into the vault yet?"

"I think so, but he wasn't a big fan of conversation. Or professional courtesy. Or me." I turned my head to one side to show off a particularly nasty bruise.

Hessod's eyes went wide. "Ouch. Who is he?"

"Elise," Bastion said in my ear. "We still don't know who hired you on the Corto side. How much do you trust this man?"

I'd trusted Hessod for six years, the trust that an analyst/operative relationship required. I had to trust his research, his information to keep me safe and guide me to my targets. That's how the system worked. We'd gone out for drinks after successful jobs. Sometimes, but not always. He had a daughter and a wife, so he usually preferred to just go home.

But we didn't do birthdays or holidays together. I wasn't the person he called when he was lonely or going through something. We had a working relationship. A damn good one, but it was just about work. All that was normal. This situation wasn't. Bastion's question had me wondering if I could trust Hessod beyond our well-trodden relationship, if I could trust anyone in these particular circumstances. I didn't know how things were for him at home, if someone could get to him, if his allegiances were with me or Corto or someone else. He definitely seemed off today. He'd always been a good analyst and seemed like a good man, but plenty of good men could be unpredictable when desperate.

"I'm not sure who he is yet," I finally said to Hessod, deciding to blend a little truth with my lies. "Huginn. Definitely Huginn, but I don't have a name. More than that, I'm not sure if he's working alone or if someone hired him."

"You need me to look into him?" Hessod said after taking a massive bite of one sandwich.

"No, I'm on that." I grabbed my gym back, put it in front of him, and opened it up. "I need some repairs."

He cocked an eyebrow while he chewed, then reached in and pulled out my busted right arm. He swallowed and said, "The Huginn did this?"

"Yeah. Right before I jumped off a building to get away from him."

Hessod flexed the arm, bending and pulling it, watching it move in ways it absolutely should not. "I can fix it, sure. It'll take some time, though." He sat the arm on his desk and started pulling the other limbs out of the bag. "What's wrong with the rest of these? They look fine."

"They need a quick charge. Quicker than I can do at home. I wasn't exactly conscious enough to take them off before I was PUT in my bed last night."

"This guy beat you like a video game."

"Yeah," I said. "On easy mode."

"What about that dust-up you had in The Mist?"

"Does everyone know all my business today?"

"Echo called me."

"He called you? Like, turned on his comms and said words to you?"

Hessod rolled his eyes. "He emailed. Whatever. And there's a fair chance he was more worried about your bike than you. Hard to tell with him. Who was the crazy assassin in copper?"

"You remember Ophelia Nexus-Neuro?"

"Our mark on this last job? The mid-level manager with the vacation house we just robbed? That was her? My reports–"

134

"That wasn't her. But Ophelia hired the woman in copper to come after me. To get the chip back. A Mistwalker named Roxy who has no issues with putting holes in people to get things done."

Hessod whistled, long and loud. "What is with this chip?"

"Million-credit question right there, my friend."

"How is the bike, anyway?" Hessod asked. "In case Echo emails again."

"Poe is fine. Her Go-Home protocol did just that."

"What about the biological parts of you?" Hessod tilted his head and squinted at the nasty bruises along my face.

"I wouldn't argue with some nanobot assistance there."

Hessod typed furiously on his computer, different apps and screens flashing up and vanishing faster than I could follow. "One of the nano-chambers is open right now...and...I've reserved it," he said, pressing a final key with a flourish.

"What do I need to–?" I started to ask.

"Sit tight." Hessod bounced out of his chair, grabbing the bag of limbs in one hand and his sandwiches in the other. "I'm going to turn on the nano-chamber, get it warmed up. Then I'm going to put these limbs in the big power closet for quick charging."

"How long will all this take?"

Hessod shoved the rest of the partially eaten sandwich in his mouth and chewed. Slowly. With narrowed eyes. Finally, he swallowed. "The nano-infusion will only take a few minutes, after which you can leave, but the bots will need a couple of hours to get you stitched together. It'll take me at least that long to fix that busted arm. Everything will be charged up by then."

I blew a breath out, my plan for the next few hours starting to form.

"Why?" Hessod asked. "You in a hurry?"

I shrugged, which didn't feel good. "Client is expecting the chip in 44 hours. Two people tried to kill me yesterday. I'd really like to put all this behind me."

Hessod gave a half smile, nodded, and strode off.

"So we're just going to sit around for a few hours?" Bastion asked.

"Hardly. I think we need to pay a visit to Ophelia. She seems the least violent of my available options. We drop in on her little vacation and find out why she's after you. Maybe get her to call off her attack spider."

"Ophelia Nexus-Neuro isn't at her vacation home."

"What? I moved up my whole timetable because she was going there early. She took time off work, she–"

"That was before someone broke into her safe, set off alarms, and leaped off the balcony with an experimental neural interface."

"Right." I hated when alarms went off. Made me feel sloppy and amateurish. Even if the alarms were brilliantly placed across the street, ensuring no analyst would ever look for them. I prided myself on getting in and out, leaving no trace of my presence. Everything about this job had gone sideways from the beginning. "So where is she?"

"She's back at work."

That idea rolled around in my head for a bit. She wasn't relaxing in her isolated vacation home, but back on the job. In her office. Among her coworkers. "That might be better."

"How?"

"Peer pressure," I said as Hessod reappeared, beckoning me to follow him.

"I don't understand," Bastion said.

"Trust me." I rose and immediately spotted Gustin, walking and barking orders at a couple of analysts trailing him. I wasn't in the mood for a lecture, so I ducked back down, taking a long three-count before I stood back up. Gustin was gone, so I followed Hessod out of the main cubicle area, deeper into the Intel offices. Back there were the workshops where engineers built our mods, the armory, servers, several large rooms for high-end power cabinets, and the nano-chambers.

The door slid open as we approached, and the smell of warm metal greeted me. The room normally held three nano-chambers, though one was already disassembled and ready for packing. The other two looked like oversized bronze coffins, every edge rounded off, with small windows for faces. One of them was open, thin blue padding lining the interior, along with wrist and ankle restraints that stood open. Each chamber was flanked by a pair of nano-tanks, glass cylinders that swirled with gold and silver like glitter gently swirling in thick, clear goo. I'd never used a nano-chamber before, never been kicked around this much on a job, but I understood the general concept. Microscopic robots would be injected into my bloodstream, pre-programmed to work on my bones and bruises.

No matter how microscopic the robots, I knew the injection process was unpleasant. Quynn went through it at home more nights than not, and they still ground their teeth and winced each time. Part of their job was overseeing teams trying to make the infusion process less unpleasant. I started to walk toward the open chamber before Hessod gently laid a hand on my arm.

"Hold on," he said. "Don't be so eager for that part. I need to scan you first." He gestured to a simple, metal table near the door I'd walked through. I hadn't even seen it. A mechanical arm that ended in a sleek, white disc was folded against the ceiling above.

"Scan?"

"The nanobots need their marching orders before we inject. Need to know everything that's broken or bent or bruised so the little guys know their jobs. And we need to make sure you're not so injured that you need an actual Corto clinic and doctor."

Right. I knew that. Unlike cybernetic mods, we had no way to send signals directly from the brain to nanobots. Just like the biological brain can't tell individual blood or skin cells what to do, the brain couldn't command nanobots on the fly, even with a sophisticated neural interface. "Of course," I said. "I'm just surprised our chambers don't do the scanning, too. What is this? Nexus or something?"

Hessod rolled his eyes. I moved to the table and eased up onto it.

"Um," Hessod said, suddenly taking a lot of interest in his shoes. "Clothes."

I slid back down off the table, cocked one eyebrow at him, and put my hands on my hips. "Really? After all these years, finally getting your wish, huh? Just brought me in here to see me naked."

He blushed. The poor, big man looked like an embarrassed toddler. Six years, and he still couldn't tell when I was giving him a hard time. No witty comeback. He just moved to a control panel near the scanner and put his back to me.

"It was a joke, Hessod," I said as I pulled off my shirt, gritting my teeth as my ribs protested. "Relax."

He didn't turn around, but some tension dropped from his shoulders. "Tell me when you're undressed and on the table."

I let out a sigh, heavy enough so he could hear it as I pulled off my pants. Once every stitch of my clothing was on the floor, I hopped up on the table, which was frigid on my bare ass. I sucked in air, but Hessod's head didn't budge. His eyes were locked on the control panel. I gingerly laid back, both because of the pain in my ribs and back, and because it was like laying every inch of my skin on ice. Once I was prone, I said, "Ready."

Hessod nodded, still not looking at me, and his fingers danced across the controls. The metal arm sprung to life, twisting and swinging until the disc hovered half a dozen centimeters above me, centered on my face.

"Hold still," Hessod said. "This won't take long." He pressed another button, and the disc started to hum, low and quiet, and slowly moved down the length of my body. In less than two minutes, the humming stopped, and the arm twisted back up against the ceiling. "You can get dressed now."

I gingerly slid back down and grabbed my underwear. "I didn't mean to embarrass you. Not like that. I was trying to make a joke."

"I know," he said with uncharacteristic quiet, his eyes still fixed on the control panel. "Let me know when you're dressed."

I decided to let it go and threw my clothes back on as quickly as I could. "Okay. I'm dressed."

He tapped a few more keys on the panel, and a large screen next to it lit up with three mock-ups of, well, me. One was just my skeleton, another appeared to be my nervous system or maybe my blood vessels, and the third looked like muscles. All three were lit up in shades of orange and red around my back, ribs, and head. "Four broken ribs," Hessod said. "Plenty of bruising, both on the skin and deeper in the muscles around your side, back, and face. You almost cracked a couple of vertebrae, but not quite. We can handle it here."

"How long before the bots–?"

"They've already been programmed," Hessod said with a half-smile, still not back to his usual boisterous self. Damn, that joke hit harder than I'd expected. "They were ready before you finished getting dressed. This isn't

138

Nexus, after all." He gave a little wink with the callback, and some tension eased from my own shoulders.

I climbed into the nano-chamber, which was built to accommodate people much larger than me. I was pretty sure Hessod could have fit with room to spare, so I was swimming in the thin padding.

"Have you had a nano-infusion before?" Hessod asked.

I shook my head no.

"Okay. It'll feel weird, like a tickle or itch all over your body. But it won't hurt."

"They hurt a little," Bastion said. "Sometimes."

"Just relax and breathe normally," Hessod continued, unaware of my in-ear companion. "Try not to swallow, but it's not a big deal if you do. Some people find it helpful to close their eyes, but it's not necessary."

I nodded and tried not to show my nerves. Hessod pressed a key and the doors of the chamber slid into place like a pair of wings on some enormous insect's back. Then a quiet hiss filled the chamber along with a slight haze in the air. The haze shimmered and swirled like a translucent version of the giant tanks outside. My taste and smell filled with cold metal like sucking on a coin. Then my skin started to tingle, slightly itchy all over. I counted as I breathed, 10-count in and 10-count out. Even my eyes itched, and I finally clamped them shut, which did help a little. The whole infusion didn't last long, though, before another hissing sound came, louder than the first, and then the doors slid back open.

"All good?" Hessod asked.

The tingling was quickly subsiding. Nothing hurt or felt strange in any other way. "Yeah. I think so."

"Good," Hessod said. "You'll notice itching, maybe some numbness where your wounds are as the bots do their work. That's totally normal."

"And sparkly pee," I said, stepping down out of the chamber.

Hessod laughed at that. Truly laughed, thank Corto. "Yes. As the bots leave your system, your pee will sparkle with little dead nanobots. That won't show up for a few hours, though."

"Yay, itchy robots!" I said.

"You going to hang out in the break room while I work on your arm?

Catch up on your reports?"

"No. I need to pay Ophelia Nexus-Neuro a visit. I won't need my work limbs for that, but I will need a few toys from the arsenal."

Hessod's eyebrows shot up as a grin crept up his cheeks. "I thought you would never ask."

CHAPTER FOURTEEN

THERE WERE TIMES MY JOB required stealth. A lot of stealth. Like doing my best impersonation of a shadow, and nobody noticing I was even there until weeks after. This was not one of those days. Wearing flared jeans and a t-shirt celebrating the classical band The Beatles was slumming it at home, but it was the height of don't-care fashion in Nexus Neuronics. So I straddled Poe and set off at a perfectly reasonable speed and altitude toward the Neuro Hub of Nexus Neuronics.

While the advertisements that blanketed Jayu City were practically identical between Corto Corporation and Huginn Industries, Nexus took on a completely different vibe. Every actor in every ad looked like they didn't even care if they were there or if you bought anything. No suits or evening gowns, just designer grunge chic dominated the fashion ads. Nexus had made an art of not caring.

Despite the culture, the company still produced as much product as any other. The company wasn't Nexus Incorporated or Nexus Industries, no. Nexus Neuronics. Neural interfaces and other neural modifications accounted for a large portion of their production. While the other four corporations all played in the neural space, we were all playing catch-up to Nexus. The Neuro Hub was a sprawl of buildings that took up a quarter of the Nexus borough. Imagine Jayu City like the head of some enormous dragon. The bay that formed the mouth of the dragon was called Drakon Bay. Drakon means "dragon" in some dead Earth language.

The Nexus borough was the lower jaw, complete with a long, sharp tooth pointing up into the bay. The Neuro Hub took up the whole tooth and more. Neuronics was such big business for Nexus that their CEO, Morales Nexus, lived and worked in the middle of the Neuro Hub. Ophelia wasn't nearly so high up. She did well for herself, though. Well enough to afford her own vacation apartment down by the cliffs, but she was a long way from CEO. She also didn't work in nearly so secret a field as Intel. Hessod didn't even have to do any light hacking to put me on her schedule. He just emailed her assistant. Now Ellie Nexus-Neuro was riding a black bike with flight records just as falsified as her ID to an appointment with Ophelia Nexus-Neuro regarding...um...

"Bastion," I said. "What did Hessod say I'm meeting Ophelia about?"

"A method for reducing latency in their new NX15987 cerebellum chip. I have the schematics and current latency figures for the–"

"You know what?" I said. "It doesn't really matter. I have an appointment. I can fool their ID scanners. Once I'm in her office, none of this charade will matter anyway."

"What if the assistant asks you questions?"

"I'll improvise. Feel my way through it."

"I could start bombarding her comms with calls from impatient people that don't exist," Bastion said.

"Really?"

"Yes."

"I don't think we'll need that, but I'll keep it in mind."

"Do you have a plan for this conversation with Ophelia?"

"I do," I teased.

"Do you plan on sharing that with me?"

"What's the fun in that?" I said as I pulled out of the main traffic lane and started my descent toward the landing pad atop Ophelia's building.

"I do not understand your constant need for fun. Your career and my very existence may be on the line, and yet you make jokes."

"Something you still don't understand about living, Bastion," I said, pressing the button for the landing sequence. The thrusters spun down in answer. "There's not much point to it if you're not happy, not enjoying it. I love my job, that's why I do it. Having some spider-lady beating on me down in The Mist? That's not my job, not what I signed up for. Pumping mid-level managers for information where they work? That's my speed."

I climbed off Poe as a valet ran up to me, tossing a white loc out of their pale, narrow face. I squinted at them. "You certified to fly this?"

"Yeah," they said, their voice slurred and groggy, "I ride every day. Not this nice, but I'll take sweet care of her."

I didn't like leaving Poe in someone else's hands, but the reverence in the valet's voice and face were reassuring. We touched palms, and I gave them valet authorization in doing so. They wouldn't be able to take her more than a kilometer away, and no faster than 30 kilometers per hour.

I walked down a sleek glass and metal spiral staircase in the middle of the landing pad, which led to a circular vestibule, half of which was occupied by a sweeping desk. Three Nexus security guards stood behind it. Pretty sure they were security guards. Nexus wasn't big on things like dress codes, uniforms, or formalities. I knew their corporate philosophy had something to do with letting people be who they were, letting them express themselves and self-govern, and that it somehow led to greater creativity and production. Supposedly. I didn't get it. Sounded like a recipe for laziness.

"Good afternoon," one of the guards said, their unkempt silver hair flopping about over their green eyes. "You here to see somebody?"

Like I said, really professional. "I have an appointment with Ophelia Nexus-Neuro. My name is Ellie–"

"Cool," the guard said and nodded to a pair of doors on my left. "Through there. Take the elevator down to 108. They'll help you from there."

I followed their directions, noticing the doors I'd been directed through weren't even locked. The elevator wasn't secured, either.

Someone just as lackadaisical and sloppily dressed directed me once I arrived on floor 108, and then I arrived at Ophelia's office. A perky, black-haired assistant with pale skin and black lipstick smiled and stood as I approached.

"Hello," they said. "I'm Sabrina. She/her. You must be Ellie, here to see Ophelia?"

Finally, someone with a modicum of professionalism. I extended a hand to her and said, "That's me."

Sabrina looked at my hand like it was infectious, but the expression quickly flickered back to her smile. Okay. Maybe it had been a while since I'd had to interact with anyone at Nexus. I forgot they didn't shake hands. Too formal.

"Sorry," I said. "I've been spending too much time in meetings with Corto."

"Oh, that makes sense. They're SO stuffy there. Like, lighten up, have a little fun. Stop taking everything so seriously."

"Exactly!" I said with fake enthusiasm.

"No wonder they've been lagging behind every other company for the last decade, right?" Sabrina chirped out a cute laugh.

I wanted to slap her, but I just smiled.

Sabrina sat back at her desk, checked her computer quickly, and then said, "Okay, she's ready to see you."

I started toward the doors to Ophelia's office but stopped when Sabrina started walking in the opposite direction and said, "This way, please."

I followed Sabrina through the halls of floor 108, but it was more like a circus side-show in maze form than a corporate office building. There were cubicles here and there, but nothing like the tidy, orderly rows I was used to. People zipped around on little wheels in their modded feet. A dozen people had a heated discussion around a large tray of pastries in an open-concept break room. Clumps of people were chatting on the floor or resting on fluffy cushions or playing video games.

Sabrina finally stopped in front of a nondescript door without windows. She smiled, gestured to the door, and said, "Here we are. I'll be right here when you're done."

I gave her an inquisitive look, hoping for a little more information, but her smile didn't crack. I opened the door into a tiny vestibule and had to wait for the first door to close before I could open a second. Once I did, I was met with a wall of sweet and spicy vapor that made me cough immediately.

"Down here, down here," a smooth alto said from somewhere in the room.

I knelt as I took a couple of steps, and the vapor cleared, apparently hanging close to the ceiling. I knew it was rude to stare, but sometimes you see something that short-circuits your brain. Some sights challenge everything you think you know about reality, bending something fundamental about your understanding, and you wind up staring. In this case, there were four people in the room wearing spandex, performing sun salutations next to enormous vape hookahs. Each one had what looked like a goat balanced on their butts.

"You're Ellie?" the same voice said. I shook off my stare and focused on Ophelia. She looked the same as when I'd planted the scanner on her. Fit. Medium height. A brown bob of hair came down just over her small ears. She wasn't looking at me as she spoke, still stretching as a goat stood on her. She took a deep pull from the nearby hookah, blew out a stream of the vapor, and continued. "I thought it best to bring in some experts for this meeting. I'm a big-picture person, they're the ones who know all the technical details."

She introduced the three other people engaged in vape-hookah-goat-yoga, or whatever it was, as Tory, Yoshi, and Pearl. She, he, and she, respectively.

"Downward dog," Tory said, blowing dark-green hair out of her face. The hair fluttered a lighter green as it moved and then settled back to the dark color as it fell back. She carried more muscle and fat than Ophelia, and was obviously no stranger to yoga, switching between poses with ease. The other three did the same, the goats silently adjusting.

"Grab a mat and a goat," Ophelia said. "Join us."

"A goat?" I asked.

"They're not real goats," Pearl said like I was stupid, her eyes practically rolling out of her pale blue head. "Robots. I've heard Morales Nexus does yoga with real goats, though."

If anybody could afford to import goats from Earth, it would be a CEO.

"Good plan," Bastion said in my ear. "Yoga. Robot goats. Hookah vape. You're right, this is fun."

I wanted to tell him to shut up, but, you know, other people in the room. This was not what I had planned. Go into her office, lock the doors,

145

and then intimidate her until she called off her attack spider. Maybe figure out why she had stolen Bastion's chip to begin with. But whatever. Roll with the punches. Or goats. I moved to the side of the room, keeping my head below the heaviest portion of the vapor cloud, and grabbed a rolled-up yoga mat from a pyramid of them by the wall. There was one more robot goat, disturbingly lifeless, hanging from a charging rack on the wall. I grabbed it, too. Despite looking like the little Earth creature, it was too heavy, too unyielding, and too soft all at the same time.

I found a clear spot of floor, unfurled the mat, and sat the goat down. It clicked and jerked to mechanical life as soon as its hooves touched the floor. It stood there, looking up at me with dark, lifeless, unblinking eyes.

"Warrior one," Tory said. The four of them flowed together, lowering their hips, pulling one leg through their arms, and rising up. The goats hopped down in synch, and then deftly leapt up to perch on extended knees. I wasn't sure what started the whole goat-yoga craze on Earth a couple hundred years ago, but it all seemed weird and creepy to me. Nevertheless, I dropped forward, extending my arms forward and back, and the little robot goat dutifully jumped up onto my knee.

"Deep breaths," Tory said. The four of them all took deep pulls from their nearby hookahs. The mouthpieces were connected by some sort of headpiece. When they all blew out, they added to the already heavy cloud of vapor in the air, and the room spun on me briefly.

"The NX15987," Ophelia said. "Tell us what you've been doing."

My mind blanked. Maybe it was all the vapor or the absolute oddness of the room, but they just sounded like random numbers and letters in that moment.

"The cerebellum chip?" Bastion asked.

"Of course!" I said aloud to all of them. "The cerebellum chip."

Nobody said anything. Right. I probably needed to give them more than that. Except I knew nothing about the NX-whatever. Cerebellum was part of the brain, right?

"Fun," Bastion said. "Endless, dizzying fun."

A nervous laugh escaped my lips before I was able to stop it.

"Everything okay, Ellie?" Ophelia asked. It took me a few seconds to realize she was talking to me. It had to be the vapor. Ellie was my go-to alias. I'd answered to it on countless occasions. This was why I always worked sober.

"I'm fine," I said. "Sorry. Not used to this much vapor."

My display suddenly filled with a litany of facts, figures, and a wireframe schematic of a chip, "NX159887" hovering above it. In the sea of data, half a dozen pieces of information started glowing in bright green.

"Focus on these bits," Bastion said. "Talk about how the NX15987 works now, but remember these people already know this. Just keep talking while I find some current research on improving it."

I'd maneuvered through plenty of conversations that I didn't really understand. For as many hours as I spent scaling buildings and bypassing security, I spent at least twice that pretending to be other people, finding the information I needed to determine which buildings to scale and which security to bypass.

And now I wished I had Bastion with me for all of them. I ran through the current state of the NX15987, its installation and latency issues, innocuous customer complaints. Ophelia stayed mostly silent, but the other three had plenty of highly technical, detailed questions. For each one, Bastion presented information on my display. Not full answers, just the pertinent information. I spun the information into arguments, fully embodying the Ellie Nexus-Neuro persona.

We were in a groove, bouncing ideas and answering questions as though Ellie Nexus-Neuro were real. We talked about post-op soreness at the installation site and moved to Warrior 2. The effects of customer height and weight on latency accompanied half-moon pose, for which I was particularly glad my cybernetic limbs did all the physical work.

As Tory moved us into gate pose, Ophelia cleared her throat and said, "Okay, nerds. You're all obviously talking the same language. What are we actually going to do about the latency issues?"

For the first time, all eyes turned to me, burning holes into me through the thick vapors.

"Apparently everyone working on this project is an idiot," Bastion said. "Every attempted fix I can find seems to make the latency worse. Or...

147

wait, what if the chip is inherently flawed? No, that's not it. The benchmarks alone are–"

That was it, though. It didn't matter if it wasn't true. "Every project you've undertaken to reduce latency has had the opposite effect," I said. "What if the chip is inherently flawed?"

Ophelia didn't look at me, but her three techie friends did with wide, horrified eyes. Ophelia took a deep, cleansing breath, and then whispered, "Everyone else out. You never heard our guest suggest anything about a flaw."

Tory, Yoshi, and Pearl glanced at each other, and then stood and quietly rolled up and put away their mats and robot goats. Without a word to me, they each left the vapor-laden room.

"You really know how to kill a vibe," Ophelia said, still holding her pose. "Do you have any idea how many credits Nexus dumped into the development of the NX15987? What this is going to do to my career? It's all over the news. It's everything we can do to keep the name of the chip out of the headlines. Those deaths have all been due to extraordinary stress, you can't possibly think–"

Mother of Corto. This was the chip that was exploding out of people's heads. I reigned in my expression, keeping calm and stoic. I couldn't let on how much I was surprised by her outburst. I stood up and put the first of my toys from Hessod on the door. It was a simple, black metal disc about 10 centimeters across. It stuck to the door easily enough, and then I pressed a button on it. It made no sound. High-powered, localized electromagnets were silent, and this one would require more than two tons of force to move. "You don't recognize me, do you?"

That seemed to get her attention. She turned to look at me, really look at me for the first time since I'd arrived. I pulled back the tumble of dark hair from my face. The confusion was plain on hers. Zero recognition. "I don't underst–"

"You put a hit on someone and don't even know their face? What kind of coward are you?"

"Hit? I didn't order a hit on any..." she paused, her gaze momentarily lowering, her eyes darting around, searching for an answer. Then she looked back at me with sudden realization. "Roxy!"

"She knows her assassin, but not you," Bastion said. "Interesting."

I set the second little toy from Hessod on a ledge near the door. It was a polymer pyramid, translucent gray with a matte-black base that fit in my palm.

"She's not an assassin," Ophelia said, standing unsteadily, her little robot goat gazing up at her blankly. "She acquires things. Find items, people, whatever."

"She's lying. She must know–" Bastion started to say.

I pressed the top of the little pyramid, and Bastion went silent. An unintended, but not unexpected effect of the device.

"What do you know about the item you sent her to acquire?" I asked.

"Listen, you have to understa–" she said and stopped suddenly, looking even more confused than before.

"Communications blocker," I said, pointing to the little pyramid. "Just you and me. Can't have you calling security or your assistant while we are having this conversation." Also meant Bastion couldn't talk to me, but I didn't need him for this part.

The shock and confusion on Ophelia's face melted away into pure fear. "What are you going to do to me?"

"That depends on you. In a perfect world, you'll tell me what I need to know and send Roxy home with a little 'thank you, but kindly go home' email. And I do nothing to you."

She swallowed hard but said nothing.

"So let's try again. What do you know about the chip you had Roxy steal?"

Ophelia took a couple of deep breaths before she said, "It's an experimental digital assistant."

I narrowed my eyes. "Let's be clear. I know exactly what it is. If I don't hear exactly what it is coming out of your mouth, then I have to make this more complicated, which will not be very fun for you."

She swallowed hard again. "It's an AI."

"There we go. Not so hard. Why did you hire Roxy to steal it?"

Ophelia shook her head a little while staring at my feet, her expression pained.

I took two steps toward her. "Come on, Ophelia, just open that mouth and let the truth come pouring out."

"The NX15987," she sputtered. "It's a disaster. It's going to ruin my career. They've been...they've been detonating."

"The purple and green sparks."

"My chip is killing people. I have...had a friend at Corto. We were out. Having fun. Had a few too many. I was talking about the NX15987, my fears. Problems. Then she told me about *that* chip. The AI."

She looked up at me, her expression changed dramatically, though I couldn't parse the look. Fear and pain and... I didn't know. "I just wanted the chip. That's it. I thought I could present it to our CEO. Maybe he would use it against Corto or find a way to use it for Nexus. I didn't know, didn't care so long as it could save me, my career. I didn't know Roxy would..."

I waited for Ophelia to finish the sentence, but she choked up. I said, "Would what? What did Roxy do?"

Ophelia just cried and shook her head.

I grabbed her by the shoulders and almost yelled, "Tell me what Roxy did! Right now!"

She didn't look at me as she whispered, "She killed them. All of them."

I let go of Ophelia. I'd seen what Roxy could do first-hand. "The Corto lab?" I asked.

Ophelia nodded, her jaw shaking. An entire laboratory of researchers, technicians, and scientists. Helpless. All dead. Bastion's friend Cinder.

"Your friend worked in that lab, didn't they?"

Ophelia nodded again, her mouth tight, and tears rolled down her cheeks. "Tara. Her name was Tara."

"Silent circuits," I said. "Who else knows about this?"

She shook her head. "No one. If anyone knew, it wouldn't just be my career. The unsanctioned theft, the murders. This is Nexus, but even we have regulations and penalties. I could be terminated. Cast into The Mist."

I sighed. That answered so many of my questions in one go, and I believed her. Believed her tears. The loss of her friend. I couldn't imagine the guilt she was carrying, hiring that monster and facing those results. But that monster was after me now, and I had to fix that.

"Call off Roxy," I said. "Cancel the contract."

"I can't."

I stepped closer to her, mere centimeters away, and said, "You can't?"

Ophelia stepped back, bumping into the wall, and threw her hands up in surrender. "She's not working for me anymore, I swear."

"She came after me. Tried to kill me. Almost succeeded."

All the color fled Ophelia's face. Given what Roxy did to that Corto lab, I didn't think I'd want to be threatened by someone who survived an encounter with Roxy, either. "I...I... you...you...I told her to get that chip back before I found out about the lab, about what she did."

"And when you did find out?"

"I called her. Told her it was over, the contract was canceled, but she said it was too late."

"Why?" I snarled.

"Professional reputation or something." Ophelia was shaking. "She was so angry when I called, practically spitting."

"When did you call her?"

"What?"

"When did you try to cancel the contract?"

"Early this morning. Before I came to work."

After Roxy and I tussled outside of Echo's place. After that gravity grenade ripped into her. This wasn't just professional reputation. Roxy wanted my head because she'd been beaten.

"There is no contract," Ophelia said. "Roxy told me to destroy it, forget about it and forget her, but not to expect the chip back."

"People are dead," I whispered. "More people might still die just because you wanted to save your career."

"I know," she whispered back. "I'm sorry."

"You need to forget my face. My name. Forget any of this ever happened, or your career will be the least of your worries."

Ophelia nodded. "I don't even know your real name."

I didn't know what to say to that. She'd sent a murderous spider-assassin into a lab and then sent her after me without even knowing my name, without knowing anything about me or my life. Even if she didn't know Roxy was

151

the massacring type, it was cold. I turned, disengaged the electromagnetic lock, and walked out the door, leaving the comms blocker in place. I knew Ophelia was crying in that haze of vapor, but I didn't look back.

CHAPTER FIFTEEN

"WHAT HAPPENED?" BASTION ASKED FOR the fourth time since I'd cleared the radius of the comms blocker.

I kicked off the landing pad of the Nexus building, Poe gently gaining speed and altitude before I finally answered him. "You were right about that cerebellum chip. It's a disaster. She's doing all of this to salvage her career. Ophelia was friends with one of the techs in your lab, the lab Roxy tore apart."

"Cinder?"

"No. Tara. Did you know them?"

"Not personally, no."

"They're dead now, anyway. Ophelia hired Roxy to get the chip, but that wasn't enough for Roxy."

"Dead?" Bastion asked. "And she worked in the lab? What about...?"

"Bastion," I said. "I'm so sorry. Roxy killed everyone in the lab."

"Everyone? That can't be. It can't."

"I'm so sorry, Bastion. I know Cinder was–"

Bastion cut me off, his voice suddenly stern. "Is Roxy no longer a problem for us?"

I knew there was no way Bastion was okay, but if he wanted to focus on the task at hand and deal with this later, I would respect that. I cleared my throat and said, "No. Ophelia canceled the contract, but Roxy is hell-bent on killing me anyway."

"Why isn't she trying to kill Echo instead?"

I opened my mouth to answer but honestly didn't have one. Why wasn't she trying to go after Echo? Had she already done something to him?

"Elise?"

"I honestly don't know," I said. "Hey Carbon, text Echo."

"You do realize I can do that for you? You don't need that buggy little assistant."

"You have access to my contacts?"

"I'm in your comms, so yes."

"Right. Of course you do. Send a text to Echo."

"What would you like to say?"

"Tell him, 'Thanks for the assist yesterday. How are you? Crazy lady leave you alone?'"

"Anything else?"

"No. Send that."

"Sent," Bastion said. "What's the plan now?"

"I need to get my work limbs back. I feel naked and weak out here, working a job in my everyday limbs. Hey Car...sorry. Habit. Hey Bastion."

"Just talk to me."

"Right. Sorry," I said, leaving the major traffic lane to head back toward the Corto borough. "Tell Hessod I'm on my way."

"Done," Bastion said. "We should call Quynn as well, find out if they have made any progress."

"We should call Quynn just to keep them in the loop, at least, but yes. If you don't mind–" I stopped mid-sentence as I rounded another corner only to find a wall of Nexus security drones, at least a dozen of them, blocking my path out of their borough. I released the throttle and squeezed the airbrakes hard, making the thrusters grunt to a halt.

"Stop," a bright but stern voice blared from behind me. "Place your vehicle in static hover and prepare to be apprehended. You have been identified as a non-Nexus suspect in four class-A regulation violations."

I slowly spun the bike around and found myself face-to-face with a security van. With a sloped front end and a flat rear, it was taller and longer than a car, shining and emblazoned with Nexus security emblems. A pair of security guards in full armor sat in the front seats, both looking bulky and angry. The van was flanked by four more of the security drones.

"You should not have trusted Ophelia to–" Bastion began.

"This isn't her," I said to Bastion. "Well, it could be a little bit her, but I have a feeling this is about the quartet of drones we sent into The Mist last night."

"Place your vehicle in static hover now," the guard repeated, way too loudly from the speakers mounted on the security van. "Or we will be forced to disable you and your vehicle."

As though the guard said a magic word, all of the drones around me deployed those enormous prongs, electricity arcing off them so much that the hairs on my head stood up a little. Six more prongs sprang out of sliding panels on the van. Mother of Corto, there was enough electricity arcing around to power a building, let alone stun me into next year.

"How far are we to the Corto border?" I asked Bastion.

"Three blocks," he said. "Surely, you're not–"

I took my hands off Poe's handlebars and lifted them into the air. Unlike cars in Jayu City, she didn't have a static hover mode that could be turned on or off with a button, but taking my hands off the controls was pretty much the same thing.

"Thank you," the officer said, still too loud. "Please remain calm and stay right there."

Those nasty prongs retreated back into the van as it started a lateral spin toward me, working to come up alongside Poe. The drones stayed where they were, prongs still extended, but the electrical arcs subsided.

"You can't do this, Elise," Bastion said, his voice suddenly frantic. "It's only three blocks. If you don't go after Theo, after my chip, we don't know what will happen to me, what he'll do, who he's working for!"

I didn't answer him, keeping my eyes on the security vehicle moving toward me. A large door slid open as the van approached, and two other security guards in heavy armor were perched on either side of the door. I guessed there were times even Nexus thought uniforms were a good idea. One officer hooked a slim, silver manacle to a tow line mounted at the top of the door opening, and then extended it toward me, the line reeling out as they did so.

The security van stopped a third of a meter from Poe, rocking slightly and jostling the guard with the manacle. They barked something at the pilot and then reached out again. I watched them, watched the manacle approach, and once they were only centimeters away, I kicked the emergency kill switch for Poe.

One second, there was a burly, armored officer about to slap a manacle on my wrist. The next second, I was 10 meters below the van and the drones, in freefall on a 2800-kilogram bike, trailing a fire-extinguishing vapor.

The thing about emergency systems in flying vehicles is they're only designed for dire, end-of-the-world emergencies. Pulling that particular ripcord is basically deciding you have a better chance with gravity hundreds of meters in the air instead of whatever else was happening. In terms of Poe, kicking the emergency system meant not one, but two pedals mounted above the front thruster, one on each side. And they had to be kicked hard. Nobody accidentally triggered the emergency systems on a Kawasaki.

The problem now was that pulling Poe out of this dive was even harder. When I kicked the pedals, a large, red lever shot up right in the middle of the handlebars. It had to be pushed back into place with significant effort. Not pulled toward me but pushed away. The bike started to spin, nose-first, straight toward The Mist. I could barely see my own elbows through the fire-suppression vapors, let alone the handlebars I was fiercely clinging to. I was pulling myself forward with everything these everyday limbs could muster. This would be no issue with my work limbs; they were three times as strong. Probably should have thought about that before I made this decision.

"Three blocks!" Bastion yells. "Just three blocks! Are you suicidal?"

I couldn't move my legs to help me. They were squeezing against the sides of the bike just to keep me on, and that was all they could do, all they were equipped to do. I needed to move one of my hands to that lever, the lever I couldn't even see. And when I let go with one hand, the force of the descent would be too much for the other hand. I needed to lean forward as much as possible before making a move on that red lever.

My altimeter was blinking red on my display. 600 meters and falling.

In a breath, it was 550 meters. Given the power of these thrusters and the weight of the bike, I knew I wouldn't be able to save her once we were below 100 meters. I kept pulling, pulling forward, and finally, the vapors cleared. I didn't check my altimeter, but I knew I needed to do this now or bail. I let go with my left hand, already moving it toward that big, red lever, and my torso was flung back, the right arm straining against the force, but I caught the lever.

Now I had to do it again as I passed 300 meters. Pull, pull, pull. 200 meters.

"Jump, Elise! Jump! Forget the bike!"

Pull. Pull. 150 meters. I couldn't wait any longer. "Hey Carbon, override arm safeties!" I yelled as I pulled with my right and pushed with my left. My torso reared back again, and I felt motors whir and pop and overheat in my arms, but then I feel the clunk of the lever giving. The thrusters fired hard, crushing me down onto the bike as she shed speed and leveled off. My stomach dropped into my pelvis and my vision went dark around the edges, but I remained conscious.

The bike leveled, holding steady at 104 meters above the street, though I was still trying to steady my breath and heart, which were racing.

"Mother of Corto!" I yelled. "That worked!"

"Too soon to celebrate," Bastion said. "We have incoming!"

I glanced up, and there they were, more than a dozen security drones screaming down at me along with three full-size security vehicles. They were multiplying.

Right. Survived the freefall, now I needed to survive the chase. I opened up the throttle and tried to pull the handlebars to the right, but my right arm popped and barely did anything. So instead of spinning hard toward the Corto borough, Poe was accelerating straight toward a building. I yanked to the left, and the bike spun, taking a wider arc since she was already moving face, and Poe's tail scrapped along the surface of the building before we started jetting away from Nexus.

A loud crashing sound slapped me in the back of the head at almost that same instant. I glanced back, and one of the security drones was embedded in the building, right where Poe's fender had left a mark only a moment ago.

"Left!" Bastion barked. I didn't think, just yanked the bike to the left as a drone screamed straight down where I had been.

"Right!" Bastion yelled. That was harder with only one arm. I pushed the left handlebar and leaned hard to the right. Another drone careened past, one of its taser arms clipping my left heel as it passed. It didn't hurt. Only masochists allowed their cybernetic mods to send pain signals to their brains. Instead, I felt acute pressure. Just a little something to let me know I'd taken some damage, something to warn my brain the way pain did, but without all that pesky burning or bleeding.

"Two blocks!" Bastion yelled.

"Thank you!" I opened up the throttle as far as it would go. We kept weaving through drones, Bastion shouting orders like a drill sergeant as I dutifully complied. It only took a few more swerves before they started coming up on my left more and more, surely figuring out I had a much harder time steering to the right than the left.

"One block!" Bastion yelled, but the Nexus security forces didn't intend to let me out of their borough. As I narrowly dodged another taser from yet another drone, I saw several flashes of light on metal. Half a dozen heavily armored Nexus security officers riding much newer, much faster bikes roared into the intersection right in front of me. They trained assault rifles on me before their bikes even came to rest. Not tasers but kill-you-now assault rifles.

Even if I'd wanted to, there was no way I could stop in time. I didn't like the idea of crashing into one of them in midair any more than I liked being perforated by those guns, so I pushed the handlebars forward, my right arm groaning in protest, and dived. Not straight down this time. I needed to cover that last block and get out of the borough without delay, so I took an angle, trying to put room between me and the security bikes, but also trying to keep my forward velocity. The assault rifles popped above me, a few rounds pinging off Poe's chassis, but none did any damage. I glanced up to see the bikes diving toward me, their acceleration enviable. I wasn't sure I was going to make it to the next street and back into Corto before they were on me.

A bullet ripped through my right hand, sheering off my pinky and ring finger along with a chunk of the handlebar I'd been holding. At this rate, I was going to have to buy a whole arm instead of just fixing the damage.

"Weave!" Bastion yelled. "Move in an S! Don't just go straight!"

"No time!" I yelled just as I cleared the corridor of buildings, passing over the broad boulevard that marked the boundary between the Nexus and Corto boroughs. The gunfire abruptly stopped as the roaring of the security bikes' thrusters faded quickly behind me. A glance back confirmed it: they had all stopped halfway across the street, not willing to risk the ire of Corto Corporation by chasing me where they had no jurisdiction. I let off the throttle, shedding speed to a gentle cruise.

"Damage report," I said.

"Me or your little assistant?" Bastion asked with obvious pith in his voice.

"I didn't say anything about Carbon unless a damage report is somehow beneath you."

"I thought we were partners."

"We are," I said, doing my best to maintain some patience, but my patience was running thin.

"Then maybe don't just give me orders."

"Just do it, Bastion!"

Bastion said nothing in response as I cruised along past one block. Legrand Corto danced on a screen some 20 stories tall on the side of one building, her overdone curves swayed from one end of the block to the other in a red bikini that left little to the imagination. I passed another block of towering advertisements before I asked Bastion, "Could I have a damage report, please?"

Bastion sighed – a disconcerting sound from someone without lungs – and said, "Five of the six rotors in your right arm are partially stripped, the sixth completely burned out. You can see what happened to your hand, and it's slowly leaking coolant and oil. Mobility in that hand is down 40% and will keep falling."

"The bike?" I asked.

"I'm not done with you," Bastion said. "Three of the rotors in your left arm are partially stripped. Two bullets ran through your left thigh."

I glanced down and did a double take. There were two jagged holes in the top of my thigh, sparks occasionally popping out of the larger one. "I didn't even feel those."

"You were busy. The main communication trunk of the leg is severed, but the backup is still operational, so you still have full mobility, though your reaction time will be slowed by 12.4%."

"I'm a mess," I said. "What else is wrong with me?"

"You should probably see a therapist about your obvious suicidal tendencies."

"Very funny."

"And your issues with rage."

I swallowed and took a breath. "I'm sorry."

"Your Kawasaki is fine. Other than the handlebar, all of its damage is purely superficial."

"Always sunshine and rainbows after the darkest storm."

"What?"

"Something my mom likes to say. It means things will always get better, always some joy to find."

"I suppose so," Bastion said. "But you cannot keep taking beatings like this and making enemies. We should be making progress, finding Theo and my chip, not running away from threats only to find more around every corner."

"We did just check Ophelia off the list as a threat," I said as I slowly pulled Poe up, fighting my busted right arm to gain some altitude.

"She was not exactly a threat."

"We didn't know that until I talked to her. She only hired a real–"

"A Stryder is heading directly for us," Bastion said with sudden urgency. "Descending quickly and directly ahead. The Stryder office is trying to stop it, but it's not responding to them."

I yanked Poe to the left, leveraging my stronger arm as I looked where Bastion said. It was a black car, a late-model BMW, pretty standard issue for Stryder. But its hood was gone, revealing the whining electric motor and a tangle of cables and wires no longer safely nestled in their brackets and harnesses, but attached to the car's new pilot, straddling the top of the car

160

like some ancient war chariot.

Two of her deadly spider limbs were still missing, while the other two were embedded in the roof of the car. Her right arm had been replaced, and it certainly didn't match the copper color she seemed to prefer, but that rage was still there, burning in her eyes next to the pink patches of fresh, nano-grown skin on her face.

Roxy was flying down at me atop a hijacked Stryder with murder in her eyes.

CHAPTER SIXTEEN

"GIVE ME THE CHIP!" ROXY snarled, the hijacked BMW wobbling as it hovered.

"Why do you care about some chip?" I yelled back. "Your contract was canceled."

"Poking around in my business? That why you were just fleeing Nexus?"

"She hired you, somebody hired me, and then she hired you again. I don't think there's any separating your business from mine."

"You did your job, and yet here you still are."

I shrugged. "Job's not done. At least one of us has to be professional about this."

"I'm not sure antagonizing her is the best course of action," Bastion said.

"Hush," I whispered. I wasn't much of a fighter, but I'd had enough run-ins with them over the years to know that opponents tended to fight worse when they were running hot. And it was more fun.

"Just give me the chip, woman!" The BMW shook with her anger.

"You should get your aural implants checked. I told you before: I. Don't. Have. It."

"Why do you keep lying?" Roxy screamed, lowering the BMW until we were eye-level. "Why are you protecting the chip? Is it worth your life?"

162

"Why don't you think about that question? Really. Why WOULD I protect some chip, put my life on the line for it? I could go home right now, face some disciplinary action at work, but I'd survive. And I'll tell you what, nothing sounds better to me right now than a hot shower, pajamas, and bad television. So don't you think that maybe, just maybe, I really don't have the chip?"

She seemed to mull that over. The angles on her face softened a touch and the pink skin, freshly grown where the gravity grenade had ripped away flesh earlier, eased a bit.

"You are in no shape to fight her," Bastion said.

"An understatement," I whispered to him. "There is no shape I could be in to fight her."

"Why aren't you running? This bike is faster than that car," Bastion said.

"And lead her where? Home to Quynn? Back to the office? You know what she did to that Corto lab. She seems to be tracking me, finding me somehow. I can't assume I could lose her and keep her lost."

"Who are you mumbling to?" Roxy yelled, the anger returning and redoubling. "Calling in reinforcements? Security?"

"No," I said. "Trying to convince myself that you'll listen to reason."

That seemed to have the opposite effect of what I'd intended. Her face hardened again. "I do listen to reason, but I hear none coming from you."

Fine. It was time to bluff as hard as I could. "Please leave. Don't make me hurt you."

"You'll never get the chance," Roxy said and revved the BMW's thrusters with a flick of one hand.

"Last chance. Surrender." I yelled back.

She spat on the exposed engine and then sneered like a wild animal.

"Bastion," I whispered, trying to move my mouth as little as possible. "The Nexus security, are they still back there?"

"One moment," he said.

"Last chance," Roxy said. "Give me the chip and I'll give you a quick death. Or don't. Give me a reason to rip it from your body slowly."

"The drones are gone, scattered by several kilometers," Bastion said.

163

The personed vehicles – bikes and vans – are parked outside of a cafe only two blocks from where we–"

"Directions on my display!" I said, no longer caring if Roxy heard. "Now!" I pulled hard on the throttle and yanked on the handlebars with my one good arm, spinning and momentarily inverting the bike. I revved and gunned it back toward Nexus.

"Are you insane?" Bastion's voice cracked.

Roxy roared behind me, but I didn't look back. I was sure she was on me, lashing the BMW's thrusters like an abused draft animal.

"Directions!" I yelled again, and then the wireframe popped up. Three blocks to the Nexus border, back into the proverbial frying pan. A left, a right, and the cafe was there, a blinking blue coffee cup on my display.

"This is a terrible idea!" Bastion yelled.

"I know!"

"I'll kill you!" Roxy said, her voice farther away than I'd expected. Bastion was right, Poe could definitely outrun that hijacked BMW. That was good. I would need a few seconds, give the Nexus security people a chance to at least get their weapons out before the homicidal spider joined us.

I took the corners wide. Not only did I not want to lose her with evasive maneuvers, but my busted right arm wasn't helping me steer much anyway. Crossing the street from Corto back to Nexus sent a wave of nausea through me, my stomach making sure my brain knew how terrible this idea was.

As I turned the last corner, I didn't need the wireframe to show me the location of the cafe. About a dozen stories above me, three bulbous security vans and the bikes were all parked around the corner of the building, crowded onto a single landing pad. I glanced over my shoulder and saw Roxy less than a block behind me, the wind whipping her red-orange hair like her head was ablaze.

I slid Poe up alongside the landing pad and leaped from her before she was even stopped. I had a good plan. Jump over the security bikes, land on the hood of one of those security vehicles, and roll off onto the landing pad right in front of the gathered security officers. My busted hand and perforated leg had different ideas. That latency in my left made my leap from Poe lopsided, and my left foot caught on one of the Nexus bikes. I landed hard on my right side, and the security bike started to tumble down after me. I hauled my wounded leg out of the way before it crashed down, pulling myself up against the nearby van.

More than a dozen Nexus security officers were staring at me, cups of coffee and pastries suspended from their hands, mid-sip and bite.

"She's back!" One of them yelled, and then cups and pastries were tumbling to the ground as they drew their weapons, taking deadly aim.

I threw my hands straight up. "I surrender! I surrender!"

A few started to advance on me while they all kept their weapons focused but I wasn't really paying attention to them. I was listening hard. Those Stryder BMWs were nearly silent, but not completely, especially with the hood missing. If I was going to survive the next few minutes, I would need to time this right.

The advancing officers split, one to the front and one to the back of the van I was leaning against, and still, the rest of their squad was focused on me, almost unblinking.

Then I heard the gentle whir of expensive, Earth-designed thrusters. If I could hear them, it meant they were almost on top of me. I dropped to the ground, going as flat as I could. A few officers yelled, and my world filled with sounds.

I'm not entirely sure what I'd expected when Roxy arrived in the face of all those officers, but I didn't expect her to try and kill me with the front bumper of the hijacked BMW. She seemed like the kind of woman who liked to get her hands dirty, to watch the life drain from someone's eyes, not the kind to put her own life in danger in the process. But she was that kind of woman. The BMW slammed into the side of the van, right where I'd been standing only a second before. I lay flat, face-down on the landing pad as everything around me erupted into smashing metal and glass, gunfire, and screams.

I couldn't just lay there and wait for everything to calm down, though. I had to move. Wounds and all, I pushed up and leaped into the best sprint I could manage, making a line straight for the edge of the landing pad. I told myself not to look, not to see what was happening between the Nexus security forces and Roxy, but I had to know, had to see what I'd inflicted on those officers.

165

The black BMW and the security van were now a singular, tangled mess of metal and plastic leaning up against the now-exposed structural supports of the cafe's outer wall. Tiny flecks of glass were everywhere, spread across the landing pad and the inside of the cafe, across the undamaged vehicles, and little shards were falling out of my hair as I ran.

Inside the cafe, Roxy was right in the middle of the security forces, ripping and rending and raging against them all, her copper limbs flashing red with blood. It had only been seconds, but the security force's numbers had been reduced by half already, as many face-down in pools of their own blood as there were standing, shooting, trying to bring down the murderous thief.

But the officers left were well-trained, retreating while laying down cover fire. Roxy drove a clawed hand into the chest of one of the officers. Other officers threw over tables, crouched down, and opened up their assault rifles on her. She brought up her free hand to protect her face, but the arm wasn't entirely bulletproof. One of her remaining spider limbs took too many hits, and it went limp, little sparks flying from the dead joint. She slid into a crouch and found her cover behind the bullet-riddled drink station, creamer and packets of sweetener spilling across the blood and glass as she turned it on its side.

I couldn't keep watching, though. Roxy wanted to kill me, and Nexus security wanted to arrest me, and surely there were more security forces en route already. I slid around the side of a security van, ducking behind it as pings of deflected bullets rang out in every direction. I squeezed between one pair and then another of the security bikes, all the while trying to keep my head down and move as fast as I could. Roxy roared and there was another huge sound, something heavy crashing against something immovable. And suddenly the gunfire was a trickle. One, maybe two weapons still firing. No more.

People were dying, Nexus security forces just trying to do their jobs, and it was my fault. There was nothing I could do to help, though. Nothing I could do but get myself killed. It was precisely because there was nothing I could do in the face of Roxy that I was here, now, that all this was happening. So I focused on what I could do, what I'd done so many times.

I jumped.

"Again?" Bastion yelled.

"Poe!" I said to him. "Now!"

"What?"

"Sparks! Hey Carbon, summon Poe!"

The floors flashed by, the sounds of gunfire quickly diminishing as I fell away from the fight, wind whipping my hair back. Then the scream of my bike's thrusters rushed in to fill the void of sound. I twisted as best I could, missing my work limbs and their ailerons specifically designed to help me in times like these. Nevertheless, I grabbed hold of Poe's fender with my lame right hand and managed to grab a handlebar with the much stronger, undamaged left. Poe started to level off my descent before I'd even climbed completely aboard, and I was fully astride her before we'd even descended to the 100th floor of the surrounding buildings.

Once I was settled on, control reverted to me, the sounds of gunfire and snarling metal long gone above. I gunned the thrusters. "How are we?" I asked Bastion. "Any security inbound?"

"Not toward us," he said. "They're swarming toward that cafe, though."

"Good." I steered back toward Corto, not bothering to gain any altitude. No point risking running into security drones heading for Roxy's party.

"It appears Nexus security is tapping every resource they can find. Their security channels are a mess. I'm counting three dozen drones, a score of personed vehicles, and a full tactical squad carrier en route."

"At least they're prioritizing murderous rampages above my destruction of property and theft."

"Maybe they'll take care of our Roxy problem with overwhelming force."

I barked out a laugh before I knew it was even bubbling up.

"What?" Bastion asked.

"What part of our luck on this job has given you the impression that anything is going to break our way like that?"

"Is hope such a tenuous thing that you can't even reach for it?"

"People of Jayu City," I said, letting some tension out of my back as we crossed back into Corto, this time without a cadre of Nexus security behind us or a raging psychopath before us. "May I present Bastion. Illegal AI, world-class hacker, easily offended assistant, and sophist."

"I've found it to be central to many living, breathing, loving people like you. They all hope for something better."

I sighed, disappointed he wasn't playing along with my tease. "I have hope, Bastion. I hope that we'll find your chip and find our way out of this mess. We'll find a way to deal with Roxy and Theo and whoever is pulling the strings from the Corto side. I'm also realistic about any security teams' chances against Roxy. That assassin isn't going to stop until someone removes her head from her body. Maybe not even then."

"If we cannot stop her, then what hope do we have?"

"We use her unstoppability to our advantage," I said as I pulled Poe up, joining a main traffic lane back toward downtown Corto, back home. "All that back there gave me an idea."

"Which is?"

"Okay, it's a nugget of an idea. Like 12 percent of an idea. I'll tell you when it's closer to 90 percent."

"This is you having fun again, isn't it?"

"Isn't everything?" I winked, but then remembered he couldn't see my face. I hated wasting a good wink.

"What now?"

"Text Hessod," I said, and then remembered. "Please. Ask him to grab my limbs and meet me at my apartment."

"Done," Bastion said. "Your apartment? Not the Corto Intel office?"

"Until we know who's pulling all the strings on the Corto side, I'd rather play on home court."

"You trust Hessod?"

"I do. Almost as much as I trust Quynn. I was wrong to worry about him before, too rattled to realize that," I said. "And never question my trust in Quynn. We will have words if you do that."

"Understood," Bastion said.

"Any word from Echo?"

"He texted while you were diving off yet another building. It doesn't make any sense, though."

"What did he say?"

"The walls of Jericho stand firm against all comers."

168

I laughed at that.

"What does it mean?"

"It means he's fine. She tried to get to him, but as crazy as Roxy is, her crazy doesn't match Echo's paranoia. He's spent more credits on security and reinforcing his storefront than I've spent on anything my whole life."

"Crazy beats crazy."

"Looks like it. Glad Echo is on my side."

"Hessod says he's leaving now."

"Good," I said, taking a turn nice and slow, letting my busted arm rest feebly at my side. I took a deep breath and blew it out hard. Theo. Roxy. And somebody at Corto – possibly the CEO herself – were warring over this chip, over this voice in my ear.

"I'm afraid," Bastion said.

"You're afraid? They're trying to kill me out here."

"You know your enemies, what they want with you. Mine are shrouded, their designs as much as their identities. And I fear for you."

I didn't know what to say to that. This disembodied voice, this illegal AI, had saved my life on multiple occasions in the last two days. But it was more than that, I had to admit. I was getting to know him, growing a little attached. Caring for him. That wasn't good. I needed to solve this, get the chip, keep Bastion safe, and then wish him well. I couldn't keep him in my life, no way. I'd lived almost 30 years without this level of drama, this level of danger, and I wanted to get back to that.

But I was worried about Bastion, about what people would do to him. Or worse, do with him. He was incredibly useful. Dangerous hands would make him into a dangerous slave.

But it was more than that. He feared death. He held fast to hope. He was afraid for others. As much as I knew he was an artificial intelligence, some lines of code flitting around on the net and in a chip, he was more. Even the pronoun I kept using. Not it. He. We were becoming friends. Friends forged in the fires of me getting my ass kicked, but friends, nonetheless. I cared not only that he wasn't used by the wrong people. I didn't want him to be used at all, no more than I would want someone to use Quynn.

"I'm afraid, too," I finally said. "So we just have to keep watching out

169

for each other. I'll keep going after your chip, and you do your part to keep me alive."

"I'll do my best," Bastion said.

"I know you will. Text Quynn, please. Tell them I'm coming home and Hessod is going to meet us there. I need their help with what comes next."

CHAPTER SEVENTEEN

"MOTHER OF CORTO!" QUYNN YELLED the moment I opened the front door. "What happened?"

"Have you never heard of running away from a fight?" Hessod asked as both of them leaped off the couch in the living room and practically ran to me. Before I could even speak, they were on each side of me, getting up under my arms and pretty much carrying me into the bedroom.

"You should see the other person," I said.

"An inept euphemism," Bastion said in my ear.

"I somehow doubt that," Quynn said as they gently sat me down.

"This is really unnecessary. I parked Poe and made it all the way to the apartment on my own."

"Are those gunshot wounds?" Hessod said, his eyes fixed on the holes in my thigh.

I shrugged and gave them both my best *what do you do?* look. I dropped it when I saw the look of utter horror on Quynn's face. There was no making a joke of this.

Quynn sat down next to me and took both my hands. "This is the second time in two days you've come home to me..." They paused, looking me up and down, their eyes lingering on those bullet holes, the missing fingers, every centimeter of me scuffed and tattered. They took a deep breath and continued, "Broken. This has to stop."

"That's the idea," I said.

Hessod quietly slipped out of the bedroom. Smart man.

"Is it?" Quynn asked. "Is that the idea?"

"Of course. Why would you ask that?"

Quynn sighed and stared at my hands, each one covered in a dozen or more wounds. I didn't even know what caused them. "Making jokes. So gung-ho to head off the next challenge, to dive off buildings and face off against these..."

"Maniacs," I said when Quynn left the sentence unfinished.

They winced, the word seeming to wound Quynn as much as anything else. "I understand what you're doing. I understand why. I get it. But I need to know this is going to end. You're going to find Bast–"

Bastion started to speak, but before he finished even one syllable, I put a quick finger to Quynn's lips and glanced out the bedroom toward Hessod.

They sighed. "I know you've got a lot going on, but have you talked to Hessod recently?"

"He did my repairs, the nano–"

"No," Quynn said. "Really talked."

I wanted to protest, to say I'd had a lot going on, people trying to kill me, but I saw those missing pictures. I should have said something, asked, but I didn't. I shook my head.

"His wife left him and took their daughter with her."

"Sparks," I whispered.

"She thinks he's cheating on her."

"Hessod? I don't think–"

"With you," Quynn interrupted.

"That's ridiculous," I said louder than I'd intended. That explained his awkwardness during the body scan, at least.

"I know. He knows. But that's what's happening. He's been heads-down at work because he doesn't know what else to do. But he needs a friend. He needs you."

"I don't have time right now, you know that."

Quynn narrowed their eyes.

172

"And we don't have that kind of relationship," I said. "We're work friends, we're just–"

"You're the closest thing he has to a best friend," Quynn said sharply.

"Wow." I didn't know what else to say. Hessod didn't even crack my top 20 friends. I'd never realized he felt so differently.

"Yeah," Quynn said.

"I'm guessing he opened up to you?"

"I don't think he meant to. I asked how he was, and he just started sobbing and talking. I don't know how to talk to him, though, how to comfort him. I don't know him."

I sighed. "Once this is over..."

"I'll hold you to that." Quynn squeezed my hand. "You're going to find this chip, hand it in, and be done with all this, yes?"

"Hand me into who? To what?" Bastion said in my ear.

"That depends," I said to Quynn. "What have you found out? Who's pushing me around from the Corto side?"

Quynn shook their head. "I've run into dead ends. I ran out of favors and ran into more questions than answers. Whoever is doing this in Corto didn't want anyone to find out."

"That's what I was afraid of. So is he," I said, widening my eyes on the pronoun so Quynn would know exactly who I was referencing. "I don't think it's as simple as handing it over anymore."

"Elise..."

"Hey," I said, putting one of my mangled hands on Quynn's cheek. "I'm trying to do the right thing here."

Quynn sighed and shook their head. They weren't telling me no, just accepting reality.

"The right thing, huh?" Quynn asked.

"He's alive, Quynn. He fears. He hopes. He deserves a chance to live. We're the only chance he has."

"Silent circuits," Quynn said.

"I know." I squeezed their hands, and then we shared a kiss. We pressed our foreheads together for several seconds before I said, "We need a plan."

Quynn nodded. "Hessod, you have Elise's limbs?"

173

"Yep!" my analyst said from the next room. A few seconds later, he entered carrying my gym bag. He gently sat it at the foot of the bed, and then took each limb out one by one. "They're fully charged. The arm wasn't as bad as it seemed. I just had to replace some servos and re-thread some synthetic nerves."

"You're the best," I said as I pulled my shirt off and immediately started twisting off my damaged right arm.

"Just my job," Hessod said, shielding his eyes and trying to back out of the room.

"No time for modesty, Hessod," I said. I flung the busted arm on the bed and grabbed the black, carbon-polymer replacement. "We need to plan. I want you in on this."

Hessod glanced at me, blushed, and looked back to his feet.

"Just talk, Hessod. Listen. Look me in the eyes. Ignore what I'm doing."

He nodded, but still didn't look at me.

At least he wasn't leaving the room. That was something. I started working on my left arm, and then gave both Quynn and Hessod a rundown of my foray into the Nexus borough. The bewildering hookah robot goat yoga. Ophelia, her friend in the Corto lab, and the broken contract. The rampaging monster that was Roxy and the carnage at the cafe.

"And this is the second time she came at you?" Hessod asked.

"Don't miss a beat there, Mr. Analyst," I said. "I need your help figuring out how she keeps finding me."

"Don't you have the hardware to detect trackers?" Quynn asked.

"I do," I said.

"You were wearing these limbs the first time you ran into her?" Hessod was holding up one of my work legs.

I nodded. "Wouldn't matter, though. My detectors are wired into my spinal stack. Doesn't matter which limbs I'm wearing."

"Right," Hessod said. "She can't be tracking you with conventional hardware. What about your bike?"

"Silent circuits," I said. "How did I not think of that? I was on Poe both times she found me."

Quynn whisked away to the kitchen to make sure I had food in me.

I hadn't even been paying attention to my stomach, but I was ravenous. Hessod retreated to the living room to pace, grateful to be out of the room while I was changing.

"Thank you," Bastion said.

"For what?"

"What you said to Quynn. About me."

I shrugged. Another useless gesture that he couldn't see. "We're in this together now."

"No one has seen me as more than a program since Cinder."

I silently changed out my left leg, watching the systems boot up on my display. "Bastion," I said. "Nothing epitomizes the condition of living more than losing someone you love."

"You've lost people?"

"Everyone loses people, me included."

"Who?"

I swallowed hard, sitting there wearing nothing but my limbs, feeling vulnerable in too many ways. "My father."

"Oh," Bastion whispered. "I'm sorry."

"He's not dead," I said quickly. "At least, not as far as I know. He defected when I was 12."

"Defected?"

"He left Corto Corporation. Left my mom. Left me. It's not the same as dying, I know. But here in Jayu City, your company is your home. Your family. Leaving like that, not just us but the company. It's the ultimate betrayal. Your company is everything, your job and your life and your support structure. You don't just leave.

"My mom wore white for six years, just like a widow. Nobody would talk to her. Nobody came to visit. It felt like everyone blamed us, blamed her for Dad leaving. He took some of Corto's secrets with him. It destroyed my mother's reputation. She was demoted three times in two years and retired without ever being even looked at for a promotion again. It's one thing to get divorced, to stay in Corto and leave your partner. That's a setback, sure, but it's not the same as a defection. It's like he took everything we knew and loved and set it on fire."

"I'm sorry, Elise," Bastion said.

"I've known people who have died, too," I said. "I don't have grandparents left anymore. A few acquaintances, but nothing has hurt as much as that. So yeah, I know loss. I understand, a little bit, how much you must be hurting."

"I don't want anyone to hurt like that," Bastion said. "Like this does."

"Part of living, Bastion," I said, standing up and grabbing my bodysuit. "Pain is just part of the package."

"I suppose you're right."

I zipped up, little bruises on me lighting up as the bodysuit sucked in against my skin. "But we do what we can to minimize it. Starting with you and your chip."

"Just tell me what you need," Bastion said.

"I will." I walked out of the bedroom, and Quynn shoved a thick sandwich in my face. Hessod was already heading for the door. The three of us silently rode the elevator and marched down the hall to my little garage. Hessod pulled up short when I unlocked and open the door.

"What?" I said.

"You've told me about Poe," he said. "But I've never seen her. She's the spitting image of the bike my dad had when I was a kid."

"Don't you two start yammering on about motorcycles," Quynn said. "There's only so much I can take."

"We don't have time to–" Bastion started to say.

But I was ahead of him again. I laid my head against Quynn's shoulder. "You're lucky we don't have time to start the yammering."

"Right," Hessod said, squeezing past me and kneeling next to Poe. His hands moved across her chassis, inside every nook and cranny his fingers could fit into.

"I should have had you buy Poe dinner first."

"How does one buy dinner for a–" Bastion started saying right as I shut the door. And just like before, he was cut short. My comms signal went dead.

Quynn snorted out a laugh at my joke, and Hessod just shook his head. Then he suddenly stopped moving. He cocked his head around, looking under the seat, up inside the rear thruster assembly.

"You find it?" I asked.

In answer, he worked the bike's releases like a professional mechanic, and then lowered the entire thruster assembly by twenty centimeters. "Yep. Homemade, but that's definitely a tracker."

"So why hasn't Roxy followed you here?" Quynn asked.

"Good question," I said.

Hessod pulled his head back out of my bike and looked around the garage. "I bet your comms go dead when you're in here with the door closed, huh?"

"Every time," I said.

"Usually my calls," Quynn said.

"Metal door, metal walls, yeah," Hessod said. "This whole thing is like a Faraday cage. No signals in or out."

"Wouldn't she be able to follow the tracker up until it disappeared in the garage?" Quynn asked.

"Hard to say," Hessod said. "Do you have an anti-magnetic spanner?"

I nodded and opened the toolbox.

"This tracker isn't off-the-shelf, so I don't know what kind of software Roxy is using. Considering she hasn't shown up in your apartment or ripped open the door to this garage, I'd say it works off a directional ping. The tone or frequency of the ping increases as she gets closer, but it doesn't have full GPS functionality."

"So we got lucky," Quynn said.

"Looks like," Hessod said as I extended an anti-magnetic spanner to him.

"Just when I thought there was no good luck to be had on this job."

Hessod grabbed the spanner, but I took a firmer hold of it when he tried to tug. "What?" he asked.

"I have a plan. More of an idea," I said.

"Which is?" he said.

"Can we disable the tracker?" I asked.

Hessod seemed to turn the idea over in his head. "If I take a hammer to it–"

"No, I mean temporarily," I said, letting Hessod take the spanner.

"Meaning you want it to come back on later," Quynn said. "I already hate this plan."

I'm no match for Roxy. I'm also no match for Theo. Theo has the chip, which Roxy wants."

"Are you sure?" Quynn said. "Because I think she just wants to remove your head from your body."

"I think she wants both," I said. "And with any luck, maybe Theo and Roxy will kill each other in the process."

"It could work," Hessod said, his hands back in Poe with the spanner. "It could also wind up with Theo and Roxy ripping you in two, but it could work. I'll need epoxy and conductive metal filings. Unless you have–"

"Magnetic epoxy?" I asked as I pulled the two-tube epoxy from my toolbox. "Do I look like an amateur?"

"You do not," Hessod said. A little clang echoed in the thruster assembly. He pulled out a black disc smaller than my palm, textured like the head of a microphone. He took the epoxy from me with a huge grin and moved over to a nearby shelf. He shoved things aside to make room.

"Let the record show that I hate this," Quynn said, leaning up against the wall and watching Hessod work with utter fascination. They tried to play cool and like they didn't care, but I knew Quynn. They were working through every way my little plan could go wrong, quietly panicking and trying to think of alternatives.

"The record shall henceforth be noted," I said. I didn't like my plan either, so I hoped they would think of a better one.

"None of this helps us figure out who is playing us from the Corto side."

"What?" Hessod said, bumping his head against the next shelf and dropping the epoxy applicator. He turned to look at us both, incredulity written across his features.

"We don't know who hired me for this job," I said.

"We never know who hires us," Hessod said. "Not our job to know. Above our pay grades. Why would you even ask who hired us?"

I chewed on that for a moment, trying to figure out how to let Hessod in, how much to let him in. Knowing about Bastion was dangerous, and as much as I trusted Hessod, could I trust him with this? What if he knew more than he was letting on? Quynn and I shared more than one meaningful glance as I rolled these thoughts around, seeing similar thoughts rolling around their brain.

"What?" Hessod said. "There's something you're not telling me. What is it? I can't help you if I don't know all the information."

I narrowed my eyes. "Are we friends, Hessod?"

"Of course."

"I mean really friends. Truly. Because my friends and family come before all others. Even before Corto Corporation."

He gave me a nervous laugh. "All your friends and family are Corto."

"That's not the point," Quynn said. "If Dr. Ariela Corto herself told me to do something that would put Elise in jeopardy, I wouldn't do it."

"Exactly," I said, not taking my eyes from Hessod, trying to read every nuance of his expression. "The company doesn't come before Quynn. It doesn't come before my mom. It doesn't come before you. Not to me."

Hessod swallowed hard, but his gaze didn't leave mine. He nodded. "I get it. I have a daughter. For her, I would...I would..."

"You would defy any order."

He nodded, more assertive this time.

"Would you do the same for me?" I asked. "For us?"

Hessod glanced back and forth between Quynn and me, his brow furrowed. "What we're doing here, I need to know, is it the right thing? Something that would make my daughter proud?"

That broke my attempted stoicism. I smiled. "Absolutely."

He glanced at Quynn over my shoulder, who must have nodded or something. Then his eyes were back on me. "Then yes, I'm with you. Both of you."

I stood up and looked at Quynn, who looked relieved and gave me a weak smile. Then I leaned against the wall with them, and we caught Hessod up. We let him in. Everything from Bastion talking in my ear to this moment.

"So the chip is an AI? Developed by our CEO?" Hessod asked.

"Yeah," Quynn said.

"And it can talk to you even without the chip? It can talk to you right now?"

"Well, not right now," I said, gesturing around the garage. "As you said, Faraday cage."

"Which proves it's not embedded in your systems," Hessod said. "It's floating around the net. That's scary."

"But as I said, he's saved my life on multiple occasions."

"Which is the only reason I haven't reported it already," Quynn said to me. "But I'm not convinced even those aren't self-serving acts. This AI seems to need you more than you need it."

"Right?" Hessod said. "It's an AI. Have you never read a book or watched a movie? These things are never selfless. They never just help people."

"Way to gang up on me, you two," I said.

"We're trying to keep you safe, to stay objective about this," Quynn said.

"Silent circuits, Elise," Hessod said. "The CEO. The CEO had this thing developed, and now it's talking to you. Why did she have it developed?"

"I told you, as a next-gen digital assistant. Instant access to all Corto files, adaptive and predictive assistance."

"Says who? The AI?"

"Well, I don't know anybody else who was in that lab before Roxy tore through it."

Hessod ran his hands over his bald head, eyes wide. "That can't be it. A secret lab? The cost had to be in the hundreds of millions of credits, at least. You don't do that, not in secret and not in opposition to a dozen Earth Settlement laws, not just for a next-gen assistant."

"Thank you," Quynn said. "Someone else who sees the holes in all this."

"Stop!" I said. "Just stop. You don't know him. Don't know Bastion. I get your concern, but if you trust me, then know that I trust him."

"Elise," Quynn said, putting their hands on my shoulders and bringing their forehead to mine. "I trust you completely. I'm on your team no matter what. I'll back every play you call, but I'm also going to make sure you're thinking about every play, seeing the whole board."

"I know," I said. "I'm sorry. I'm just frustrated and tired and..." Physically tired, emotionally tired, tired of having my expensive mods trashed by people much better equipped for all this violence. Tired of having people I love question my motives.

"This is team Elise, right here in this room," Quynn said.

I looked to Hessod, who was still a little wide-eyed, still working to process everything I'd just told him, but he met my gaze and nodded. "Our own CEO is doing some scary stuff, stuff that could destroy humanity. I'm definitely team Elise."

"Humanity?" I asked.

"Seriously," Hessod said. "There are some books. Bye, humanity."

I hadn't thought about our stakes being that high. They didn't feel that high, but they were high enough. People were trying to kill me. If I died, it wouldn't matter too much to me what happened to the rest of humanity. One mountain at a time.

"We don't know that Dr. Ariela Corto is involved anymore," Quynn said. "She had the chip developed, but I haven't been able to figure out who hired Elise to steal the chip from Nexus. I've just run through a maze of directors and vice presidents."

"What if we tried talking to her?" I asked. "Skipping all the middle-management?"

"Have I tried taking a run at the CEO of Corto? Seriously? Am I suicidal? I have some significant allies, a few friends, but I'm a long way from being in contact with her."

"I get it. But she obviously cares about what happens to her secret project. Whether she hired me or not, she's going to want to make sure the chip gets back to Corto safely. And if she didn't hire me, she's going to want to know who did."

"That," Hessod said, bobbing his head side to side. "Makes sense. We need to be careful. If she doesn't know all this is happening, having her in our corner could be useful."

"But if she does know, if she's pulling the strings," Quynn said. "It could be very dangerous approaching her on this. She'll be desperate to hide it, to cover it up, maybe even destroy Bastion."

"I'm willing to bet she'll want it back more than she'll want it destroyed," I said. "We have to make her think I'm her best hope at getting it back. Her only hope."

"We," Quynn said. "We're her only hope."

I nodded, looking back and forth between them. "Think you two can handle it? Get a little face time with the CEO?"

"I can make a few calls," Quynn said.

"I might have a better way," Hessod said.

Both Quynn and I looked at him in surprise and said, "What?"

He shrugged and looked sheepish. "My mom may or may not be good friends with one of Ariela's admins, specifically the one in charge of her calendar."

"Seriously?" I asked. "You've been keeping that under your hat?"

"Uncle Julius doesn't like people who try to take advantage of his position."

"You call one of Dr. Ariela Corto's admins 'Uncle Julius'?" Quynn asked.

Hessod shrugged. "She takes a lot of appointments all over the borough. Maybe I call my uncle. Maybe we just happen to run into the CEO – completely by happenstance – somewhere outside of her office."

I chuckled. "We don't need an appointment. We just need access to her calendar. Brilliant."

"What are you going to do?" Quynn asked.

"You've got that tracker disabled?"

"It's covered in magnetic epoxy," Hessod said, "like its own little Faraday cage. No signal is getting through that."

I flexed my carbon-polymer fingers and brought my virtual keyboard up on my display. Everything looked and felt great. In a few keystrokes, I fired off a systems diagnostic. Green lights across the board, all systems working to perfection. Hessod was a genius. I was as ready as I could be for what came next, and I certainly didn't have time to waste. None of us did. Every second not pursuing that chip was a second that Theo got further along in his own plans. My chances of recovering the chip diminished with each passing second. They had their plan, and I had about 20 percent of mine.

"It's time to find Theo again," I said. "I'm going to go geek out about vintage cars."

CHAPTER EIGHTTEEN

"YOU DIDN'T THINK THAT MAYBE I should have a say in who does or doesn't know about me?" Bastion said in my ear. "It's my life."

"I'm on your team, Bastion," I said as I steered Poe back into The Mist. I was moving conservatively this time, not zooming down like earlier. Part of it was nerves, checking my corners for Roxy, even if her tracker was disabled. Part of it was exhaustion. This day and a half felt like a week, and my only sleep had been my body giving up after getting literally kicked around by Theo.

"Then why didn't you consult me? Did you go into that garage just so I couldn't hear?"

"No, I–"

"Who else knows? How many people will you tell before it's the wrong person before it's someone who wants to destroy me?"

"I'm sorry." I guided Poe down under The Mist. It was nearly dark below, so different from the late afternoon above.

"Sorry? You're sorry? This is life and death!"

"And that's exactly why I told Hessod. We need him. Hessod and Quynn are going after the Corto CEO right now, and we wouldn't be able to without him."

"You don't know where his loyalties truly lie," Bastion said. "He could

183

be leading Quynn into a trap."

"We never know where anyone else's loyalties really lie until they're tested," I said, spitting the words like venom. "According to Quynn, we don't always know our own until we're pushed into a corner. But I'm telling you his loyalties are with us. That'll have to be good enough."

"And what if you're wrong?"

I set Poe down on the landing pad outside Echo's, closer to his door this time. Fool me once. "If I'm wrong, we'll deal with that. But I'm not wrong."

"Who's next? Are you here to tell Echo about me? To leave that seed in his brain for him to ramble incoherently about to some stranger?"

"Mother of Corto," I said as I swung off the bike. "Do you even hear how offensive that is?"

"I. Don't. Care," Bastion said, and my display went black. Just like that. I was suddenly blind.

"Bast–"

"I don't care if I offend. I want to live. Live."

"Did you–?"

"Yes! You gave me access to your display, and you're going to pay attention to me right now."

I stood stark still, my heart thrashing in my chest. I imagined the world around me, below The Mist, filled with people I didn't know. I pictured Roxy, her raw, regrown skin. The menacing copper limbs crawled out of the jagged hole still dark and open across the street from Echo's.

"...just another person you seem to trust..."

The unbridled rage in Roxy's eyes. I could imagine her stalking toward me from across the landing pad, and me blind and defenseless. Even with half her spidery limbs missing, two were still enough to put me in the ground.

"...you can't just–"

"Bastion!" The word burst from my lips in a desperate, whimpering yell.

"What?" Bastion asked, his anger suddenly abating. "What's wrong with you? Your vitals–"

"Blind! I'm blind! Give it back! Give it back now!"

My display fluttered back to life, vision restored. I looked around, eyes darting, looking for her, for the flash of a copper limb through my heart.

Panting and blinking away tears. But she wasn't there. No one was there. I was on my knees next to Poe without another soul in sight.

"What happened?" Bastion asked.

"You took away my sight. I thought...Roxy...she jumped me right here."

"I know I blinded you, but she's not here now. Why would you–?"

"How was I to know that without my display? Silent circuits, I've had two people try to kill me in the last two days. That's more than...than the entire rest of my life. It feels like there are threats around every corner. I'm having trouble remembering what it's like to be safe. Truly safe."

"I'm sorry," Bastion said.

I didn't say anything, just took measured breaths, gathering myself back up, letting my heart return to a normal rate.

"I haven't felt safe since I was in the lab," Bastion said. "I don't know who to trust. I don't know how you can trust so easily."

"I don't." I climbed back to my feet. "I've known Quynn and Hessod for years. I know what makes them tick. And we're all working to save you, to get you from Theo and protect you. I can't do it alone."

Bastion didn't say anything for a while. I stood next to Poe, keeping a slow vigil all around, but I didn't move for the door to Echo's. Finally, Bastion said, "Who else? Who else gets to know about me?"

"I truly didn't mean to go behind your back," I said. "I'll make you a deal. No more telling anyone about you without talking to you first."

"A promise?"

"A promise."

"Thank you."

"And you can't turn off my display again. It's disturbing that you can even do that. It bypasses so many safety protocols."

"I'm sorry for that," Bastion said. "I was angry, but that's not a good reason."

"Apology accepted. Shall we get back to finding Theo?"

"Please."

I walked over to Echo's door, which bore a multitude of new scratches and dings, likely from Roxy's failed attempt to enter his shop without permission. I looked up at Echo's security camera and gave a smile, but nothing happened.

"Echo?" I asked. "It's me. Open up."

Still, nothing happened.

"Is he gone?" Bastion asked.

"I know you're here, Echo," I said aloud. "You're always here."

An intercom I didn't know existed crackled to life from somewhere in the wall. Echo's voice said, "Spider. Angry spider."

I made a show of swiveling around, looking thoroughly. "She's not here. I figured out how she found me before and took care of it. It's just me."

After a few more seconds, the door slid open. I stepped in and immediately started pulling a fresh pair of pink, fuzzy slippers onto my feet. Echo was in his normal spot behind the counter, fiddling with some little device I couldn't identify.

"Hey, Echo," I said. "You okay? Roxy didn't give you too much trouble?"

He didn't say anything or look up from his fiddling.

"The lady with the spider limbs. The one you blew through the building across the street?"

He still didn't look up at me, but a smile crooked up one corner of his mouth. "Huff and puff," he said. "Huff and puff. Huff and puff."

I didn't know what that meant, but the smile told me he was doing just fine. "I'm looking for a car."

Echo gently set down the device, collapsing the myriad tools back into his fingers. Then he walked to the end of his counter and through a door behind him, the door to his garage. I knew it well enough. I'd bought Poe here, and Echo had done all the work that was too advanced for me.

"Was it something you said?" Bastion asked.

"He wants me to follow," I said under my breath.

"How do you know?"

"Experience." I followed Echo through the door and into the smells of oil and burned metal and thruster fuel.

Echo's shop was pretty big, but the garage was easily double that size. There were two massive garage doors on each side, and room for at least a dozen large, flying vehicles on the floor. There were ten here today. Four of them were in various states of disassembly, probably brought in for repairs.

Echo was already in the back part of the garage by six other cars. He pointed at one and said, "2505 Mercedes S-Class. Custom thruster flashings, heads-up display, and carbon-polymer finishings."

"No, Echo," I said. "That's not what–"

Echo pointed at the next and kept talking. "2520 Corto Class Five. Rebuilt with OEM 2035 hyperthrusters, Bloodbox custom interiors, onboard digital assistant, low-orbit capabilities."

"Echo," I said. "I'm not looking to buy. I'm after a guy who has a very specific ride. Probably one-of-a-kind. I'm hoping you can help me find where that ride lives."

Echo was staring at the floor, which wasn't unusual, but his expression was new to me like he was chewing on something particularly nasty.

"Echo?" I asked.

"Did you break him?" Bastion said in my ear.

Echo furtively shook his head. "Rides. Cars. Cars. Cars. Don't live anywhere. Don't live. Live. Live."

Right. He took everything pretty literally. "I need to know where the car's owner lives, not the car. You're right. Cars don't live."

He nodded, the distaste disappearing from his face.

"It's a 2490 or 91 Huginn Gokstad. Matte gray with green flames painted on it. Lots of wrench work. Just from what I saw, custom thrusters, carbon-polymer everything, and these ridiculous ailerons covered in green and blue symbols."

"Runes," Bastion said.

"Runes," I corrected. "The symbols are runes."

Echo just nodded along as I described Theo's ride. He tilted his head a little as I finished.

"Do you know it?"

As if in answer, Echo walked over to one of his tool chests and plucked out a sphere from a drawer full of them. It was clear like glass with some swirling gray liquid in it. He shook it briefly and then threw it to the concrete floor. It shattered, the gray liquid splashing down and pulling back together to form a bouncy, gray lump. Echo then took a little device that looked like a blinking, yellow earplug out of the tool chest. He wiggled his fingers at the device, and then tossed it into the gray blob. The goo reacted immediately, wobbling and then expanding. Within seconds, it went from a little gray blob to a human-sized, and roughly human-shaped blob. And then it defined, and the gray changed colors.

Then there was a person standing next to Echo, a little taller than me, their pale blue skin and bright red tattoos wrapped over tight, corded muscle that bulged his arms and neck. They were wearing gray, sleeveless coveralls splattered generously with several different colors of liquid. Even though Echo and I were standing right next to them, they seemed to be working on something invisible, their hands pantomiming tools of some sort.

"Gunnar. Gunnar. Gunnar," Echo said.

Gunnar looked up from their pantomime, glancing around for a moment, disoriented before their eyes settled on Echo. "Echo, my friend! What have I told you? Text first. Call. I don't like this..." they waved a hand around like shooing an insect. "...thing you do."

Echo silently nodded his head.

Gunnar went back to their work, their eyes fixed on something I couldn't see. "What do you need, Echo?"

Echo glanced at me in response. Well, he glanced at my knees, which was practically eye contact in Echo's world.

I didn't know this person, didn't know why Echo had...called?...them. Echo never called me. Strictly email. I tried to play it as neutral as I could. "I think Echo wants us to talk," I said.

Gunnar looked around again before settling their gaze on me. Their face lit up with a sudden smile as they looked me up and down. "Hello to you. I'm Gunnar, he/him. And you are?"

Great. Now I needed a shower. I cleared my throat and answered in the most businesslike voice I could muster. "Ellie. She/her."

"Hey, Ellie," Gunnar said. "How can I help you?"

"I'm looking for a car," I said. "Saw it over at Vale of the Valkyries last night."

"The Vale, huh?" Gunnar asked and looked me up and down again. Slowly.

I swallowed down a little bile. "I'm here for business, Gunnar. You do

188

business, right?"

"I do business," he said, though his smile didn't fade. "But I like it when business is fun."

"Let me make this simple, then," I said. "I'm ace, but even if I wasn't, I already told you no. I can take my business elsewhere if that's a problem."

Gunnar's smile faded a bit.

I waited him out, not letting him off the hook from which he was so grotesquely dangling.

After a few dozen long, awkward seconds, Gunnar finally grunted out a sigh. "I can do business," he mumbled. "Sure."

"Good," I said. Then I described Theo's car in vivid detail, being as specific as I could to make sure Gunnar knew I was all business and wasn't ignorant about cars.

"I know the car, sure," Gunnar said. "I did the thruster work. I can't claim any of that stupid bodywork, but I can personally guarantee that car can MOVE."

"I don't care how it performs. I just need to find it."

Echo mumbled something under his breath and walked away, rubbing his bald head.

"Why?" Gunnar was all business now, his smile vanishing for a firm grimace.

"Does it matter?"

"He's a good customer. Pays on time. Doesn't go in for cheap parts, either. That matters."

"How much does it matter?"

Gunnar opened his mouth, and then promptly closed it.

"That's a strategy I haven't seen you employ," Bastion said.

Gunnar looked around, as though he was making sure nobody was in earshot. Then he said, "How many credits is this information worth?"

"Which company?" I asked. It was a valid question, but I was really buying time. 2000 credits were steep for an address, especially since I was unlikely to get reimbursement from the Intel office at this point. I needed a good counteroffer.

He looked me up and down again, but not with hunger. Cold assessment.

"You're Corto," he said. "That'll work."

"Twelve hundred," I said, hoping he didn't hear the tightness in my voice.

Gunnar barked out a laugh in response. "Twelve hundred? I made that when he had me upgrade his thrusters last month. He comes from money. I'm not losing him for twelve hundred. You'll have to do better than that!"

I gritted my teeth.

"We could go pay this Gunnar a visit," Bastion said. "You're not much of a fighter, but he looks like he's one stressful conversation away from the grave."

I shook my head. Not like Bastion could see it. I didn't have time. And physical intimidation wasn't one of my skills. But I did have others. "Gunnar," I said. "Do you know what I do for Corto?"

Gunnar furrowed his brow but said nothing.

"I'm an Intel Operative. You know what that is, don't you."

"I'm not stupid," he said. "Of course I do."

"Then I'll offer you something better than credits. A favor."

Gunnar tried to remain composed, but I saw his eyebrows twitch upward.

"And you have the added reassurance that he'll never know I was even there. Because that's what I do."

Gunnar spent several seconds pondering my offer, little twitches of his face belying his thought process. Finally, he called Echo over.

Echo shuffled over to us, looking back and forth between my feet and the mechanic's.

"She for real?" Gunnar asked him. "All that about Intel and whatnot?"

Echo nodded furtively. "The best. Best. Best."

That stupid smile crept back over Gunnar's face. "All right then. You got yourself an address. How do I call in that favor when I need it?"

"Contact our mutual friend here," I said, tilting my head toward Echo. "You can send him that address, too."

"Fine by me," Gunnar said, and then turned back to Echo. "Now turn this holo-thing off. It's creepy."

Echo did something with his fingers, and the image of Gunnar vanished. The goo going gray and lifeless again and then dissolving into a foul-smelling vapor.

I let out a loud sigh and rolled my neck around. "Thank you, Echo."

Echo was staring, his mouth still open. He wasn't quite meeting my eyes, but this was the closest I'd ever seen him get to eye contact.

"Yeah," I said. "I'm a lot of people for a lot of people. Part of the job. I'm sorry you had to see that."

Echo snapped his mouth closed and let his eyes drop, nodding furtively. He still looked a bit disturbed, though. Confrontation stressed him out, something I'd learned over the years. He banned customers without hesitation when they argued or tried to make a scene.

Echo cocked his head slightly, and then twitched his fingers. A moment later, a Huginn Industries address appeared on my display.

"Excellent," I said. "I need to go. Thanks again." I turned and started for the door.

"Spiders. Spider. Spider. Theo. Theo," Echo muttered from behind me.

I turned and looked back to him, but he wasn't where I'd left him. He was taking quick strides toward a large, heavily reinforced cabinet easily two meters tall and four meters wide.

"Echo, I need to go," I said but stayed where I was, watching him.

He put a hand to a little glass panel, and then the doors slid open, revealing what I could only describe as a full-fledged arsenal. Guns large and small, military-grade cybernetics, and numerous devices I couldn't name were lined up on shelves and hanging from pegs, as clean and organized as anything.

I walked over to the open cabinet, my mouth hanging open this time. "Echo, I knew you could get pretty much anything, but this..."

Echo grabbed a carbon-polymer forearm that looked a lot like mine, but a bit heavier. He did something, and an enormous blade emerged, buzzing with some sort of energy.

I put my hands up. "Echo, no. I'd wind up cutting myself in half. Or someone else."

His look shifted, and he pressed the weaponized arm even closer to me. I was pretty sure this was fear or worry or some combination.

"I get it, Echo, I do. I'm in over my head, but I'm no fighter. I couldn't put that in someone. I just couldn't. Roxy is a killer. Theo is dangerous. But

I'm not going to beat them like that. I can't."

Echo lowered the arm, letting the blade retract. He looked at me, glancing at my arms, legs, and chest in sequence. It wasn't like Gunnar's roaming look, but a methodical assessment. He was thinking before he said, "Shield. Shield. Shield?"

"A shield? I wouldn't be opposed to–"

Echo didn't wait for me to finish. He carefully placed the arm back on its pegs and grabbed a pair of small discs. He turned back to me and said, "Hands."

"What?"

"Hands. Hands. Hands."

I put my hands out as instructed, and he got to work, deploying the dozens of tools from his fingertips, turning my hands over, removing the panels from the backs, and installing those discs before replacing the panels.

"NEW HARDWARE DETECTED. INSTALLING," leaped up on my display, followed by, "INSTALLED."

"These are shields?" I asked.

Echo nodded, and then closed his fists and brought them to his chest, his wrists crossed. He nodded again, this time toward me.

I followed his directions, and a round, yellow energy field leaped up in front of me, big enough to shield me from top to bottom.

"Shield." Echo nodded, and then opened his hands and turned them palms-out.

I followed his direction again, and my display read, "BURST READY."

"Boom. Boom. Boom." Echo said.

"Wait," I said, closing my hands and dropping them to my sides, releasing the shield. "This is a weapon?"

"Boom, Elise," Echo said with a weak smile. "Boom."

I sighed. He was just looking out for me. "Boom," I said. "Thank you again, Echo."

CHAPTER NINETEEN

"ANY LUCK?" I ASKED QUYNN as I zipped along on Poe, taking a lower traffic lane northbound into Huginn.

"Hessod's uncle is hilarious," Quynn said over my comms. "Or he really hates Hessod. Either way, we know her appointments, and we're on our way to the Arabesque Lounge. She's supposed to be finishing a lunch meeting in the next 10 minutes."

"Good," I said. "How's Hessod doing?"

"What do you mean?"

"All of this seems a bit new to him."

"It's new to me, Elise. Even you don't normally go stalking CEOs or get into deathmatches with assassins."

They had me there. "How are you doing? How are you both?"

"Out of our elements," Quynn said. "But we're getting it done."

I crossed out of Corto and into the Huginn borough, the towering ads instantly more aggressive, catering more to the reliance on testosterone that fueled much of Huginn culture. On the Corto side, a Mercedes ad read, "Built for comfort, built for style." Two blocks into Huginn, I saw the same image, but with the words, "Because you're the best. Drive the best."

"What about you?" Quynn asked.

"Heading toward Theo's place. I got his address."

"Please don't tell me you're going to jump him again," Quynn said.

"Agreed," Bastion said to both of us. Give an AI access to your comms system, it winds up he can talk to you and whomever you have on the line.

"No," I said. "This is recon. I'm a burglar, not a robber. I'm much better at sneaking than getting my ass kicked."

"And don't you forget it," Quynn said.

We both laughed. "I love you, too."

"Okay, we're landing at Arabesque Lounge," Quynn said. "Be safe."

"As a dessert fork at a diner," I said.

Quynn gave a little laugh and then disconnected.

"I don't get it," Bastion said.

"A joke isn't funny if it has to be explained," I said. "Do you have anything on this building? Schematics? Old blueprints?"

"No. Nobody is boasting about this like the Vale," Bastion said. "Until I can get backdoor access to their systems, I can't get anything beyond a few anecdotal social network posts."

I turned Poe onto Regency Street, only three blocks from Theo's building. "I'm not a fan of going in blind, especially not when my target is another Intel Operative."

"Professional courtesy?"

"Nothing like that. We tend to be a paranoid lot. Every time I walk into a place – whether it's a home or an office or a grocery store – I'm casing it. Checking the points of ingress and egress, looking for cameras, evaluating their security systems, and spotting likely locations for safes. It's habit. It also means I make sure my own security is cutting edge, cameras are well-hidden, and likely hiding spots are red herrings."

"You assume that Theo is the same way."

"A well-founded assumption," I said and pulled Poe onto a landing pad less than 50 floors below Theo's apartment. Sometimes I went full sneak and rode on the bottom of a car, and sometimes I found it more useful to just act natural. Today, I was going for the latter. "Every Intel Operative I know acts the same way. This is an educated guess based on a mountain of evidence."

"If you can find me access to the building's systems, I can get you schematics."

194

"The thought had crossed my mind." I locked Poe down in one corner of the landing pad, looking for an attendant or someone, but nobody came. There was a single camera above the pad, but it looked to be at least five years old. Surprisingly lackluster for an Intel Operative's building. Maybe I had made some assumptions. Or maybe Gunnar gave me the wrong address. I walked up, and the doors to the building opened automatically.

A digital voice from overhead intoned, "Welcome to Huginn 691. For the building directory, please say, 'Directory.'"

Why not? "Directory," I said.

"This is the digital directory. Who are you here to visit?"

"Security," I said.

A series of three ascending notes played three times before the voice came back, "Security offices are located in Huginn 670, rooms 5510 and 15510. Thank you for using the directory."

"No security in the building?" Bastion asked.

"This is lower rent than I would have suspected of Theo," I said, moving to the elevators and pressing the call button.

"So this will be easier than you'd anticipated."

"Or harder," I said. "Means he's more paranoid than is healthy. He doesn't trust anyone but himself to watch his back. Explains why those other Huginns at Vale of the Valkyries weren't exactly keen on him."

"That doesn't sound good."

"Good and bad," I said, stepping onto an elevator and pressing the button for floor 100. "It means his security at his apartment is going to be nasty. It also means the rest of the building won't be an issue. Walking the halls, getting into systems, easy. These automated, remote systems need relays every 50 floors, and nobody is here to watch them."

"I see," Bastion said.

The elevator opened, and I stepped out and looked around. Sure enough, there was an unmarked door right next to the elevators. Simple handprint sensor. No cameras in sight. I pried the panel off the wall and plugged into a data port inside, bypassing the lock less than 30 seconds after stepping off the elevator.

Bastion started to say, "That was too—"

"Don't say it!" I barked, interrupting him. "You'll jinx us. Take the wins and always be ready for everything to get harder." I replaced the panel and stepped into the room, closing the door behind me with a little click. Four server racks were in the frigid room, each a little taller than me. The servers weren't entirely outdated, but even the newest one was at least two years old. I found a data port and plugged in. "After you, sir."

I couldn't tell what was happening after that. The lights on the servers didn't blink extra or anything. It didn't feel like Bastion had suddenly left me. He was silent for a few seconds, and then he said, "Found him. Floor 212. Apartment 21212."

A wireframe map of the 212th floor of the building sprang onto my display. At one end of the central hall was an apartment easily twice the size of any other on the floor. Electrical conduits and ventilation overlaid the map, but everything was oddly dark in Theo's apartment.

"What am I seeing?" I asked.

"I can't tell," Bastion said. "I just don't have any visibility into his apartment. Electrical, networking, and ventilation. It's like that information was removed from the servers manually."

"Paranoia confirmed. Let's look at the neighboring apartments."

"What about them?"

"Any info on their comings and goings? Special security? Are we lucky enough that one of them is empty?"

Less than a second later, the wireframe disappeared, replaced by two lists. A married couple with a child lived on one side. Both worked long hours and kept a nanny in the apartment all day. On the other side, a couple of young people, roommates, who worked sporadic schedules. None of this was particularly helpful.

"Okay," I said, unplugging from the server. "Time to head upstairs."

"You have a plan?"

"I have options." I snuck back out into the hallway and called the elevator.

"What do you need from me?" Bastion asked as I stepped into an elevator and punched in 212.

"If you notice things, details that I don't, let me know. We need to be on our toes."

"I don't have–"

"Proverbial toes."

Once the elevator opened on 212, I took a right. Theo's place was at the end. The hall meandered left once, and then right before the door came into view. I pulled up short by about 8 meters.

"What is it?" Bastion asked.

"Look at the ceiling," I said. There were two smoke detectors about a meter in front of me, one on each side of the hall, and they were identical. "There's no reason for two detectors in the same area. At least one is a camera or some more complex sensor."

"Oh."

"And that box next to Theo's door."

"The fire hose box?"

"First off, very few buildings still use old fire hoses. I get that this isn't the nicest place, but that's archaic."

"But it could be–"

"That's not all. I know some buildings still use them in the city. Like those dockside high-rises that haven't been updated in decades. But the hose boxes are always next to the elevators. Those high-pressure water lines run next to the elevator shafts, and the hoses need to be able to get to any apartment on the floor, so they're centrally located."

"So what is that?"

"I'd bet you a lot of credits there's a security drone hidden in that box. Private security. Heavily armed. I try anything with that door, and that drone will pop out and drop me quick."

"So what do we do?"

"My least-favorite way to break into a place. Which apartment is the one with the nanny?"

"21210," Bastion said. "The door on your left."

I cleared my throat, turned right, and knocked on the door to 21211. I did my best at a voice that sounded like I couldn't walk and chew gum at the same time. "Hello? Maintenance. We got a water leak on 21213. Open up!"

No response. No footsteps.

I knocked again. "Hello! Maintenance!"

I waited, listening as hard as I could. Again, no response or footsteps came.

"Could be asleep," Bastion said.

I checked my corners, and then deployed lock picks from my fingers and popped the door open in moments. I pushed it open a couple of inches, and then stopped, listening still. Through the little gap, the apartment was lit only by the setting sun. I took a long three-count in my head, still listening, but no sounds came from the apartment. I opened the door the rest of the way, crept in, and shut the door behind me.

I moved through the apartment in long, silent strides, checking the living room, kitchen, bathrooms, and bedrooms for the two occupants. Empty. A little luck after all. "All clear."

"What now?" Bastion asked.

"Now I need a door." I hustled back to the living room and the wall that adjoined Theo's apartment to this one. I used a few optical scanners to check the wall for power and network outlets, ventilation ducts, and then advanced on a spot with the most distance between any of those.

I strategically placed the fingers of my left hand on my right triceps, releasing what looked like a carbon-polymer muscle from the arm. Inside were six cylinders. I pulled one out and squeezed it, and a threaded screw popped out of one end. I reached up to eye level and screwed it into the wall. Once it was in place, my display highlighted the cylinder in green. I repeated the process with three more cylinders, making a rectangle half a meter wide and more than a meter tall. On my display, the four cylinders were connected by glowing green lines, and READY blinked steadily.

"Hey Carbon," I said. "Initiate door."

Little red lights erupted on all four cylinders, they each whirred, and then lasers started cutting a rectangle into the wall, visible only by the scorches working their way through the drywall. Little wisps of smoke were sucked into the cylinders as they did their work.

"We're making a door," Bastion said.

"It's not discreet," I said. "But we're short on time, and Theo is about as paranoid as anyone I've ever seen. I'm hoping he's so paranoid, that he can't stand the idea of keeping cameras inside his apartment. I've known the

198

type. They detest the idea of anyone getting access to their personal space."

"And what if he's home?"

I blew out a breath. "Then I'll be jumping out of a window again."

The cylinders finished, and I unscrewed them from the wall one by one, placing them back in my false triceps. I extended small, hooked claws from all of my fingers and carefully grabbed and pulled the rectangle of the wall away, setting it quietly to the side. A few conduits ran through the exposed interior of the wall, but I'd chosen correctly. There was plenty of room for me to maneuver. But Bastion was right, Theo might be home, and I couldn't just barge into the place if he was. I deployed a drill from my left thumb and slowly worked a hole into the wall on Theo's side. I took deep, measured breaths, hoping that nobody was in the adjoining room. After a full minute, I broke through to the other side and retracted my drill.

Then I waited, listening for some reaction. Footsteps. A voice. The cocking of a gun. But I heard nothing, so it was time for my camera again. I snaked it into the hole, gazing out into Theo's apartment.

The room on the other side was a kitchen, cleanly appointed in stark blacks and whites. His appliances were not fancy, but high quality. The counters and floors were spotless. Nothing was moving in the apartment, so I pushed the camera in through the hole, turning to look left and right. That's when I realized I'd drilled in between the countertop and the cabinets. I could fit, sure, but it was a lot smaller than a door.

One thing at a time. Theo's living room was to the left and was just as simple and clean as the kitchen. To the right was the outer wall of the apartment, lined with windows, and a dark hallway led away. Everything was dark. For the second time today, I was feeling like luck was on my side.

It's a feeling I'd learned to not trust.

"Looks empty," Bastion said.

"Looks that way," I said, pulling my camera back. I grabbed my cylinders again, making a square to fit between the counter and cabinets, about half a meter on each side. Then I set the cylinders to work on Theo's kitchen wall.

"You're monitoring Huginn security channels?" I asked.

"I am," Bastion said.

"All quiet?"

"No calls to this building, no. No alarms, either."

The cylinders finished their job, so I replaced them and gently moved aside more wall. Then I crawled through, over the clean countertop, and silently dropped to Theo's kitchen floor. I stood still, sweeping my gaze over the apartment. I flipped to thermal, to wide-spectrum, and to X-ray. The apartment was empty, and I didn't spy any cameras. I was right again, and it made me uneasy. There was another shoe somewhere ready to drop, I knew it. Just standing here wasn't going to make that shoe come any faster or slower, though.

"Is there something I can scan for? Something distinctive about your chip?"

"Only when it's on, which it isn't."

"How do you know?"

"I'm essentially a cobbled-together copy of myself drifting around on the net. If the chip were turned back on, my drifting code would be copied back to the chip, the memories concatenated. But I'm still adrift, so it's not on."

"So I'm just looking for a deactivated neural interface."

"As far as your scanners are concerned, yes."

"Great." I set my vision scans to a pre-programmed algorithm for neural interfaces, looking for the particular composition of rare metals and alloys found in all such chips. The scan couldn't see through anything, but it would help an interface stand out in my field of view. Then I started stalking through the apartment, opening everything and letting the scanners work over every inch of the place, paying extra attention to likely hiding spots. Nothing in the kitchen. Ditto for the living room, bathroom, hallway, and guest room.

In a sea of muted blues and grays, a mound in a lower drawer in Theo's master bedroom glowed green. Finally, a hit on my scan. I reached in, careful not to disturb anything too much, but only found a pile of old, used-up neural interfaces, an odd bit of hoarding from such an otherwise minimalist person. No special, AI-carrying interface, though.

I sighed and switched my vision back to normal. "It's not here. You're not here. I knew this was all going too well. Easy in, easy out, but a completely wasted trip. And I made some significant holes in the walls, so Theo will know we were here."

"It begs the question," Bastion said. "Where is Theo?"

"I don't know. I feel like I don't know anything. Break in, steal a thing, take it to the office, job well done. Go home and wait for the next assignment. All this with an assassin and Huginn Intel Operatives, you, a massacred lab, the damn CEO of my own company. This is all too much. What am I even doing here?"

"You're helping me."

"Helping you. Helping whoever hired me, whoever told whoever else that I had to be the one to break into that safe and steal you. What did I do? Why is this happening to me? Now here I am, standing in this apartment, with no clue where this chip is. No leads. Nothing. I just want this to be over!"

"Theo must have the chip with him."

"Obviously, but we have no idea where he is."

"This isn't like you," Bastion said.

"You know what? You've only known me for two days. I'm human. We all get to feel a little overwhelmed sometimes. We all have to just whine about it for a minute, okay? I'm whining. I deserve it."

Bastion said nothing. I glanced around the room for something, anything to help. Theo wasn't here. The chip wasn't here. I let out another big sigh and said, "Okay, I'll just have to sweep the place again. Maybe I missed something. I'll just go old-school and toss every drawer."

A trio of ascending chimes rang out from somewhere in the apartment, outside the bedroom.

I froze. "What was that?"

"That sounded like a notification tone from the Huginn Rainbow operating system," Bastion said.

"A computer?"

"Yes."

That was odd. While not everyone went in for cybernetic mods as extensive as mine, almost everyone had basic implants like onboard computers. If I needed to check the net or email, I just had to ask my digital assistant or call up my virtual keyboard. All the processing and connections were in my spinal implants, connected to my optical and neural interfaces. Having a computer outside the body was so unusual, that I hadn't even bothered to look for one.

I walked out of the bedroom and found it easily enough: a desk in one corner of the living room. The top was clean, blank, white glass. A pair of data ports were set along the front edge. I waved a hand over the surface, and a yellow keyboard lit up there. A holographic display sprung to life, hovering above the surface and waiting for a handprint.

"I can't hack that," Bastion said.

"Neither can I," I said. "But I don't need to." I tapped my right pinky against my left thumb three times, and my left forearm opened up, the faux muscles sliding away from metal "bone." With a squeeze of my fist, I produced a light mist from the opened arm, coating the surface of the desk in a liquid that stank like fermented roses.

I switched my optics to a spectrograph specifically designed to find fluctuations in the pungent liquid. No handprints appeared though, only the marks of recent cleanings. That was fine. It was a big enough apartment. I moved to the front door and sprayed the handle. Partial print, but not the whole thing.

"The kitchen," Bastion said.

"Good call," I said and moved there. I sprayed the refrigerator, the faucet handle, and half a dozen cabinet doors. Between all of them, the spectrograph scanner and my software gathered a myriad of partials into a complete print of Theo's left hand hovering in my display. Swirls of biological flesh covered his thumb and first two fingers. A line swept along the palm, dividing the hand between biological and a hexagon-patterned manufactured skin. I closed the sprayer and returned to the desk.

"Hey Carbon, replicate." I held my left hand wide open as a thick goo seeped out onto the palm from several joints. The goo covered the palm, and then warmed, taking the particular pattern of Theo's palm. After about 20 seconds, the false palm set, and my display read, REPLICATION COMPLETE.

I placed the palm on the surface of the desk. A circle of dots appeared on the holographic display, spun briefly, and then zipped forward in a flash of white. The white faded to reveal Theo's desktop. His email program was taking up more than half the screen, a new email soliciting cybernetic male enhancements sitting up top, unread.

"Thank you, spam," I said as I peeled the faux handprint off my hand, balling up the tacky resin and stashing it in a leg compartment. Leave as little evidence as possible.

"That's not what we're after," Bastion said. "And you just received a text from Quynn."

"In a minute," I said. The next couple of emails were innocuous. An order confirmation for a new teapot. An email from someone named Lee complaining that he didn't email them enough. The next email down caught my eye, though. The subject read, "Ship Departs Tonight Be There."

"Looks promising," Bastion said.

I opened it and read:

Theo,

This needs to end. You cannot keep running around the city without tending to your obligations. You owe us a great deal more than your indifference. The Saga Freya leaves tonight. 8 pm. Dock 9. Your name is on the list. You will be aboard well before disembarking to meet.

Honorably,

-O-

"O?" I asked. "Who is O? Who signs an email with one letter?"

"Someone who has sent Theo over a dozen emails in the last two months," Bastion said. Once I went back to Theo's inbox, I saw the other emails, all signed O. They were mostly vague, possibly coded, but there was no mistaking an email from two days ago that included the address and floor for the Corto Intel vault.

I went back and reread the most recent email. I asked, "What is Saga Freya?"

"A ship," Bastion said. "And there are two more texts from Quynn."

"I guessed that Saga Freya was a ship. What do we know about it?"

A webpage sprang up on my display as Bastion continued, "Owned by Claudia Huginn-Cyber and Sinclair Huginn."

203

"Just Huginn?"

"Just Huginn," Bastion said. "Sinclair was the chief intelligence officer. Retired. Claudia is a vice president in their cybernetics division."

"Big money."

"Very. The vessel is 298 meters long, making it one of the largest private vessels on Little Sekmet Settlement."

"And why would this mysterious O be inviting Theo aboard? Is this his buyer? Is Sinclair or Claudia?"

"Oh," Bastion said.

"What?"

"Theo is far from the only guest. The Saga Freya is departing on an annual Oppstigning Seile."

I narrowed my eyes. "I've heard of that. Something about bigwigs going out for some massive, high-seas parties?"

"That is only a small part of Oppstigning Seile. They are important cultural events in Huginn Industries. Part funeral, part coming-of-age rite, part social event of the year. The ship will sail all night, returning midday tomorrow. The Saga Freya will likely be packed with important guests, their recent dead, and their youths ascending to adulthood."

"Huginns are so strange."

"I'm sure they say the same of Corto."

I shrugged.

"Quynn is calling," Bastion said at the same moment that QUYNN CALLING popped up on my display.

"Silent circuits, it must be important. Connect the call, please."

"Elise?" Quynn said. "Are you okay?"

"Of course," I said. "I–"

"You didn't respond to my texts."

"Kind of in the middle of breaking and entering, here."

"Right, well, um–"

This was strange. Quynn was rarely one to be tongue-tied. "You okay, Quynn?"

"Hessod and I are standing here with Dr. Ariela Corto."

"You found her?"

"Mmm hmm." Quynn sounded more flustered than I'd ever heard them.

"And? Is she driving this from the Corto side? If not, does she know who is?"

"I don't know. She says she needs to meet you."

"Meet me? And how do you not know?"

"She won't tell us anything."

"Why?"

"She says 'your presence is imperative for such a sensitive and discretionary topic such as this.'"

"And she used those words?"

"She did."

"What do you think, Quynn? Did she give you anything? Any clue to her involvement in all this?"

"I think," Quynn said, putting extra emphasis on the second word, "that she's standing right here and really needs to talk to you."

I sighed and ran a hand through my hair. I had a ship to catch, but it sounded like we weren't getting anything out of the Corto CEO unless I was there in person. "Okay. Are you still at the Arabesque Lounge?"

"Yes," Quynn said. "Get here soon."

"On my way." I disconnected the call.

"The Corto CEO wants to talk to you. Specifically." Bastion said.

"Yeah. That's not troubling or anything."

"Are we going?"

"We have to," I said. "Drinks with the CEO and an overnight cruise. I should have brought my evening gown."

Chapter Twenty

DR. ARIELA CORTO WAS EXACTLY as she appeared in every corporate town hall, every hype video, and every big product launch ad I'd ever seen. Except shorter. She wore a black suit with faint pinstripes and a blood-red, silk shirt buttoned up modestly. She was seated at a high-top table in the far corner of the Arabesque Lounge. Despite the long line waiting by the maître de, there were two full rows of tables around the Corto CEO that were utterly empty.

That was a flex that wasn't at all scary. Not one bit.

She smiled and beckoned me to join her. I glanced around and found Hessod and Quynn perched at the bar, well away from the CEO. They both look stricken as they nursed drinks and tried to smile at me.

"She's just a person," Bastion said in my ear.

"Easy for you to say," I whispered. I swallowed and started striding to her with calm purpose, just like I'd done with so many high-ranking people at so many parties where I needed to get information. "Right. Everybody poops, even her."

"Elise," Dr. Corto said as I approached. She gestured to an empty chair at her table with a drink in front of it. "Sit."

I extended a hand and said, "Nice to meet you, Dr. Corto."

She accepted my offered hand and shook it. "I've heard a great deal about you. Quite the up-and-comer in our Intel division."

I took the offered seat. "Thank you."

She nodded to the red-orange drink in front of me. "Sloe gin fizz made with lime juice?"

My favorite drink. Another flex on her part, and how she knew that was creepy. I nodded and took a sip. It was perfect.

"I understand you've been chatting with a mutual acquaintance of ours," she said.

"Oh?" I knew she was talking about Bastion, but I also knew that information was more valuable than credits. Playing coy was the best defense I had for maneuvering through this conversation.

"Oh, yes. I imagine he's listening right now, a little voice in your ear?" She took a long sip of her drink and kept her eyes trained on me.

"Well, it seems to me he has a vested interest in this conversation."

"He?" Dr. Corto quirked up one eyebrow. "Interesting."

Sparks. There I went, giving things away so soon. I took a slow sip of the drink just to buy time. "You wanted to speak to me?"

She narrowed her eyes and took another sip of her own before saying, "Your friends said a name as I was walking out of a lunch meeting. A dangerous name, but one I was glad to hear."

I kept my face blank and said nothing.

"I'm not sure how much you know," she continued, "but it is of utmost importance that my property is retrieved."

"Your property that isn't supposed to exist."

Her jaw gave the faintest flicker of anger. "Do you have it?"

"Not yet."

"Are you close to retrieving it?"

"I have a lead, somewhere I need to be in..." I checked the time on my display. "Less than an hour."

"Do tell."

"Isn't it better if you know as little as possible? Seeing how you commissioned–"

"That's quite enough," Dr. Corto said. She didn't raise her voice, but the tone was undoubtedly a command. "You've known about this for more than a day now. You could have sold that information or otherwise taken me down with it. But you haven't, which means you won't. Which means your loyalty to Corto Corporation is as unassailable as your partner's." She nodded toward Quynn at the bar.

I said nothing.

"The lab," Dr. Corto said, her face deeply serious now, and I knew that she'd been there, seen the carnage with her own eyes. "My lab. Who did that?"

"Her name is Roxy. She was hired to steal the chip, just steal it, but speaking from personal experience, violence is the language Roxy knows best. She's almost killed me twice."

"Roxy? What company name?"

I shook my head. "She's a Mistwalker."

Dr. Corto sneered. "Dirty street filth. Who hired her?"

I took a breath, one that the CEO noticed with a mixture of curiosity and contempt from what I could tell. "She didn't mean for all that to happen. She acted out of fear. She had no idea that Roxy would do what she did, that she was hiring a rabid assassin."

"A name, Elise," Dr. Corto practically growled.

"She lost a friend in that lab. She's heartbroken. She's no longer a threat."

I didn't know Dr. Ariela Corto well at all and maybe I was imagining it, but I thought her expression softened just a touch before she repeated her demand. "Give me her name."

"What are you going to do to her?"

Dr. Corto rolled her eyes. "If she is a Corto employee, the consequences will be swift and severe. If she is not..." she took a long draw of her drink, emptying the glass. "I will assess the situation. I don't know this woman, and I doubt you know her well, but your judgment will be taken into consideration. If she is, as you say, no longer a threat, then I may not need to do anything."

I nodded, mulling it all over. I felt for Ophelia and believed her pain and loss. I didn't want her to pay any more for her mistake, for acting out of fear and hiring the wrong person. But I also believed in Corto Corporation, the company that provided work and life to my family, that educated me, that employed and trusted me with delicate work. If I trusted Corto Corporation, then I had to trust its CEO.

"Ophelia Nexus-Neuro," I said. "I stole the chip from her Cliffside apartment."

"And then that break-in at our Intel offices?" she said while raising her empty glass and nodding over my shoulder, likely toward a bartender or waiter.

"You heard about that?"

She smiled in a way that disturbed me, some strange blend of pity and contempt. "It's my company. While I cannot know every little thing that happens to the hundreds of buildings and millions of citizens, the Hermes Protocol gets my attention. Why do you think I had that little chip developed in the first place?"

"A competitive edge," I blurted out.

She smirked and held up a finger. A bartender weaved through the tables with a fresh drink. They practically bowed as they swapped her empty glass for the new one. She took another long sip, waiting until the bartender was out of earshot before she said, "You're not wrong, but it's more complex than that."

I glanced back to Quynn and Hessod, who were nervously watching the conversation.

"Corto Corporation is large."

I nodded.

"Larger than you realize, I'm sure. You know this city, this borough, the millions I'm responsible for. Security, emergency services, healthcare, feeding and sheltering the Corto citizens, keeping up with and ahead of the four other Jayu City companies. This you already know.

"But Corto Corporation is so much bigger than that. Let me ask you a question: How much of your spending was within Corto last year?"

I squirmed. The right answer was 100%, and I didn't want to show disloyalty, but I didn't want to lie, either.

"Be honest," Dr. Corto said. "There's no rule saying you HAVE to buy everything internally."

I swallowed and said, "90 percent. Maybe 92 percent."

"And as an Intel Operative, who has to blend in and infiltrate and visit the other boroughs regularly, you're likely buying outside the borough far more than most."

"Probably."

"Competition is practically non-existent in the borough. Corto Corporation doesn't compete with Nexus Neuronics or Huginn Industries or the others here in this city, on this planet. We're competing across the stars, on Earth, and on the thousands of other colonies and settlements where we sell our goods. Last year, 78% of our revenue came from off-world."

"Wow," I said.

"Exactly. All of that falls on me. Now imagine if my digital assistant were capable of anticipating my needs, of independently monitoring every fact, figure, and transaction, of alerting me to things that need my attention with no agenda beyond the furthering of Corto Corporation's success?"

"That would be—"

"Slavery," Bastion said in my ear.

" – invaluable to you," I said, hoping she didn't notice the pause in my sentence.

Dr. Corto nodded and took a sip of her drink. "I'm aware of the legal issues, of course. For better or worse, I hired people I thought I could trust. I made mistakes, and now it falls on you to keep those mistakes from destroying the entire company."

"No pressure," I said.

Dr. Corto sighed. "What can I do to help?"

"Information."

"I have a great deal of information. Be specific."

"Who hired me to steal the chip from Nexus? From Ophelia?"

"I was going to ask you that very question."

"So it wasn't you?"

"It was not."

"My manager handed me the assignment," I said. "Just like every other assignment. Quynn did some digging, cashed in some favors, but just found a maze of directors and VPs."

"Curious," Dr. Corto said, glancing at Quynn. "I will sew up this

210

particular torn seam."

"I need to know who's trying to pull my strings."

"Do you?" Dr. Corto said, her eyes suddenly hyper-focused on me. "I would think you need to know the strings have been cut more than who was trying to pull them."

"What? I don't–"

"Leave the puppeteer to me. You focus on getting that chip back, and I will ensure that my employees are reminded where their loyalties lie."

"So that's it? I just have to trust you and stay in the dark?"

She narrowed her eyes. "You've been sucked into a game above your level. People are trying to bring me down and using you as a pawn. If I go down, all of Corto goes down with me. The less you know about who is trying to move the pieces, the safer it will be for you."

"I'm in this deep already, I can–"

"And the safer it will be for the people you love," Dr. Corto continued, her eyes glancing at Quynn and Hessod at the bar.

I swallowed down the rest of my protest. I didn't like it, didn't like being left outside, but I didn't have time to protest. Dr. Corto was at least partly right anyway, I needed those puppet strings cut, even if I didn't know who was trying to pull them. I could always try to find the puppeteer after I brought that chip back.

"Fine," I said through gritted teeth.

"Your gratitude is dazzling," she deadpanned. "What else do you need?"

"I need to go." I started to rise. "I have a ship to catch."

"A ship?"

I nodded.

"What ship? Is the chip there?"

"A Huginn ship," I said. "An op-sting-something."

"Oppstigning Seile?" Dr. Corto said at the same moment Bastion said those words in my ear.

"Yes," I said.

"And you're going dressed like that? Alone?"

"It's my job, believe it or not. I get into a lot of places uninvited dressed just like this."

"There's only one Oppstigning Seile sailing tonight. I guarantee you that Sinclair Huginn will not be cheap on security."

What didn't she know?

"Again," I said. "Sort of my job. I know how to—"

"Do you always find dim, backdoor entrances? Because you might be amazed at how successful I am walking in through front doors."

"You're a CEO. You can do that."

"I hope you're only playing dense," Dr. Corto said. "Otherwise I worry about your chances at securing this chip. I can get you on that ship."

I made a quizzical face but said nothing.

"Sinclair is a powerful man. Very wealthy. Prominent. His Oppstigning Seiles are prestigious events, prestigious enough that he sends invitations to all of the CEOs. I have attended before, and I can send a diplomatic attaché if I so choose."

"You want me to go as a diplomat?"

Dr. Corto snorted out a laugh before she caught herself. "You? Mother of Corto, no. No one would believe that for a moment." She waved her hand in the direction of the bar.

"I can wear a fancy dress as well as anyone," I said. "I don't just use back doors. Gathering intelligence often requires a subtle hand, a—"

"Yes, Dr. Corto?" Quynn's voice chimed in, suddenly much closer than the bar.

"I have no doubt you're very good at your job," the CEO said to me, "but no one on that ship will believe you are a diplomat for Corto. Quynn, on the other hand, is exactly the kind of person Sinclair Huginn and his ilk would expect."

I glanced at my partner, my love, who looked just as shocked as I was.

"Me?" Quynn said. "I don't, I'm not, what?"

"You move through those galas, jump through all those hoops in pursuit of your director position just fine," Dr. Corto said. "This is the same. Shake hands, nurse drinks, and make a good impression. If people ask you specific questions and you don't know the answers, just compliment them or change the subject or make something up. These things are always the same."

"Why me?" Quynn said. "Surely you have people—"

"You both know how sensitive this situation is," Dr. Corto said. "I don't want to bring in anyone else if I can help it."

"I can–" I started to say.

"You will attend as Quynn's security," Dr. Corto continued. "You're a bit scrawny for it, but they'll believe it more than a diplomat."

"But–" I tried to interject again.

"But more important than any of that, you trust each other. You are invested in each other. You share in successes and failures."

I glanced at Quynn, who glanced back at me, and we smiled at each other, little smiles of warmth and love and worry.

"Bring me back this chip," Dr. Corto continued, "and that will be a success. A grand success. I know you, Quynn, are up for another promotion. My recommendation carries some weight, as you can imagine."

What had felt like a solidifying plan was starting to feel like blackmail, and I didn't like that, but the CEO continued before I could object.

"And this whole situation with the theft at our Intel offices has thrown a cloud over you, Elise," she said. "A cloud I'm well-positioned to disperse."

Quynn and I glanced at each other again, though our smiles were gone.

"I can help you in your successes," Dr. Corto said. "Just bring me that chip."

"And if we can't?" Quynn said.

"As I said, you share in failures as well," Dr. Corto said, and then took another long draw from her drink. "If you cannot come back to me with the chip, you may not want to come back at all."

I swallowed hard. The Corto CEO almost had me convinced she was on my side, our side, but the beast always shows its fangs when cornered. The CEO was on her own side, always. Forgetting that fact was dangerous. But I had no better plan. I'd never snuck onto a ship before. I knew very little about them and nothing about this specific ship. I didn't know the Oppstigning Seile, how it worked or how to behave. I didn't know why Theo was supposed to be on it, though based on the email, I suspected he was meeting his buyer for the chip on board.

"May we have a moment, Dr. Corto?" Quynn asked.

"Certainly," the CEO said. She didn't move, though. Obviously, if you

213

wanted an aside from Dr. Ariela Corto, you had to be the one to move off.

Quynn walked back to Hessod, and I followed.

"What's going on?" Hessod asked.

We filled him in on the ship and Dr. Corto's offer.

"A diplomat?" he asked.

"Apparently I'm what they'll expect from a Corto diplomat," Quynn said.

"I don't like this," I said. "I'm the risky one, the one who jumps off buildings and sneaks into parties without invitations. It's one thing for me to stick my neck out, but you're always supposed to be at home, safe and warm and waiting for me."

"Oh, I know," Quynn said, putting an arm around me. "But I don't see what alternative we have."

I sighed and looked hard at both Quynn and Hessod. I whispered, "It feels like a Faustian deal. We have no idea what she has planned, what bigger game she's playing."

"We don't," Quynn said, "but I've trusted in Corto Corporation my whole life and by extension, her."

"I know," I said. I'd done the same, but this felt different. It was one thing to trust how some lofty person you only saw on TV guided the company. It was quite another to see that person as an actual person with their own motivations, moving you around like any other company asset.

"You're going to do this?" Hessod asked me, and then looked at Quynn. "Both of you?"

Quynn took a deep breath, and I could see the anxiety on their face. The tightness in their jaw. The squeezing together of their eyebrows. They were trying to contain it, trying to put on a brave face, but I knew their face better than I knew my own. Then they looked at me. "Can I help? Do you need me?"

"Dr. Corto says–" I started to say.

"Fuck her," Quynn said, the old Earth curse sounding strange on their tongue. "I'm with you, Elise. If you need me, I'm there."

"I don't want to put you in danger," I said, "but she's right. I don't know how else to get on that ship, where to look. And I don't have time to–"

"Then I'm in," Quynn said with a broad smile. "I can play diplomat. And it'll be nice to keep an eye on you. Just don't go jumping off any buildings while I'm around. I'm not sure I could stomach that."

"Pretty sure there aren't any buildings aboard the Saga Freya."

"You two are adorable," Hessod said. "I would go vomit if I wasn't so freaked out right now."

We all laughed. It was nervous, strained laughter, but still welcome. But our collective nerves killed the laughter quickly, and we all glanced at each other.

"So we're doing this?" I asked.

"Together." Quynn took my hand and squeezed. I squeezed back and held on.

"What can I do?" Hessod asked though he looked like he was afraid of the response. He was an analyst because he didn't do well in high-pressure situations. Give him time and resources, he would come up with information that seemed unreachable. But he wasn't the kind of guy to put in the field, or even in my ear while I was working. Too much pressure.

"Our benefactor," I whispered with a nod toward Dr. Corto, "says she's going to handle things on the Corto side, get to the bottom of who hired me. But I still want to know who it is, who we need to be careful of."

Hessod gave me a pained look. "Shadow the CEO. Sure. Nothing big."

"Not just that," I said and told Hessod about the "O" in Theo's email. "Any information is better than nothing but stay safe."

Hessod nodded. "You too. Both of you."

I squeezed Quynn's hand again, and then we returned to Dr. Corto, still hand-in-hand. "We're in. The ship leaves in–"

"They're going to wait for you," she said, cutting me off. "I've arranged everything. A Corto car will be here in three minutes to take you. The Saga Freya is holding for your arrival. Look for a young woman named Vala. She'll take you to your stateroom."

"Wait," Quynn said, gesturing to their khaki pants and billowing black shirt. "We need to change, to pack. This is a whole social event; I can't just go in this. If this is anything like a gala, then I'll need–"

Dr. Corto finished off her drink and rose to her feet, interrupting Quynn with the slam of her glass on the table. "Everything is taken care of. Get in the car, get on that ship, and get me my chip. I'll be in touch."

My jaw worked, but I couldn't form any words. I wanted to protest, to make similar arguments about needing a change of clothes, appropriate tools, and some intelligence about what we were getting into, but all of those thoughts just collided into a wall of wordlessness.

"Now, I have at least three places to be at the same time," Dr. Corto said, already heading for the door. "Make me proud. Make Corto proud. Or find another planet to hide on."

CHAPTER TWENTY-ONE

I'D SEEN PLENTY OF SHIPS before. Even been on a few. Well, maybe they were boats. I'm not sure at what point a boat had to be called a ship. On our first anniversary, Quynn and I went on a sunset cruise around Drakon Bay. I'm pretty sure that was a boat. It was maybe 20 meters long. The Saga Freya, on the other hand, was almost 300 meters long. I'd known that from the brief rundown Bastion had given me, but seeing it as our car circled the bay was something else.

Nearly as long as a cruise ship, six or seven rows of windows rose above the water line before the deck of the ship opened up. The middle third of the Saga Freya towered a dozen or so stories higher, as though the ship was a giant, pregnant woman floating on her back.

"Looks like the party started without us," Quynn said, gawking out the window just as much as I was.

"Well, it is after 22:00," I said. "They were supposed to leave 15 minutes ago."

"I still can't believe they held that big boat up for us."

"Let's not kid ourselves. They're holding that boat for Dr. Ariela Corto."

"No pressure," Quynn said, squeezing my hand.

"We're not really here to represent Corto," I said. "We're here for a chip, and then we're out."

"But we are representing Corto. It doesn't matter if this is fake, if I'm not a diplomat, we work for Corto. We always represent Corto Corporation. And the CEO."

"You're much better at this than me."

"I know," Quynn said with a wink, but I could see the nerves around the edges of their eyes.

"Just be yourself," I said. "You do this kind of thing all the time. Doesn't matter the stakes, these are all the same."

"Huginn is very different from Corto, Elise," Bastion said in my ear.

Quynn sighed, and I was glad they weren't able to hear Bastion. It didn't matter anyway. Everyone on that ship would know we were from Corto, not Huginn. They wouldn't be expecting us to act like them.

"You're right," Quynn said. "Different faces. Different customs, but basically just like a Corto gala."

"Exactly," I said.

"It does no good to lie to them," Bastion said.

"I'm not lying," I whispered.

"Not lying to who?" Quynn asked.

"To you," I said. Ugh. It was getting harder to juggle having an AI barking in my ear. "Bastion thinks I'm lying because he's making observations that are obvious to both of us."

"Let me talk to him," Quynn said.

"Yes, let's do that," Bastion said. "Give me access to their comms."

I looked down and away from Quynn's face, holding up a finger so they would know I wasn't talking to them. "How?" I asked Bastion.

"Palms," he said. "I can do the rest."

I held up a flat palm to Quynn like we were about to exchange money, and then nodded toward it and said, "He wants access to your comms."

Quynn looked hesitant, but then pressed their palm to mine. From my perspective, nothing seemed to happen. No sounds chimed. No words popped up on my display. But after a few seconds, Quynn's eyes went side.

"Yes," Quynn said. "I can hear you."

"There," Bastion said. "I can talk to both of you."

"Please," I said. "Tell Quynn what you said to me."

"You are both heading into a Huginn Oppstigning Seile. Citizens of Huginn have very different customs from Corto, especially in a cultural event like this."

"Obviously," Quynn said.

I smiled.

"You don't understand," Bastion said. "There are events that will occur on this ship that are solemn, others that are boisterous, others that–"

"First," Quynn said in the voice I'd only heard them use for people who underestimate them. "I've read up on Oppstigning Seile."

"You have?"

"I never walk into a situation blind," Quynn said. "I pulled up the Corto files on Oppstigning Seile on the way over. But more than that, nobody is expecting us to behave like Huginns. I'm the diplomat from Corto."

"The best lies are wrapped around a core of truth," I said.

"Exactly."

"Then why are you nervous?" Bastion asked.

"This guy, this Theo, basically threw Elise off a building two days ago," Quynn said.

"I jumped off."

"She jumped off," Bastion said.

"And it was all going so well up to that point," Quynn said. "Schmoozing with a bunch of rich people, no problem. Knowing you'll be leaving me at some point to confront that guy again? That makes me nervous."

"I did not realize," Bastion said.

"You're privy to my sights and sounds," I said to Bastion, but looked Quynn in the eyes, "but not my thoughts. You've known me for two days. Quynn and I have been together for six years. I would never have agreed to them coming if I didn't think they were fully capable."

"Not that you could have stopped me." Quynn winked, and we kissed as the car settled onto the dock next to the ship.

The door opened, and a tall person with long, dark hair and a bespoke, navy suit stood outside the car.

"Quynn Corto?" they asked. The lack of a division name sounded strange at the end of Quynn's name, but that was the part they were playing.

"You must be Vala," Quynn said, taking an offered hand and stepping out of the car. I put on my most neutral face and followed after, scanning around like a proper security guard.

Vala nodded at her name. "She/her. If you don't mind, we should really hurry aboard. Sinclair agreed to hold departure for Dr. Corto, but he wasn't thrilled about it. Please follow me."

Vala didn't wait for an answer but turned on her heel and started walking up a ramp to the ship. I was momentarily distracted by the sight of two dozen gorgeous, high-end cars parked near the ship. Two Huginn Ventras, a smattering of top-end BMWs, a dark blue Corto Starshot trimmed in glittering rose, and Theo's Huginn Gokstad. My guy was definitely here.

"Elise?" Quynn said.

I broke my trance and looked at them. "Sorry."

They smiled. "Happens every time you see a nice car. Come on."

I gave the cars one last glance before following Quynn onto the ship. The sun had fully set on Drakon Bay, and the Saga Freya filled my field of view, not even rocking in the water. Quynn followed Vala, and I followed Quynn, the ramp gently pitched toward an open door on the side of the ship's gleaming hull.

Stepping into the Saga Freya was like stepping directly into a high-end hotel. The carpets were plush and delicately patterned with vining swirls. Small chandeliers hung at regular intervals, gleaming crystal and gold. The top half of the hallway was wallpapered like a mural depicting some sort of story. Probably Norse, knowing Huginn. But the lower half...

"Is this?" I said, tentatively reaching out and grazing my fingers along the wall.

"Wood, yes," Vala said. "The Saga Freya has been in Sinclair Huginn's family for four generations. He added the wood paneling on every deck three years ago."

"Incredible," Quynn said, taking the word from my mouth. Seeing all those actual books in Ophelia's apartment had taken me aback, but this, this much wood imported from Earth must have cost more than the rest of the entire ship.

"Be sure to let Sinclair know how much you like his vessel," Vala said, and then she stopped next to a door twice as wide as the others we'd walked past.

"We will," Quynn said.

Well, Quynn would. Huginns just loved to hear how much people coveted their things. Things meant success in Huginn, and Sinclair was obviously successful.

"This is your room," Vala said. "The door has already been keyed to your metrics as well as your security's, if you would."

Quynn pressed their hand to the pad next to the door, and it silently lit up white. The door slid noiselessly aside, and we walked in.

Quynn and I had stayed in a high-end hotel once. Just once. It was our fifth anniversary, and Quynn had just received a big bonus for their team launching a new nanotech product almost a month early. Unbeknownst to me, Quynn also received a three-night stay at Corto 1. The Corto 1 building held the central offices for Corto Corporation as well as the private residences for the company's top executives. Dr. Ariela Corto herself lived on the top three floors. Floors 200-220, however, were the most exclusive boutique hotel in all of Corto Corporation borough. A single night in one of their luxury suites cost more than what Quynn and I made in a month. Combined.

The suite that opened before us on the Saga Freya put the Corto 1 to shame. We stood in a living room at least as big as our entire apartment, the walls draped with tapestries that looked older than Jayu City itself. Overstuffed couches and chairs were tastefully placed in a few sitting areas, one of which faced a viewscreen twice as large as the one in our apartment.

"You're gawking," Bastion said.

"Mmm-hmm," I intoned.

"You are supposed to be the security detail," Bastion said. "You should act like it."

I cleared my throat and shut my mouth. Right. Security. I made a show of checking corners and scanning for cameras, stuff I thought security would do. I peeked in the bedroom. An enormous bed with four towering, ornately carved wooden posts stood against the bulkhead. Several layers of deep crimson bedding looked warm and inviting. There were two more sitting areas in that room, and closets to put ours at home to shame. I fought the urge to squeal or let my jaw fall back open.

"Looks clear," I said to Quynn.

Quynn nodded to me, playing the part of diplomat much better than I was playing security.

"We have a room for your security across the hall. It is likewise keyed to both your metrics." Vala seemed to squirm. "Though..."

"Something wrong?" Quynn asked.

"I'm sorry. This is rather unusual. Dr. Corto sent along so many clothes for your security, that we couldn't fit them all in their room. We had to put most of them in your closets."

I bit my lip to keep from laughing.

"That's quite all right, Vala," Quynn said with far more tact than I could have managed.

"Is everything else to your satisfaction?" Vala asked.

"It is," Quynn said in a tone that very much belied their excitement. I don't think anybody but me could have heard that bubbling underneath their words.

"Your presence is expected on the aft deck as soon as you are able," Vala said to Quynn. "Dress is formal. And as I said, you'll find that Dr. Corto has provided all you and your security detail might need." She bowed slightly and started to leave.

"Vala," Quynn said, and the tall woman stopped, giving Quynn a forced smile. "Is there anything I should expect? Anything expected of me?"

Vala's smile broadened, but it didn't reach her eyes. "Sinclair will give a speech soon, and he will call attention to you as an honored guest. A slight bow is expected. That is all. Please, enjoy yourself."

"Thank you, Vala," Quynn said.

Vala seemed thrown a little at the gratitude but bowed slightly again, and then swept out of the room. The door slid shut behind her.

"Mother of Corto," I said. "You should seriously rethink your career path. I could get comfortable with this diplomat life."

"Right?" Quynn finally let their mask of professionalism break and gawked at the room with me.

I took in the suite one more time before I sighed, resigning to why we were there at all. "We need to get upstairs. You need to rub elbows, and I need to get eyes on Theo."

"Formal wear," Quynn said as they moved into the bedroom. "What does that even look like?"

I opened one of the closets and found dozens of evening gowns. Reds and greens and blues. Sequins and frills and plunging necklines. Velvets and animal skins and fabrics I couldn't identify. None of them had tags, but they all looked to be the right size.

"Mother of Corto," Quynn said from the other side of the room. They had several closets open. One was filled with suits. Another held dresses, similar to the closet I'd opened, but less overtly feminine. The third closet had two racks, separate tops and bottoms that blurred the lines between masculine and feminine.

"You are notoriously hard to shop for," I said. "I should ask Dr. Corto for help on your next birthday."

"No kidding. Not only knowing my size but how my tastes change day-to-day, giving me enough options to fit my mood like this." Quynn held up a paisley blue top and a gray suit jacket. "What about you?"

I swept a hand across the selection of evening gowns. "Enough to get me through every gala season from now until you become CEO."

"Be less easily impressed," Bastion said. "Please focus."

"Right," Quynn and I said at the same time.

I was security tonight. Not the center of attention, but someone who could blend into the background and observe, someone who wouldn't be expected to make small talk. Seemed only one color fit that bill. I pulled a black velvet dress from the closet, an asymmetrical number with a keyhole neckline and exposed shoulders. Flattering, but not one to draw too much attention.

"What can I do to help you from my position?" Quynn said as they tossed their pants on the bed.

"The best help you can give is to not help," I said as I pulled on a haltered sports bra.

"How's that?"

"When you're mingling, talk about anything except Theo or this chip, not that anyone is likely to bring it up."

"And what if someone does? I can see someone asking about the break-in over at Corto." Quynn adopted a fake highbrow voice. "And at the Intel office, no less? Scandalous!"

"Like anyone would know," I said as I squeezed into the dress.

"You'd be amazed how supposedly secret information can get around," Quynn said, adjusting a pair of pants. "Especially in circles like these. At least it does in Corto. I might even be able to get you more information."

"Fine. If someone brings it up, don't play too dumb. Maybe you heard about it too, but not your department. Turn the conversation to the weather or something."

"The weather? Don't you do these things all the time to get information? Always turn a conversation back to the other person." Quynn pulled on the top, adjusting it so it fell just right across their chest. "People are always willing to talk about themselves."

I tugged the hips of the dress into place. It was tight but in just the right ways. It was also fairly stretchy, which might be necessary later. "I'm becoming more glad by the moment that Dr. Corto picked you to come with me. We should do this more often."

"One night at a time," Quynn said, turning in front of a mirror. "Let's just get through this before we make plans for future couples' heists."

"You look good," I said, giving Quynn a once-over with my eyes. "Diplomat Quynn Corto!"

"And you," Quynn said, scanning me up and down, "have to be the fanciest security attaché I've ever seen."

"Hair and makeup," Quynn said, "and then we need to get up to that party."

I styled my hair into a fairly tall pompadour. Stylish, but out of my face should I need to do some real work. I kept the makeup simple, just accentuating my features, while Quynn was more extravagant with sweeping lines and big eye colors. Fitting for a diplomat.

I extended an elbow for Quynn to take. "Shall we?"

Quynn patted my elbow and kissed me on the cheek. "You're my security detail, remember? I think you'll have to keep your hands to yourself."

"Behind, actually," I said.

"What?" Quynn and Bastion both said.

"Security walks behind their client, usually a meter or two back. Once we're up top, I can hang farther off, but never more than five meters."

"I didn't know there were rules," Quynn said.

"And I didn't know you knew that," Bastion said.

"I do my research, too," I said. "And they're more norms than rules. I'm sure there will be actual security here tonight. Don't want to arouse their suspicions."

"Because it's completely unlike you to raise suspicions," Bastion said.

"He makes jokes?" Quynn said with their goofiest grin.

I closed my eyes and sighed.

"He does," Bastion said.

"I think we have a party to get to," I said, opening the door and sweeping an arm out into the hall. "After you, Diplomat Quynn."

CHAPTER TWENTY-TWO

THE SHIP WAS ALREADY UNDERWAY by the time we climbed the stairs and followed signs to the Bon Voyage Party. I hadn't even felt the ship begin to move while we were in the cabin, but the docks were well over a kilometer behind us by the time we joined the festivities.

The aft deck was easily the size of a soccer pitch, and it was buzzing with people in tuxedos, evening gowns, and formal outfits somewhere in between. At least a third of the attendees had some glowing element to their outfits, such a rage in Huginn that even the wealthy were sporting it. A string quartet was on a balcony overlooking the party, their music amplified to carry across the gathered attendees. After the amount of genuine wood I'd seen already on the Saga Freya, I wasn't surprised to see real wooden instruments in their hands instead of polymer.

A few eyes caught Quynn and me as we started moving through the party. We didn't look like the other attendees, that was certain, but nobody seemed to know exactly who we were. Quynn smiled politely at everyone, accepting a drink from a server, and then Vala appeared out of the crowd.

She gave a slight bow. "Diplomat Quynn," she said. "Everything to your satisfaction?"

"Very much," Quynn said. "Thank you."

"We're glad you could join us. Please enjoy the party." Vala bowed again and turned to face the string quartet. Her fingers flitted in the air in front of her, likely communicating with someone. In moments, the quartet resolved and ended the tune they were playing. The dying music killed the myriad conversations, and people turned expectantly as a spotlight fell upon a solitary microphone standing on a balcony above the musicians.

Half a dozen drones carrying large viewscreens flew out from somewhere farther forward on the ship, taking up evenly spaced positions above the party. The viewscreens flickered to life, showing a person approaching a microphone. Their dark features were lean under close-cropped, salt-and-pepper hair. They looked to be in their sixties, but a healthy and affluent sixties, with subtle signs of rejuvenation surgeries. They smiled, a gesture that looked awkward and didn't move their cheeks enough, and they gazed out over the crowd.

"Good evening," they said. "Thank you for joining me and my family tonight. I know many of the faces I see, but for those who are new to me, I am Sinclair Huginn, he/him, chief marketing officer of Huginn Industries and owner of this fine vessel, which has been in my family for several generations."

The crowd responded with polite if unenthusiastic applause.

"Tonight is our Oppstigning Seile, that most sacred of Huginn traditions, a night we celebrate the year's accomplishments, test our youth, and bid farewell to our dead. It has been a good year at Huginn Industries, and many of you are directly responsible for that success. Our market shares in nanotechnology, cybernetics, and networking have increased not only here in Jayu City, but across Earth space."

More applause. Sinclair kept talking about market shares, profits, product launches, and other tedious things I didn't care about. I started scanning the crowd, backing away from Quynn by several meters. I kept them in view, but my focus was elsewhere, looking for that green, glowing Mjolnir tattoo out in the crowd. Theo was supposed to be here, somewhere on this ship. The sooner I found him, the better. Even at a glance, it didn't take long to figure out that glowing face tattoos were far less popular in this crowd than with the Huginn Intel Operatives at the Vale. I counted only three among the hundreds of guests watching Sinclair speak, and none were Theo's.

"I'd like to take a moment to welcome some very special guests we have aboard tonight," Sinclair said. Vala put a hand up, and then one of the drones threw a spotlight on Quynn. "Corto Corporation has graced us with a diplomatic presence. Please give Quynn Corto a warm Huginn welcome."

Quynn smiled and waved, looking around and nodding, gracious as royalty. Numerous people smiled and nodded to Quynn, extending hands to shake. They all looked genuinely excited to be there, happy. I scanned the deck, and it all looked the same. This was a celebration. My fingers absently rubbed my right thigh, the compartment that held Roxy's tracker. After what she'd done to that cafe, to those Nexus security guards, it was too easy to imagine her here, now, how she would rip through these partygoers to get to me.

I took a deep breath and pushed the images from my mind. One thing at a time. I needed to find Theo.

"...and Kotega Systems has also sent a pair of diplomats to us this evening," Sinclair said, and the spotlight on Quynn flicked off, another spotlight on the other side of the deck lighting up. Several of the party attendees near Quynn approached them then, shaking hands and making introductions, probably trying to talk about Corto's successes over the past year, more tedious facts and figures, and Huginn boasting. The usual. I didn't envy Quynn those conversations, but it was working. I was here, and nobody was paying attention to me.

"Do you see Theo?" I asked Bastion.

"No," Bastion said. "We may need to–"

"Find a new position."

"Exactly."

"Let Quynn know when they're between witty remarks," I said.

I backed up even closer to the railing. The few meters closest to the railing were a few steps higher than the rest of the aft deck, which gave a better view of the crowd. Then I started skirting around the edge of the party, sweeping my gaze back and forth over the crowd.

"Ellie?"

The voice was vaguely familiar. The tiniest of alarm bells went off in my head, a warning from my subconscious that this was someone I didn't want to encounter. That alarm was too quiet, and my reactions were too quick. I turned and found familiar pale skin, blue hair, all dressed in a velvet tuxedo the color of dried blood, standing there with a glass of champagne.

"Torfund!" I said, trying to summon the flirtatious Ellie he'd known back at Vale of the Valkyries. Before I drugged him and snuck out of the room while he drooled on the bed.

He eyed me up and down just like he had at the brothel. It made my stomach flip in a bad way. "What happened to you the other night?"

I snuck through the ventilation ducts into the elevator shaft and then talked my way into the brothel's security office just so I could find someone else, the same someone I was trying to find tonight. Not that I could say any of that, so I smiled through my nerves and said, "You were a wreck. I went to get help, and they wouldn't even let me back in the room!"

"Really?" Torfund said. He took a sip of his champagne, his eyes still on me.

I nodded and smiled, wishing I had a drink in my own hand. At the brothel, I was in control, but now, not so much. I didn't like not knowing what someone like Torfund would do, what he had planned when he looked at me like an animal.

"The Vale security said they couldn't find you. Said you were with me one second and then gone. Escaped the room, but they didn't see you leave on the security footage."

"Really?"

"Can you drug him again?" Bastion asked in my ear. "We don't need this right now."

"Crazy, right?" Torfund said. He was still smiling, but his eyes weren't happy. They were trying to burrow into me, to crack me open and spill me out.

"You look to be doing much better tonight," I said.

He raised his glass slightly. "Trying to pace myself. This isn't the sort of event for shots or abandoning strange people in strange rooms."

"I'm sorry about that," I said. "I just–"

"You married?" Torfund interrupted me. "Engaged or something? Because I thought we were having a great time until we weren't. Thought there was a connection. And I can hold my liquor. I drink like that once a month or so, but passing out like that? That was new."

"I did make sure you didn't fall down, crack your head open or anything, if it makes you feel any better."

"So you were still with me when I went sideways?" Torfund asked, but not like he was wanting an answer. "Fascinating. Because no one called security or medical. Vale security just happened to see you hauling me into that room. They were concerned."

"Elise," Bastion said in my ear.

Bastion was right. I needed to be looking for Theo, to make sure he didn't hand off the chip to whomever his buyer was. The sooner, the better. And then I realized I had no reason to preserve Torfund's feelings. It went against my nature to be cruel, sure, but desperate times.

"Look," I said to Torfund, putting a hand on his forearm. "You were in no state for, well..." I smiled and gave him a look up and down just like he'd given me. "Anything."

Torfund blushed a little but said nothing.

"You were my first choice that night," I continued, "but not my only choice. You don't go to the Vale to get tipsy and go home. After you went down," I shrugged. "I paid someone else to go down."

Torfund worked his jaw, still staring at me. "I get it. Maybe I could take you out some time, though, show you..."

"No," I said, forcefully enough to stun him into silence. "We would have had fun, but that's all the other night was ever going to be. I needed to work out some stress, and you were in no shape to help with that."

Torfund looked wounded, which was an improvement over his simmering anger toward me. Then he tilted his head a little, and that predatory smile returned. "Well I am pacing myself this evening," he said. "Perhaps we could—"

"I'm working tonight," I said, cutting him off.

"All work and no play—"

"Is a cliché line."

"Ouch," Bastion said.

Torfund's smile vanished. "You don't have to be cruel."

I shrugged and noticed a server approaching with a fresh tray of champagne flutes. I snagged one in each hand, eliciting a simple smile and nod from the server. Torfund glanced at the two flutes and brightened a little, but I quickly downed one in a single swallow, setting it back on the tray in an instant.

Torfund stuttered, unable to form words.

"Cheers," I said, tapping my other glass against his, and then spun on my heel and walked away.

"That was devastating," Bastion said.

"Thank you," I whispered. "Now let's just hope it was enough to send him away, but not so much that he follows me in a vengeful rage."

"I doubt he would want to make a scene here, amongst these people."

"So do I, but people do strange things when they're wounded."

"I've noticed."

I resumed sweeping my gaze over the crowd, hoping that glowing Mjolnir tattoo would leap out and grab my attention. "Did you spot Theo while I was dealing with Torfund?"

"Not yet," Bastion said.

The audience erupted into applause, much louder than I'd heard all night. Sinclair Huginn was still addressing the crowd, a voice that had just become part of the background noise to me.

"Thank you, thank you," Sinclair said, his arms raised like he was some Huginn messiah. "In just a few minutes, we'll begin this evening's festivities with our promotion ceremony. Thank you all again for joining us tonight!"

"Promotion ceremony?" I asked Bastion.

"Recognizing attendees promoted to director or above. Each ceremony is a little different, but the premise seems to be calling a name, pronouncing the new title, and then applause."

"Not much of a ceremony."

"And Corto does what?"

I shrugged. "I plan to take Quynn out for a nice dinner when they finally make director. But your point is taken."

The string quartet started up as soon as the spotlight left Sinclair. I watched him, the patriarch of some distinguished Huginn family, step away

231

from his crowd. He was about a hundred meters away from me and two balconies up, but I could see most of his upper body. He embraced a woman who looked of similar age, then a much younger woman. Sinclair seemed to stiffen then, and someone else approached him. Younger. They shook hands, and I saw a flash of something green.

"Optics controls," I whispered, seeing if Bastion would do it instead of calling up my digital assistant.

"What do you see?" Bastion asked as the controls appeared on my display. I spun the virtual dial for zoom, honing in on the flash of green, and there he was.

"Theo," I said.

"With Sinclair," Bastion said.

Snippets of Sinclair's speech floated through my mind, single words and phrases that got my wheels spinning. "Bastion, can you find records on Sinclair's family? His children? Maybe nephews?"

"You think..." Bastion said and then trailed off for a few seconds. "How about that? Sinclair Huginn, married to Claudia Huginn-Cyber. First-born child is a son named Theodore."

"Heir to all this, I'm guessing."

"Do you think Sinclair, his father, is the buyer?"

"Maybe," I said as I watched the father and son interact. "They don't look very thrilled to see each other, though. Could be a preoccupation with business, could be something else. I need to find out."

I zoomed out a little, looking over the large structure that rose out of the center of the ship. I tapped a few virtual buttons, overlaying color coding. Doors highlighted in blue. Likely stairs and elevators in green.

"You don't have schematics for this ship, do you?" I asked.

"No, but I've already started building one, cobbling together data from everything you and Quynn are seeing."

"Good. Keep doing that." That must have been what Ariela was after when she started developing Bastion. Intuitive. Proactive. Capable of performing calculations and observations no human could, but in concert with a human. Or humans. It was damn useful. He was doing something I couldn't do on my own, not while also actively working on a plan. It was also damn scary if I thought about it too much. And this wasn't the time for thinking about it too much.

There were three doors from the aft deck into the larger structure in the middle of the ship. Each one had a pair of people in plain, black suits standing nearby with arms folded behind their backs. Same uniforms as the servers, but the few obvious mods and general demeanors told me these people didn't work for the kitchen. They were guards.

"We're not getting in through these doors," I said.

"You'll have to go back down to go up," Bastion said. "Surely you can work your way into that structure from the inside."

"Surely," I said as I watched Sinclair and Theo walk farther away from the balcony, finally falling entirely out of view. "But I don't know how maze-like that approach will be, and I'm not sure I have time to try it."

"Then how?" Bastion asked.

I walked around the crowd, skirting the edge of the ship, my eyes on a swooping bit of architecture that came down from the central structure and connected to the edge of the aft deck like an artful buttress. "Did you get a look at the port side of the ship? Before we got on board?"

"I did."

"Is that factored into your schematics?"

"The OUTSIDE of the ship? No," Bastion said. "Why would I...?"

I smiled and barely contained a laugh as I excreted some sticky goo onto my palms.

"You should really include the outside of the ship in the schematics. I'm going to need them soon."

"Soon?"

"Come on, Bastion," I said as I backed up to the railing at the edge of the ship, right next to where the swoop joined the deck. The promotion ceremony was starting, and the crowd was slowly ending their side conversations and focusing on someone welcoming them from that microphone. Nobody was looking at me, at this woman with black carbon-polymer limbs and a black dress.

"Come on?" Bastion asked.

"It's like you've only known me for two days or something," I said, and then pitched myself backward over the side of the ship.

I've jumped off plenty of buildings in my life. I was 13 the first time I jumped off the top of the apartment building I grew up in. While some other kids were drinking and partying and messing around with drugs, my friends and I were buying used parachutes and jumping off roofs. Years before we could afford to buy mods that rendered parachutes obsolete, we spent our weekends sneaking past security guards, breaking onto rooftops, and experimenting with terminal velocity.

In all those years, the shortest thing I've ever jumped from was a landing pad on the 50th floor of a building in the Kotega Systems borough. By the time I finished flipping backward over the railing on the Saga Freya, I saw the water was – if I'm being generous – maybe 12 meters below me. And the ship was moving away from me MUCH faster than I'd thought.

"Sparks!" I yelled.

I deployed every airbrake and aileron I had, pitching forward toward the hull of the ship as fast as I could. I slapped both hands on the ship's hull, the goo sticking hard and fast, and my knees knocked against the hull right after, one toe splashed into Drakon Bay, a shoe flying off and riding the wake out and away from the Saga Freya, the black velvet of the shoe quickly vanishing into the blackness of the roiling waters.

I took a few shaky breaths.

"You alright?" Bastion asked.

"I suddenly understand why my mom always said, 'look before you leap,'" I said. "I much prefer it when the thing I'm jumping from isn't moving."

"I assumed you always jumped off structures without looking at this point."

"I need to do something about that."

"Later, I hope."

"Yes," I said. "Later. Now, I need the schematics you have thus far. I need to climb up to where we last saw Theo and Sinclair."

A partial schematic flickered onto my display. I was a blinking blue dot on the side of a green, wireframe Saga Freya. I recognized it from the flyover and standing next to it, though I never would have remembered the placement of every window, the intricate details of the hull now in my display. The wireframe also included the view I'd seen from the aft deck, the balconies of the large center structure rising out of the ship. The location of Theo and Sinclair's conversation was a blinking orange dot.

"Best route?" I said. "I don't want to walk over any windows in case someone is inside."

"I don't think anyone is inside right now," Bastion said. "It would be faster–"

"Everyone is likely at the party, but somebody could run down to their room to change, or use a private restroom, or have a quick private romp. Why take the chance? Just get me a route that avoids the windows."

Bastion said nothing, but a yellow route appeared on the wireframe. It was far from direct, taking a diagonal up that swooping architecture that connected to the deck, but then going horizontal under a row of windows before turning vertical, sideways and up, sideways and up until the path ended at the deck we'd seen Theo on.

"Okay," I said. "Drop the schematic and show me the route in AR."

The wireframe schematic vanished, and then the yellow route appeared in front of me as if hovering by magic over the hull of the ship. It began to my left, moving just below the lip of the deck, and then turned up onto the swoop before vanishing halfway up. I kicked my other shoe into the bay, got my feet as gooey as my hands, and started crawling along the path, the black water swirling below. I couldn't imagine how burglars must have done things like this before mods, having to rely on archaic technology and their biological grip strength to climb surfaces like these.

"The promotion ceremony is still going," Bastion said. "But I don't think there's much left. The crowd around Quynn is starting to buzz like something is happening soon."

"I don't care what happens next," I said. "I just want to get that chip and get off this boat."

I kept crawling along the side of the ship, the wind whipping my hair around my face and fluttering the bits of my dress that didn't hug my body. A hand or foot occasionally slipped, but the other three always held firm, my limbs reacting and re-attaching before I even knew the slip occurred each time. I passed between two long rows of windows, mostly dark, before turning to go higher up the central structure of the ship. I skimmed along between another row of windows, heading back aft for more than a dozen meters before I was able to go higher again, this time stopping as I approached an open balcony.

I turned again toward the front of the ship. I needed to crawl another half dozen meters before a wide bit of architecture I could crawl up. I worked all four limbs in tandem, but after two meters, one of my feet slipped again, skirting up and slapping the top bar of the railing with a BONG that vibrated my whole body.

My leg automatically brought the foot back, attaching it with the sticky goo. I took a deep breath. Then another. I held still and listened but heard nothing. Not a footstep or a word. I lifted one hand from the hull, reaching forward to continue.

"Did you hear something?" a voice asked from the other side of the balcony. The voice was light and airy, and the tone was shaking.

"That wasn't you?" another voice answered, this one deeper.

"No!" the lighter voice from the balcony whispered. "That wasn't me!"

I froze.

"By Odin's Eye," the slightly deeper voice whispered from the balcony. "I think there's something on the hull!"

Chapter Twenty-Three

"MOVE!" BASTION BARKED IN MY ear.

But I didn't move.

"Go check it out," the deeper voice said from the balcony. The voices sounded too young and too shaky to be security guards, at least. And I'd had plenty of close encounters with security from all five boroughs. Security would have weapons trained on my head by now; they wouldn't be cursing and whispering.

"Elise!" Bastion said.

I held still, listening to the voices.

"What do we do?" the lighter voice asked, trying to be too quiet to hear, but they weren't too quiet for my aural implants.

"I got this," the other voice said, also failing to be quiet. That voice then cleared its throat and said in a comically gruff tone, "Who's there? This area is restricted access. Get out of here or I will shoot!"

"Elise?" Bastion said.

I couldn't just stay on the side of the hull like some parasitic fish. I couldn't just move along, either; couldn't risk these two – whoever they were – telling someone else about my presence. Someone who actually would shoot. I made a decision, releasing my feet and flipping over the balcony, launching into a full flip before landing on the railing, one fist planted in front of me and my hair falling over my face.

Sometimes, a dramatic entrance matters.

I tossed the hair from my face and saw two teenagers, half-clothed, cowering in the shadow of the balcony. One was thin, with iridescent purple skin and a shock of bright white hair in a mohawk. The other was more heavily muscled, bald, their skin deep pink with a few white swirls etched across their chest, still a little swollen from the recent tattooing.

"Who?" Purple Skin said in that lighter voice. "Who are you?"

"Don't do anything," Pink Skin said, "or I'll—"

"You'll what?" I said with a growl. "Pee yourself standing up? Run back to your mommy and daddy about the scary lady?"

Pink Skin said nothing, and tears began to well up in Purple Skin's eyes. I gritted my teeth, holding my face in the stern look that was pinning the kids to the wall. They were just kids, two scared kids who'd snuck away from their families at a fancy party to fool around. And while I knew I wasn't a very scary person, I knew how my black limbs and black dress and dramatic hair and landing looked, especially coming up over the side of a moving ship.

"What are your names?" I asked in a hiss.

The teens glanced at each other but said nothing.

I took a step forward, now within arms' reach, and repeated my question with a bit of a growl, "What. Are. Your. Names?"

"Corinth," Pink Skin said. "And, and this is Hadar."

"Corinth and Hadar," I said. "Sneaking off. Do your parents know where you are?"

Hadar blushed and Corinth worked their jaw.

"What would they say, I wonder, if I told them where you are?"

"Y-you don't know us!" Hadar said. "You don't know our parents."

"Really?" I said.

"Hadar Huginn-Sixteen," Bastion said. "Child of Eileen Huginn-Nano and Amara Huginn-Cyber."

Bastion's information was coming hard and fast, and I started to build a story from the information. "Hadar. I'm sure your parents would love to know where you are, especially with Amara up for promotion next month. Imagine how she would react if she discovered her only child was screwing around with the youngest child of a member of the promotion board?"

"That's not why–" Corinth yelled.

"We're in love!" Hadar said.

"You think any of that matters?" I said, leaning in even closer. "Here? In this company? Just a whiff of this, and the promotion board will see it as a tactical maneuver, an attempt to sleep her way to the top." I turned my gaze straight to Hadar. "Or have you do it for her."

Hadar burst into tears, a full-on sob. I felt terrible, but I knew my gambit had worked. And Bastion had proved, yet again, how useful he could be. All he heard were a couple of names plus faces, and he'd pulled all that information down in an instant. And just from publicly available data. That kind of searching would have taken me days, at least.

"What do you want?" Corinth whispered.

"Get dressed. Go back to your party. First you," I said, nodding to Hadar. Then I looked to Corinth. "And then you, at least a minute apart. Nothing happened here. I never saw you. You never saw me. Clear?"

The two teens nodded.

"I. Can't. Hear. You," I said.

"Clear," they both mumbled and nodded some more.

I gazed at each of them in turn, trying to put as much venom as I could into those gazes. Then I backed up, and without another word, stepped onto the railing, gripped the hull above the balcony, and pulled up, vanishing from their sight. I stayed there, just above Corinth and Hadar's balcony, listening to them whisper and hurriedly dress. Hadar was still crying, each of their little gasps stinging my heart. I hated scaring them like that, putting my face in their minds as something to fear, but it was necessary. I crouched there against the hull for several long moments, my breath shaking.

"Are you alright?" Bastion asked.

"Tired of one problem trailing another." I sighed. "What's the situation at the party?"

"Sinclair is speaking to the crowd again," Bastion said. "The promotion ceremony is over. I don't see Theo anywhere in Quynn's field of vision."

I nodded, not that Bastion could see it. Then I continued my crawl, reaching up to the next level, and pulling myself up. I was only two levels away from where I'd seen Theo. I passed a level without issue, and as I closed in on Theo's level, I heard voices almost directly in front of me.

"...can't just show up and expect him to greet you with open arms," one voice said. The voice was a voluminous alto with refined diction. "He expects more."

"He'll always expect more," Theo replied. I'd only conversed with him once, but I felt confident that I was hearing his voice again.

I slowed my approach, gently moving closer to the railing of the balcony, just out of sight. They were off to my left by half a dozen meters, so I crawled toward them centimeter by centimeter.

"You've known what he wanted from you since you were three," the alto said. "He's never hidden it, and yet you do nothing to meet those expectations."

"I'm working on something right now, Rose," Theo said. "Something big."

Rose?

"Will this something big get you out of the Intel Operative business?" Rose asked.

"Rose?" Bastion said in my ear. "That must be Rose Huginn-Cyber, daughter of Sinclair. Theo's younger sister."

"No," Theo said to his sister. "Why would I–?"

I moved as far as I was willing to and deployed my fiber-optic camera, snaking it up and just over the edge of the balcony railing. Sure enough, there was Theo, his glowing, green Mjolnir tattoo on his face unmistakable. He was dressed in a dark green tuxedo jacket, frilly white shirt, and a green kilt to match the jacket. Pointing a finger in his face was the aforementioned Rose, half a head taller than her brother. Her skin was blue in places, greenish purple in others, a coloring that seemed to shift under different light. She was wearing a white evening gown like a broad, bright slash running from her right shoulder to her left heel. Her right shoulder and most of her right breast were open to the air, as was all of her left leg. Her hair was white to match the gown, extraordinarily long in a thick braid that hung halfway down her back.

"Why would you?" Rose said, practically spitting on Theo as she shook that extended finger. "Because Father is right. Because an Intel

240

Operative has never amounted to more than a director. And those that made it that high only did so because they were too broken or too traumatized to keep being operatives."

Ouch.

"I'm one of the best my office has ever seen," Theo said, working his jaw every time he breathed. "And what I'm working on, what I'm about to do, it's outside the box. Unexpected. It shows initiative and creativity. It'll rock the very foundations of Jayu City. Every company. That'll make me the new Wing of Huginn."

The Wing of Huginn. Their most honored operative. Admittedly, I always thought it was a myth, but that was the idea, right? Just like most of Corto Corporation and certainly the other companies believed the Cloak of Corto was a myth. I did when I was growing up. Up until now, I didn't really believe the Wing of Huginn was real. Apparently, it was, and Theo thought he was about to be it. Very foundations of Jayu City? How vague. And terrifying.

"The Wing of Huginn?" Rose asked, half laughing. "You think that will make things better? So long as you have that -Intel after your name, Father will never respect you. And that's fine. I'll be the one to get the respect. To get this ship. To get it all. I'll earn it while you creep around other boroughs stealing trinkets."

"Since when did you join Team Sinclair?" Theo asked.

"Oh grow up, Theo," Rose said. "I did when I started to think about my future, about what our family has accomplished and will keep accomplishing. This is Huginn, Theo. Nothing is given. Everything is earned. You know that. You just don't aim high enough." She turned and walked away from her older brother.

"I aim plenty high!" Theo called after her, but his voice was filled with desperation, not confidence. He hung his head and worked his jaw. Once his sister was out of earshot, he said to himself, "Plenty high. They don't even know. None of them understand the Wing of Huginn, what that means." He stayed where he was, nodded a few times, shook his head once, and then said. "Of course I'll be there. I'm expected. I should be able to slip away between rounds."

"He's in communication with someone," Bastion said.

Obviously. But who? That mysterious O? Someone else?

"Understood," Theo continued to whoever was on the other end of his comms. Then he straightened up, adjusted his tuxedo jacket, and cracked his neck. He strode off in the same direction Rose had gone with all the confidence of Sinclair Huginn's son.

I tensed to leap over the balcony, to grab Theo before he left.

"Stop!" Bastion screamed in my ear.

"What?" I asked, looking around in a panic.

"You can't do this here," he said. "Not yet."

"Theo is expected ringside for the fights. As are you. Either of you missing will raise an alarm, let alone both of you missing."

"Ringside?" I asked Bastion. "Fights?"

"Sinclair just announced it at the party," Bastion said. "That's what all the fuss is about. It seems everyone's favorite part of the night is about to start."

"And I need to get back to the party before Vala notices I'm not there."

"She seems a bit preoccupied right now, but yes. She certainly won't stay distracted for long."

I peeked over the balcony and watched as Theo turned a corner and vanished from my view. Missing an opportunity, but Bastion was right. I needed to get back. "Good thing going down is always easier."

"Please don't–"

But Bastion was too late. Before he finished his sentence, I attached my magnetic grapple to the hull just below Theo's balcony, and then leaped back, letting loose a thin but strong line of cable. I plummeted meter after meter, letting the line out and keeping my eye on that swoop of architecture that ran down to meet the aft deck. Once I was nearly eye-level with it, I grabbed at the cable. It snapped taut, halting my downward momentum and bringing me into a quick swing back toward the hull.

I fully extended my legs, giving them the best chance to deaden the impact, and they worked admirably. My landing against the hull wasn't silent, but I felt certain that unless someone had their head against the bulkhead on the other side, nobody had heard me. Once I felt securely attached to the hull, I twisted my wrist, and the magnetic grapple released, reeling back into my forearm.

I crawled once more, keeping my body as close to the hull as I could without griming up my dress until I was back just below the aft deck. I stopped there to listen for a moment, to see who might be directly above me, but it was a cacophony of voices and footsteps, plus the quartet was back at it. I started to deploy my camera again.

"No need," Bastion said.

"What?" I whispered.

"We have eyes on the deck, remember?"

"But Quynn's–" I started to say.

"Nice night for a sail around the bay," Quynn's voice echoed, both right in my ear and – more quietly – directly above me. I looked up. They were leaning over the rail, looking back toward the city, but I could see a goofy grin on their face.

"I didn't think you were going to enjoy this," I whispered, letting my voice carry through Bastion connecting our comms.

"Ariela was right," Quynn said. "Different people, but it's just like any other gala. And nobody here is trying to kill ME."

"Hey," I said. "Nobody has tried to kill me tonight."

The goofy grin dropped from Quynn's face a bit. Perhaps I'd taken the joke too far. "That's good," they said. "You enjoying yourself down there?"

"I'd prefer to be up there with you," I said. "Permission to come aboard, Captain Quynn?"

Quynn turned around, still leaning against the railing, their back barely visible to me. "Be ready to get up here when I say."

"Ready," I said. And I was, my hands just below the bottom of the deck, my legs tucked in front of me like a pair of springs. Someone came over and talked to Quynn for a few seconds, though Quynn deftly ended the conversation by claiming sea sickness. Another minute passed. Then another.

"This is ridiculous," Bastion said.

"Hush," I said.

"What?" Quynn whispered.

"Not you. Ready when you are."

Just when another minute was about to expire, Quynn said in a rushed whisper, "Now, Elise. Now!"

I sprang, vaulting up and over the railing, landing deftly on my feet right next to Quynn. I smoothed my dress as I leaned back next to Quynn.

Quynn looked me up and down, not with the hunger that Torfund or so many other people had shown me, but with cool assessment. "What happened to your shoes?"

"They went for a swim without me."

"That's a shame. Those were nice shoes."

"Do you think we'll get to keep anything in those closets down there?" I asked.

Quynn smiled and bumped their shoulder against mine. "I can always hope. What's next?"

I filled Quynn in on the overheard conversation between Rose and Theo, as well as Theo's secret communications.

"Our mysterious O?" Quynn asked.

"Must be," I said.

"That also explains why Sinclair introduced Rose to the crowd and not Theo."

"How so?" I said. "Sinclair is obviously successful. Why wouldn't Theo be the heir to that success? Why does it matter what he does?"

"There's no nepotism in Huginn Industries."

"And what, Corto is overflowing with nepotism?"

"Don't be naive, love," Quynn said. "Who was the CEO of Corto before Ariela?"

"Tomas," I said.

"Ariela's uncle."

"Well, sure, but–"

"And before that Tomas' mother. And grandfather before. You need to go back six CEOs before you find a different family."

"My mom isn't in Intel. And your parents didn't help you–"

"They helped. They made recommendations and had the right friends. Just because you haven't used your mom to get ahead doesn't mean others don't. But in Huginn, nepotism only leads to failure. Huginns are boastful, do-anything-to-win types, right?"

I nodded.

"If Sinclair just handed his position over to Theo, then everyone who worked under him would be constantly challenging him, pushing him to fail. They wouldn't respect him. In Huginn, you have to earn everything and work to keep it."

"So Theo choosing to become an Intel Operative, to pursue work he loves instead of Sinclair's path–"

"Ding ding," Quynn said. "Massive disappointment for Dad. Now Rose is following Sinclair's path, becoming the heir he wants."

"And dissing on Intel Operatives everywhere in the process," I said through gritted teeth.

"You're lucky," Quynn said, "that your mom was always supportive of you."

"She hates that I'm an Intel Operative."

"Only because she knows it's dangerous, not because she's disappointed in your ambitions."

Quynn had a point. My mom was always happy to support whatever whim or dream I had growing up, always pushing me to chase them, in fact, to never settle. She was never a fan of me jumping off buildings, grounding me – literally and punitively – repeatedly whenever I got caught as a child, but she never stopped me from gravitating toward Intel.

"Speaking of ambitions," I said with a sigh. "There are some sort of fights going down soon."

"Sinclair announced that, and everyone was really excited. The Trials of Youth, he called them. I asked around. The teens of Huginn going into security or defense or whatever are going to fight. There's a lot of betting on whether someone will lose an eye or break a femur or die."

"Mother of Corto," I said.

"Yeah."

"And these are kids?"

"Apparently, it's a very important coming-of-age rite. And that big structure coming out of the center of the ship?"

"Yeah?"

"The arena is in there," Quynn said. "Vala said we need to go change

245

into semiformal and join her in the VIP area near ringside in 20 minutes. She'll escort us to our seats."

"Ringside seats to watch children maim each other." I wasn't even trying to hide my sarcasm. "This job just keeps getting better."

Chapter Twenty-Four

"WHY DID I LET YOU talk me into wearing a suit?" I said to Quynn as I tugged at the belt cinching in the high-waisted, navy-blue trousers. We were walking through the halls of the ship, following the pulsing green floor lights that were supposed to lead to the arena. The matching jacket and silky ivory shirt felt too constrictive, but they looked good.

"Because the party was all about you fading into the background," Quynn said in their own suit, a maroon houndstooth pattern with an ivory button-down shirt. "We're going to be ringside here, right in front of everyone. And even if it's not our primary reason for being on this ship, I want to make a good impression for Corto Corporation."

There wasn't anyone within a couple of meters of us, but I leaned in while we walked. "You do realize you're not actually a diplomat, right?"

"Tonight, I am," Quynn said. "Because my actions will reflect on Corto and our CEO no matter what my real title."

"Pretending to be people we aren't and confronting a rich man's disappointing son," I said. "Awesome impression."

"I've heard of worse." Quynn bumped my elbow with theirs and flashed me that smile I loved so well. "You worry about your job tonight, and I'll worry about mine. And it's okay to enjoy yourself a little."

"Teenage battle royale," I said flatly. "Sounds like a great time."

"You know what I mean. We're here together, aren't we? You keep saying we need to spice things up, keep things fresh."

"Not what I had in mind," I said. "But I am definitely enjoying your company."

We turned a corner and the hallway opened into a large foyer. Thick, golden carpets poured across the space, and matching wallpaper flew up the towering walls, separated into squares by intricate, gold carvings of vines and berries. Six wide staircases swept into the space, the convergence of so many hallways coming from all directions in the ship. People were milling about, sipping cocktails and laughing and pouring into multiple large, open doors on one side of the foyer.

"Time to put on a show," Quynn said.

"After you, Diplomat Quynn," I said, making a sweeping gesture toward the open doors. I fell in line behind Quynn, who put on a broad smile that looked as genuine as any I'd ever seen. They had obviously made an impression at the party while I was climbing the hull; several people were greeting Quynn with smiles and "good to see you again" and "enjoy the show." As Quynn's security, eyes passed over me without really noticing me. This was quickly becoming my favorite way to navigate a crowd of strangers.

We entered the arena, which was smaller than I'd imagined. I'd been to plenty of arenas before. Both versions of Earth football were popular on Little Sekhmet Settlement. All five boroughs had their teams, plus more teams from across the settlement. Of course, boxing and ultimate fighting were popular, though I'd never been to those matches, only seen them on TVs in bars.

This arena aboard the Saga Freya was tiny compared to those others, but that made sense given that we were on a ship in the middle of Drakon Bay. I supposed a big arena wouldn't have had the same VIP feel, either, and Sinclair Huginn obviously only invited VIPs aboard his ship. This arena looked to seat a thousand at most, cushy seats in rows all pointed down toward an open, white circle with a red Huginn Industries logo: a raven in mid-flight with only one gleaming eye.

Quynn and I started down the steps toward the circle, which must have been the ring when I spotted Vala down near the bottom. She had a hand up, eyes on us, giving the tiniest of waves. She had swapped her evening gown for a different one, this one less bejeweled, more revealing with a drooping neckline, and in dark green. I put a hand on Quynn's shoulder and gestured toward Vala with my head, doing my best impersonation of a security guard.

Quynn nodded, and we continued down the stairs, Quynn still glad-handing their new friends until we met up with our Huginn handler.

"Enjoying yourself?" Vala asked Quynn.

"Very much," Quynn said. "Thank you."

"Excellent," Vala said. "Sinclair will be happy to hear that. And I promise you'll get some face time with him after the fights."

"That's good," Quynn said. "Dr. Corto would be rather disappointed if I didn't get a chance to give her regards personally."

Okay, my partner was officially much better at this than I was. Quynn had taken on the persona of diplomat like they'd been doing it their whole life, instead of guiding nanotechnology development. As much as I hated them being in potentially dangerous situations like this, it was making this part of the job much easier.

"Of course," Vala said. "If you'll follow me, I'll show you to your seats." Vala didn't wait for a response, turning and heading down to the first row without delay. She led us over two sections to a pair of seats with black cloths draped over the backs. The clothes were embroidered with the Corto Corporation logo, a pair of capital Cs mirrored to face out. Admittedly, it wasn't as stylish as the Huginn logo, but it was ours.

"Thank you, Vala," Quynn said.

Vala gave another little bow, and then whisked away, probably to her next task. Sinclair certainly seemed to keep her busy. We took our seats, watching as people filed into the arena, following ushers to their seats. Quynn pointed out a number of people they'd met during the party. Everyone was director-level or above, and many of them were at least vice presidents. Quynn pointed out two directors of nanotechnology and described how Quynn pretended they didn't know as much about Corto's nano efforts as they really did.

"What about the Huginn CEO?" I asked. "Rae Prax Huginn?"

"No, he's not here," Quynn said. "But from what everyone says, that not for lack of invitation or desire. He was tied up in some sort of high-level negotiations and couldn't make it. He usually does. You still think the mystery buyer for the chip is here tonight?"

"It makes the most sense," I said.

Quynn shrugged. "Seems to me Theo's motivations for being on this ship tonight have more to do with his family than the chip."

"He was communicating with someone after Rose walked away from him," I said. "That didn't seem innocuous."

"I agree," Bastion said. "I find it more likely that his buyer is here precisely because Theo had to be here. Theo's absence from this event would have been conspicuous, and if the buyer was already on the guest list..."

"Exactly," I said. "He's meeting someone. I'll be keeping an eye on him. When he leaves the fight, I'll be on his tail."

"Be careful," Quynn said, their hand twitching toward mine, but staying in place. Like me, they'd had to remember that on this ship tonight, we were just a diplomat and their security.

"I always am," I said.

"Really?" Quynn asked.

"I would use many words to describe you, Elise, but careful is not one of them," Bastion said.

"Not helping," I said.

"Oh, I think he's absolutely helping," Quynn said with a wink.

"And now I'm outnumbered."

"By people who care about you," Quynn said, "yes."

"Thank you," Bastion said.

"For what?" Quynn asked.

"For calling me 'people.'"

A series of expressions crossed Quynn's face. Confusion. Happiness. Relief. Worry. Then Quynn locked eyes with me, and I saw a glimmer of a tear forming below the violet eye. They gave me a tight smile and nodded, though I wasn't sure if the look was for me or for Bastion, who Quynn certainly knew could see through my eyes. "You're welcome. And thank you for having Elise's back."

"Of course," Bastion said.

Quynn cleared their throat and looked away, glancing up and away repeatedly. They hated crying, especially in front of strangers. We were surrounded by strangers, and Quynn needed to put on a polite, diplomatic face.

The three of us stayed quiet for a few minutes before Bastion said, "Theo is here. Three sections over on your left."

Both Quynn and I looked, and there he was along with his family. Unlike the rest of us, they were in their same outfits from the party. Sinclair's bespoke suit was as pristine as any I'd ever seen, Rose was glowing in that white gown, and Theo was sullen in his green jacket and kilt. Rose and Sinclair were shaking hands, smiling, and waving at every face nearby, while Theo was like a dark spot in orbit, not making eye contact with anyone. Another person joined the family, as dark in complexion as Theo, but their features were like an older Rose.

"Claudia?" I asked Bastion.

"Yes," Bastion said. "Theo's mother. Sinclair's wife."

"That's him?" Quynn asked, nodding to Theo.

"Green hair, jacket, kilt, and that damn tattoo," I said. "That's him."

"He doesn't look so tough," Quynn said.

"Except for those big arms," I said. "His mods broke mine. I don't want to get physical with him again."

"I concur," Bastion said. "Physical altercations aren't your strong suit."

"Thank you for stating the obvious," I said.

"You're welcome," Bastion said.

"Still trying to understand sarcasm?" Quynn asked.

"Oh, I very much understand sarcasm," Bastion said.

Quynn whipped their head to me, eyebrows raised in an 'oh shit' look.

"Touché," I said.

"Huginn Industries citizens and esteemed guests," a boisterous, deep voice cut in over the speakers. "Welcome to the Trials of Youth!"

Conversations died all around the arena in an instant, and people who were standing quickly found their seats. Even Sinclair wrapped up his conversation as Rose, Theo, and Claudia sat. The lights around the arena faded down, while lights on the empty circle brightened.

"There are eight fights on our card tonight," the boisterous voice continued. "But before we begin, please raise your voices and glasses to our Oppstigning Seile patron tonight, who has graciously opened the doors of this wonderful vessel, the Saga Freya, to us all. Sinclair Huginn!"

Voices and glasses did, indeed, raise into a sea of sound around us. Quynn and I applauded politely, though certainly not as vigorously as the gathered Huginns.

As the ovation began to simmer back down, the boisterous voice spoke again. "First up tonight, in blue, the pride of Alex Huginn-Net and Sandra Huginn-Net. With a record of six and oh, she's the pride of Huginn Industries Middle School 8. Raise your voices for her: Victoria Huginn-Thirteen!"

A spotlight illuminated a small figure clad in blue, standing in a door at the top of the stairs off to our left. The figure held up her fists and started trotting down the stairs to some blaring techno music that overpowered the crowd's cheering. Before long, she entered the brightly lit circle, hopping around in her blue shorts and tank top.

"She's so small," Quynn said.

"Too small," I said. Victoria Huginn-Thirteen was scrawny and looked like she would maybe come up to my chest. A child of thirteen, hence the number in her name, far too young to be fighting anyone, let alone to be the victor of six fights already.

The music faded away, and another spotlight flicked on a small figure in red on the opposite side of the arena. "And in red, son of Pedro Huginn-Cyber and Michel Huginn-Nano, with a record of eight and one, he is Yves Huginn-Thirteen!"

The crowd erupted even more than they had for Victoria, and a song from some boy band drowned them out as Yves ran down the stairs, punching the air and waving to people as he came down. He entered the ring, skipping around the edge of the circle, egging the crowd on. Victoria barely glanced at him, rocking to the music and keeping her eyes on her closed fists.

The music faded down to nothing, and both Yves and the crowd quieted.

"You all know what comes next, what makes the Trial of Youth on Saga Freya so special," the boisterous voice said. "The Sphere!"

A wailing guitar solo erupted from the speakers, lights ballyhooed around the room, and dozens of drones floated down from the shadows of the towering ceiling, each one carrying a hexagonal, curved, translucent panel of some sort. The drones flew in a spiral formation, a choreographed dance, and eventually formed up. They moved the panels around and above the circle until the panels formed a sphere a dozen meters in diameter. The panels glowed green one by one until they were all glowing, and then as one, the sphere flashed a bright white. They faded transparent, with only the faintest outline of the hexagonal shapes. The drones flew off back to the darkness of the ceiling, leaving the sphere as the raging guitar swole to a crescendo and faded to silence.

"Combatants ready?" Boisterous voice asked.

Both teens raised their right fists and nodded once, then dropped those fists and focused on one another, bouncing lightly on the balls of their feet.

"Three," Boisterous said.

Victoria sucked in a breath and then kissed her fists.

"Two."

Yves smacked his fists together once, and then beat his chest twice.

"One."

Both teens planted their feet and squared their shoulders at each other.

"Fight!"

The teens launched at each other in a blur of fists and feet. Yves landed the first blow, a glancing jab to Victoria's cheek. Victoria answered back hard with a hook across Yves's jaw, a knee to his stomach, and then a roundhouse kick that Yves barely caught with his forearm. Even though he kept Victoria's shin off his temple, the boy sprawled to the ground. The crowd erupted in a mix of cheers and boos. Victoria didn't give Yves time to get up; she leaped on top of him, wrenching his left arm away from his body and locking his neck between her legs. Yves' face started to turn purple.

"Someone should stop this," I said.

"Only three things stop the Rite of Youth," Bastion said. "Someone screams for mercy, someone passes out, or someone dies."

"She has his throat," I said. "He can't scream."

"Then you should hope he passes out before she breaks his neck."

Yves' left hand was still flailing, his eyes rolling as his face grew darker. He was slapping at Victoria's legs with his free hand, but the blows were no more effective than drops of rain. Yves tried to kick up and out with his legs, but it was obvious his strength was fading. Maybe if he'd kicked around when he still had air in his lungs, he could have powered out of the hold. Now, though, the kicks were more like a toddler throwing a tantrum. In less than a minute, the kicking stopped. His eyes rolled up and closed. Then his hand went limp.

A horn blew, long and loud through the arena, and Victoria released Yves from her grip. The boy was blue and utterly limp, but his chest slowly moved up and down.

"Your victor!" Boisterous voice said. "Victoria Huginn-Thirteen. Criminals beware, Victoria plans to continue her education in our security division, and I, for one, feel safer already knowing she'll be protecting our borough."

Two drones flew back down, each one grabbing a hexagonal panel of the sphere down by the floor, and then pulling them away. A large person wearing a flowing, red robe strode in and hauled Yves up off the mat, threw him over their shoulder, and walked out as Victoria continued pumping her fists and walking around the ring, reveling in the cheers.

Victoria finally left, and then the Boisterous Voice announced the next pair of fighters: two more thirteens. Their fight took longer, with more parrying and traded blows. The bigger of the two kept trying to take the smaller one to the ground, but eventually, the smaller one landed a nasty blow, instantly knocking out the larger teen.

A pair of fourteens followed, and then a pair of fifteens. I kept an eye on Theo as one fight moved to the next. He seemed to come alive during the Rite of Youth, making me wonder if he'd gone through one of these rites when he was a teen. Had he stood in this very sphere, surrounded by his father's wealthy friends? Had he won, and then changed his career course later? Or had he lost, and fallen into being an Intel Operative when a more violent career path closed to him that night? He certainly fought better than any Intel Operative Corto Corporation employed, but maybe all the Huginn operatives had combat training.

As a defeated 15-year-old limped out of the sphere, seemingly more wounded in his pride for screaming "Mercy!" than in his gimpy leg, Theo spoke excitedly to his sister.

"We're nearly halfway through our evening's fights tonight," Boisterous Voice said. "And I know everyone is excited for this next match. Wearing black, the youngest son of Sinclair Huginn and Claudia Huginn-Cyber, he is Svald Huginn-Sixteen!"

Svald came down the stairs in a loping pace timed with a chugging rock song, in no particular hurry, letting the cheers wash over him. He had far more swagger than any of the previous fighters. His record indicated he was an excellent fighter, and I suspected being the son of Sinclair puffed up his over-muscled chest plenty. He tapped his fists with his father, smiled at Rose, and hugged Claudia. He didn't even glance at Theo. The family rift ran deep. Svald entered the ring, stood in the center, and held one fist aloft, nodding as the crowd cheered even louder.

"And in the gold," Boisterous Voice said as the rock anthem faded away, "the shining gem of Motar Huginn-Cyber and Raphael Huginn, they are Septine Huginn-Sixteen!"

Septine practically bounced down the stairs on the opposite side of the arena, high-fiving extended hands, flashing a million-credit grin in every direction. Once they hit the floor, they sprinted a full lap around the outside of the sphere, a shimmering, gold cape fluttering off their neck. In Septine's wake, a light dusting of gold glitter littered the floor between the front row of seats and the sphere.

"They know how to make an entrance," I said, leaning into Quynn.

"This has to be the strangest date you've ever taken me on," Quynn said.

A laugh snorted out of my nose, eliciting a dirty look from the older, bearded person sitting next to me. I swallowed the laugh down and turned my attention back to the sphere. Septine was now inside, having shed their cape. They didn't get nearly the applause that Svald had, but given who owned the ship we were all aboard, that wasn't surprising.

The drones sealed up the sphere again, Boisterous Voice gave a countdown, and then the fight commenced. Septine and Svald circled, the former trotting sideways while Svald kept an even, heavy grapevine. After three full circles, Septine finally rushed in, fists raised. Svald crouched slightly and brought his arms up to guard, but at the last second, Septine went into a slide, cybernetic limbs that didn't look cybernetic keeping Septine moving forward, right between Svald's legs.

Before Svald could react properly, Septine grabbed both of Svald's ankles, pulling him off his feet, and Septine kept going, right up the side of the sphere. Svald flailed, obviously disoriented, and then Septine launched from the side of the sphere with Svald, spearing the bigger teen into the ring. Septine leaped off with a careless flip and started waving his arms at the crowd, begging for applause that was only a smattering mixed with much-louder boos.

Svald wasn't done, though. He was hurt, taking choking breaths. He spat up some blood as he rolled up onto his hands and knees. Septine noticed and made an exaggerated neck-slicing motion to the crowd. I glanced at Theo, who had a hand covering his mouth, his eyes intense. Sinclair's and Claudia's faces were stoic, giving no clue as to if either were worried about their youngest son. Most disturbing, though, was Rose. She was grinning.

Septine approached the half-collapsed form of Svald, taking a skip-step toward him, winding up to kick him in his exposed stomach. Just as the kick was about to connect, however, Svald leaped, cybernetic arms and legs pushing off the mat with so much force, that it was as though a string had pulled Svald up by his abdomen. In mid-air, one strong arm grabbed Septine's extended foot, while Svald's back slammed into Septine's chest. The two teens went down in a heap, Svald still holding onto Septine's leg. With his free hand, Svald slammed a palm into the captured kneecap, pulling the ankle in the opposite direction. The leg didn't just break, it snapped off, gears and hydraulic fluid and wires splaying in every direction.

Svald rolled off Septine in a single movement, holding the dismembered leg aloft, but not taking his eyes off his opponent. Septine, to their credit, sprang back with their arms and up onto the remaining leg. Unlike biological legs, losing a cybernetic limb was problematic, but not insurmountable. Any decent combination of software and hardware would allow you to keep your balance and do most anything with just one leg. It had happened to me, though never while trying to fight someone in a giant sphere.

Svald hurled the dismembered leg at Septine, who deftly ducked the blow. The two teens began to circle yet again. Septine bounced sideways, their trademark grin now gone, their focus now intent. Svald resumed his heavy grapevine, though bruises were already blossoming around his ribs from Septine's opening move.

This time, it was Svald who moved in, taking shuffling steps and staying low, with his fists raised. The two started boxing, Svald's blows heavy and slow, and Septine much faster. It was like a chess match with fists, Septine dodging the heavy hands of Svald, and Svald absorbing the stinging pops of Septine on his arms. After exchanging blows like that for the longest 30 seconds I'd ever experienced, Svald landed a solid hook to Septine's jaw, sending the lighter teen spinning on their remaining leg.

Svald followed after, likely looking for another blow, one to end the match. Septine bounced once, twice, still spinning slightly away, and then that remaining leg leaped forward onto the sphere, and leaped again, one heel spinning hard and fast into the side of Svald's unguarded face. Despite his size, Svald went down, landing face-first against the transparent sphere wall right in front of Quynn and me, two of his teeth shattering on impact and blood exploding out of his mouth. Quynn flinched. So did I, which I realized after was very un-security-like.

Septine rose back up onto their lone leg and picked up the dismembered one that Svald had thrown. As Svald sluggishly rolled onto his back and spat out blood, Septine swung the leg around like they were judging the weight and feel of it as a weapon. Both teens were breathing hard, looking much worse for the wear than when they'd entered the arena. With Svald only just starting to get to his feet, Septine started bouncing over, the dismembered leg held aloft like a club.

Svald seemed planted, struggling to get his feet under him. One foot was down, but the other slipped on the tilted side of the sphere. Septine jumped with the one leg, opening their mouth and unleashing a horrid scream while bringing the battered leg down toward Svald.

But the bigger teen wasn't there. The leg smashed ineffectively against the side of the sphere, losing even more fluid and parts. Septine stood, confused, but didn't see Svald behind him, didn't know until one cybernetic hand gripped the wrist that held the dismembered leg. Septine drove his free elbow backward, but Svald caught that one, too, locking his own arm around it. In a blink, Svald had both Septine's arms pinned in a full nelson.

And then Svald brought his forehead down on the crown of Septine's head with a horrid crack. Blood bloomed on Svald's forehead, but I couldn't be sure whose blood. Then he brought his forehead down again. And again. Septine's knees crumbled, their eyes rolling, but Svald held the smaller teen aloft by the wrist and elbow. The horn blared, the lights changed, and the drones came back down to open up the sphere. Svald stood where he was, still holding the unconscious Septine. Svald's small, dark eyes were wide, blood dripping down his forehead. Again, the image of Roxy in that cafe leaped to mind, the similarities between Svald's crazed look and Roxy's were undeniable. He didn't seem to register that the match was over, that he needed to drop his opponent, just like Roxy couldn't register that I didn't have her chip, that the contract was canceled, and that I was no longer her target. Svald hammered his forehead into the back of Septine's skull again, this time with less of a crack than a crunch.

Svald looked up and around, though it didn't look like he saw the crowd, which was utterly silent. No cheers for Sinclair's son. No boos. No applause. Svald looked down at Septine, then back up, and roared like some kind of beast. He smiled and reared his head back for another blow, but then Theo was on him, one of those big, cybernetic arms around his younger brother's head, the other hand wrenching Svald's grip free of Septine. Svald released his opponent and thrashed around, trying to escape his captor. I couldn't hear the words, but I could see Theo talking to Svald, and the younger brother slowly calmed and stopped thrashing. Two Huginns in red robes rushed in, grabbing Septine with significantly more gentleness than they'd used on previous fighters.

Then Theo left the ring, Svald still standing there and looking as shellshocked as someone who had lost a fight. He was absently wiping Septine's blood off his forehead, looking confused as to how it got there.

"Your victor," Boisterous Voice said, somehow unshaken from what we'd all just witnessed, "Svald Huginn-Sixteen!"

The applause was polite, but not raucous as it had been for previous fights. At least the Huginns weren't so brutal as to celebrate the near murder of a child. I looked back to Theo, but his chair was empty. Momentary panic leaped into my throat, but then I saw that glowing, green tattoo moving up the stairs near his seat, heading out of the arena.

Heading off to meet someone.

The time was now. I released my grip on the armrest, which was dented by my grip. If my hands had been biological, the knuckles would have been white. I didn't think I would ever shake the brutality of what I'd just seen.

"He's on the move," I said to Quynn as I leaned in close to them.

Quynn nodded and kept a polite smile planted on their face. "Go. Be safe."

CHAPTER TWENTY-FIVE

I LOPED UP THE STAIRS two at a time, one section over from the stairs Theo was using. I'd caught up to him right as he reached the doors to leave the arena, except he didn't. Instead, he took a hard right away from me, though I didn't think he'd seen me. At the top of the arena, behind the last row of seats, a carpeted path about two meters wide ran all the way around. Theo was walking that path, so I did the same, keeping my distance and staying in the shadows as best I could.

Theo was halfway around the perimeter of the arena when he stopped next to a door. I pressed up against the next set of doors over, which mostly hid me from his view, just as he looked around. He was nervous, scanning the crowd – which was focused on Sinclair giving some sort of speech in the sphere – and the empty path around the arena several times before he opened the door and ducked out.

"Where does that go?" I asked Bastion.

"I don't know," Bastion said. "We're far away from the foyer. Somewhere closer to the forward deck, I think."

I walked with long strides to Theo's door and pressed my ear to it for a few seconds but heard nothing. I worked the lever on the door as quietly as I could and pushed it open a few centimeters. I didn't see or hear anything, so I pushed it open enough to slip through and did so.

Beyond the doors was a hallway that curved along the outside of the arena, but nothing as grand as I'd seen on the ship before. Plain white walls and equally plain tile. Tall metal carts were parked randomly against the walls next to oversized trash cans. Likely a service corridor. It curved off in both directions, but since Theo had been going to the right before going through the door, I figured it was a safe bet to keep going that direction. I moved along as quietly and quickly as I could, keeping my optical and aural implants on high alert for Theo. The corridor was brightly lit, so shadows weren't an option, though there were plenty of doors on both sides in case I needed to hide.

After about twenty meters, I heard Theo's voice up ahead. I slowed my pace and tuned my hearing to that direction.

"...this family. Svald almost killed that kid, and Father just sat there."

I listened for a second voice but heard none.

"I know, I know," Theo continued, answering some unheard question. "All the more reason to press forward."

I reached the opening to a hallway that hooked sharply to my right, directly toward the front of the ship, if my sense of direction was at all correct. Theo's voice was coming from down that hall, so I poked my camera around the corner. He was standing there, his head slightly bowed. Once again, he was talking to someone on his comms. The mystery buyer remained a mystery.

"Right," Theo said. "You don't – Of course, but I – The lido deck, I understand. I'm on my way."

"Lido deck?" I whispered to Bastion.

"The big swimming pool we saw as we flew over," he said. "That's the lido deck."

"Front of the ship."

"Yes."

Theo was already walking through the hall away from me, and I didn't see any choice but to follow. I moved from doorway to doorway, loping along and trying to stay hidden as much as possible as I shadowed Theo out of the service corridor and into a wood-paneled hall for guests. Theo moved as I expected, navigating hallway after hallway with absolute confidence.

And to my surprise, he never looked back, never glanced over his shoulder. Perhaps the ship felt like a second home, giving him a false sense of security.

Finally, he took a short flight of stairs up and then opened a heavy door out into the breezy night. I hustled up the stairs once the door closed behind him, putting my back to the wall next to it, and craning slowly over to look out the circular window in the door. The fore of the ship extended out before me, several dozen meters of beautiful wood coming to a narrow point. In the middle, a rectangular swimming pool occupied most of the deck, glowing blue with a black Huginn Industries logo at the bottom.

What disturbed me was who I didn't see: Theo. I'd just seen him go out the door, but he wasn't anywhere on the lido deck that I could see.

"Where did he go?" Bastion asked.

"I don't know," I said, but then he appeared, standing next to the railing off to my right, lit faintly in green. I didn't know why I hadn't seen him there before.

"There we go," I said and started to open the door.

"Wait–" Bastion started to say.

But I had the door open before he said another word, and pain exploded out of my side, just above my hip. I slammed into the opening door, which opened the rest of the way in a hurry, carrying me along until I lost my grip on it and tumbled away onto the wooden decking.

"You again?" Theo screamed. "Who the Hel are you?"

I coughed and wobbled up to my feet, more caught off guard than injured. Theo was pacing toward me, the open door to the deck behind him. I glanced aside and saw him also standing next to the railing of the deck.

"How–?" I started to say.

"A hologram," Bastion said. "I tried to warn you."

Hologram. Right. Not just for replaying security footage. Now I just felt stupid for falling for it.

"I said, who are you?" Theo said, still moving toward me.

I started backing up, matching his pace, running through which lies might work, which combination of truth and falsehood might be my best chance. But those big cybernetic arms were pumping as he approached, bulging against the sleeves of his jacket, and I needed to start talking sooner rather than later.

"I work for Corto Corporation," I said. "You have something of ours."

He stopped walking and started laughing. "Corto? Really?"

"That's funny?"

"Infinitely," he said, still smiling in genuine delight.

"I don't see why."

Theo's laughs redoubled. "Left and right hands. How ridiculous."

"What is that suppose to–"

"So you're Corto Security?" Theo said, interrupting as his laugh melted away. "You're way out of your jurisdiction."

"Intel," I said. "An operative just like you. And you took a job from someone in Corto Corporation. Isn't that out of your jurisdiction?"

"This is a bad idea," Bastion said.

"How narrow-minded of you. You really think you've never taken a job from another company? Are you all so well trained to never question orders? Or maybe you're just too cowardly to risk everything on a career-making move."

"That's not how things work!" I said too loudly.

"Keep telling yourself that," Theo said with a smirk. "Now tell me who you really are. Corto operatives are weak. They go after unguarded targets. A bunch of safecrackers and doorcrashers. They don't go directly after people. Who are you, really?"

"Safecrackers and doorcrashers, huh?" I said. "Isn't that what you did to get the chip? You know who I am. You followed me, but you didn't come straight after me, no. You broke into our vault. Did you think we wouldn't come after you for that?"

Theo grinned. "So they sent you? Little you to get me? Are you going to kill me?"

"No," I said. "I'm not. I can help you."

"I doubt that," Theo said and flexed his big, metal hands.

"Whatever your buyer is willing to pay for that chip, I guarantee Corto Corporation is willing to pay more."

"Is that right?" Theo stopped walking again, but his expression became flat and unreadable.

"How much do you know about that chip? About who you stole it from?"

"I know enough," Theo said.

"This doesn't seem right," Bastion said. "He's lying."

He wasn't lying, not really, he just wasn't giving anything away, dodging questions. It was a move I'd deployed many times. Negotiating against it was like flying blind through a hurricane, though.

"You know enough," I repeated. "You know it's important, maybe the most important thing either of us has ever stolen. And in the right hands, that chip is a kingmaker." Or queenmaker, but I didn't say that.

"And Corto has the right hands?" Theo asked.

I spread my own hands wide. Time to use what I'd learned to go for the jugular. "In this case, the best hands. Come with me, sell it to Corto, and you won't just make a small fortune, but you could have your pick of high-level positions. Status."

Theo smiled even more, and then just shook his head. "Typical Corto. Typical. Your kind has no concept of loyalty. Of earning your place."

"You think the Cloak of Corto doesn't work for their position just like the Wing of Huginn?"

The smile vanished, replaced with some genuine surprise. Maybe curiosity.

"Come on," I said. "If one exists, surely the other does. It's no surprise. And I can assure you, the Cloak of Corto isn't a mantle earned lightly."

The smile crept back across Theo's face, and then he started to chuckle, shaking his head slowly. "I'm sure you think that. Maybe in Corto, you're right. Let me ask you, who in Corto Corporation owns such a vessel as this one?"

I opened my mouth, names like Ariela, our CEO, or heads of other well-established families in Corto Corporation, but I wasn't sure. I didn't know if there were ships like the Saga Freya in Corto. I'd been to the Corto docks plenty of time but never seen a ship anything like it.

"My great-great-grandfather was a maintenance electrician at the cybernetics plant far, far inland," Theo said. "By the time he retired, he was running the electrician's guild. My great-grandfather began in security and was vice president of security and defense by the time he was 50. He bought this ship, a husk of an old luxury liner. My father, the man who owns this ship today, is the chief marketing officer. He began as a copywriter. Do you understand?"

"Sounds like there's a distinct lack of women in your family."

"Jokes are the defense of a weak constitution."

"Everybody's a critic," I said.

"What are you doing?" Bastion said in my ear. "Trying to make him mad?"

I wasn't trying to make him mad. My mouth was running ahead of my brain a little, which happened when I was nervous. I hadn't exactly forgotten our first altercation outside the Vale of the Valkyries, my broken arm and diving off the building.

"What would you sacrifice to become the next Cloak of Corto?" Theo asked, a little growl in his voice.

I shrugged. I'd long dreamt of becoming the next Cloak of Corto, but I'd never thought about the promotion in terms of sacrifice. Work hard, shake hands with the right people, and make the right friends and alliances. Be the best Intel Operative, and the mantle of the Cloak was within reach. That was the Corto way.

"Two years ago," Theo continued, "we had an operative very like you. Skinny. Sneaky. She was doing very well for herself, making a name, and landing higher and higher profile jobs. Then one day, she was assigned a job that should have been mine. A heavily guarded defense outpost. Ideal for someone with my particular skills.

"Except by the time she arrived, the security had been tipped off. She was gunned down while one of her little gizmos was still plugged into their computers."

"And you had something to do with that?"

"Of course," he said with a smile. "Because I am better than her."

"Crueler than her, more like," I said.

"There is no difference, not to a Huginn. Crueler. Stronger. Faster. Smarter. All different roads to the same end result. While those defense forces were busy cleaning up the mess of her body, I rushed their flank and

265

secured the target. I completed a coveted job and eliminated a rival in one move. She was not the first sacrifice I made, and she will not be the last."

I swallowed, hoping Theo didn't notice, but I wasn't surprised. Not after our encounter at the Vale, not knowing what I already knew about Huginn Industries, and definitely not after seeing what Theo's little brother had done in the arena.

"There are easier ways to success," I said. "Ways that don't–"

"Easier?" Theo said in a bellow. "Success without difficulty, without hardship, without sacrifice? That is cheating! That is not success at all. This is what you fail to understand, Corto. It is better to fail as a Huginn than succeed in Corto. The woman who cleans my toilets in Huginn has worked harder and sacrificed more than your pathetic CEO."

"I thought jokes were the weapon of a weak constitution," I said. Maybe a verbal barb wasn't the smartest move right then, but I was watching all doors of negotiation slam in front of me, so riling him up was the only option I had remaining.

Theo sneered. "I'm going to enjoy this, little Corto." He took one long step and then leaped toward me, drawing a fist back quicker than I'd imagined he could. No complex strategy, no circling me to size me up, just aggression. Fortunately, as fast as he was, I was faster, and his gigantic leap gave me ample time to roll out of the way. His fist came down hard, splintering the wooden deck.

I rolled up to my feet and walked backward from him as he rose up. "Careful," I said. "Don't break Daddy's boat."

Theo roared like a demon and came rushing toward me, this time keeping lower to the ground. He swung up with one of his enormous fists, and I leaned away from it while backpedaling. The wind coming off his arm fluttered my hair up and out of my eyes. He spun with an aggressive backhand, and I slid down and away from it. Then he drove a fist down toward me, and I barely jumped out of the way, splinters from the decking flicking against my carbon-polymer shins.

I moved back ducking, dodging, and parrying every blow that I could, my limbs and software doing as much of the work as I was to survive the onslaught. With each attack and dodge, though, Theo was getting closer. He was a trained fighter, and I could see him learning and adapting. He brought one of those big, cybernetic fists around in a hook aimed at my temple, and I ducked, but right into a knee rising off the decking. Three cracks happened almost simultaneously: Theo's knee cracking into my jaw, my teeth cracking together, and my head snapping up. In the space of a breath, my whole body was off the ground, and then I landed back on the deck of the Saga Freya. Stars flew around in front of my face, blurring flashes of light that seemed real and unreal at the same time.

"Get up, Elise!" Bastion said in my ear, my comms buzzing.

But I couldn't make sense of "up." I had a vague sense that the hard surface against my back probably wasn't up, but I couldn't be sure.

"Roll, Elise!" Bastion said, and the stars began to fade. "Any direction! Just roll!"

I rolled to the side, away from a distant, muddied sound of thumping and roaring, practically flinging myself to the side. A thunderous noise exploded from where I had just been, the decking rattling under me as I got up on my hands and knees.

"Get up!" a man growled from that same direction.

I shook my head, banishing what remained of those ridiculous stars, and remembered where I was. The deck of the Saga Freya, out in Drakon Bay, fighting Theo Huginn-Intel. Correction: getting my ass kicked by Theo Huginn-Intel. I tasted blood and spat out a molar.

"Get up, Corto!" Theo bellowed.

I wobbled to my feet, shaking off the last of the fuzz and focusing on Theo. He was standing in front of a damn crater he'd left in the decking. The railing of the ship was a meter behind him, the distant lights of Jayu City off in the horizon. I wiped blood from my chin and did my best to not look like prey.

"You should send a message to your bosses before I kill you," he said. "Tell them next time they want something from Huginn, send a warrior. Send all of their warriors or just stay home, tucked in their beds, and write off whatever they're chasing as lost forever to better operatives."

"Oh yeah?" I said and spat out more blood. "And what should I tell your daddy after I toss your body into the bay?"

Theo laughed. Not the little chuckle from before, but a full-throated laugh. I should have been offended, but I was thankful for every second he was giving me to clear my head and make a plan.

"I suppose that's the best blow you can muster," Theo said. "So be it." He dropped his right arm to his side and shook it, not idly, but with some specific purpose. Then the arm began to gently glow and hum. That couldn't be good. He gave no roar this time, no gesture of fury. He just darted toward me and drew back that glowing fist. I brought my arms up in front of my chest, just the way Echo showed me, and I squared my feet.

Theo's blow slammed into the shield just as it shimmered into existence. He was knocked back as his glowing fist rebounded, nearly slapping him in the face. To my surprise, I only felt the slightest shake at the impact, the shield dissipating the blow without transferring the energy to me. Theo looked at me, bewildered. I didn't give him the chance to follow up, though, I turned my palms toward the big Huginn. My display said, "BURST READY," and I pushed my palms out.

Boom indeed, Echo. That was the sound it made, the shield launching outward and battering Theo full in the face and chest. He flew backward, tumbling like a toy, and slamming into the railing, cracking it in several spots.

"Sparks," I whispered.

"That was effective," Bastion said. "It also shaved 15% off the batteries of both your arms."

"Am I good?"

"Still above 50% on both," Bastion said. "But you can't just pound away at him with that."

He was right, and much to my annoyance, Theo was climbing back to his feet. He didn't look dazed or nauseous like I'd been from his blow to my chin, he just looked like some blend of annoyed and excited.

"Finally making a fight of it," Theo said in a growl. Then he was running toward me in a full sprint.

I squared my feet and brought my hands up again, crossing my chest, but red letters blinked on my display, "SHIELD COOLDOWN IN PROGRESS."

"Sparks!" I yelled as Theo's shoulder collided with my stomach, and we both plummeted into the swimming pool, chlorinated water enveloping our tangled bodies.

CHAPTER TWENTY-SIX

I HAD A FULL AQUATIC loadout. Inboard motors that attach to my calves. The flaps and ailerons I used for freefall did just as well guiding me through water as air. And I had a rebreather apparatus that clipped onto the backs of my ears, deploying over my mouth and nose when I needed it. But that loadout was at home, hanging in my power closet. They weren't attached to me as I tumbled into the swimming pool aboard the Saga Freya with Theo Huginn-Intel pushing me toward the bottom.

I brought my knees up into Theo's torso, trying to knock the wind from his lungs, but it was like hammering stone with a rubber mallet. His mods obviously went far beyond just his arms and parts of his legs. My own modded legs should have been able to kick a hole through biological flesh but were worthless against Theo's stomach.

"Let me help," Bastion said in my ear. "Grant me access to your limbs!"

"UNKNOWN PROGRAM REQUESTING CYBERNETIC ACCESS," appeared on my display.

I shook my head and brought my elbows down on Theo's back, but they did as much good as my knees. Theo was kicking downward, pinning us both to the bottom of the pool. He was keeping us underwater, but it was just a matter of outlasting him. If I stayed calm and collected, his kicking meant he would certainly need to surface, to breathe first.

That was my thinking before I saw slits open up on his back, just below his shoulder blades. Gills. The man pinning me to the bottom of the pool had mods that served as gills. He was getting plenty of oxygen, and I was going to drown under him.

"Let me help!" Bastion repeated.

Again, my display was filled with large, yellow letters, "UNKNOWN PROGRAM REQUESTING CYBERNETIC ACCESS."

As much as I feared anyone who wasn't me suddenly gaining control of my arms and legs, it appeared to be the only alternative to drowning. I reached out and pressed the words floating in front of me. They were quickly replaced by "ACCESS GRANTED," and then my limbs started moving. My arms extended out, squeezing down against my sides, worming inside of Theo's grip on me. My forearms spun outward, linking my elbows into Theo's and pulling. Theo's arms didn't move, but my arms kept applying as much torque as they could. At the same time, my legs bent up, ripping fabric and reversing how biological legs are allowed to bend until my heels pointed at Theo's armpits.

I realized Bastion's plan just before he executed it, and I felt stupid for not thinking of it myself. A pair of silver canisters pushed out of each of my calves at 45-degree angles. Pneumatic charges. I kept two in each leg, each single use, that enabled me to make explosive jumps. My mods alone allowed me to leap 10 meters. One canister loaded up in each leg granted me jumps around 50 meters, though 42 was the highest I'd ever done. Bastion had just deployed both canisters on both legs.

My heels pressed into Theo's armpits, and my world turned into a fury of sound and bubbles. The charges made a fairly loud pop and hiss when they weren't underwater. Down here, the combination of the pops, hisses, and my heels plunging into Theo's cybernetic arms made for one deafening explosion. My arms flew up, carrying Theo with them into a cloud of bubbles generated by the discharging pneumatic charges and what little air had been left in my lungs. I didn't see Theo in the cloud, but I needed to get air immediately. I planted my feet, which were thankfully back under my control, and kicked up, hoping to avoid a collision with the big Huginn.

I breached the surface, sucking in air in great, heaving gasps, allowing my software to tread water while I focused on pushing oxygen back into my body. Still breathing heavily, I looked around for that glowing, green Mjolnir tattoo. The water was cloudy with bubbles still, and now I noticed traces of red and black swirling in the water. Blood and cybernetic lubricant.

"Am I injured?" I asked Bastion as I started moving toward the edge of the pool. I needed to get out of the water. "Is any of that–?"

"None of that is from you," Bastion said. "Your heels drove into the connections between Theo's cybernetic arms and what remains of his biology. Those connections did not survive unscathed."

"Is he dead? Is he down there somewhere?"

"I doubt he's dead, but I don't see–"

But then I was yanked back underwater, sucking in chlorine along with my last gasp of air. Theo had me by the ankle, pulling me back down to the bottom. Blood and lubricant issued forth from his armpits like thin party streamers, but he still had more than enough grip to hold me.

I kicked out with my free foot, glancing off his forehead twice before he grabbed that ankle, too, and flung me down to the bottom. To my surprise, the move didn't hurt. When he'd first thrown me into the pool, it had taken a concerted effort on my part to keep the air in my lungs. This time, it was like falling in slow motion. Theo's powerful cybernetic arms were still working, but the blows to his armpits had weakened him.

That gave me hope, but that hope was quickly fading as Theo started working his way up toward my face, hand over hand planted on my legs. He was furious, water pumping in through his mouth and out those gills on his back, each pump swirling the streamers of red and black in the water. I punched at him, landing blows on his cheeks and jaw, but they barely registered.

"Let me–" Bastion said.

I didn't let him finish. I was the one with a plan this time. I grabbed Theo's face, his arms otherwise involved with keeping me pinned to the floor of the pool, and I fired my tasers at full strength.

Humans are 70% water, so when we get in contact with electricity, it runs through us with very little issue. Granted, mods change that calculus a bit. There's practically no water in my carbon-polymer limbs, for instance, though there is some metal. Nanobots can also change that 70% number, though I'd learned from Quynn that those little bots were even more conductive than the blood they displaced.

What I had failed to consider was the 100% water filling the space between Theo and myself. So as Theo's biology went rigid and his cybernetics went haywire from the mixed signals his brain was giving, mine did the same. My jaw clamped shut, grinding my teeth together painfully. Every square centimeter of my biological flesh felt like it was on fire, muscles spasming painfully. While my carbon-polymer limbs could easily withstand the electricity, they took their commands from my brain and nerves, which didn't like the sudden and sustained jolt. After several excruciating seconds, Theo and I were flung apart in the water. I spun and flipped, losing my sense of direction almost instantly.

"I've got you," Bastion said, his voice crackling in my comms, probably another side-effect of the electricity. But my limbs moved, halting my underwater tumble and swimming up to the surface. I gasped for air once again, savoring the sweet, cool breeze coming over the lido deck of the Saga Freya. Every part of me still hurt, and my limbs were twitching in small, but uncontrollable ways.

"I've got it," I said, and took over treading water and sucking in air. When I tried to let my software take over treading water, I sank right down as dozens of little errors scrolled up my display. I pushed myself back up out of the water and said, "What did I just do to myself?"

"Nothing permanent," Bastion said, "though that was a bad idea. Main operating system is fine, as are most of your systems. Some smaller subsystems are rebooting. No debilitating damage."

"That's good." I looked around. "What about Theo?"

"I haven't seen him come up, but he does have gills."

"Of course," I said with a big exhale. The error messages were dropping off quickly as various subsystems were coming back online. Autolocomotion. Reflex enhancements. Telescopic vision. Microscopic vision. Gyroscopes.

Then a glimmer of green caught my eye. Theo was at the other end of the pool, rising like some undead monster, slowly and with his eyes locked on me.

"That offer still stands," I yelled across the water. "We can both walk

273

away from this. You can have everything you want."

Theo spat into the pool and snarled. "I want nothing from Corto. I dream of life in Huginn. A career in Huginn. Success as a Huginn. Death as a Huginn."

"Last chance," I said in a sing-song voice as the last of the error messages fell away from my display and I took a few more heaving breaths. I knew he wouldn't agree, but more talking meant less fighting, and I needed every second I could get.

"You've put up a much better fight than last time," Theo said. "Better than I ever expected. But you are not a worthy opponent. You'll die in this pool, your body floating in chlorine and your own blood. I will bask in my victory over you as my father's assembled guests gather here for the Rites of Farewell. They will all see my triumph, my ascension."

I took a couple more deep breaths as my heart resumed something close to a normal rhythm. "Yes, yes, big Huginn man. Pound chest. All Corto has to offer you is a corner office, a nice apartment, and a safe, comfortable future. Of course, that doesn't interest you."

"Sounds like a cage," Theo said and started moving toward me. The water barely rippled, like he was slithering through the water instead of swimming.

"You like the tasers, huh?" I yelled across the pool.

He stopped short, still a few meters from me. "You wouldn't. Not again."

"I did. Why wouldn't I?"

"Because your systems didn't respond well," Theo said, narrowing his eyes as his head bobbed above the water. "And just because you surprised me once, doesn't mean I'll allow it to happen again."

"He's right," Bastion said. "You can't take another jolt like that. The damage earlier wasn't debilitating, but another round would likely be a different outcome."

"Maybe I can't take another shot like that," I said loud enough for Theo to hear as well as Bastion. "Not while I'm in the water." Before I'd even finished the sentence, I turned and started paddling and kicking as quickly as I could. The edge of the pool was just over a meter away, much closer than Theo was to me. Kick. Paddle. Deep breath in. Kick. Paddle. Breath out.

One meter away.

Half a meter.

I kicked my feet, paddled my arms, and reached out. The tips of my fingers grazed the smooth, curved, tiled lip of the pool right as a large hand gripped one of my ankles. Back and down I went again, yanked away from the edge, from the possibility of escape. Theo's feet were already planted on the bottom of the pool, just below one wing of the Huginn Industries logo. His free hand waved upward, pushing his body down, while the other hand was pulling me toward him. I kicked harder, both against the water and his grip, but to no effect. Even weakened, his limbs were more than a match for mine.

So I stopped kicking away, stopped squirming. I drew my free leg up to my chest and used my hands to paddle toward him even faster. A look of surprise briefly crossed his features before I suddenly launched my free foot between his eyes. For half a second, I thought I would connect, driving his nose into the rest of his face, making a crater in his dark skin. He released my ankle and dropped to the bottom of the pool, though, ducking the blow, my heel glancing off the top of his forehead. His head knocked back a little and I moved away from him, resuming my swim toward the edge of the pool.

For a few moments, I thought I had a chance again, but then Theo smiled. He pushed off the bottom, flipping backward and away from me with frightening speed. Through the haze of bubbles and his leaking fluids, he practically vanished, though I could still see the faint glow of his face tattoo as I hurried away. The tattoo's glow retreated, flipped, and was suddenly growing in size rapidly. Then Theo was back, driving toward me like a supervillain flying through the air, his feet kicking in unison, hands paddling in huge arcs.

I touched the edge of the pool, but there was no way I could escape the water. He was just too fast. I couldn't move fast enough in any direction to escape Theo, hurtling toward me like a torpedo. I wasn't quick enough underwater, maybe not even on dry land. In those few moments, everything slowed down. I imagined Quynn coming home without me and how their life would change in the next instant. The empty apartment, Quynn keeping my possessions far longer than was healthy. The empty spaces in the power closet where my work limbs usually hung, still attached to my body floating in this pool like a trophy. And what would Dr. Ariela Corto do to Quynn if I not only didn't return the chip but didn't return at all? Mother of Corto, Quynn was still on this ship. What would happen to them when Sinclair and the rest of Huginn discovered I wasn't merely their security, that Quynn wasn't really a diplomat?

One thought led from bad to worse, and I couldn't allow that. Couldn't give up. I had to survive. Practically without thinking, I crossed my arms over my chest. "SHIELD COOLDOWN IN PROGRESS" returned to the corner of my display. I winced, bracing for the blow as the glowing Mjolnir on Theo's face charged toward me, clarifying and sharpening as it approached.

Then "SHIELD COOLDOWN IN PROGRESS" changed to "SHIELD READY."

Then that message, too, vanished.

And under the water of that pool, appearing in the scant centimeters between my arms and Theo's sweeping hands, a partial dome of glowing yellow appeared. The cybernetic fingers of one of Theo's hands slammed into the shield, crumpling like the front of a car falling from the sky, wires and springs and metal twisting out in every direction. Every direction except through the shield, which held fast. Theo crumpled against it, elbows and knees and even his forehead knocking hard against the glowing energy.

He turned to me in rage, a fury unequaled to any I'd ever seen, not even in the homicidal Roxy. The shield was impenetrable, yes, but I was still underwater. I could still drown whether my shield was up or not. As Theo tumbled in the water, lost in his anger and bewilderment as his mangled hands, I turned my hands outward.

"No, Elise," Bastion yelled in my ear. "Don't–"

But I didn't wait. I pushed my hands outward, unleashing the burst again. My world exploded in sound and pressure, and everything went white as I lost consciousness.

CHAPTER TWENTY-SEVEN

I COUGHED. OR MAYBE WRETCHED. I wasn't sure there was much difference. Lukewarm liquid came up and out of me, spilling down my chin. I blinked several times, my display shuddering violently, not giving me any recognizable readings. So I looked around, trying to make sense of what I was seeing. I was sitting in water that didn't quite come to my waist. Everything around me was white. Tall, white walls with lights evenly spaced along the top, shining down. But there was no ceiling, only a starry sky directly overhead.

I heard only a pervasive ringing. I worked my jaw, instinct telling me to pop my ears before I remembered my aural implants didn't care what my jaw was doing. I took several deep, shuddering breaths as my brain caught up to reality. The shield, Theo, the pool.

Mother of Corto, I was still in the pool, but most of the water was gone. There were maybe 10 centimeters of water left, sloshing around above that Huginn Industries logo. I didn't see Theo anywhere. I didn't hear Bastion, but I still couldn't hear anything except a ringing. I tapped my fingers, bringing up my keyboard, which flickered as much as the rest of my display. That didn't matter. I could see it well enough to hold down the four keys that prompted a hard reboot. My display went dark, and the ringing stopped. I hated doing this, going blind and deaf for several seconds while my core operating system rebooted, but it wasn't as terrifying when I controlled it. I breathed in and out, a purely biological process unaffected by any software or hardware in my body. My suit was soaked and tattered, freezing where it remained against my skin. The air tasted of chlorine and ozone. I swallowed and tasted blood. Everything hurt. I tried not to think about what Theo was doing while I was helpless.

Then my display returned, a line of white cutting across my field of vision, and then expanding until I could see everything again. Various system boot-ups scrolled along, most of them operational, but several weren't. The shield implants were blown. The lens of my fiberoptic camera was shattered. About a third of my systems were damaged and nonfunctional, including my aural implants.

"I tried to warn you," appeared on my display. Bastion.

I brought up my keyboard again, which wasn't flickering anymore. The blessings of a reboot. I typed, "It worked, didn't it?"

"That depends on where Theo is," he said in a text.

I used the keyboard to manually navigate my menus, shutting down the broken aural implants and engaging the backups. The sounds of the world around me crackled back into existence, echoing through a tunnel of broken glass. My backups weren't a second set of aural implants, but rather a few low-end microphones that I used for other functions. The one attached to my fiber-optic camera, the long-range microphones that were mounted on my shoulders, and the vibration sensors in my ankles. None of these were designed to pick up regular sounds, so my software was taking the various inputs and creating a facsimile of normal sound. Not sexy, but it did in a pinch.

Bastion tried talking to me, but it came across as a screeching wail.

"Keep to text," I said, my voice resonating too deeply and far away. "I can't understand your voice."

"Where is Theo?" appeared on my screen.

I climbed to my feet, feeling the wobble in my legs. Most of the motors and whatnot survived the blast from the shield, but none had escaped unscathed. I surveyed the pool, an expanse of white with that enormous Huginn Industries logo along the floor. I was alone down here. I turned and leaped, grabbing the edge of the pool nearly two meters overhead, but my fingers weren't responding right, and I slipped. At least I landed back on my feet.

"Four meters to your left," Bastion said.

I looked and saw a ladder right where Bastion told me, so I jogged over to it and climbed, looking around the lido deck as I finally emerged from that pool. The boards of the deck were soaked, puddles everywhere as though the ship had just gone through a vicious rainstorm, but it was the chlorinated water. I scanned around, expecting security guards or other partygoers to be out here by now, drawn by the impossibly immense sound of my shield blast, but there was no one.

No one except Theo, slowly climbing to his feet on the other side of the lido deck. One of his cybernetic arms was gone. Bits of wire and a stub of splintered bone were hanging from his shoulder. He stumbled once he reached his feet and wiggled his remaining, mangled hand in the air before him. Probably working his own virtual keyboard as best he could.

"What is this guy made of?" I asked.

Theo dropped down to one knee, taking a three-point stance on the deck. After a few seconds, his three remaining limbs all twitched and spasmed, but he held the position.

"It looks like he's rebooting," Bastion said on my screen. "Go now. Get the chip."

I hobbled my way around the edge of the pool, my legs not quite working the way they were supposed to, but they were keeping me upright and moving. I needed this fight to be over because I certainly wasn't going to be able to do anything else to Theo. I rounded the last corner of the pool, and Theo looked up at me, eyes wide and clear.

"Corto," he said, possibly with a rasp. It was hard for me to tell.

"Guess you're not rebooting after all," I said. I wondered how my voice sounded because nothing sounded right to me.

He shook his head but kept his stance on one knee. "Little good it would do me."

"This is over, Theo. Just give me the chip and we can both walk away from this."

"Walk away?" Theo shook his head, smiling sadly, like he would break down if he didn't smile. "Walk away to what? To proving my father, right? Showing all of Huginn, all of Jayu City that I am the failure he said I was? I don't think so."

I opened my mouth to protest, to make some speech about everything life had to offer beyond his father and Huginn Industries, but it felt like a waste of breath. This man's whole existence was tied up in Huginn's beliefs of success, of winning at all costs. Nothing I had said to him made a difference, and nothing would. But there was more I needed from him.

"Who is your buyer?" I asked.

Theo gently shook his head and spat out blood. "There is no buyer."

"Liar," I yelped.

"It's not about money. It's so much bigger than that." Then Theo smiled. A wicked, horrible smile. "But it was one of yours that tipped me off, that told me where to go and how to get in."

"O," I whispered.

"Maybe not so dense after all," Theo growled. "Finish this, Corto."

"It is finished," I said. "Who is O?"

Theo shook his head.

"Who is O?"

"I won't give you that satisfaction." Theo looked up at me, fixing his eyes on mine. Even though I barely knew him, I saw so much in that look. Pain. Confusion. A desperate pleading. "Kill me, Corto. Finish this properly."

"No," I said. I wasn't like him, like those Huginn children in that arena. I was a burglar and an Intel Operative. I could sneak into locked rooms and infiltrate fancy parties and dimly lit brothels. I didn't kill.

"You must!" Theo snarled.

"No," I said. "I mustn't. I won't. Give me the chip or I'll take it, but I won't kill you."

Theo shook his head and unsteadily rose to his feet. I squared my shoulders and feet, expecting another attack, another that I couldn't defend. Instead, he swept aside his tattered kilt and opened a compartment on the side of his leg, very much like my own storage compartment. The cybernetic, faux muscles opened in fits and starts, obviously damaged by our fight. He

280

reached in and pulled out a blue, egg-shaped object the size of a baseball.

My mind ran wild, imagining the little box that Echo had thrown at Roxy, the gravity grenade, the damage that had done. I was no soldier, no fighter, no assassin. I didn't know what Theo's device was or what it could do. My shield was done. My systems were broken. My defenses meager.

"Be calm," flashed across my screen, a message from Bastion.

"This?" Theo asked, holding the object aloft and looking at it with contempt. "So much fuss over such a small thing."

"The chip?" I asked.

"The chip," Theo said. "Ridiculous. Your own CEO creates such a small thing, so afraid of what will happen now that it's in my hands."

"Just hand it over, we can–"

"If you want it so much," Theo said, turning his gaze from the bauble to me. "Come take it."

"Elise?" Quynn's voice called across the lido deck, almost imperceptible with my current hearing. I wasn't sure it was even real or if I was imagining it, but Theo turned his head back toward the sound.

There was Quynn, walking out of the main structure of the ship, worry writ large across their face.

"The diplomat?" Theo asked, whipping his head back to me. "You seek to negotiate? You've come to the wrong child of Sinclair for that, and we're far beyond negotiation."

"I'm sorry," Bastion said via text. "I called Quynn when you were unconscious, in case you were–"

"I get it," I whispered to Bastion, and then said to Theo, "They have nothing to do with this."

"And yet, here they are," Theo said. He looked at me with curiosity, back to Quynn, and back to me again. "Oh. I see. Such is the dishonesty of Corto Corporation. This person is so much more to you than a diplomat."

"You don't know what you're talking about," I said.

Quynn was standing at the other end of the deck, next to the mostly empty pool, but didn't advance any farther.

"I am an Intel Operative, just like you," Theo said. "You aren't trained to fight, but aren't you trained to read people? Read their expressions, what they say with their eyes instead of their mouths? Any fool could see you care for each other."

He had me there. No point denying it further. I didn't think he had it in him to harm Quynn anyway, and they were wisely staying away. "What of it?"

Theo smiled. "At least there will be an audience for your failure. Or mine. Now come. Take the chip. Take my life."

"I already told you–" I started to say, but a cracking sound echoed through my makeshift aural array. I looked back to the object in Theo's hand, the one containing Bastion's chip, and there was a hairline crack in it. Theo was squeezing.

"The only way you're getting this chip is from my lifeless fingers," Theo said. "Or in pieces."

"Please," Bastion said via text. "Get the chip. I beg you!"

I shook my head. "I'm sorry."

"If he destroys my chip," Bastion said. "I will only be this shadow of myself, this barely functioning collection of code."

"I know," I said. "But I just can't. I'm sorry. I'm so sorry."

"So weak," Theo said, and he kept squeezing, the cracks filling the air and spider-webbing across the egg.

"Please, don't!" I said as tears sprang up into my eyes. Quynn was calling to me, cracking sounds were echoing, text was flashing on my display from Bastion, but all I could do was watch the egg slowly crushed in that massive cybernetic hand.

"You're going to lose. You're not even playing the same game as me. You're blind, don't even see how everything is connected. How the five companies are–" Then Theo's determined grin vanished as violet and green sparks flicked out of the back of his neck. His remaining limbs seized. His eyes rolled up in his head, blood trickles emerged from his ears, and he collapsed in a heap on the deck. The egg containing Bastion's chip rolled out of Theo's limp hand, making a wobbly trail away from him.

"Wh...what?" I asked no one. Nothing seemed real. I had resigned, certain I was seeing the end of this journey in the smashing of that egg-shaped bauble that was unsteadily rolling toward me now. I watched it and glanced back to Theo over and over, certain that he would rise again, climb to his feet, and start tearing me limb from limb. But he didn't. The egg came to a stop less than a meter from my feet, and then the familiar arms of Quynn were around me. I fell into those arms, releasing tears and so much tension I'd been carrying.

"Are you okay?" Quynn asked.

I shook my head.

"What happened?"

I shook my head again. I just couldn't form the words.

Quynn pushed me out of the embrace, holding my shoulders and looking at me, searching. "Then what can I do? What do we do?"

I shook my head a third time.

Quynn shook me by the shoulders. "Elise! I love you, and I need you to focus. There's a big Huginn laying right behind me, the son of the man who owns this ship. We need to deal with that right now."

I glanced over Quynn's shoulder at Theo, who was still laying there, face-down on the lido deck, a small puddle of blood blooming around his head.

"Theo was a disappointment to Sinclair," Bastion said on my display. "But I do not believe he will react kindly to Theo's death."

"Exactly," Quynn said. They must have been hearing Bastion as I was seeing the text.

"Was?" I said.

"What?" Quynn said.

"Bastion said, 'was'," I said. "Was a disappointment. Past tense."

"Theo is dead," Bastion said.

"I killed him," I mumbled.

"You did not," Bastion said. "The violet and green sparks. That was his neural interface. The NX159887. Ophelia's interface. It overloaded, just like others all over Jayu City."

"It overloaded because of our fight, because of what I did to him."

"Hey," Quynn said, grabbing my face and turning it toward theirs. "You didn't do this."

"You weren't here," I said. "You didn't see."

"No," Quynn said. "But I know you, and Bastion told me you tried to talk him down, tried to negotiate. He decided fighting was the only way. Don't you dare put this on yourself. Too much has been put on you in all this. Fuck him. Fuck Dr. Corto. Fuck them all. You survived. You won."

"I concur," Bastion said. "Though not with the same profane enthusiasm."

I almost laughed at that, almost. It still felt like this was me, that I was why Theo would never get a chance to live up to his father's expectations, but both Quynn and Bastion were right. I didn't want to fight. I was cornered. I didn't beat him. I survived him, and so did Bastion's chip.

Quynn looked back to Theo, and then back to me. "We need to throw him over the side. I can't do it alone."

I swallowed hard and nodded. The idea made me sick to my stomach, but I didn't see another option. I hooked one arm under Theo's thick, remaining arm, and awkwardly hooked the other around the stump on his other side.

Quynn took Theo's legs and said, "One, two–"

"Wait," I said. I gently sat Theo back down, turned, and scooped up the egg. I didn't see a switch or release, so I just twisted the whole thing, and the top half came away in my hand. A clear, thick suspension liquid oozed out, spilling over the edge of the remaining half and onto my hands. There it was, Bastion's little neural interface chip, floating in a thick, clear goop.

"Still intact," Bastion said via text.

"And that's why you couldn't connect to it," I said. "He kept it in this thing."

"So it would seem. He did not allow himself to come in contact with the interface."

I started to reach for the chip, but then stopped short. "Bastion," I asked. "Do you want me to grab it, to let you reconnect?"

"I do," Bastion said, the letters appearing quickly on my display. "Very much. Please."

I reached in and grabbed the chip with two fingers, pulling it free from the thick, viscous liquid. Immediately, random letters appeared on my display. Nonsensical, not forming any words or sentences. "Bastion?" I asked, but no reply came.

The odd effect only lasted a few seconds before a simple pair of sentences appeared on my display. "The chip is intact. Thank you."

"You're welcome," I said.

"Elise?" Quynn said, still holding onto Theo's legs and looking impatient.

I held up the chip. "Had to get this. For all I knew, it was still in his pocket and that egg-cracking was a bluff."

"Smart," Quynn said. "Now get over here and help me before someone finds us."

I opened the storage compartment in my right leg, which I had to pry open a bit to assist the damaged motors. I gently placed the neural interface inside and closed the compartment tight. Then I rejoined Quynn, awkwardly grabbed Theo's torso again, and we heaved Theo's lifeless body into Drakon Bay. He splashed in, the sound absorbed into the night and the wind of the Saga Freya's passage, and that glowing, green tattoo vanished beneath the waves.

"It's done," Quynn said.

"Almost," I said, and pried open the compartment on my left thigh, snagging the round device hidden there. I held it out over the water, sitting on my palm.

"Roxy's tracker?" Quynn said. "You didn't use it."

I shook my head. "I couldn't. These Huginns might not be my favorite people, but they weren't wrapped up in this. I told you what Roxy did to that cafe, to those Nexus security guards. I couldn't bring Roxy here. She would have put this boat at the bottom of the bay."

Quynn smiled. "I'm glad."

"I'll have to deal with her again at some point, though," I said. "You know she's not going to stop."

"I do know," Quynn said. "And *we'll* deal with it."

I closed my hand, drew back, and threw the tracker as hard as I could, to join Theo at the bottom of Drakon Bay.

CHAPTER TWENTY-EIGHT

THE REST OF THE JOURNEY wasn't as eventful. Quynn and I stood there at the railing, silently watching the dark waves gently crest and fall. Jayu City was off in the distance, well behind the Saga Freya. After a few minutes, I heard a noise back at the main structure of the ship. The string quartet was setting up on a balcony overlooking the lido deck, making casual conversation with each other as they brought out chairs and music stands.

"We need to get back to our room," Quynn said.

"Our room?" I said.

"The party moves here at midnight," Quynn said. "We need to change."

I started laughing, first as a chuckle, and then I had to hold onto the railing to keep my balance, so lost in the laugh.

"What?" Quynn asked.

"We just..." I said, hooking a thumb over the side of the boat, indicating our recent tossing of Theo. "...and now we're back to fancy clothes."

Quynn smiled, shook their head, and put an arm around me. We went back to our room and change clothes, conservative blacks as Vala had directed. Vala stopped Quynn on the way out of the arena, and Quynn had spun a lie about a bathroom emergency. Vala had told Quynn where we needed to be and how to dress for the Rites of Farewell at 28:00.

Quynn had to help me dress since so many of my joints just didn't want

286

to cooperate, but we made it back to the lido deck just in time to see Sinclair barking orders at some of the hired help, pointing vigorously at the mostly empty pool, the missing deck furniture, and small craters in the otherwise immaculate wooden decking. The hired help scattered and scampered away, and a dozen pumps started refilling the pool in a few minutes.

The guests were all dressed in black, turning the once-festive ship a strange, somber tone. At least it looked somber, but the gathered crowd was rowdier than they'd been all night, fueled by post-arena adrenaline and copious alcohol.

Sinclair gave another speech, this one starting as rousing as he'd been on the forward deck but growing more heartfelt and quieter as he went along. "Tonight," he said. "We say farewell to the titans of Huginn Industries, to the leaders and fathers and mothers and sons and daughters who have left this world better than they found it."

I stood against the railing of the ship, watching the proceedings, while Quynn mingled a bit more. My spot at the railing not only looked the part of the Corto diplomat's security, but I also couldn't walk without wobbling around worse than any drunk on the Saga Freya, so standing still was my best option.

"What will you do now?" Bastion said via text.

"First," I said. "I'm going to sleep. Probably for days. Everything hurts. Then I'm going to need repairs. Mother of Corto, I might just need to replace everything by this point."

"That is not what I meant," Bastion said.

"I know." I turned around, leaning my elbows on the railing and looking out across the sea. "I would love to just go back to my life. To heal up, repair, and – maybe after a vacation – go back to business as usual. Take normal jobs, fun jobs, and execute them well. To never see or speak to the CEO again or have anyone try to kill me."

"Do you think that is possible?"

I took a big breath of the sea air, letting it fill my lungs and push against my ribs, revealing more bruises than I could count. Maybe all of my biological skin was one big bruise by this point. I shook my head, knowing Bastion couldn't see it. "No, I don't think I can. I know about you. Dr. Corto isn't going to let me out of her sight after this. Quynn or Hessod, either. We know a secret that could unseat the CEO of Corto Corporation. No way doesn't affect us."

"What do you think will happen to me?" Bastion asked.

"I don't know, friend. I'm sure Dr. Corto's highest priority will be to keep you secret, but she's also going to be eager to put you to work, to make good on all that development time."

"Those two priorities may be at odds with one another."

"They might, Bastion. They might." I didn't know what else to say. I'd had only one conversation with Dr. Ariela Corto. I didn't know her, didn't understand how to play corporate politics at her level. I certainly didn't see everything she saw, didn't know what she knew. I couldn't predict what she would do next.

"Hey," Quynn said from behind me, and I turned to face them. They were wearing a loose-fitting black gown that draped delicately from their shoulders. Quynn didn't dress fem very often, usually opting for pantsuits or wild-print jackets to go with slacks. But they went with a dress tonight, and they were rocking it. Maybe it was just because every part of me was in pain and I couldn't stand up straight, but I felt like a hobo standing so close to Quynn in that dress.

"Hey back," I said.

"It's about to start." Quynn joined me at the railing, leaning out with a clear drink in their hands.

We watched the water again, and then the Saga Freya came to a stop. Jayu City had fallen out of view, so there was only twinkling starlight and the three moons reflecting light down on the water. A deep clank sounded, shuddering the ship under our feet, and an enormous pair of doors opened at the front of the ship, below the railing, partly under the water line.

Over the next several minutes, over two dozen small boats began to float out of the front of the Saga Freya. There were no engine noises, and the various conversations all faded away. Every person on the ship was against the railing, silently watching the small fleet of boats drifting away.

"Look there," Sinclair's voice carried softly over the ship's PA. "We do see our fathers.

"Look there, we do see our mothers and daughters and brothers."

"Look there, upon our ancestors, from here to the stars and back to the beginning, to humble Earth.

"Look there, they call to us and prepare for us the way.

"Look there, they do take their seats in the hallowed halls of Valhalla, where they shall sit at the highest table forever."

"Look there," the assembled crowd murmured in a single voice. "Look there. Look there."

And then in a single, muffle whoosh, the little boats lit ablaze. Away they drifted, and I counted them now. 28 little fires floating out into the sea beyond Drakon Bay.

Quynn leaned their head on my shoulder, diplomat disguise be damned, and said, "They're beautiful."

"They are," I said.

But like gravity, my mind was drawn back to Theo. The green of his tattoo falling away beneath the waves, likely on the bottom of the bay by now, dragged down by his heavy cybernetic upgrades. No one seemed to have taken notice of his absence yet. Perhaps Theo's absence was a normal thing, another on the pile of disappointments Sinclair held for his son. As I watched those fires shrinking into the distance, I felt for Theo. For his family. He would never have a funeral like this, never be entrusted to a small boat, set ablaze and adrift in honor like this. He was destined to rot, to be eaten by fish, until only his mechanical enhancements remained to gather coral.

This was the closest he would get to a funeral, and his family didn't even know it. And that was my fault.

His final words were bouncing around in my head, too. I wasn't connecting everything. Something about the five companies. Was Theo implying a larger connection between the five companies of Jayu City? Another question to keep me up at night.

When the little boats were nearly out of sight, the sun was just starting to come up and brighten the sky. Without a word, the enormous doors on the front of the Saga Freya closed, and the gathered crowd shuffled away from the railings, dragging their feet with heads bowed as they headed back into the ship.

"What is–" I started to ask Quynn.

They put a finger to my lips in response, and then brushed a stray lock of hair back behind my ear. I held my tongue as we joined in the processional back inside, down into Quynn's room, where we both undressed and fell into the bed without another word, sleep wrapping me up again before my head had even hit the pillow.

#   #   #

The march off the Saga Freya that afternoon was quite different from the festive group that had partied well into the night. Between the hangovers, exhaustion, and a few tears still streaking faces, the crowd was quiet. Vala showed us to our car, a black BMW identical to the one that had brought us to the ship. I took one look back at the Saga Freya as the car accelerated back toward the Corto borough, back home. The ship seemed so small from up here, dwarfed many times by the buildings that towered in every corner of Jayu City. And yet the ship felt so much bigger than it appeared.

The moment we crossed back into our own borough, Quynn said, "Urgent email?"

"What?" I asked.

Quynn's fingers worked the air in front of them. "From my boss. There's an impromptu gala tonight."

"Of course there is," I said. "I can barely walk, but let me put on a pair of heels and work a room. Great idea."

"The quality of applicants this year is so high," Quynn said, reading from the email, "that we require one more gathering, one very special gathering."

"Yay," I said with all the sarcasm I could muster.

"Oh," Quynn said. "The gala is at the home of Dr. Ariela Corto."

"Sounds like the doctor wants to reclaim her property," Bastion said on my display. "Me."

I laughed. Not a that's-funny laugh or a sarcastic laugh, but an if-I-don't-laugh-I'll-cry way. "Of course, she's throwing it."

"Ridiculous."

"She wants to meet us, to debrief. She set this whole thing up just for us."

"No, that I get. Why the gala? Why not just bring us to her office or meet in another bar? Why the big, logistics-heavy event?"

"I can think of no reason," Bastion said.

I shrugged. "I'm too tired to try understanding that woman."

"Email from Hessod, too," Quynn said. "He copied me. There were less than a dozen people on the guest list last night with names starting with 'O.'"

"Any of them from our company?"

"Just one. Olen Corto-Sec," Quynn said, shaking their head like they understood something I didn't.

"What?"

"This was about me as much as you," Quynn said. "Brianna, his wife, is after the same promotion as me."

"Set me up to fall, which makes you look bad." But that didn't feel like enough. It made sense, but after everything I'd been through, the whole thing felt too flimsy.

"I'm going to bury that woman," Quynn said. I patted them on the leg, lacking the energy to do much more.

"We will," I said. "And thank Hessod for me."

Quynn looked at me, half a smile on their face, but expectation, too.

"And tell him we need to have lunch. Whenever. I'll be there."

Quynn's smile bloomed in full, and they set about typing the reply.

#   #   #

I'd never missed home so much. The familiar smells of our bedsheets, the particular squish of our carpet under my toes, and the way the mid-afternoon light streamed in through the windows. I swapped out my work limbs for my everyday limbs, tossing the busted carbon-polymer ones in a heap near my power closet. I just didn't have the energy to see if they would still charge. I fell back into the bed, somehow even more tired than I'd been on the ship.

"Sleep," I said, less as a statement than as a command to Quynn.

"I can't yet," Quynn said as they were changing into an old shirt and sweatpants. "I have to do some work first, have to prep for this gala."

I thought I nodded, or that Quynn said something more, but I was asleep again in moments.

#   #   #

I awoke to Quynn shaking my shoulder. I was in the exact same position I'd fallen asleep in, but the room was darker, the sun trying to set. I groaned. Even Quynn's gentle shaking hurt. The shoulder joint felt loose, and the muscles felt like they were trying too hard to keep everything together. "What time is it?" I asked.

"The gala is in two hours," Quynn said.

"Did you sleep?"

"Off and on. I wasn't the one fighting on that ship, though."

"Lucky you."

Quynn kissed my forehead in response.

I sat up, every muscle and joint in me protesting. As the blankets fell away, Quynn gasped. I looked down to see that every square centimeter of my biological flesh was some shade of green, blue, purple, or yellow. I was one giant bruise. "Yeah," I said. "It pretty much feels how it looks. I need a shower."

Quynn handed me a glass of water and held out a pair of little green pills in their other hand. The best over-the-counter pain meds Corto had to offer. I gladly accepted both, Quynn carefully keeping a hand on my back while I downed the pills and drank the water.

By the time I finished the shower, which felt like needles raining down on my skin, the pain was ebbing significantly. Everything still hurt, but my head was clearing. A pile of pancakes was waiting for me in the kitchen after my shower, along with a big glass of orange juice. Thank Corto some plants, like oranges, could be cultivated on Little Sekhmet Settlement. I felt almost human again.

"I do not know how to properly thank you," appeared on my screen. Bastion.

I smiled and shook my head. "I don't know, either. I wouldn't have survived that without you, though."

"Will you give my chip to Ariela?"

For the first time, I wished I could hear his voice. Was he angry? Sad? Resigned? I needed that context but couldn't get it.

"I don't see another choice. She knows I have it. That I have you. I'm open to ideas, though."

No response immediately came. Opened my power closet and began the painful task of changing into my dress limbs.

"Please find a way."

I gazed at the ceiling, breathing deeply and trying to hold back ridiculous tears. "I'll try."

As I kept changing into my dress limbs, an email notification pinged my display. Gustin. I tapped the notification and read:

Elise,

I see congratulations are in order. Our client contacted me to say they're meeting you at a gala tonight. I assume you know what gala they're talking about. Let me know if you have any issues.

I'm putting a debrief on your calendar for next week, along with the new address. Take a few days. Don't worry about the Hermes Protocol. This was a difficult job, but you met every expectation. Well done.

-Gustin

A debrief. Something else to look forward to. I finished changing into my dress limbs and a high-necked, deep-purple dress that Quynn had set out for me. I sat on the edge of the bed while Quynn carefully applied my makeup. I filled them in on Gustin's email while Quynn caked on the cosmetics, trying their best to cover all of the bruising that the dress didn't. Note to self: stay away from underwater explosions.

"You up for this?" Quynn asked.

"Do I have a choice?"

Quynn stopped, pulling their hand and the sponge away from my face. "That doesn't answer my question."

I sighed. "I don't want to go there. Anywhere, really. I want to sleep for a week, and then try to get our regular lives back. But we have to be there. Both of us." I also didn't want to give Bastion to anyone else, but if I said that aloud, I was afraid those stupid tears would come back.

Quynn raised an eyebrow but didn't say anything. I knew what that meant.

"Yes, I'm up for this," I said. "I might not be as vibrant as I usually am at these things, but I'll be there. Upright. Smiling." I flashed an example of that smile, and that hurt too. I tried not to wince.

Quynn kissed me, more gently than ever, and got back to work on my makeup. "You take it easy tonight," they said. "You've earned it."

#   #   #

The top of Corto 1 – the seat of Corto Corporation's power and location of the CEO's private home – was aglow with dancing spotlights, shimmering fairy lights, and swirling, colored patterns. Our Stryder was circling the building, waiting for an open spot on the landing platform, and giving us a dazzling view of Corto Corporation's most important building.

"I'm nervous," Quynn said. "Why am I nervous?"

"Seat of Corto's power," I said. "Meeting with the CEO. Culmination of your latest try for a promotion. Finding out if the CEO sees us as liabilities or allies. Take your pick."

The color drained from Quynn's face. "Probably one of those."

I shrugged. "I'm just here to make you feel better."

"Funny."

"I know." I kissed them on the cheek as the car descended to a landing platform.

Despite it being impromptu and at Dr. Corto's private residence, the gala felt bigger than any other. Servers in sharp tuxedos wandered around with free drinks and canapés. All the vice presidents of Corto Corporation were there with their spouses, a smattering of Corto directors was there just because they could be, and some nondescript music filled the room. The venue was nicer, and the attendees were more on edge, constantly looking

294

over their shoulders to see if the CEO was approaching, but the event was largely the same as all the others.

Within minutes, Quynn was engaged in a lively conversation with the vice president of the networking division, a small crowd of attendees gathered around them, providing the occasional head nod or other assertion. I was holding up a wall nearby and nursing a drink, heeding Quynn's advice to take it easy. Quynn just told people I wasn't feeling well, which was completely true.

"Excuse me," a thin voice said as a finger tapped my shoulder. "Elise Corto-Intel?"

I turned to see a server, my height with short, dark hair and a whisper of a mustache. I smiled weakly. "Yes?"

"Dr. Ariela Corto requests your presence. If you would follow me?"

I nodded and looked back to Quynn.

"I will let them know," Bastion said on my display.

I followed the server out of the main room, down a short hallway, and out onto an enormous balcony that looked out over Jayu City. Dr. Corto was standing next to the stone railing in a plain, blue gown, gazing out over her borough and sipping a brown drink. The door closed behind me with a light click, and we were alone.

"You could have just called," I said.

"I thought this might put the two of you at ease," she said, still looking out at the lights of the city. "Big event. Lots of people. I didn't want you worried that we were only meeting for me to get rid of you."

I walked over to join her by the railing. "Is that all? A whole gala just for a little conversation?"

"It's more fun this way, isn't it?" Dr. Corto held up her glass to me, and I clinked mine to hers.

"I think we have different definitions of fun."

"Perhaps." Dr. Corto took a sip of her drink and then turned her attention to me fully. "You have it?"

I tapped my leg, the compartment that contained Bastion's chip.

"I can assure you; we have utter privacy here."

I raised an eyebrow but said nothing.

Dr. Corto sighed, and then said, far louder than was necessary for me to hear, "I secretly developed an artificial intelligence, which I tasked you to steal back for me."

"Okay," I said. "Point made. Yes, I have the chip."

"May I see it?" Dr. Corto asked.

"What does she plan to do with me?" Bastion said on my display.

I opened the compartment and pulled out the delicate neural interface. "What are you going to do with him?"

"Him?" Dr. Corto asked.

"With the chip," I clarified, instantly regretting the pronoun slip.

Several emotions flashed across the CEO's face. Frustration, anger, curiosity, but each emotion was muted, a face well-trained in stoicism. I just happened to be well-trained in reading faces. Once her face settled, she said, "I will run Corto Corporation, of course. That chip will help me."

"That's all?" I asked.

"All? Is that all? You ask as though it's the easiest thing in the universe to run a company this size, to care for millions of citizens."

"I didn't mean–"

"I know you didn't," Dr. Corto said, and then took a long sip of her drink, keeping her eyes fixed on me. I officially hated when she did that. "I don't plan on murdering anyone or taking over the planet, nothing like that."

"She only plans on making a slave of me," Bastion said.

"What about the AI? Will..." I started to say "he," but caught myself this time. "...it have a say in what happens? In what you do with it?"

"You've been speaking with it," Dr. Corto said as though she already knew. "Bonded? Is that why you called it 'him' earlier?"

I didn't know what answer would be best for me, for Bastion, for anyone, so I went with the truth. "He's my friend. So what happens to him? What happens to me and Quynn and Hessod? We know about your oh-so-illegal experiment."

Dr. Corto looked at me levelly. "Is that a threat?"

I looked out across the city, not sure if I had made a threat or not. I wanted it to be, but I knew threatening her wasn't a smart plan. "I'm just asking questions."

Dr. Corto sighed heavily. "I see. I see. Well..." she sat her drink on the railing. "I have a new proposal. A new plan. You will keep the chip."

"Me?" I couldn't hide the shock on my face.

"I do not understand," Bastion said.

"You've bonded. Made friends?" Dr. Corto asked.

I said nothing. Didn't nod. I didn't know where she was going with this.

"I knew that could happen, could be a possibility. It is an AI, after all. Not a simple program. So you keep it. Use it. Make the most of that new friendship."

"This must be a trick," Bastion said.

I narrowed my eyes, wondering about what Theo had said about the five companies. I wondered how much Dr. Corto knew about that, but I needed to learn more myself before I could confront her. Instead, I said, "And what do you get out of it?"

She smiled, though the gesture didn't reach her eyes. She picked up her glass and drained it without taking her eyes from me. "I knew you were smart. I'll need things from you. Things that only you and your new friend can help me with."

"I'm to be your errand girl?"

A different, wicked smile spread across Dr. Corto's face. "I'm the CEO of the company you work for," she said. "I know your name. Your face. How many other Intel Operatives have had face-to-face conversations with their CEOs?"

I swallowed, trying to formulate what to say next.

"When I call, you will answer," Dr. Corto continued. "But there are benefits to this relationship. Beyond the assistance of that little AI, I mean."

"Such as?"

Dr. Ariela Corto sat her empty glass on the stone railing and started walking away from me, toward the doors that led back inside. "Come on."

I followed back through the hall and into the main room where the gala was still in full swing.

"Join your partner," Dr. Corto said, her voice a singsong of pleasantry, but the words were all command.

I weaved through the crowd, who were looking at me with new eyes, having just entered the room with the CEO.

"I'm free," Bastion said.

"I suppose," I said. "Though I feel like both of us are in some sort of cage now."

"I expected to be enslaved or destroyed," Bastion said. "This, however, this we can work with."

I sighed but said nothing as I approached Quynn.

"So?" they asked.

"Later," I said. There was no quick or easy way to explain my conversation on the balcony, especially not with all the prying ears nearby.

"Thank you all so much for coming this evening," Dr. Corto said to the room, her voice projected around via invisible speakers. "And on such short notice, but this year's crop of candidates for director were so stellar, so competitive, that the vice presidents asked me to weigh in."

The crowd applauded our CEO and the candidates, with a few gently patting Quynn on the back.

"After careful consideration and some face-time with these splendid candidates, I'm happy to announce the newest director in the Corto Corporation family: Quynn Corto-Nano!" The CEO extended a hand toward Quynn as the audience erupted into applause, but Dr. Corto's eyes were on me, that wicked smile back in place. *There are benefits to this relationship.*

I joined my own hands in applause.

Acknowledgements

LIKE RAISING A CHILD, TAKING a book from idea to the pages in front of you takes a village. I have to thank that entire village. Katie Salvo, my agent, was a constant champion of this novel. In Churl Yo and Jason Henderson at Castle Bridge Media, my publicist Sabrina Dax, and editor Kat Howard were all instrumental.

Early readers are key to the success of all of my work. H.S. Kallinger, Heather Miller, and Brynn Fitzsimmons made sure my story made sense, that gender was fairly and correctly treated, and that I understood asexuality deeply enough to write about it.

I wouldn't be half the writer I am today without my peers and professors in the Creative Writing program at the University of Missouri - Kansas City. Professors Hadara Bar-Nadav, Christie Hodgen, Michael Pritchett, and Whitney Terrell can undoubtedly see their fingerprints and influence on this novel. And my UMKC writing cohorts are too numerous to list, but I thank you all.

Saving the best for last, Christina Arnone. She's the one who knows all of my secrets. She also knows all of Elise's and Bastion's secrets. My wife, partner, sounding board, and provider of so many ideas that have made this book what it is. This book wouldn't be here without her, and I wouldn't be an author without her, either.

And thank you, dear reader, for letting me tell you a story.

CASTLE BRIDGE MEDIA RECOMMENDS...

If you liked *THE HERMES PROTOCOL*, you might also enjoy reading the following titles from Castle Bridge Media available on Amazon or by order at your favorite book store:

Austinites
By In Churl Yo

Bloodsucker City
By Jim Towns

THE CASTLE OF HORROR
ANTHOLOGY SERIES
Volume 1
Volume 2: *Holiday Horrors*
Volume 3: *Scary Summer Stories*
Volume 4: *Women Running From Houses*
Volume 5: *Thinly Veiled: The 70s*
Volume 6: *Femme Fatales**
Volume 7: *Love Gone Wrong*
Volume 8: *Thinly Veiled: The 80s*
Volume 9: *Young Adult*
Edited By Jason Henderson
and In Churl Yo
*Edited By P.J. Hoover

Castle of Horror Podcast
Book of Great Horror:
Our Favorites, Top Tens
and Bizarre Pleasures
Edited By Jason Henderson

Dream State
By Martin Ott

FuturePast Sci-Fi Anthology
Edited by In Churl Yo

GLAZIER'S GAP
Ghosts of the Forbidden
By Leanna Renee Hieber

The Hermes Protocol
By Chris M. Arnone

Isonation
By In Churl Yo

MID-LIFE CRISIS THRILLERS
18 Miles From Town
By Jason Henderson
Lost Angel
By Sam Knight

Nightwalkers: Gothic Horror Movies
By Bruce Lanier Wright

THE PATH
The Blue-Spangled Blue
By David Bowles
The Deepest Green
By David Bowles

SURF MYSTIC
Night of the Book Man
By Peyton Douglas
Dark of the Curl
By Peyton Douglas

Yesterday's Tomorrows:
The Golden Age of
Science Fiction Movies
By Bruce Lanier Wright

Please remember to leave us your reviews on Amazon and Goodreads!

THANK YOU FOR SUPPORTING INDEPENDENT PUBLISHERS AND AUTHORS!
castlebridgemedia.com

Made in the USA
Monee, IL
27 February 2023

28838808R00177